Ebola

William T. Close was born in Greenwich, Connecticut and attended Harvard College. After serving in France during the Second World War he trained as a physician and in 1960 he travelled to Zaire where he practiced medicine and surgery for the next sixteen years. During the ebola outbreak in 1976, he supervised logistics for the international medical team, and during the 1995 outbreak, he has worked as an unofficial liaison between the Centres for Disease Control and Prevention in Atlanta, the Zairian government and many concerned international organizations. He now practices family medicine part-time in Big Piney, Wyoming. He has been married for fifty-two years and has four children and six grandchildren.

EBOLA

William T. Close, M.D.

ARROW

Published by Arrow Books in 1995

1 3 5 7 9 10 8 6 4 2

c William T. Close, M.D. 1995

The right of William T. Close has been asserted under the
Copyright, Designs and Patents Act, 1988 to be identified as
the author of this work

First published in the United Kingdom by
Arrow Books Limited
20 Vauxhall Bridge Road, London, SW1V 2SA

Random House Australia (Pty) Limited
20 Alfred Street, Milsons Point, Sydney,
New South Wales 2061, Australia

Random House New Zealand Limited
18 Poland Road, Glenfield
Auckland 10, New Zealand

Random House, South Africa (Pty) Limited
PO Box 337, Bergvlei, South Africa

Random House UK Limited Reg. No. 954009

A CIP catalogue record for this book is available from the
British Library

Papers used by Random House UK Limited are natural, recyclable
products made from wood grown in sustainable forests. The
manufacturing processes conform to the environmental
regulations of the country of origin.

ISBN 0 09 967461 0

Printed and bound in Great Britain by
BPC Paperbacks Ltd, a member of The British Printing Company Ltd.

ACKNOWLEDGMENTS

Special thanks to the following people, all of whom played an important role in the writing of this book:

Bettine, my wife, whose constant support over fifty-two years made this book and all that went into it possible.

Sandra Lambert and Susan Lehr for their pursuit of excellence in the text and story. Melina Mans for her sensitive translation of letters and other documents from Flemish into English.

Dr. Ruppol, Dr. Miatudila, Dr. Massamba, Prof. Guido van der Groen, Dr. Karl Johnson, Dr. Joel Breman, Dr. Margaretha Isaacson, Dr. David Heyman, Prof. Patyn, Dr. Peter Piot, Dr. Pierre Sureau, and all the other colleagues who added to the story.

The Sisters of the Sacred Heart of Mary for their open-hearted collaboration as we remembered together those nuns killed by the virus during the epidemic.

Finally, a very special thanks to a Sister called Veronica in the book who made it a lie to say that "it is impossible to look into the heart of a Flemish nun."

AUTHOR'S NOTE

Yambuku is a real place where the Sisters of the Sacred Heart of Mary from 's Gravenwezel in Flanders and the Fathers of Scheut have a large, successful mission. A lethal epidemic, caused by a new virus called Ebola, did indeed devastate this outpost of peace and efficiency toward the end of 1976.

At the time of the epidemic I was spending a final three months in the Republic of Zaire, winding up my sixteen years as a physician and surgeon to the Zairians and their president. For reasons of language and past experience, I became involved with the extraordinary group of nationals and foreigners who dealt with the disease.

Gradually the events of the epidemic, and the people involved in its discovery, those it killed and those who survived, became an abiding passion, and my accounts of those days also captured the imagination of my daughter Glenn Close. In 1987 we traveled to Europe and Zaire, and for the next three years I continued my research into the human aspects of the tragedy. As we continued our work, the impact of the disease on the forest people and the missionaries struck us as a story worth telling.

At first, all I had were fragments of information. So I began weaving them into the long interviews I recorded with some of the participants. Then I added private letters, diaries, and scientific field records. With the strands of my own impressions and facts gathered during the years I spent in Zaire, I have created the fabric of this novel.

Hundreds of people of varied backgrounds and cultures were involved in this epidemic. Sometimes I have blended two characters into one; much of the dialogue is what I imagine the characters would have said, and the chronology has been simplified. The events, however, and their impact on those who died and those who survived, are true.

PROLOGUE

Fly due east toward the coast of Africa, six degrees below the equator, altitude one thousand feet above the sea. Twenty minutes before landfall, the water becomes mud brown as a giant apron of silt and pulverized vegetation spreads out into the Atlantic, marking the outflow of the Congo River. On the horizon, the domes of cumulus clouds boil up from a thin line of hot green haze into blue sky. Sand spits marking the entrance to the river are just ahead. To the right, tucked into a small bay, is the old Portuguese settlement of St. Antonio do Zaire, now part of northwestern Angola. The ebb tide has stranded a row of outriggers on the yellow beach.

On the left, seven miles north, sitting across a sandbar, is the village of Banana. A few palm trees bend in the offshore wind; rusted corrugated sheds and a handful of huts huddle around an old wooden jetty. The Zairian pilot boat has pulled out from its berth to make its daily run to the dark island of Bulabemba, guardian of the mouth of the river. A World War II coastal artillery battery, camouflaged by thick vegetation, rusts in the earthworks. VIP political prisoners are housed in the old barracks. Water, the color of strong tea, laps at the stained shoreline and flows sluggishly through thick mangrove swamps. Two soldiers shake their rifles up at the plane.

1

Bank away from the cattle ranches on lush green islands below and follow the course of the river as it continues inland to Boma, the first port city, and on to Matadi. Here the river narrows, and suddenly the engines roar as you climb out of the spume thrown up by the cataracts in the Cauldron of Hell. These are the first of many formidable rapids cut through the Crystal Mountains and extending inland for 160 miles. In the deepest, narrowest gorges, giant whirlpools suck whole trees into their vortexes and spit them out like toothpicks.

Fly low over Monkey Island, isolated between cataracts formed by massive boulders in the riverbeds. The Zairian capital, Kinshasa, and the beginning of the Stanley rapids are ahead. Steer clear of the paratrooper camp next to the fountained gardens and zoo of the presidential domain. Army headquarters and the bare pedestal of the old monument to Henry Morton Stanley are over on the right. Beyond the bay where the river barges are built, fly parallel to the right bank and its manicured lawns. Ambassadors and the regime's favored few live here in mansions tucked among stately palms and hibiscus, their terraces draped with bougainvillaea, their gardens shaded by full-leafed mango trees.

Now head for the lines of rusting river barges. Along the southern shore of the river's vast Malebo Pool clusters of purple hyacinth float in smooth, brandy-colored water between grassy stretches of sun-baked silt.

This is where Kinshasa's population of two million lives in slums sprawled over twenty square miles from the river to the hills guarding the Bateke plains. Check in on the radio with the Ndjili tower and ease off to the northeast, dropping down to five hundred feet. Maluku, its deserted steel mill one of many monuments to faulty planning, flashes by. Fly past the sacred brown slash in the wooded hills inhabited by the *ndokies*, spirits, that guard the entrance to the pool and on to where the inky waters of the Black River merge into the Congo.

A long, sleek pirogue, its gunnels inches from the water, streaks out from the bank. Tall, slim men in long pants and open shirts stand in the bow and stern of the narrow craft, and a woman dressed for market in a red cotton print skirt down to her ankles sits between stacks of manioc and smoked fish. The men bend at the waist, and their powerful arms and shoulders pull long paddles in synchrony through the water.

As the river widens, follow the main channel, which weaves between forested islands. Wild buffalo, grazing in a swampy clearing, toss their heads and run for cover. A bull stands his ground ready to charge, then is hidden by the wing. Climb to ten thousand feet and set a course over the forest for Mbandaka, capital of the Equateur Province. After an hour, Lake Tumba glitters in the distance beyond the swamps and forest to the east, and Irebu, where Katangese gendarmes were imprisoned and perished of malaria and dysentery, passes slowly below. The Ubangi, flowing into the Congo from the north, is just ahead, and in five minutes you will cross the equator. Check in with the tower at Mbandaka, then follow the great river, now three miles wide, northeast then east as it continues to receive tributaries from the Congo basin. Another hour puts you over the town of Bumba. Now, head north to Yambuku, fifty miles away.

Look down on the mantle of green which hides the ground—part of the three million square miles of great trees and swamps that form the jungle belt of the African continent. This is the equatorial forest where massive trees crowd out the broad-leafed undergrowth in damp soil, where the fluting of boles spreads into buttresses that

writhe over the soggy floor from the base of the hardwood
giants. Trunks push up through the understory to a hundred
feet or more before branching into a spreading crown. At
ground level, the light is dim, the atmosphere moist, heavy,
and still. Calls of invisible birds, the yell of a monkey, and
the whine of insects accentuate the brooding silence.

Descend to a thousand feet and circle the village and the
Catholic Mission of Yambuku, carved out of the forest by
Belgian missionaries in 1935. Over the years, its church
and schools and, more recently, its hospital served over
sixty thousand people in the region. By 1976, the hospital
had 120 beds and a medical staff of seventeen—no doctor,
but a highly trained Zairian medical assistant and three
Flemish nursing nuns. There was an active prenatal and ob-
stetrical service, and the outpatient clinic treated over several thousand people each month.

During the late seventies, Zaire was struggling to crawl
out of the morass of "Zairianization," a euphemism for ex-
propriation, followed by "radicalization," when the control-
ling power attempted to correct some of the more blatant
abuses of their fellow citizens. Businesses, large and small,
had been seized by President Mobutu and some of his family and supporters. The resulting mismanagement created
administrative chaos and economic disaster for a country
already bled dry by a privileged few. By September 1976,
however, the president undertook far-reaching efforts to
undo the damage. Foreign investors were encouraged to return to their plantations, factories, and businesses with a
promise of regaining 60 percent of their assets. But vast
wounds had been inflicted on the economy and public services. State funds for essential supplies and maintenance of
government facilities in all sectors had been siphoned into
private accounts in Switzerland and spent on prestigious
monuments to greed and jet aircraft for the army. Schools

were empty shells, hospitals were without medicines or instruments, and roads were left unrepaired after rain damage isolated large areas of the interior. Except for the capital, the country was returning to the bush. Zaire's reputation as a difficult—if not impossible—place to work was worldwide.

The Mission of Yambuku, with its schools, farms, and hospital, was still an island of efficiency and commitment in the midst of a dense, rain-soaked forest. At the end of August 1976, a lethal hemorrhagic disease, later known as Ebola fever, exploded out of the Yambuku hospital, devastating the mission and surrounding villages. An oasis of peace and order became a focus of terror and death.

CHAPTER 1

The night storm had cooled the air. A gray mist hid the tops of trees around the mission. The day had started with matins at five, followed by breakfast in the refectory. Bread, gamy from bugs in the flour, was dipped in strong coffee made from beans grown locally and dried by the sun on a concrete slab in front of the guest house. Goat cheese, slices of bacon from the mission farm, and ever-present bananas were polished off with relish by the Sisters of the Sacred Heart of Mary, a small order of nuns drawn from farms in the Flemish countryside near Antwerp. Swaying harmonies of an African choir and the beat of drums came from the church where Father Dubonnet was celebrating Mass. A boy herded thin cows with wide, pointed horns down a path between tall rows of palm trees planted by the first Flemish colonizers. Passing a small cemetery where white Catholic missionaries were buried, the cattle and the boy ambled into a rough pasture wrested from forest years ago. The boy climbed to the top of a giant termite hill to watch the sun rise out of the mist.

Mango trees planted beside the buildings caught the morning sun on their dark, shiny leaves. In the yellow brick hospital pavilions that lined each side of the dirt road people were beginning to stir. A young girl carrying a bucket of wash water chased a chicken out of the maternity ward, then strode around to the back to empty her pail into the high grass. Along the path that connected the hospital to the convent, a woman leading an old man stopped to ask a worker for directions to the dispensary. Behind the convent, children trudged across a bare patio from their dormitories to the classrooms; others played a hand-clapping, skipping game as their friends watched. The bell on the convent's back porch clanged with authority, and a nun on a red Vespa without a muffler skidded around the corner of the schoolhouse. The children jumped up and down, cheering, "Vero, *oyeh*! Vero, *noki-noki*." *Noki-noki*—quickly, quickly—was the nickname they had given Sister Veronica. Hopping off her scooter, she tugged her gray skirt down to where it belonged. The students ran from her laughing as she clapped and chased them inside, shouting, *"Noki-noki."* Across the playground, Sister Augustina, the Mother Superior, frowned and released the bell cord.

African mission workers waiting in line outside her office greeted Augustina quietly with *"Mbote, ma mère,"* as she walked past them and sat at her desk. She called them in by name, one at a time, to stand in front of her and receive orders or advice or answers to questions. Augustina had the build of a Flemish farm woman, big shoulders and an ample bosom. The dark hair in front of her veil was streaked with gray.

Sister Veronica, having left the Zairian teachers in charge, hurried to the convent and into her superior's office. A woman with a bruised, swollen eye was standing in front of Augustina's desk.

"I will talk to your husband myself," said Augustina. The woman turned and walked out, rewrapping her loose skirt and tucking it in at the waist, a grim smile on her battered face.

"Do you know her husband?" asked Veronica.

"Only by sight."

"He's one of the grave diggers. An animal when he's drunk."

"I will talk to him," said Augustina. "Sister—"

"I'm late for the radio," interrupted Veronica. "Do you have anything for Lisala?" At age forty-five, Vero's energy and zest for life were packed into a short but shapely frame.

"Yes. Tell them we need more fuel for the generator. Ask them to send up more than two barrels so we aren't caught short."

"Anything else? I have the supply list to call in."

"There is something else, Veronica. Sit down."

"I'm late for the radio."

"I know. You said that before." Veronica sat and took a deep breath. "That's better. Now, I want you to calm yourself. You make more noise than all the children put together. And, as I have told you much too often, you must have the exhaust repaired on that Vespa."

"I've written to my father. If the new muffler's not stolen on the way here, Luc will have the scooter purring like a kitten."

"All right. Go call Lisala," said Augustina, shaking her head.

Veronica rushed out of the office past Sister Antonie, who flattened herself against the wall and gazed up toward Heaven. Disregarding the waiting Africans, Antoine tucked in her blouse and smoothed the skirt over her flat posterior before stepping up to Augustina's door. She tapped lightly, almost apologetically.

"Come in, Sister," said the Mother Superior.

Antonie entered demurely. She waited with her head cocked a little to concentrate on the instructions she would receive for the day as she contemplated the intricate wood carving of the Madonna on Augustina's desk. Her small eyes and narrow nose gave her a mousy air.

"After you help Lucie with the new mothers, Fermina needs your assistance with inventory in the pharmacy. This afternoon you had better count the linen in the laundry again."

"Very well," said Antonie, with a slight inclination of her head.

"Is there anything you need, Sister, anything I can do for you?" asked Augustina.

"Nothing at all. I am content in my work, but thank you for asking," replied Antonie, taking a step back then turning and walking to the door with her hands folded as if she had just received communion. Augustina watched her leave, then shuffled papers on her desk before calling in Casimir. The laundry man, wearing a khaki skirt, shorts, and white apron, came forward timidly. His lean, sad face was the prelude to another report of missing sheets and pillowcases. Augustina was sure that he sold the linen in Yandongi, but she had never been able to catch him stealing.

Veronica turned on the radio; the humdrum voice of Jules, the priest who communicated on a regular schedule with all the Catholic missions in the province, filled the closet-sized room. Jules was calling each station in alphabetical order and was somewhere in the *M*'s. The transmission varied in pitch and volume against a background of crackles. Vero adjusted the dials on the old transceiver, and the reception improved. She checked the water level in the two ancient batteries that powered this unreliable link with the outside world and reminded herself to fill them before the generator down by the spring was turned on for a few hours after sunset. Veronica liked fiddling with the dials and keeping the batteries filled with rainwater, but sometimes she felt that the requests and directives relayed over the air from Lisala intruded into their work at the mission; and Father Jules tolerated no discussion. Sister Lucie, the midwife at the hospital and Veronica's best friend, could imitate him to perfection. She claimed that when he called Heaven even the angels stopped to listen. Veronica sat on the stool and gazed at the mission grounds while she waited. The approaching rainy season would mark her twentieth year in Yambuku.

During the rebellion, when most of those who could read and write had been killed, the population was apathetic or too frightened to go back to the fields. Veronica had said to the priests, "It is useless to ask the blacks to pray when their stomachs are empty. God does not want anyone to go hungry. If the natives are too lazy to grow food for themselves, then we must help them." So she organized the Catholic Agricultural Cooperative, and the villagers came together again and now produced some of the best rice and coffee in the country. Her father in Belgium, a farmer himself, had been proud of her work and had sent her the red Vespa on which she made rounds. Strictly speaking, the scooter belonged to the mission, but Veronica was the only one who rode it except for Father Dubonnet. She smiled as she thought of him. He was a simple man who lived in great poverty. Thin, with the head of an ascetic, his eyes were deep set under bushy eyebrows, and crow's feet spread to his temples. A long white beard, stained with tobacco below his mouth, hid his chin. His real name was Jef Maas, but he was thought to resemble *monsieur le docteur Dubonnet*, whose patriarchal and bewhiskered head, poking up from a wing collar and black tie, graced the label on a bottle of tonic for weak blood that bore that name. The elixir, which was 30 percent alcohol, had been appreciated during the colonial years as a cure for anemia and any other strength-sapping condition.

She loved his sermons. He did not preach hellfire and repentance but spent much of his time in the villages, helping a little here and there, performing simple ceremonies that might bind the people in their moments of joy and help them through their times of grief. He drank *masanga* and smoked *bangi* with the elders. He and the forest people seemed to have an understanding of each other. When he spent a night in a village he slept on the ground, sharing a reed mat with fleas and bedbugs. No amount of teasing could keep him clean.

Jules's voice over the radio calling Yambuku interrupted her thoughts.

"Yambuku here. Go ahead," she replied.

"Nothing for you, Yambuku. Nothing for you," intoned the priest.

Veronica depressed the button on the microphone. "We have messages for you, Lisala."

"Ready to copy, Yambuku."

"We need a sack of flour, without bugs if possible. A sack of sugar. A can of kerosene. Salt for us and the villagers. Five liters of brake fluid, and a platinum screw for a Vespa one twenty-five. Sister Augustina asks that you send us more than two barrels of diesel fuel for the generator. She does not want to run out when mud holes make the roads impassable. Over to you."

"Your list will be given to the father in charge of supplies. Anything else?"

"Another jigsaw puzzle would be appreciated. Over."

"I will do what I can. Over and out," said the priest. Yambuku was the last mission on the list. Veronica switched off the radio. Another twenty-four hours of freedom from headquarters.

* * *

The morning was cloudless and fresh. Vero tucked her skirt under her knees and sped down the packed dirt road to Yandongi, her right hand twisting the throttle open, her left hand on top of her head to keep her veil from blowing off. Two women were coming toward her, the taller striding along well ahead of the other. Veronica slowed down, then stopped.

"What good luck to see you. My little sister from Bongolu is with me," said Nza, shaking hands with Veronica and pointing back to where a small, delicate-looking woman waddled toward them, clutching her bulging belly.

"Come on, Ngasa, here is Sister Veronica," said Nza, urging her forward. "Vero, this is Ngasa Maliboso. We call her Ngasa Moke because she is so small." The younger woman shook hands but was too out of breath to speak.

"She may be small, but that's no pygmy baby she's carrying," said Veronica.

Nza put her arm around Ngasa's shoulders. "Sister Veronica and I work on agricultural affairs together in Yandongi," she announced.

"You do all the work, and I do the talking," said Veronica. "But I'm happy to see you, Ngasa Moke. You must not let Nza make you go too fast. It's not good for you or the baby."

"She forgets what it's like," panted Ngasa Moke.

Nza leaned forward from her waist, loosened the sling around her baby, and, grabbing an arm, pulled him forward. She wiped his nose with her thumb. "You're right, my little sister. It will be much easier when you carry him on your back instead of in your belly." She handed her child to Veronica. "Ngasa still has a couple of weeks to go. I'm taking her to the maternity clinic for another of Sister Lucie's *ntonga*—injections."

Veronica held the baby up at arm's length. "This one is going to be a big, strong farmer and president of the cooperative." She kissed him on his pudgy cheeks.

"Thanks to all of you," said Nza.

Ngasa Moke wiped her face with a corner of her *elamba*, the long cotton print cloth snugged around her waist. "I had a miscarriage in Bongolu."

"Well, I'm glad you are coming to us," said Veronica. "I'm sure this time you will have a beautiful, healthy baby."

Nza leaned forward, and Veronica lowered the child onto the mother's broad back. Nza pulled the cloth tight and straightened up. "We had better keep going. Sister Lucie does not like her mothers showing up late."

Veronica watched the two women head off to the hospital. She smiled with satisfaction—Nza's sister had come from thirty kilometers up the road to have her baby with Lucie. She restarted the Vespa, gunned the engine a couple of times, and took off toward Yandongi—her veil streaming, her plain silver cross on its black cord blown over her right shoulder. Speeding toward the tunnel through the trees that separated Yambuku from Yandongi, she flashed past a woman daubing mud on a hut, who shouted, "Vero! *Mbote, ma soeur.*" A girl in the manioc patch beside the hut laughed and broke into a dance, throwing her arms above her head and kicking up dust.

As she raced on, Veronica was filled with the exhilaration of speed and the exulting confirmation of her calling as a missionary nun. She sang out her praise to God above the roar of the engine. Suddenly the wind ballooned her skirt; she slammed on the brake and stopped. Luckily no one was around. She tucked her skirt under her thighs and rode on in a more dignified fashion.

* * *

Sister Veronica represented the best of a long line of Belgian missionaries who, together with administrators and soldiers, had colonized and ruled the Congo after the Berlin Conference in 1884 had granted it to King Leopold II of Belgium as his personal property. Administrators, army officers, and missionaries were deployed from Europe to "civilize" and Christianize the people of this huge, mysterious part of the "dark continent" over seven times the size of Belgium.

In 1960, Baudouin, king of the Belgians, returned the Congo to its own people under the leadership of Joseph Kasavubu, a descendant of the kings of the Kongo Empire at the mouth of the giant river of the same name. Patrice Lumumba, a firebrand nationalist, became Prime Minister. When the West turned against him, he flirted with the Soviet Union. The United States reacted. The prize was diamonds, gold, uranium, copper, and other strategic minerals necessary for the war machines of the great powers. The Congo became a central playing field in the Cold War.

Five days into its independence the Congo exploded as the army mutinied and Belgians fled by the thousands. A few weeks later, mineral-rich Katanga Province, under Moise Tshombe, seceded from the Leopoldville government. Those with interests in the huge commercial potential of the province supplied administrators and army cadres to Tshombe. At the urging of the United States, the United Nations launched operation "Rumpunch" against Tshombe's white officers and were defeated. A month later another bloody operation by the U.N. called "Morthor" ended the secession, and the blue-helmeted troops were denounced throughout the world for their brutality. Tshombe went into exile.

The Cold War turned hot and violent. Lumumba was assassinated; men trained in China and Eastern Europe backed a rebellion, actively supported by Castro's Cuba, that eventually controlled more than half the country. It was only after Tshombe was returned to power with the blessings of General Mobutu, who had become president in a bloodless coup in 1965, that the rebellion was finally extinguished with the help of mercenaries from Europe and southern Africa. Tshombe became Africa's pariah for his use of mercenaries, and he was eventually kidnapped and held prisoner in Algeria where he died, supposedly of a heart attack.

In 1971, Mobutu renamed his country Zaire and changed his name from Joseph-Désiré Mobutu to Mobutu Sese Seko Kuku-Ngbendu Wa-Za-Banga, which may be translated as "the all-powerful warrior who leaves fire in his wake and advances from conquest to conquest with no force or person able to stop him." All Zairians changed their Christian names to those with an authentic African ring. Mobutu "Zairianized" all industry, down to the smallest Portuguese shop in the interior. A feeding frenzy among his family and supporters followed, and, in short order, little remained of the country's economic resources. Mobutu tried to reverse the trend by inviting Europeans to return to their enterprises. Unfortunately, the cupboards were bare and few accepted his invitation. Travel in the interior came to a halt as bridges collapsed and abandoned roads turned to rivers of mud during the rainy season. Hospitals closed and patients returned to their villages. Doctors sought work in the cities, but even there medicines and supplies had become an unaffordable luxury. Unpaid teachers abandoned their classrooms and worked in the fields to feed their families. Yet a few missionary schools and hospitals like Yambuku continued to function effectively in a country ravaged by the greed and corruption of the privileged handful around Mobutu.

* * *

Sister Lucie stepped out of the maternity pavilion. A man who had been sitting under a mango tree came up to her.

"Your baby is doing well, but your wife lost a lot of blood. We'll have to keep her a few days and give her shots to build up her strength." The man turned around and went back to the tree. Lucie chuckled. She had been delivering babies in Yambuku for fourteen years and could count on one hand the number of times she had been thanked for what she did. As a nurse and midwife, struggling for hours over a delivery or a sick child was normal; you were not thanked for doing your job. Gratitude came only if you did more than was expected.

Across the way, patients were already waiting outside the dispensary. Over her shoulder she called to her Zairian assistant, a tall, graceful young woman in a low-cut white blouse and a long skirt wrapped around her slim waist.

"I have to run over to the dispensary. Stay close to our last patient and call me if she starts bleeding again."

"Yes, Sister. Oh, look, here comes Nza," said the assistant. The women met and shook hands.

"You poor woman, you must be exhausted," said Lucie to Ngasa. "Nza, take her in and give her some water and a bed. I'll see her later." Fingering the ruffles of Nza's tight green bodice, she added, "You're as healthy as ever. Plenty of milk too." Pictures of the president in his leopard-skin hat decorated each of her large, productive breasts.

"A new *Movement Populaire elamba*?"

"Yes. My husband and I have been appointed to the Regional Council," said Nza proudly.

Sister Fermina, the nurse who took care of the children and shared the responsibility of the dispensary with Lucie, joined them. Fermina lifted the child. Her brusque manner

and no-nonsense narrow face softened the moment she cradled the baby in her arms.

"He will carry you on his back in a few weeks," she
said, kissing him on his forehead. "Come over when Sister
Lucie is through with you. I would like to weigh him for
my records." Fermina returned the child to his mother and
marched off to her pavilion.

Lucie hurried to the dispensary. Brown hair pushing out
from her veil framed a round, happy face. She seemed
younger than her forty-two years. As she approached, those
who were sitting or lying on the ground stood up or were
pulled to their feet by others and joined the line of patients.
Mabalo Lokela, a dignified man dressed in a conservative
abacos, a tailored jacket with short sleeves, approached the
waiting group and, after greeting everyone, took his place
at the end of the line.

Lucie sat at a desk near the entrance and motioned the
first person to come in. She opened the register which listed
patients' names, sex and age, village of origin, and the
symptoms—or disease if known—that needed attention. On
a wooden table next to the desk an enamel tray held glass
syringes and needles, three vials of injectable medicine, a
metal tongue depressor, and an ear speculum. Another tray
held two stainless steel kidney basins, one containing
Dettol, a disinfectant, the other, water. A small glass jar
was filled with cotton balls.

The first patient, a woman supporting her left breast in
her cupped hands, stepped up gingerly and sat on the stool
beside the desk. A young girl, balancing a thin infant with
big eyes on her hip, stood next to her.

"*Mbote, mama. Sango nini?*" asked Lucie. How are
things?

"*Nazali na pasi awa,*" said the woman, pointing to her
breast with her chin. I have pain here. Lucie leaned forward

and gently pulled back the neckline of the woman's bodice, revealing the dark, shiny bulge arising out of the breast. The nipple oozed a little pus.

"Your children?" she asked, glancing at the girl and the infant.

"*Iyo.*" Yes.

"Can the baby suck on your other breast?"

"*Iyo.*"

After recording the patient and her abscess in the register, Lucie called Sukato, a male nurse.

"Take her to the surgical pavilion. The abscess needs to be drained." Turning to the woman, she added, "Masanga-ya, our medical assistant, will take care of you." The girl hiked the baby higher on her hip and moved aside; her mother pushed herself out of the chair slowly and followed Sukato down the steps.

The next patient was a thin woman with *pulupulu,* diarrhea. The dry skin on her forearm stayed in a ridge when Lucie pinched it; this meant the woman was dehydrated. Lucie put the back of her hand on the woman's forehead. Diarrhea with fever was dysentery and was treated with antibiotics; patients with diarrhea and no fever were treated for worms. Here there was no fever, so Lucie wrote "Vermox" on a slip of paper and told her to go to the pharmacy. The woman left, pushing past an old man eagerly awaiting his turn. He hobbled in and sat on the stool.

"*Mbote, tata.*" Hello, old father. "*Sango nini?*"

"*Pasi na lokolo.*" Pain in my leg.

"Show me." He pulled his knee up, extended his leg, and lowered his foot onto the table. A deep, suppurating ulcer had eaten its way into his ankle.

"Since when?" asked the nurse.

"*Teeeeeee,*" said the old man, pointing a gnarled finger behind his head.

"I know," she said. "Since the beginning of time. You are Tata Boni, the old soldier. You come in to see Sister Fermina every week." He gave her a toothless grin and sat a little taller on the stool. Lucie patted the thick sole of his foot; he removed his leg from the table. Her note in the register read: *Tata Boni, very old, male, chronic leg ulcer, vitamin ointment.* Although nothing would really help heal the wound, she had to give him something—he would not expect to leave empty-handed—so she handed him a slip for the pharmacy. The old man pushed himself up from the table, snapped to attention, and saluted. Lucie returned the salute with a smile. "Until the next time," she said, as he did a staggery about-face and hobbled down the steps.

Next, two women with infants on their backs came in, dragging a screaming child between them. Lucie raised her voice above the noise. *"Nini?"* What?

One of the women heaved the boy up from the floor and buried his face in her bosom. The screams became muffled gurgles.

"Makila," she said, pointing to his rear end. Blood.

"Pulupulu?" asked Lucie, feeling the fever in the child's head. Diarrhea?

"Te." No.

Lucie thought for a moment. *"Kisi ya basenji?"* she asked. Native medicine? The women looked at each other in fear.

"Why?" asked the nun. The women said nothing. The one with the sick child rocked him against her chest. Just then Sukato returned; Lucie called him over.

"This child was given native medicine and is now bleeding from the rectum. Ask them what was used and how it was given." There was a rapid exchange between Sukato and the women in a different dialect; it sounded like Budja, and they spoke too fast for Lucie to understand.

"Their *nganga*, the healer of Bongolu, gave them leaves to boil for an infusion that they put into his rectum."

"Why?"

"Does it really matter? Maybe fever," replied the male nurse, avoiding the sister's eyes.

"That *nganga* should be thrown in jail."

"I know you may not believe me, Sister," he replied, "but to our people, he is a wise old man, who lives at the edge of the forest. He has helped many of us."

Lucie dismissed the subject with a shrug of her shoulders and snapped, "Well, put this child in a bed and run some saline into him. And give him a shot of nivaquine for good measure. He probably has malaria." Sukato herded the women out; they chattered with relief as they followed him to the pediatric ward.

Although Lucie was a good midwife and was comfortable taking care of pregnant women and their infants, she would be glad when her turn for this month ended in the dispensary and Sister Fermina took over. The missions were chronically short of trained personnel, who were being asked to do more and more as government services ground to a halt or were diverted for private gain. Lay volunteers were coming to Africa to work in some of the mission hospitals, but they wanted nothing to do with the religious orders. They had their own opinions and lifestyles.

Next, a man was helped in by his wife. He was leaning forward, both hands pressed into his groin, supporting a large hernia. The couple was from Yaongo, thirty-two kilometers west of Yambuku. After examining the man, Lucie gave the woman a slip of paper and pointed them toward the surgical pavilion.

After three more patients, it was Mabalo's turn.

"Good morning, Mabalo. I'm glad to see you. Please sit down," said Lucie. He was the president of the parish committee and had helped Veronica push her agricultural cooperative through the channels of the church's African hierarchy. A respected teacher, he was greatly appreciated by the sisters and the priests.

"Good morning, Sister," he said, wiping his face with a large handkerchief.

"Sister Fermina told me you had a good trip up north and were able to buy some fresh meat. Too bad the bridge to Gbadolite was out; you might have seen the president and brought back a present for the mission," said Lucie with a grin. She looked at him more closely. "You aren't well. What's going on?"

"I came back with a headache, which I blamed on drinking the *lotoko* my wife's uncle gave us in Abumombazi. Yesterday I took a nap at noon and awoke with a fever, and my headache is worse."

Lucie leaned forward and felt his forehead. "You do feel hot. Any chills?"

"Some. I think it is just malaria. I do not have any nivaquine at home, or I would have taken it and not bothered you."

She saw distress in the small lines around his eyes; beads of moisture appeared on his forehead and upper lip. "You could never bother me. You should have come yesterday," she scolded. "Let me examine you." She turned him toward the light.

"Open your mouth." His tongue was dry and coated. She slipped the metal tongue depressor in and saw that his throat was red. She felt his neck and under his chin for lymph nodes.

"Now, slip off your shirt and let me listen to your chest." She put the stethoscope in her ears. "Deep breath, through the mouth. "Again ... keep going. Good. Now the front." His heart was beating fast and hard. She put the stethoscope on the table. "Stand up, please." She thumped him lightly over the liver. He stepped back. "Does that hurt?"

"Yes, it does!"

"Sorry, but I had to see if your liver is tender. Please," she said, indicating the stool. Mabalo slipped into his shirt and sat down. Lucie started to write in the register.

"I have to put down your age."

"Forty-four."

"And you are from Yalikonde but live here with Sophie and the baby."

"That is correct," said Mabalo.

"You are right—you have malaria. I'll give you a shot of nivaquine; it works faster than the pills. You'll feel better quickly." Lucie reached for a glass syringe and needle on the enamel tray. She sucked disinfectant up into the barrel, then rinsed it out with water. She drew out a dose of the antimalarial from a vial, wiped off Mabalo's upper arm with cotton dipped in Dettol, and injected the medicine.

"That should do it." She pulled out a small plastic envelope of tablets from the desk drawer. "Take these aspirin for the headache and fever, and say hello to Sophie."

Mabalo wiped his face again as he got to his feet. "Thank you for the shot, Sister," he said. "I will give Mbunzu your message."

"Oh, that's right—it's hard to remember all your new names since the president's campaign for authenticity."

Mabalo laughed. "Our old names were Christian names given to us when we were baptized. Our 'new names' are the ones we were given at birth: they tell who we are."

"That is fine," said Lucie, smiling at the teacher but not really understanding what he meant. "But you are still good Christians!"

"Well, Christians anyway," answered Mabalo. They shook hands and he left. Lucie rinsed the syringe with

Dettol and then with water and put it back on the table, ready for the next patient.

Outside she heard a commotion. Looking out she saw Nza surrounded by Ngasa Moke and three other young pregnant women, who were slapping their thighs and laughing wildly. Nza was holding forth. "And do not worry about the sting of the shots, they are no worse than a mosquito. They are powerful and will strengthen your babies. I know; I have been through it. When your time comes, you will climb onto the table and put your feet in metal rings and scrunch down with your bottom till you think you are going to fall off the end. Then the sister will say, 'Breathe in, uh—uh—uh—and out, whoo—whoo—whoo—and push, push, puuush!' She stands on a stool so she can press on your belly and soon the baby comes and it is all over. Now, come on, practice the breathing." The four mothers-to-be formed a semicircle in front of Nza.

"Together," said Nza, raising her arms like the choirmaster on Sundays, "Breathe in, uh—uh—uh—and out, whoo—whoo—whoo." After several cycles of *uh—uh*'s and *whoo—whoo*'s, the four women strutted around shouting, *"Pusa, pusa, puuusa,"* then convulsed into fits of laughter.

Lucie clapped with delight. Nza saw her, held her hand up to stop the chorus, and yelled, "Enough!" She pointed to the sister, and her pupils' shouts became giggles.

"None of these young women have had babies here before, so I was just telling them what to expect," explained Nza.

"I can see why they have you organize party rallies," said Lucie, still laughing.

Then she called each of the four young mothers in turn and marched them to the examination table behind a screen. She weighed each woman, checked her blood pressure, measured the dome of her abdomen, and listened to the fe-

tal heartbeat. All four were healthy, in the bloom of moth-
erhood. They were excited by their pregnancies. If their infant lived for the first week or ten days, it was given a
name. If it lived on to adolescence and the ceremonies of
initiation, the child became a full-fledged member of the
family. Thus the mother's place in the clan was guaranteed
and respected if she bore children. A barren woman was
not ostracized, but it was understood that her husband
would find another wife who could give him children, often
leaving the childless one bitter and unfulfilled.

After the examinations, Lucie led the women to the table
for the all-important shots that would give them healthy
children. She picked up a 10-cc syringe, loaded the barrel
with vitamin B complex, and, after carefully wiping off the
skin over their upper arms, gave each one 2.5 cc's. The
women grimaced as they stepped up for their shots, fearful
of the needle but proud to be suffering for such a good
cause. Their ordeal would add to their authority as mothers.

On the day after his injection of nivaquine, Mabalo resumed teaching French to the older children then, in the
evening, hoeing weeds in his field of manioc and coffee.
During the five days following his treatment, he felt better,
but during the fifth night, his fever and headache returned
with a vengeance. Hot steel rods seemed to run down the
muscles next to his spine and into the backs of his thighs.
Squeezing his head between his hands, he crawled out of
bed stiffly and slowly, so as not to awaken Mbunzu, and
crept over to the washstand in the dark. He found the plastic bag of aspirin and swallowed three with a little water
from the jug. He held his head again, feeling it would explode if he moved too fast. He made his way to the couch
in the front room and lay down, rolling onto his side, hugging a pillow to his head and pulling his knees up to relieve

the agony in his back. At first light when he awakened, Mbunzu was sitting next to him, a worried frown on her face.

"I must have worked too much in the fields," he mumbled. She said nothing, walked over to corner of the room, dipped the end of a towel in the water bucket, and brought it back. He wiped the perspiration off his face and neck and pushed himself up.

"You had better go back to the dispensary," said Mbunzu.

"I will, after my first class." His head swam when he moved, but the aspirin had taken the edge off his pain.

Sukato was behind the desk at the dispensary that morning. Mabalo told him that he had received a shot of nivaquine a week ago and that he had felt better until yesterday. Sukato asked the teacher to wait. He walked over to the maternity where Lucie was about to deliver a baby. She ordered him to give Mabalo a full dose of quinine, since some people in the forest had a malaria that responded poorly to nivaquine. Sukato injected the medicine into the teacher's arm, then handed him more aspirin. Mabalo went home, certain now of a cure.

Over the next four days, Mabalo's fever persisted and the headaches were unrelenting. He lost his appetite. Mbunzu was with him all the time. She put cool cloths on his forehead and made broth from goat meat, pressing him to eat and drink. Each time visitors came, Mabalo struggled into the front room and talked with them until they left. Once, after a fellow teacher had stayed too long, he collapsed into bed. Mbunzu was furious. She scolded him, wagging her finger in his face. "You need to rest! I will tell those who come to see you that you cannot be disturbed."

"No. I am an elder and a teacher." His face was haggard. "I cannot escape from those who rely on me." He turned with his back to her.

"They will kill you!" She looked down at his pain-racked body and whispered, "Then your family will accuse me of not taking good care of you."

During the afternoon of September 5, Mbunzu saw that her husband's condition was deteriorating. His throat was hurting terribly; swallowing was almost impossible. She asked Mabalo's mother to find Sister Vero—she would know what to do.

Late that evening, Veronica strode into the house and was shocked to see Mabalo lying on the couch, moaning.

"A friend is here to see you," said Mbunzu, laying a hand on his shoulder and helping him up.

"Just resting a little. How are things with you, Sister?" he asked feebly.

Veronica ignored his ritual politeness. "You should be in the hospital, Mabalo."

"I do not want to go to the hospital. Too many sick die there."

"That's silly. People die when they do not go to the hospital in time to get treated."

"I have had two *ntongas* in a week. I am sure they will—"

Mbunzu interrupted. "He has not eaten anything for days, and he insists on seeing everyone that comes."

"Mabalo," Veronica spoke very quietly, "if you go to the hospital, they can put saline in your veins, and you will get well sooner." She knew she could not bully him.

"I will go tomorrow if the fever is still with me."

"I'll speak to Sister Lucie when I get back to the convent. Mbunzu, you must get him to Masangaya first thing in the morning." Veronica said good night and left. She felt helpless, and returning to the convent went directly to the chapel. She prayed with all her heart that Mabalo's health would be restored by morning.

That night, Mbunzu kept the kerosene light burning low in the back room. Mabalo slept fitfully. Mbunzu lay on a floor mat, cradling their baby in her arms. Around the middle of the night, Mabalo was seized by waves of nausea, and he vomited and retched until there was nothing left inside him. The throbbing in his head exploded every time he moved. Mbunzu went to him and wiped his mouth, then cleaned up the mess in the bed with a damp towel. The baby screamed. She dried her hands on her dress, picked up the child, and put him to her breast. The child suckled for an instant, then slept. A dog barked, and angry voices came from the house at the end of the road. A woman shrieked in the night, then silence fell. Mbunzu stared at the lantern's yellow flame, too frightened to move.

At first light, Mbunzu took the baby to Mabalo's sister. She washed her husband, pulled him up from the bed and, wrapping a *liputa*, sarong, around his waist, half dragged and half carried him to the operating room pavilion. She lowered him carefully onto the steps to wait for the medical assistant.

In the early glow before sunrise, Masangaya left his house and headed for the hospital. He saw Mabalo crumpled in front of his office and ran the last few steps.

"Mabalo, my brother, I did not know you were so sick. Come in; I have a bed you can lie on." Masangaya and Mbunzu carried the teacher into the office and eased him down.

Bracing himself on the wooden sides of the cot, he whispered, "I hurt all over."

Masangaya pulled up a stool and sat next to his friend. Mabalo's temperature was 39.5°C (103.5°F), blood pressure normal, but his pulse was 130. His breathing was rapid and shallow, his skin dry and hot. He was hunched over on the edge of the cot with his eyes closed. Mbunzu stood next to a screened window that let in the early morning light. She chewed on the corner of a handkerchief balled up in her fist.

Masangaya encouraged Mabalo to open his eyes. The whites were red with bloodstained crusts in the corners. Using a small flashlight, he examined Mabalo's mouth; his tongue was dry and coated with thick green mucus. Dull gray patches of exudate covered his soft palate and the back of his pharynx. After listening to Mabalo's heart and lungs, Masangaya helped him lie back on the cot. His fingers explored the teacher's abdomen, finding tender areas over the liver and spleen where even gentle pressure made Mabalo tighten up.

Mbunzu reminded him, "He has had nivaquine and quinine over the past few days."

Masangaya sat back and thought for a moment. "He must have something more than malaria, although malaria is bad enough and can make a man this sick. But the injections should have made him better, if malaria was the problem. He will be more comfortable and I can take care of him better if we put him in the private room off the medical ward. He needs fluids and stronger medicine."

The move was made, and Masangaya started an IV of saline. He handed Mbunzu some pills. "Give him these slowly with little sips of water. I hope he can keep them down. I will check back in a while."

Other patients were waiting for the medical assistant, but

Masangaya wanted to talk to Lucie about Mabalo. He told them he would return soon as he hurried over to the maternity pavilion.

"Good morning, Sister. Working early this morning," he said, as they shook hands.

"Like you," she answered, smiling at him. "Have a seat."

"Mabalo's very sick."

"Vero told me about him last night. I'm glad he came to see you on his own."

"Mbunzu must have carried him over. He was too weak to climb the two steps into my office." He paused. "The malaria shots have not helped."

"That is strange. What will you do?"

"I hospitalized him, started an IV, and gave Mbunzu some chloramphenicol and aspirin to get into him. I do not know what he has, but the rehydration should help."

"You don't think he was given native medicine by a *féticheur*?" she asked.

"I doubt it; he is as Westernized as I am. But, of course, one can never really be sure." He raised his eyebrows and cocked his head like the sisters did sometimes when they spoke of African ways.

Later in the day, when Masangaya gave Mabalo another liter of fluid, the patient was passing black watery stool. The first IV had done little to relieve his dehydration.

During the night, his abdominal cramps became even more severe, doubling him up, and making him cry out. He vomited dark brown bile that looked like coffee grounds and continued to pass tarry liquid in the bed. Mbunzu washed him and changed the sheet over the rubber mattress. It was a long night, and she was relieved when dawn crept into the room through the window.

* * *

Masangaya and Lucie came in early. The room reeked of vomit and fecal blood. Mabalo was on his side in the fetal position.

"He just fell asleep," whispered Mbunzu.

Quietly, Lucie replied, "We will be back later." They left, and she followed the medical assistant into his office.

"A little coffee?" asked Masangaya, lighting a small oil burner under a blackened kettle.

"Why not," replied Lucie.

"At least he is resting," said Masangaya, rinsing out two cups in the cold-water sink next to his desk. "I don't know what else to do. I am afraid we might lose him."

"Oh, *mon dieu*! I hope not. But like you, I cannot think of anything we haven't tried."

Masangaya reached into the medicine cabinet for a can of Nescafé. Lucie gazed around the small office as spartan as her own. A canvas army cot covered with a stained pad was next to the wall behind her; a plain wooden table and chair filled the space at the other end; and under a narrow window, an old metal cart for the burner and its kettle made up the furnishings. The only personal effect was a faded photograph in a cheap metal frame hanging above the table. It showed a smiling group of young African and European students posing next to a plump older white couple in front of a café in Brussels.

Lucie watched Masangaya preparing the coffee. This big man—the backbone of the hospital—had been trained in Léopoldville, where the practical aspects of medicine and surgery were stressed. Afterward, because of his high grades, the Belgians awarded him a scholarship to the Institute of Tropical Medicine in Antwerp. He had run the Yambuku hospital for the past six years. The hair at his temples was turning white. To the sisters he was an effective and compassionate man, soft-spoken, and easier to work with than most of the young doctors that passed through the mission hospitals and thought they had the answers to everything.

Masangaya's reputation for good care was widespread, and people came from far to see him. The villagers considered him a learned elder with special knowledge of diseases and white man's remedies. Unlike many Western doctors and nurses, he was not in conflict with the traditional healers. He knew that they had important roles to play in the lives of the people. Masangaya was called *"monganga"*—an expert in white medicine.

"When he awakens I will give him more antibiotic and more saline. How is our supply of IVs?" he asked, handing Lucie a cup.

"We have one case of liter bags left. I will ask Vero to radio Lisala for more," replied Lucie. She sipped her coffee thoughtfully. "When Sophie—I mean, Mbunzu—wakes up, I'll send her home. Mabalo's mother can sit with him today. Mbunzu needs to nurse her baby; she can come back this evening."

"That's good. But remember, Mabalo is a *mokumi*—an honorable man. There will be many visitors."

"We should not allow them in the room," said Lucie firmly. "There's not much space, and it will be very hot."

"We cannot keep them out. If Mabalo is dying, and I think he is, they will want to be with him. He is esteemed as a teacher and a judge and will continue to be important to all of us when he becomes an ancestor."

"I know you are right," said Lucie, "but . . ." Masangaya turned to face her. His irritation showed for an instant, then he smiled. She handed him her cup. "Thanks for the coffee. I have to get back to my pregnant women," said Lucie, knowing that discussion would be useless.

* * *

During the day, Mabalo's mother sat next to her son's bed. His friends and fellow teachers, the president of the cooperative, and his neighbors came, packing into the little room. Some sat on the other bed; others leaned against the wall or squatted on the floor. Each one watched silently for a time, then took their leave of Mabalo's mother, holding their right forearm with their left hand in a sign of respect. Their place was taken by a person from the group waiting outside the ward for his turn to sit with the teacher and keep the vigil with others. Each new visitor coming into the crowded room shook hands all around, then approached Mabalo, taking his hand and saying softly, *"Mbote, mokumi."* The stifling heat seemed unnoticed. No one spoke; their presence alone sufficed to mark their affection.

And so the day passed. Toward evening, Mbunzu returned to relieve Mabalo's mother, the visitors left, and she was again alone with her dying man.

Mabalo was now too weak to turn over in bed. Mbunzu washed him when he soiled himself and wiped the bloody mucus that oozed from the corner of his mouth. Pulling the chair over she sat next to the bed, resting her elbows on the mattress, and spooned drops of water between his cracked lips. His hand wavered when he tried to reach up and touch her face. She held it and pressed it to her cheek. He smiled and she rocked gently, holding on tight as her tears washed over their fingers.

The door opened. Veronica tiptoed in and put her arm around Mbunzu who, burying her face in the nun's skirt, poured out her misery in soul-racking sobs. Veronica prayed for the agony to end. Slowly the light faded, and Vero helped Mbunzu onto the other bed. She lit the lantern on the table and tiptoed out. Mosquitoes and clumsy moths gathered around the smoky lamp. Mabalo's labored breathing was the only sound in the little room. Outside the open window, all was quiet except for thunder rumbling in the distance. Around midnight Mabalo's mother returned and lay on a mat under his bed.

During the small hours of the morning, Mabalo went into a coma. Mbunzu, her head resting in her arms on his bed, was asleep. Suddenly she awakened with a start and stared at Mabalo. Then throwing back her head and raising her fists to the ceiling, she let out a long cry of anguish. Mabalo's mother, awakened by Mbunzu's scream, threw herself on her son's dead body and wailed, *"Papa akufi, akei!"* He is dead, he is gone! Friends who had been sleeping outside came in and fell on the body, sobbing. One of them ran to Masangaya's house. Mabalo died just one week after receiving the shot of quinine.

Masangaya controlled his own tears with difficulty as he waited for those beside the bed to grieve. Later, he covered the body with a sheet and, with Mbunzu and Mabalo's mother following, helped the men carry their friend home for the laying out of the corpse. News of the teacher's death spread like the wind throughout the mission and beyond.

By noon, there was a large gathering of Mabalo's friends and family. Some wanted Mabalo buried at the mission, but those from Yalikonde protested angrily. A fight broke out and, after much screaming and shaking of fists, the villagers and the family won the right to carry away their *mokumi* and lay him to rest according to custom among his ancestors.

Mabalo's funeral was a big affair, lasting two days. People came from all over the district to pay their last respects. He was laid out in his best suit on a wooden cot surrounded by candles and flowers. Mabalo's wife, mother, and three other women sat next to the body. They kept up a steady keening, getting up from time to time to caress the dead teacher's face. Others who had been close to Mabalo hugged the cadaver and spoke to it as was the custom of the Budja.

Late in the evening, the men lifted the teacher's body into a coffin. Just before the cover was hammered in place, Mabalo's brother leaned over and, with a large handkerchief, wiped the crusts and fluids from his mouth, his nostrils, and the corners of his eyes. Then, walking to the cooking fire in the yard, he threw the handkerchief into the embers and watched as it flared up and became ash. Now the family could be sure that any of Mabalo's spirit still lingering in his body would return to the ancestors. Only his shadow would remain.

CHAPTER 2

The second death came the day after Mabalo was buried. While her husband was recovering from his hernia operation, Nsembo Ndombe had been receiving shots for fatigue in the dispensary. After several days, she began complaining of fever and severe headaches. Sister Lucie treated her for malaria, but Nsembo quickly developed intractable vomiting and bloody diarrhea. The usual treatments for dysentery were ineffective. On the same day, four women from villages around Yambuku were hospitalized with symptoms similar to those that had killed Mabalo and Nsembo. Mission workers who lived in villages surrounding Yambuku reported to the nuns that some of their neighbors and friends were very sick; others were already dead.

In her office, Sister Augustina gathered the hospital registers going back to June 1975. She searched for patients admitted with headache, fever, nausea, vomiting, and diarrhea, as well as bleeding. In August, a little over a month before Mabalo's admission, she found three successive patients who had died from postpartum hemorrhage, but she doubted their relevancy. She searched the earlier months and underlined the names of four more patients with some form of bleeding. She would go over these later with Masangaya and the nurses.

The next three days brought more admissions with symp-

35

toms of what was now being called "the fever." Three out of six of the African male nurses became ill; the three who were still on their feet worked double shifts. The wives and husbands of most patients stayed to feed their spouses and help the nurses, although soon they too developed early symptoms of the fever and had to be hospitalized.

The day after her husband was buried, Mbunzu awoke with a headache. She swallowed a handful of Mabalo's left-over pills and, after feeding her baby, pulled the curtain over the window and lay down next to the child. Her back and thighs ached, and she slept fitfully. Around the middle of the morning, Mbunzu heard the familiar noise of Veronica's Vespa pulling up to her house. She turned to the wall and pretended to sleep. The machine was shut off, and the door opened, then closed. She felt a hand on her shoulder.

"How are you?"

"Fine."

Veronica put her hand against Mbunzu's cheek. "You do not look fine, and you feel hot."

Mbunzu covered her sleeping child with her arm, keeping her back to the nun. "I am all right—just tired after yesterday."

"You must go to the hospital now and not wait until you are worse," said Veronica.

"No," answered Mbunzu. Her husband had been right: you went to the hospital to die. She had dragged him there against his will. She would not obey the sister's orders again. The door opened. Veronica looked over her shoulder and saw Mabalo's mother in the entrance. She acknowledged her, then turned back to Mbunzu.

"I'll take your baby over to Sister Fermina and come back for you."

From the threshold, the old woman announced, "I will take care of the baby and Mbunzu."

Veronica ignored her. She squeezed the young woman's arm. "Come on," she urged. But Mbunzu pulled away. Veronica straightened up, frowned at the mother and child, and brushed past the older woman without a word. The Vespa's engine was kicked into life, and its racket filled the room, then faded in the distance. Mabalo's mother closed the door to keep out the cloud of dust.

Within weeks, the old woman would be dead, as would Mbunzu's mother, her sister, and her baby. All would perish in the same agony as Mabalo.

Dr. Howard Fields, chief of the Special Pathogens Branch of the Centers for Disease Control in Atlanta, was in his office finishing an activities report of his maximum containment laboratory. It had to be on the director's desk before lunch. His telephone rang.

"There's a doctor from Germany who wants to talk to you," said the center operator.

"Put him on." The line crackled, and the caller gave his name.

"Dr. Fields, I'm phoning from Hamburg's Institute of Tropical Medicine. Hans Spiegel, a virologist here in Hamburg, says he knows you. He suggested I call about some information we have just received from a German construction crew working on roads in south Sudan. They are reporting an unidentified disease raging through the area around the town of Maridi, and apparently many are dying. The news reached us by telex from the German embassy in Khartoum. None of the Europeans in the Sudan have caught the disease, and they are heading out of there as fast as possible. Have you heard about this?"

"Not a word."

"We here at Hamburg have limited experience in this sort of thing and wondered whether CDC could do something to clarify the picture."

"There's nothing we can do unless there is a request from the U.S. embassy in the Sudan or from the World Health Organization. Why don't you ask WHO to investigate?"

"We have few interests in the Sudan, but I will see what we can do. Thank you for the suggestion and for your time."

Dr. Fields hung up and dialed the number of the Epidemiological Intelligence Service. He relayed his conversation with the German to the director and went back to his report.

Masangaya, Fermina, and Lucie needed sleep. In addition to working around the clock with fever patients, Masangaya had his usual load of surgical emergencies: injuries from work or the village bars, an assortment of broken bones, strangulated hernias, and abscesses. Fermina's pediatric ward was full of children whose parents had been admitted to the medical service. She and Antonie had been up two nights in a row giving aspirins and sponging down three of her infants who had spiked fevers. It was Fermina's week in the dispensary, but she had Sukato see most of the outpatients. Lucie was busy delivering babies at all hours, and on Friday, following early hospital rounds, she visited leprosy patients in their huts.

On Sunday, September 12, Sister Lucie rested in her room after lunch, then went back to work. But in the evening, after helping Masangaya start IVs and pass out antibiotics and aspirins, she was dead tired when she finally crawled into bed. She felt hot, but did not take her temperature, and blamed exhaustion for the ache in her temples.

After a restless night, she awakened as usual at quarter to five for matins. The throbbing in her head was now fierce. Her eyeballs and back hurt, and she felt sick to her stomach. Lighting the candle on her bed table, she eased herself up, then shuffled stiffly over to the corner sink. She put on her glasses and was shocked to see how haggard she looked. "Holy Mother of Jesus, help me! This is not the time to get sick," she mumbled. Reaching for the bottle of nivaquine, she gulped down four, grimacing at the bitter taste. *It must be malaria! The other disease hits the Africans, not us.* Still, panic rose from her belly. She rummaged around in her toilet kit, found a thermometer, and shook it down; then she put it under her tongue and leaned against the sink. After a couple of minutes, she read it: 39.5°C (103°F).

"Oh, Holy Mother," she whispered, "please let it be something else." She winced from a sudden spike of pain, and images of Mabalo during his last days flashed across the red screen behind her eyelids: the bloody vomit, the black stools, the smell. "Stop it!" she said out loud to her image in the mirror. "It could be anything."

She took off her glasses and splashed cold water on her face. That was better. She dampened a washrag, squeezed it out, and carried it back to her bed. She lay down, lowered her head carefully to the pillow, and laid the cool cloth across her eyes.

Lucie knew she was very sick; but typhoid started the same way, as did malaria and hepatitis ... and something could be done for them—antibiotics, IVs, vitamins, and tonics. She also knew that she was a strong, healthy woman with a good appetite. The Blessed Virgin and she would win this battle. Her panic eased slightly. She gazed at the cross above her bed. *Mary, Mother of God, intercede for me and give me the grace and strength to fight off this thing. There is so much I need to do ... so much.*

The sisters were at their morning prayers in the chapel a few doors down the hall from her room. She heard their chanting. Augustina would be kneeling on the first prie-dieu, contemplating the wooden crucifix above the altar, her broad, straight back a comfort to the sisters kneeling behind her. Lucie heard Veronica's strong voice as she read from a familiar homily by St. John Chrysostom: " 'The waters have risen and severe storms are upon us, but we do not fear drowning; we stand firmly upon a rock.' " Veronica's voice rang with conviction as if she had written the passage herself: " 'Let the sea rage, it cannot break the rock. Let the waves rise, it cannot sink the boat of Jesus. What are we to fear? Death?' "

Lucie recited along with her, scarcely moving her lips, " 'Life to me means Christ, and death is gain. ...' " She pushed herself up. *I must go to the chapel.* Her head seemed to explode, and she lay back down. With the room swirling and the final singing from the chapel surging and fading in her ears, she pressed her head into the pillow, fighting off tears of frustration.

After morning prayers, Veronica and Fermina hurried to Lucie's room. Fermina sat on the edge of the bed and, putting her fingers on Lucie's wrist, felt her racing pulse. *"Ça ne va pas,"* said Fermina softly.

"Ça ne va pas du tout," whispered Lucie. It is not going well at all.

Fermina wiped the sweat from Lucie's face with a towel she took from Veronica. *Please, Blessed Mother, make her well. How I have needed Lucie's sunlight. What would we do without her?* She knew the others thought she ran the pharmacy and supply room like a martinet, but Lucie understood and valued her sense of discipline. Lucie's humor and love could smooth the rough edges when the sisters were tired or irritable. Standing, she pulled the sheet up, folded it over, and tucked it around Lucie's shoulders. "Now, you rest. I will get you some breakfast. You must eat to keep up your strength."

"You know that I cannot stay in bed. We all have too much to do," protested Lucie.

"Your only duty is to rest and get well," replied Fermina sternly. "I will be back with tea and biscuits."

"And I will bring you some of the sausage from my uncle in Schilde," said Veronica. "That will give you energy."

"That will make her vomit," snapped Fermina. "I will be back in a moment, then I will check your new mothers."

"Merci, ma soeur."

Monday, September 13, and the following day, Lucie lived on aspirin. Neither Veronica nor Fermina could keep her in bed. She continued to see her patients in the prenatal clinic and deliver the babies of the women whose time had come. At 2 A.M., the night watchman banged on Lucie's door with the shaft of his long spear, announcing that Nza had arrived with her sister, who was about to give birth. Lucie sat up. Her head was pounding as she lit the candle on her bed table. A shaking chill went through her body, and every joint ached. She pulled a uniform over her head. After swallowing three more aspirin, she set out.

Nza was lighting the kerosene lamps in the delivery room, and her sister was lying on a mat when Lucie arrived. They helped Ngasa Moke onto the delivery table. The baby's head was crowning, and after a half dozen good pushes, a new baby boy made his entry into the world of the African forests. Lucie clamped, cut, and tied off the cord. Handing the child to Ngasa, she excused herself and ran into the bathroom. There she fell to her knees and, hanging on to the toilet bowl, retched up the acid and aspirin in her stomach. After ten minutes she returned to the delivery room, light-headed and trembling.

"Sister, you look awful!" said Nza.

"Probably just *la grippe*," replied Lucie, leaning against the end of the table. The umbilical cord hung out of Ngasa. The afterbirth was taking its time. Nza pushed down on her sister's belly, and Lucie pulled on the cord. When the placenta was finally delivered, it squeezed out in a gush of blood. Lucie injected Pitocin into the new mother's arm to contract her uterus. A half hour later, the bleeding slowed to spotting. After settling Ngasa, the baby, and Nza into beds in the empty maternity ward, Lucie walked heavily back to her room. She gulped down a few more aspirin, fumbled with the knot on her bloody apron for a few moments, then gave up and collapsed onto her mattress. It was 3:30 in the morning.

Lucie awoke with a start after less than two hours of sleep. She had missed matins. Struggling to the sink, she washed her face, pulled off her sodden uniform, and dropped a fresh one over her head. As a wave of nausea and vertigo seized her, she grabbed on to the sink to keep from falling. Then she felt the support of a strong hand.

"You should be in bed," said the Mother Superior severely.

"I know, and I will be as soon as I recheck Ngasa. She lost a lot of blood."

During the rest of the day, Lucie stayed in bed. Earlier Fermina had stormed into her room. "What is the matter with you! Do you really think you are the only nurse that can deliver babies around here? Do not move out of that bed without my permission."

"I'm worried about Ngasa's bleeding. I pulled pretty hard

on the cord. There may have been a tear in the placenta. I couldn't see very well."

"I just came from your service. She is not bleeding anymore; besides, Antonie is watching her," replied Fermina. "So relax. We cannot have you running around like an idiot when you need to rest." Lucie said nothing; she was too weak to argue.

The next morning at 4:30, Lucie forced herself out of bed. It was her turn to read the lesson, and she had looked forward to it all week. She lit the candle and moved to the sink. In the mirror she saw the reflected white forms of the other nuns glide past her open window. Hurriedly she splashed cold water on her face and was fumbling with a bobby pin to attach her veil, when there was a knock on the windowsill. Lucie turned and saw Augustina pointing first to her, then to her bed. The rules of the convent allowed no speaking until after matins. Lucie turned back to the mirror. She opened the pin with her teeth, but her fingers were trembling, and it dropped into the dark bowl of the sink. With a second pin, she tried again slowly and deliberately. Her arms ached with the effort, and she leaned against the sink to rest.

The service started as soon as all the nuns were kneeling in their places. When the moment came for the reading, Lucie rose slowly to her feet and, clasping her breviary, stepped into the aisle and bowed her head to the altar. At the lectern, she turned. A whisper of shock passed through the sisters when they saw her face. She steadied herself, then opened her book to the reading for the day. In a faint voice, she said, "The epistle for today's mass is my favorite: I Corinthians 13." She paused and took a deep breath and, closing her eyes, recited by heart: " 'Love is patient and kind; love is not jealous or boastful; it is not arrogant or rude. Love does not insist on its own way; it is not irritable or resentful; it does not rejoice at wrong, but rejoices in the right.' "

She took off her glasses and wiped her face. Slowly and deliberately, she continued: " 'Love bears all things, believes all things, hopes all things . . . endures all things . . . ' "

She stopped and grabbed the lectern, then quickly stepped down. Holding a hand over her mouth, she ran out into the gray dawn, braced herself against a palm tree, bent over, and vomited. Sinking to her knees, she retched convulsively as Augustina reached her and held her head. When the worst was over, the Mother Superior put an arm around Lucie's waist and all but carried her back to her room. Fermina was right behind them and helped Lucie rinse out her mouth and wash her face.

"After you have slept, I'll come back with some broth. It will stay down if you drink it in sips." She arranged Lucie's pillow and eased her down on the bed. Veronica stood at the threshold.

"I brought Masangaya to see you. May we come in?"

"Of course."

"Mbote, ma soeur," said the medical assistant.

"Mbote, my friend," whispered Lucie, "you are up early again this morning."

"Not as early as you, from what Sister Veronica tells me. Now, what is going on?"

"Malaria or the flu. I don't know. . . ." Lucie forced a smile. "Maybe even too much native medicine?"

Masangaya looked at Veronica. "A truck could run over her, and she would still joke."

"I'm sorry, that was a bad joke. I feel terrible. My head pounds every time I move."

"Any diarrhea?"

"Yes, some."

"Blood?"

"No. No blood."

"Sore throat?"

She swallowed. "A little."

Masangaya glanced at Veronica, whose eyebrows were raised in a question. He turned back to Lucie. "I'll give you a liter of fluid so you won't become dehydrated."

"I don't want any needles," said Lucie, lifting her head off the pillow and regretting it immediately.

"You cannot drink enough to make a difference," said Masangaya.

"No needles. I will drink. The sisters will see to it."

"Very well. We will try that today and see how it goes," replied Masangaya. "Vero can keep in touch with me."

"Thank you. I will do what you tell me," said Lucie.

"I'm sure you will, if you agree. But that is why you are a good nurse," replied Masangaya.

He left the room, followed by Veronica. They walked out onto the path leading to the hospital and stopped. "What do you think?" asked Veronica.

"I do not think it's malaria. I don't know what it is. I have asked Dr. Amene to come up from Bumba."

"Will Lucie die like the others?"

"I hope not, but I am afraid it is a possibility. I'll be back to see her later after I've made rounds. There are many fever patients."

Veronica stared after him. Lucie might die! They would have to do something—get her out of here! Where was the nearest Belgian doctor? *We cannot just watch her die.* She ran back to the convent and into the refectory. Augustina, Fermina, and Antonie were already there. She mumbled a quick grace and made the sign of the cross, praying that Lucie would live.

Antonie poured coffee while they smeared margarine over thick slices of bread. Each was preoccupied by their sister's desperate condition. Augustina was composing a message to be sent to Lucie's family through Sister Adeline, the order's Mother Superior in Antwerp. Fermina was making a list in her neat, bold handwriting of all that needed to be done on her service and in Lucie's, in order of priority. Veronica slammed her knife on the table and blurted out, "Masangaya thinks Lucie has the fever and could die."

"No!" gasped Antonie. A knock on the door startled them. Sukato appeared at the threshold.

"What is it?" asked Fermina.

"I thought you would want to know, two women and a child died early this morning. The families have taken the bodies. People are dying in Yalikonde and Yandongi and even farther up the road."

"Thank you, Sukato. I will come in a moment," said Fermina, dismissing him.

"We must get Lucie to a doctor," said Augustina. "We could drive her to Binga. Maybe the doctor there could help."

"You know the doctor in Binga's no good. He's drunk most of the time," countered Fermina.

"Dr. Amene is on his way, but I think we should send a message to Yalosemba and ask Sister Matilda to come as quickly as possible. She is the most experienced nurse in our congregation," said Veronica.

"I agree. Matilda taught us most of what we know, and with Lucie so sick, we really need her," said Fermina.

"Matilda will certainly know what to do," said Augustina. She checked her watch. "It's almost time for our radio contact with Lisala. I'll ask Father Jules to pass the message to Yalosemba. We'll send a vehicle for Matilda this morning." She stepped outside and called to one of the gardeners to tell Luc to come with the Land Rover.

"I will take Lucie her tea," said Veronica, getting up.

"See if she will eat some papaya; it is good for the stomach," suggested Fermina. "I will check on her later."

Dr. Amene arrived in the evening. He was young but a hard worker and had none of the arrogance of big city doctors. He and Masangaya examined seventeen fever patients before turning in for the night. The doctor slept on a cot in the front room of Masangaya's house across the road from the convent. The next morning, after an early breakfast of coffee and bananas, the two men were back at work. Three patients they had seen only a few hours previously were now dead. One was the head of maintenance of Veronica's cooperative; the others were close friends of Mabalo's, as well as teaching colleagues of Veronica's. The fever was killing the workers who washed the floors in the hospital, and the smell of vomit and bloody stool was overpowering.

Masangaya sent for the two ward orderlies who were still strong enough to work and ordered them to mop up the mess. One of them complained that he was sick. Masangaya saw the man's sunken eyes and felt his forehead.

"Clean this place, then come to my office. I'll give you some medicine," he said. "We will be back in a few minutes to start IVs."

Amene and Masangaya entered the maternity pavilion, which was empty except for Nza and Ngasa Moke and her new baby. Most of the beds still had dirty linen on them. There were bloodstains on the plastic mattresses and peanut shells and old banana peels on the concrete floor. The doctor and the medical assistant shook hands with Nza and congratulated Ngasa, who smiled and rocked her infant, pressing him to her breast. The baby searched for the nipple, found it, and sucked hungrily.

"*Mobali?*" asked Masangaya. A boy?

"*Iyo,*" replied the proud mother. The two men smiled.

"*Botikala malamu,*" said the medical assistant. Stay well.

"*Bokende malamu,*" replied the two sisters. Go well.

Masangaya signaled to Nza that he wanted her to follow them. Outside, he turned to her and said, "We have many sick with a bad fever—some have already died. You must take your sister home as soon as possible."

"But my neighbors in Yandongi are sick with this disease, and we hear that it is spreading," said Nza. "Ngasa lost much blood last night. Sister Lucie gave her a shot early this morning. I will try and take her home tomorrow or the next day. She needs the injections to build up her blood."

"Listen to me, Nza," said Masangaya. "You get her out of here as soon as she can stand. Do you hear me?"

"Yes, *monganga*. I will do it," she replied.

Nza stayed with her sister for another hour, then hurried back to Yandongi and her own child, promising to return later with food. She resolved to say nothing to Ngasa Moke about the rumors that were growing each day. The talk was in whispers; the cause of the killings, a mystery. The district elders and *ngangas* had gathered to discuss the sickness and deaths. Surely they would find out what forces lay behind the spreading menace and tell the villagers what to do.

Later in the day, Nza walked toward the maternity pavilion balancing on her head a bundle in which she had tied a plate and an enamel pot filled with *mwambe*. There were more visitors than usual around the medical ward. Some were weeping; some were sitting on the steps holding their heads. Four men came out carrying a body wrapped in a stained sheet. A woman shrieked like an animal caught in a trap and threw herself onto the corpse. She was pulled away. After ripping off the blouse that covered her breasts, she fell to her knees, pounded the ground with her fists, and covered her head with dust.

Nza grabbed the bundle off her head and ran. Ngasa Moke was sitting on the edge of the bed with the child at her breast. She was startled when her sister rushed in.

"You're all right!" said Nza, out of breath.

"Of course, I'm all right," replied Ngasa Moke. "He's a strong baby, and I have plenty of milk." She frowned. "What was all that noise? Why were you running?"

"I was worried about you. There is so much sickness now," replied Nza, sitting down on the bed. She put the bundle on her lap and untied the knot; unfolding the kerchief, she took the top off the enamel pot, releasing the strong, appetizing aroma of chicken cooked in palm oil and peanut sauce.

"I brought you some food. You need to eat well to make milk." She produced two spoons from the folds around her waist, lifted the pot off an enamel plate, and scooped out the most succulent parts of the chicken for her sister. Nza ate her share right out of the pot and finished ahead of Ngasa. The noises outside had faded, and the sun was at the level of the trees.

"I will take you home tomorrow," said Nza, wrapping up the plate and the pot.

"Thank you for being such a good older sister. We will be ready to leave with you after I get my injection." The sisters kissed each other, and Nza set off for the long trip home.

* * *

The next day Nza strode into the ward around noon, with a bright piece of printed cotton for her sister. Ngasa Moke was lying on her back, holding her head and moaning. The baby, wedged between his mother and the metal frame of the bed, was crying loudly.

"What is going on?" demanded Nza, alarmed.

"I hurt all over, and my body is burning up," whimpered Ngasa Moke. Nza picked up the screaming baby and felt her sister's forehead.

"You have a fever."

"Makila," said Ngasa Moke, pointing between her legs.

Nza lifted the sheet and saw that her sister was lying in a pool of bright red blood.

"Has Sister Lucie seen you?" asked Nza, now thoroughly frightened.

"No. One of the workers told me the sister is sick."

"Oh, that cannot be true. Sisters do not get sick. I'll go find her," said Nza, handing the baby to his mother and hurrying outside. One of the Zairian nurses was heading for the medical ward. She ran after him.

"Excuse me, my brother, can you tell me where I can find Sister Lucie?"

He stopped. "She is resting, but Sister Fermina will come later."

"Is Sister Lucie sick too?" asked Nza, calling after him.

The nurse ignored her and disappeared into the building. Nza returned slowly to Ngasa and her child, thinking hard. The mission no longer provided security. If the sister was sick and patients were dying in the hospital as well as in the villages, a frightening power was at work. She thought of her *nganga* in Bongolu. He had saved the family during the rebellion and become a wise *tata*. What would he counsel them now? Neither she nor Ngasa had followed his advice to stay in Bongolu to have their babies. The nuns

here knew how to use special medicines; they had helped
her have a normal baby after losing two. But this was a
white mission. They had their ways of doing things—good
things—but their ways were not the ways of her ancestors.
The nuns had no power over this *ndoki*. Ngasa Moke was
lying in the hospital, burning up and bleeding. She might
die because Nza had brought her to the missionaries.

Nza returned to her sister's bedside. "We are going home
to our mother."

"I cannot," whimpered Ngasa.

"You must! Sister Lucie is ill, and something is killing
people here. This is not our place. We need to be in our
own village with our family and our *nganga*."

"I cannot move," wailed Ngasa Moke, clutching her
head.

"I will carry the baby. We must go to my house in
Yandongi. My husband can get us a ride on a truck going
to Bongolu. Come on now!" Nza grabbed her sister's arm
and pulled her up. Ngasa cried out, but Nza made her
stand, stripped off the blood-soaked wraparound, and
quickly wiped her with a towel. Nza wrapped the *elamba*
around the sick girl's waist and tucked the free end in at the
hip. Ngasa Moke sat down heavily on the edge of the bed,
moaning and rocking.

"I cannot," she whispered.

"Of course you can," said her sister, yanking her to her
feet. "You will die if you stay here, and so will your son."

Nza picked up her bundle and the baby, then, putting her
strong right arm around Ngasa Moke's waist, dragged her
down the steps out of the maternity ward.

"Now stand up and walk," she ordered, releasing her sister. Ngasa clung to Nza's arm and obeyed. No one in authority saw them leave, and others they met were burdened
by their own despair and gave them no thought. The two

women proceeded slowly past the medical pavilion, past the dispensary, past the big mango trees and a palm tree whose fronds supported a flock of weaverbirds and their small hanging nests. When the weaverbirds scatter, so does the tribe.

Slowly, heavily, they continued to the end of the mission and onto the road that led to Yandongi. They passed through the coffee plantation and the mission farm. The morning sun, already hot and white, had dried the road, and the two women made steady progress; but after half an hour, Nza's arms and shoulders ached from the burden of her charges.

"Only a few more steps, and we will be able to rest in the shade," promised Nza, leading them into a green tunnel cut through trees and dense stands of bamboo. The baby slept on her left arm, and her sister staggered alongside, her fingers locked around Nza's right elbow. The vegetation met over their heads and kept out the heat of the sun but trapped the humid, stale air in which rotting plants exhaled their heavy stench. Flies converged voraciously on their faces and arms in search of moisture and blood. Ngasa Moke was deadweight. They would have to stop.

Nza turned into a small break in the foliage that bordered the road. She lowered her sister to the ground and put the bundle under her head. Ngasa Moke, rolled onto her side, pressed her fists into her middle, and curled up in a ball. Nza sat and lay the newborn in the cradle formed by the wraparound between her thighs. Sweat poured off her forehead and, mingling with tears of desperation, dripped onto the ruffles of her bodice. The baby slept. The ground cover hid them from the road.

Sister Fermina walked into the maternity ward. It was empty.

"Elles ont pris fuite," she said to herself impatiently. They have escaped.

Three beds with dried blood on dirty sheets were near the entrance. At the other end of the long room, big iridescent flies sipped from a dark pool in the middle of a rubber mattress. The place smelled of blood and feces. Only the buzzing of flies and the clucking of a curious hen at the door broke the silence.

Fermina turned her back on the filth and stomped out. The chicken squawked and ran, flapping wildly.

On September 16, nine more died in the hospital, including a young woman and her daughter that Masangaya had just started to rehydrate. Antonie ran between Lucie's labor rooms, where two women were about to deliver, and pediatrics. Fermina had sent Tata Embu, her old irreplaceable assistant, home to rest. In spite of all she and Antonie could do, children, cleaned up only minutes before, lay again in their vomit, glassy eyed, too weak to brush the flies from their faces. Three toddlers had died during the middle of the day, when the noon sun made a stinking oven of the ward.

Later in the day an ancient truck rattled up to the convent, and a white-haired African climbed down from the cab. A chief's bronze medallion, given by the Belgians before independence, dangled from his neck. He wore a feathered headdress. Slowly, with the help of an attendant, he climbed the terrace steps to Augustina's office. After a formal greeting to the Mother Superior, the old man sat down. He announced that members of three families were very ill in his village and that the leaders of other villages along the road to Bumba had asked him to report that many women and children and even some men were either already dead or dying.

"Our *ngangas* tell us to allow no one to enter or leave

the villages. This we are starting to do. Have the medical authorities passed on any other advice?" asked the chief.

Augustina was about to answer when, without knocking, Father Gérard strode in. "I saw your truck drive up, old friend," he said. The chief stood, and the men shook hands.

"I bring sad news from my village, Father. Whole families are losing blood and dying."

"I am sorry to hear that," said Gérard. "Most of your villagers are good souls who do not deserve to be punished for the evil of others."

The chief squinted up at the tall priest who had been with them for so long and carried the title of *nkumu*, "person of note," rarely given to a white man.

"The first man to die was Mabalo Lokela, a teacher and the president of your Catholic committee," said the chief.

"Yes," replied Gérard, "I am afraid that sometimes the innocent die for the sins of others. The sinners must repent and be cleansed."

The chief bowed slightly. "We have a saying, 'If you try to cleanse others—like soap, you will melt in the process.'"

Gérard laughed. "I should have remembered that 'you do not teach the paths of the forest to an old monkey.'"

Augustina cut in. "You two could fence with your proverbs all day. The point is not who or what is to blame but what we are going to do."

"I am planning a high mass to expiate the sins of the population and to pray for an end to the scourge," announced Gérard.

As they spoke, a man appeared at the door, waving a piece of paper. Augustina took it, thanked him, and read aloud: "'In Benzari, a woman and five men have just died.'"

The chief turned to the priest. "I hope, Father, that your

prayers and medicines will be effective. But, as in the rebellion, my people will be isolated behind the same bamboo poles and fetishes that kept the *simbas* out. Father, Reverend Mother"—he bowed formally to each—"I must get back to my village. Stay well." They shook hands.

"Go well," replied Augustina.

As the sun set behind the mangoes and palm trees, and the sky filled with the evening's cumulus buildup, only four patients were still in the hospital. Then, shortly after sunset, during the brief time the mission generator provided lights for the hospital, six more arrived. Two of them died within an hour of their admission.

After supper and evening prayers, the sisters gathered on the convent terrace. Lucie was getting sicker by the hour. All she would eat now were petit beurre biscuits dipped in tea or very thin slices of smoked bacon. Fermina and Veronica divided up the night so one of them would be with her while the other slept.

Mbunzu, Mabalo's widow, was now very ill. Veronica went to her house again, but she remained adamant, refusing to go to the hospital. Dr. Amene stopped by later in the day to take some of her blood to send to Kinshasa where tests could be done and, perhaps, a diagnosis made. It took Amene four jabs and some digging around in Mbunzu's muscular forearm to find a vein. After filling his test tubes, he plugged an IV into the same needle and taped it to her arm. She glowered at him, then turned her face to the wall. Embarrassed, he apologized for hurting her, but the needle was old and the bevel blunt with usage. After he left, Mbunzu stared at the water dripping from the plastic bag; it had not helped Mabalo, what made this doctor think it would help her? With her other arm, she yanked out the needle and pulled the baby to her breast, finding solace in his rhythmic, resolute sucking.

Death's pall hung over the mission. Those who died, including the three male nurses, were buried quickly without ceremony. Others clung to life in stinking wards or on a mat in a worker's hut. Relatives huddled in corners or slept under the bed of a spouse or child. The world beyond the forest was still unaware: no white person had died. Those who watched and waited clung to the hope that strong medicines would arrive. They felt certain that the fathers and sisters would stop the dying.

CHAPTER 3

After the night storm, the morning sky was clear as the Land Rover prepared to leave Yalosemba for the eighty-kilometer journey to Yambuku. Matilda had a last word with her Zairian nurses, who were worried she might catch the Yambuku disease. "What long sad faces!" she teased. "Don't worry about me, those bugs will run off as soon as I arrive." Then she climbed into the front seat next to her driver, Luc, and smiled at the thought of seeing her good friends—two of whom were the best nurses she had ever trained.

It was slow going, for in low places the road became a stagnant pool of water hiding deep ruts under the surface, and, even with Luc's skill and four-wheel drive, they were stuck three times. The first was after they'd traveled only twenty kilometers. Luckily, they were within sight of Yangome, where Matilda was well known. The men from the village dug them out, after she had lanced a boil on a screaming child and examined a shy girl whose round belly jutted out so far from her thin body that she waddled on her heels.

The second time they were not so lucky. They had been bouncing along on a stretch of road through secondary forest growth where coffee and bananas had been cultivated until the soil was exhausted and abandoned. The hole appeared shallower than it was. Matilda had to hike up her skirt, roll up her sleeves, and help Luc shovel through the ridge of heavy, waterlogged earth holding the Land Rover captive. Half an hour later, they were on their way again.

At Yalitaku, twenty-six kilometers from Yambuku, they were stuck fast up to the axles. Luc pushed on the horn; two men came out of a hut, glared at him, and shook their fists.

"What is the matter with them?" asked Matilda.

"I will go see."

The men yelled, *"Longwa, kende,"* as Luc waded heavily toward them. Go away, go away. One of them leaned over and picked up a rock.

"Yo, kobwaka te," said Luc, stopping at the edge of the mire. Hold on. "We need to come through."

"You are from the Yambuku Mission. You carry the disease that kills the young mothers."

Other villagers, some armed with sticks and machetes, were gathering behind the first two men. Luc was tall and well built, with the quiet way of men who are sure of their strength. A N'Gbandi from the north, like his distant cousin the president, he towered above the Budja villagers. He held up both hands and continued to approach.

"I have with me Sister Matilda, the nurse from Yalosemba. I am taking her to Yambuku to cure our sick. You know her; she is wise in white medicine."

The group parted for an old man with gray fuzz around his bald pate and linear tribal markings on his forehead.

"Mbote, mbuta muntu," said Luc, holding out his hand. Good day, respected elder.

The old man ignored the gesture and squinted up at him. "It is not a good day. Two of our young mamas returned from the maternity at Yambuku hospital and died last night.

One had given birth to a dead baby, and the other woman's child cannot be awakened and does not eat. Our people will not travel to Yambuku and, as in the days of the spotted fevers, no one will be allowed into the village."

"That is a sound decision. Sister Matilda and I should be the last you let through. If we have to turn back and drive to Yambuku through Modjamboli, it will take us two days. During that time, more of our people will die."

A man called out from behind the chief, "Don't let them through." Others grumbled their agreement.

"You will not pass until I confer with the heads of families and the fathers of the dead women," said the chief. He turned around and stomped back through the gathering. The men followed, leaving Luc standing alone. He returned to the Land Rover.

Matilda stepped down and reached in for the shovels. "They will not help us because they know we do not pay," she said, passing one of the shovels to Luc.

"Not this time, Sister." He told her what the chief had said. "Let's dig out while they have their palaver."

The sun beat down on them, and the smell of hot mud mingled with the odor of fermenting manioc by the road. Matilda's nose and cheeks were smeared with mud from slapping flies between each shovelful. As the clamor of voices reached them from the village, they dug at the earth under the vehicle until the Land Rover's wheels rested in the ruts. Matilda gathered an armful of leaves from the banana trees next to the road and stuffed them under the wheels.

Luc, breathing hard, suggested, "You drive. I will push." The mud sucked at his feet as he stepped to the back. Matilda climbed in, her long skirt splashing mud on the front seat and floor. The tailpipe was just below the surface, and when she started the engine, the exhaust gurgled like a motor boat. The Land Rover lurched forward and hung up again, the wheels spinning and spraying mud all over Luc. Again they attacked the central ridge to the end of the mire. This time Matilda was able to drive clear and stop on dry land. As Luc caught up with her, the racket from the meeting stopped, and the chief, followed by a small delegation, walked down to the road.

"We will let you through if the sister will see the sick infant. Then we barricade the road," he announced.

"That is fine," said Matilda. "Take me to the child." She glanced at Luc. "You look like a ceremonial dancer covered with red paint. You can wipe off; I will not be long." Luc watched the white-haired sister striding barefoot up the road and smiled.

The chief led Matilda to a small hut and pointed to the entrance. She bent over and stepped in under the palm leaf roof. An old woman sat on a wooden stool, rocking a bundle wrapped in a towel.

"*Mbote, mama.*"

"*Ahh.*"

"*Lakisa ngai mwana.*" Show me the child.

The old woman pushed aside the cloth covering the infant's head. Its eyes were half closed, and only the whites showed deep in the sockets. Matilda ran her fingers over the hot little head and felt the depressed fontanel. Thick bloody mucous bubbled from the nostrils as the child gasped for air. Matilda's eyes met those of the woman briefly; doom hovered in the dark corners of the hut.

The chief approached as she came out. She shook her head. He understood and said with quiet authority, "That the infant dies is normal; that the mother dies is not. Go quickly to the mission and stop the deaths."

Luc drove slowly through the village. The clean-swept yards in front of the houses were deserted; not even a dog came out to bark. Glancing in the rearview mirror, Luc saw men placing long bamboo poles across the road. He was relieved that there were no more villages to go through on the last leg of the drive.

They arrived in Yambuku as the sun was setting, and Luc honked the horn as they drove up to the convent. Veronica came out of Augustina's office and ran down the steps.

"Welcome to Yambuku," said Veronica. "By the looks of it, you had to dig your way here." The two sisters embraced. "I have put you in the spare room next to Augustina's office. We can have supper and talk after you have cleaned up."

"How is Lucie?"

"She's not well at all. She feels awful," answered Veronica.

"I would like to see her before dinner. I won't be a minute."

While she waited, Veronica sat on the low wall between the corridor and the garden. Dusk had fallen. A high-pitched wail signaling another death came from the hospital buildings. Far off, carried by a lingering sigh from a hot, tired land before it slept, came the beat of a drum—fast and slow, fearful and sad. Down by the workers' quarters, the generator sputtered, and the handful of lights hanging from the beams came to life as the diesel hit its stride. Moths and mosquitoes swarmed around the bulbs. The keening from the hospital stopped. Veronica was relieved that Matilda had arrived; she would know what to do.

The window of Lucie's room was open to let in the cool evening air. The glow from a lightbulb in the corridor cast a soft yellow light into the bedroom which, like all the others, was furnished with a plain armoire, a cold-water wash-stand, and a small table and straight chair. Over the metal cot covered with a thin mattress on sagging bedsprings hung a plain dark wooden cross. A bed table held a candle-stick and matches and Lucie's only personal possessions: her glasses and a picture of St. Thérèse of Lisieux.

Lucie was asleep. Matilda put her finger to her lips, as the two nuns stepped quietly to the foot of the bed. Matilda gasped. Lucie was lying on her back, her nightgown open to her breasts, a white cotton sheet covering the rest of her body. Her face, usually so bright and healthy, was damp and gray. Her breathing was shallow and rapid, and the gap between her two front teeth, which had given her the look of a little girl, was filled with dried blood and mucous. She opened her eyes and squinted up at the tall silhouette before her.

"Here's an old friend to see you," said Veronica.

Lucie wiped her eyes with the corner of the sheet and reached for her glasses on the bedside table.

Matilda moved toward her. "Do not disturb yourself, Lucie. It is me." She took the sick nun's hand and held it.

"Matilda, what a surprise!" She swallowed and closed her eyes tight, trying to shake off the pain. "What brings you here?"

"I heard that you might need some help. And I wanted to get out of Yalosemba and stretch my legs a little."

"I'm so happy you have come. I feel very stupid being sick."

"It has been impossible to keep her from going to work," said Veronica.

"There is so much to do," whispered Lucie.

"You rest now. We'll have you better soon."

Lucie smiled up at her mentor. "You bring me hope."

Matilda squeezed her hand. "Sleep now. The others are waiting for us in the refectory. We will be back after supper. Can I get you anything?"

"Nothing, thank you."

"In a little while then."

After dinner Masangaya and Dr. Amene came in, shook hands around the table, and sat down. Sister Augustina started. "With so many people dying daily, and now our dear Lucie stricken, we are all grateful that you are here, Matilda. We need to review the past weeks and figure out what needs to be done."

Augustina studied her notes, then began. "Mabalo Lokela died ten days ago. Since then, more people have come into the hospital with the same symptoms, and many have died. I have searched through the registers for patients with bleeding. I found only four." She put her finger on the paper and read, " 'In May of this year, a twelve-year-old boy was in for two days, vomiting blood. In July, a thirty-year-old woman was hospitalized for twelve days with bloody diarrhea, and a fifty-year-old woman was admitted, vomiting blood. In August, an eighteen-year-old woman came in, also vomiting blood.' In reviewing the records, I was struck by the fact that we have no idea what happened to these four patients, none of whom were from our immediate area. They must have either been removed from the hospital by their families or simply left. None of the others who have died in the hospital since January had any bleeding."

Fermina interrupted. "There was also the stranger who claimed he was from Yandongi. He came in at the end of August with bloody diarrhea and nosebleeds."

"What happened to him?" asked Matilda.

"He was removed in the middle of the night by people no one had ever seen before," replied Fermina. "We have not been able to find out where he went or whether he is dead or alive."

"So, you mean that the only people who were taken out of the hospital or left on their own were those who had some bleeding?" asked Veronica.

"That is what the records show," replied Augustina.

"Curious," said Matilda. "But let's concentrate on our current patients. What other symptoms do they have?"

Augustina turned to Amene. "Doctor, could you tell us what you have seen in the last few days?"

He scanned the notes in front of him, cleared his throat, and said, "I came up from Bumba three days ago at the request of my medical brother, Masangaya. This afternoon we reviewed the crisis at the hospital since Mabalo Lokela, the forty-four-year-old teacher, became ill on September second and died six days later. At first it was thought he had malaria, then a bleeding gastric ulcer. We know that his wife, Mbunzu, became ill two days after he died. So far she is alive, and, although she has fever and much pain in her head and body, she has not had any bleeding from her stomach or her bowel. Her seven-week-old boy seems well, but we heard this evening that Mabalo's mother has spiked a high fever and complains of headaches.

"On September fourth, a thirty-eight-year-old man from Yaekanga, twenty-eight kilometers west of here, in the hospital for a hernia repair, became febrile and started to vomit blood. He died three days later. A thirty-year-old woman from the same village, hospitalized for leg ulcers, came down with similar symptoms on the ninth. She is still in the hospital.

"Nsembo Ndombe brought her husband to the mission from Yaongo for the repair of a large inguinal hernia. Masangaya operated on him on September second; the patient did well. While he was recovering from his surgery, his wife received injections for fatigue—the usual vitamin B complex and calcium. Four days later, she came down with fever, headaches, and vomiting; three days after that, she died. Two other younger women from Yaongo who had been followed in the prenatal clinic died only four days after they became ill. All the patients suffer from the same severe symptoms and have the same rapid death. The affliction is characterized by high fever—thirty-nine degrees Celsius or higher; vomiting of blood—most often digested—but some red blood in a few cases; diarrhea, with bloody mucous at the onset, becoming pure blood toward the end; sometimes bleeding from the nose; retrosternal and abdominal pain; decreased mobility and heaviness of the joints; and a rapid evolution toward a stuporous state and death in three to seven days." The doctor paused and drank some coffee.

"Yesterday a man and his wife died in the medical ward as we were trying to start their IVs."

"Were they from the mission?" asked Augustina.

"Yes. Mabwanza, the president of the cooperative, and his wife," replied Masangaya.

"I tried to get them to you sooner, but they would not listen," said Veronica.

"I know. They told me that. It wasn't your fault, Sister," replied the medical assistant. He continued, "Two of Bozage's children have also perished."

"The director of the boys' boarding school?" asked Augustina.

"That is right."

Augustina added, "Masangaya had the boys' school evacuated yesterday. All the students were sent back to their villages."

Matilda nodded. "Good. And what about the girls?"

Masangaya replied, "I've sent word to their families, but

it will take time before they respond. It is too dangerous to send young women home without escorts, and none are available."

Dr. Amene continued, "This morning after rounds, Masangaya and I made a quick trip to Yandongi. I picked up a child to examine him, and he died in my arms." The doctor looked around the table. "We have seen no one who has recovered from the disease."

"What treatments have you tried?" asked Matilda.

"Rehydration with saline, chloramphenicol, penicillin, and the usual antimalarials," replied the doctor. "I think you have something to add," he said, turning to Masangaya.

"Yes. Almost all the people who are dead have been in the hospital or been seen in the dispensary. Some were at Mabalo Lokela's funeral. Over the past two weeks, twenty-five people have been admitted with the symptoms described by Dr. Amene. Over half of them—fifteen to be exact—have died, some immediately, others after about seven days. We counted six patients still alive in the medical ward this evening before coming over here. Two days ago, a man from Yamolembia was carried in by his family and died two hours later. When the family took the body, three of his friends from the same village left the hospital in spite of being very ill. Another man fled during the night."

Augustina said, "Abata, one of our teachers, came into the hospital the day after Mabalo was admitted. He ran off to his village the day Mabalo died."

Veronica added, "Two of the social service teachers are sick in the workers' quarters."

"Although we have tried to keep word of Sister Lucie's condition from the people, they seem to know what is going on. I think a sister being ill is increasing their fear," said Masangaya.

"Those who die as soon as they reach the hospital cause fear as well," said Dr. Amene. "Early this afternoon, a woman, eight and a half months pregnant, came in from Yandongi. She gave birth to a stillborn child and died two hours later. Her family ran off, and two of the workers had to deal with the body. So you see, Sister," he said, turning to Matilda, "the situation is desperate and chaotic. It is difficult to keep track of who is sick and who is dying."

"This is much worse than anything we have seen before," said Matilda. "What do you think is killing all these people?"

Masangaya answered, "I don't know what the organism is, but, as I've said before, most of the people struck down by the disease have come from the hospital or have been in direct contact with people who have been at the hospital. Some of the young women who have been followed in our prenatal clinic have come in with the fever and died."

Dr. Amene added, "It appears that death is caused by bleeding in the intestinal tract. We do not have a way of determining what the organism is. Those who have the disease and have run away from the hospital will probably spread it to their villages. We urgently need help to determine the infecting agent and how it is spread."

"Where have most of the people been buried?" asked Matilda.

"Usually right outside their houses, although in one village they have been buried inside," replied Masangaya.

The scraping of Augustina's chair as she stood up cut through the heavy stillness around the table. She reached for the coffee and poured the last of it into Matilda's cup. She looked around to see if anyone wanted more; no one did, so she sat down.

"What are we going to do about Lucie?" asked Veronica.

Masangaya replied, "Dr. Amene and I have been discussing her. We think she should be sent to Belgium as soon as possible. The Institute of Tropical Medicine in Antwerp has the means to make a diagnosis. If we knew what disease was causing the epidemic we might be able to deal with it better."

"That certainly makes sense," said Augustina.

Matilda agreed. "We can drive her to Bumba in time for the noon flight to Kinshasa. I will go with her as far as Bumba."

"We will notify Lisala, as soon as they come on the air in the morning. I'm sure they will approve," said Augustina.

Veronica cut in. "I wouldn't call Lisala until Lucie is headed down the road; then they won't have a choice."

Augustina frowned at her. Veronica shrugged.

Matilda addressed Masangaya and Dr. Amene. "After Lucie is on her way, I will go to Lisala and persuade the authorities that we must have more help."

The doctor and the medical assistant agreed, then left to collect the medicines and IVs needed for the trip.

Midnight came and went. The evening storm had moved on, leaving only distant grumbling and sheet lightning flashing across the tops of trees. Water dripped from the roofs, forming puddles and gullies in the soft earth. The night was heavy with sodden heat.

People everywhere were huddled together, held tightly and silently by the terror that possessed the mission and villages. Those suffering in the medical ward slept intermittently. In the convent, the sisters were restless, getting up to change out of their clammy nightgowns.

Fermina kept her vigil in the wicker chair by Lucie's bed. She fingered her rosary and repeated Hail Mary's, as she fought to keep awake. It was 3 A.M. Moths darted in and out of the light cast by a kerosene lantern on the washstand. The shrill, staccato clicking of insects, the eerie call of a night bird, and the short *ngok, ngok*s of the bush babies drifted in from the forest. The room was filled with the rasp of Lucie's labored breathing. She awakened, lifted a hand off the sheet, and pushed her swollen tongue between her lips in a sign for a drink. Fermina nodded. She lit another kerosene lamp on the table, adjusted the flame, and picked it up along with the pitcher.

"I will get you some fresh cold water," she said, heading for the icebox in the refectory, relieved to be able to do something.

Returning to the room, Fermina put the lamp on the table, poured water into a tumbler, and approached the bed. Lucie's eyes were wide open; the whites were stained with bloody, viscous tears, filling the inner hollows and overflowing into the creases at the corners of her mouth. Red mucous oozed from her open mouth and flaring nostrils, as she fought for air. Fist-sized red blotches had appeared at the base of her neck and on her upper chest. Fermina dropped the tumbler and ran out of the room and down the corridor, pounding with all her strength on the bedroom doors and screaming, "Come quickly, she is dying, she is dying!"

The sisters, terrified by Fermina's shouts, rushed out of their rooms and converged at Lucie's bedside. Matilda checked her pulse and blood pressure. Veronica dripped water from a spoon into her mouth, while Antonie picked up the pieces of the broken tumbler. Lucie swallowed with great pain. Fermina, who was out in the hallway trying to control her sobbing, was led to her room by Augustina. Matilda and Veronica conferred in whispers. Veronica would stay with Lucie now; the others needed to rest so they could take over in the morning.

The agony of breathing, and swallowing, and living continued.

At 4 A.M. the forest was silent and dark. The nocturnal creatures now slept; dawn had yet to awaken those that moved and fed by day. The night air was replaced by a gentle, cool breeze which announced the approaching sunrise. A cock crowed, and somewhere, a mangabey, high in the forest's upper canopy, whooped and gobbled to start the dawn chorus proclaiming a new day.

The lamps in Lucie's room had been turned down, and their small blue flames cast a penumbral glow into the corners and over the bed. Veronica sat next to one of the lanterns and wrote a letter to her own sister, Gabrielle, and the other nuns in the mission at Binga.

19 September 1976
Dearest Sisters:

I have to let you know bad news. Sister Lucie is very ill. There is an epidemic over here. The doctors have not yet found what it is. Each day is like a month. Lucie has been confined to bed since Wednesday with a high fever, which does not fall. She has inflammation of all mucous membranes and her throat, vomits constantly, and has black stool.

Yesterday Sister Matilda came from Yalosemba, and we decided to send Lucie to Belgium. It is now a quarter to five. Lucie was to leave for Bumba at 5 A.M., but it is impossible now. She is at the end.

Do not come over. Surely barriers to isolate our area will be put up soon. More than twenty people have died at the hospital. We do not know how many more in surrounding villages.

Lucie stirred and pointed to the bedpan on the chair next to the table. Veronica put down her pen and came over to assist her, but Lucie collapsed the moment her feet touched the floor. Veronica called out for help, and moments later, she and Antonie had Lucie back in bed while Fermina rushed to summon Father Gérard. Matilda could not find a pulse. She pushed down briskly and rhythmically on Lucie's chest, and after a minute, she heard a faint heartbeat through her stethoscope. Quickly she reached into her bag, retrieved a syringe, drew up a dose of adrenaline, and injected it into Lucie's arm. Her heartbeat became stronger, and she opened her eyes.

Augustina leaned over and, with her lips close to Lucie's ear, asked softly, "What do you want us to tell your parents?"

"I do not know, I do not know," sobbed Lucie feebly.

Father Gérard came into the room, his sparse white hair disheveled, his cassock, like a bathrobe, open to the waist, the straps on his sandals unbuckled. He sat next to the bed, took Lucie's hands, folded them together, and held them in his. He bent his head and prayed in a soft murmur, his eyes shut tight, holding back tears. "Courage, Sister. We are all here with you."

The priest turned and, looking at Antonie, said, "Please bring my sick-call bag—it is in my room—and the viaticum and the purple stole from the church."

Still covering Lucie's hands with one of his own, he reached into the pocket of his cassock and pulled out a crumpled handkerchief. Gently, he pushed a wet lock of hair from her forehead and wiped away the bloodstained tears.

They had known each other for a long time. Big and strongly built, he had the carriage of a soldier. His gray-blue eyes could be hard. A thick white beard gave fullness to his jaw. His approach to religion was uncompromising, his sermons full of hellfire. Punishment with penance was exacted for each sin admitted in the confessional. He was self-righteous, having little compassion for those he considered weak or sloppy like Father Dubonnet with his dirty cassocks and ascetic ways. Gérard had the discipline of a Jesuit rather than the softness of a parish priest from the Order of Scheut. Father Gérard was a strong man, in the tradition of those who came to subdue and civilize the Congo. He was with the sisters in Yalosemba when the *simbas*, the rebels, tried to come through the mission. The story of his heroism had become legendary and was repeated around cooking fires.

Gérard went out unarmed to meet the rebels in the pasture behind the church as they emerged from the trees. There were six of them, armed with spears and two muzzle-loading poopoo guns used by native hunters. He stood like a prophet, his arms stretched out to them, the wind blowing his beard across his shoulder and shouted, "Go ahead, shoot me, but you will not touch the mission or the people in it." Two *simbas* raised their rifles. Flames shot out of the muzzles with the hiss and crack of black powder, and lead balls smacked into the turf less than a meter away from the father. He bent over and dug the bullets out of the earth and dropped them into the chest pocket of his soutane.

"Now, fire again!" he shouted. "But do not touch the mission." The *simbas* glowered at him for a moment, then, after a quick consultation, turned and ran back to the forest. When Father Gérard returned to the convent, he ordered the sisters to be ready to leave in half an hour. He drove them to Lisala, where they stayed until the immediate danger was over.

Years ago, Lucie confessed to Father Gérard that she had been attracted to a young Belgian health officer who had spent a few days at the mission. The priest imposed a ten-

day penance of prayers to be said in the middle of the night
on the concrete altar step of the chapel. Not long after that,
Lucie caught the priest sneaking a bottle of communion
wine into his room. With a laugh, she told him that she was
relieved to see that she was not the only one with a weakness of the flesh. Although the other sisters respected
Gérard, they feared him. She saw through his façade and
loved him.

"Sister," began Father Gérard, "you have lived a life
pleasing to God and the holy angels. Do you have anything
to confess?"

Lucie nodded. Sister Augustina, taking the cue, led the
others out into the corridor. The priest leaned over to hear
her.

Lucie whispered, "I have been impatient with my sickness and disobeyed Sister Augustina when she ordered me
to stay in bed." She thought for a moment. "I am afraid to
die," then added, "There is nothing else."

The priest said, "Make a good act of contrition, *ma
soeur.*"

"Dear God, I am heartily sorry for having offended You.
I detest all my sins. . . ." Her voice lost its strength, but her
lips formed the words. When she was through, Father
Gérard extended his fingers over her head. "I absolve you
from your sins in the name of the Father and the Son and
the Holy Spirit," he said, making the sign of the cross. He
tried to hide his anguish, but the tears rolled down his
cheeks and into his beard. Looking over his shoulder, he
nodded to the sisters who came back into the room, followed shortly by Antonie, who gave the priest his bag, the
viaticum, and the stole. The nuns knelt around the bed.

Father Gérard kissed the stole and put it around his neck.
He placed his hands on Lucie's head and prayed silently.
Then dipping his right thumb in the sacred oil, he made the

sign of the cross on her forehead, saying, "Through this holy anointing, may the Lord in His love and mercy help you with the grace of the Holy Spirit. Our Father, who art in Heaven . . ." The sisters joined him in the Lord's Prayer. After giving communion to Lucie, he blessed her and the other sisters in the room.

Matilda stepped to the bedside. Lucie's breathing was coming in short gasps, and her pulse was thready and rapid under Matilda's fingers. Fermina leaned on the back of Gérard's chair, weeping. Veronica, Augustina, and Antonie prayed silently at the foot of the bed. Outside, the palm trees and mangoes were a black filigree against the pale dawn sky. The rooster in the barnyard flapped his wings and crowed, and the hens scattered from his sharp beak.

Lucie whispered hoarsely, "My feet are cold."

Veronica raised the sheet and rubbed her ankles. Gérard released her hands and sat back in the chair. Suddenly, Lucie took a deep breath, cried out, and died as the air left her body. The red blotches on her chest and at the base of her neck turned livid. Released from the struggle for air and the grip of pain, her body relaxed in the bed as it had after a hard day's work when the rewards of sleep were merited and came easily.

Fermina cried out, "She is gone!" and ran from the room.

In a strong voice, Father Gérard called out, "Saints of God, come to her aid! Come to meet her, angels of the Lord!"

The nuns responded, "Receive her soul and present her to God the Most High."

In the gray light of early morning, everything was quiet inside the medical pavilion. Four of the patients were sleeping or in a coma; the others were awake, pain racking their wasted bodies. Most of the visitors were asleep on the floor. Outside, the night fires had gone out. People were curled up, wrapped in their clothes or pieces of cloth. A mission worker, whose wife was in the ward, had been watching the convent from behind the bougainvillaea near the terrace. He had heard Fermina pounding and shouting to awaken the other sisters and had seen Father Gérard arrive. When he heard Fermina's cry, "She is gone!" he ran back to his wife in the medical pavilion. His mother was sleeping under the bed.

"Sister Lucie just died," he said, in an urgent whisper, shaking both women awake. "Nothing can be done here. We must go."

The man and his mother supported his sick wife as they left the ward. A woman sitting at the entrance asked, "What happened? What are you doing?"

"The whites cannot save their own. There is no hope here," said the man over his shoulder, as he and the two women hurried to put distance between themselves and the hospital.

The word of Lucie's death raced throughout the mission. "*Tolongwa awa, noki-noki.*" We must flee quickly from here. "The sister is dead. The *mindele* have nothing to stop the dying. The whites will die themselves."

Within minutes, the hospital was practically empty. The patients fled in all directions, some carried on the backs of relatives. Those who lived nearby went back to their villages. Others, from far off, dragged their sick into the forest and built stick and leaf shelters near a stream, as they had done during the rebellion. There, hidden from the dangerous spirits at the hospital, they would wait for the terror to pass or die in isolation. Only a few stricken hospital workers and a handful of patients without family or friends remained in the medical ward.

* * *

Veronica sat on her bed, trying to draw comfort from the cross on the wall, the unfinished letter to Gabrielle in her lap. She thought of the last outing she and Lucie and the other nuns had taken along the Dua River that meandered through the forest. With much laughter and splashing, they had pulled the pirogue out of the water and picnicked in the shade of a giant hardwood. Soon, Lucie's family would sit together in the kitchen of their Flemish farm, silent and devastated. A light rap sounded.

"Come in," she said. The door opened a crack.

"May I sit with you?" It was Antonie's timid voice. "I do not want to be alone."

Veronica nodded. Antonie came in and paused, uncertain and self-conscious, in the middle of the room. Her eyes were swollen and red. She had a towel over her shoulder and a bottle of something in her left hand.

"Sit down, Antonie. You make me nervous just standing there."

"I will . . . later, but I think we should take showers and wash off with Dettol," said Antonie, almost apologetically.

"You are probably right," responded Veronica vacantly.

"Here," said Antonie, handing over the bottle of disinfectant. "There is enough for both of us. You go first. I'll burn our nightshirts after we are through."

Augustina, after showering, had retired to her office to write Lucie's family. She sealed the letter, then went to the chapel and, kneeling, buried her face in her hands. Fermina and Matilda, still in their night robes, watched over Lucie during the early hours of the morning. Father Gérard continued to mumble prayers from his breviary, and the two nuns sat in silence. When the priest had finished praying, he left to make arrangements for a coffin and to plan the funeral. The women washed the body and dressed it with great care. Not Gérard nor Fermina nor Matilda took the time to disinfect themselves.

Around the middle of the morning, Father Gérard and two mission workers brought a plain wooden coffin into the corridor outside Lucie's room. Veronica, who had returned to sit with her friend, helped Gérard lift the body off the bed and lower it into the coffin. The workers carried it to the convent's front porch. Augustina was waiting. Veronica walked down the steps into the flower beds and, picking some red roses and pink bougainvillaea, placed them carefully around Lucie's head. Then she sat in a corner chair with her prayer book and pad of paper and thought about the evenings when the sisters had come together on this terrace to talk over the events of the day, to drink a glass of wine—when it was available—and to laugh at Lucie's jokes and imitations.

After a while, Veronica continued the letter she had started to Gabrielle.

Lucie died at 5:10 A.M. She has gone to Heaven. Pray for her.

I went to confession this morning and presently am sitting on the terrace next to our beloved sister's coffin. She is now at peace. People from the mission and the villages come by quietly to pay their last respects.

To die now would be ideal, because if we live through this crisis, some of our routine work which brought us such a sense of accomplishment and satisfaction before the epidemic will appear common and dull. I am doing everything very intensely now. Our liturgy seems to be drenched with death. We are now more aware of the things we read in the psalms and prayers, closer to them.

We have been under much stress and, in normal times,

there would have been harsh words. But we are all doing our best to help one another.

I think about death. Life is so short. I pray that I will accept death when my turn comes and that I will die well.

Pray for Lucie, my dear sisters. And pray for us.

At 3 P.M. the coffin was closed. The school directors and mission workers crowded around to help carry the coffin into the church and place it in front of the altar. Mass was led by Father Gérard and Father Dubonnet. Augustina hesitated to let the sisters attend the funeral because of the risk of exposing them to more contamination. But they all went and sat in the choir with Lucie's coffin. The church was packed with Africans, who wept and sang in harmony to the beat of the drums.

"Who will help us now at the parents' house?
Who will make the baby food for the orphans?
Who will forbid our husbands' drunkenness?
Who will give us good advice?"

The African leader of the liturgy had prepared the Mass of Glory because he thought of Sister Lucie as a saint. Father Gérard gave a powerful and sometimes emotional oration about her life. During the Mass, the skies opened and a heavy rain began to fall.

When the service was over, the sisters and the priests filed out of the church, followed by the congregation. The people sang and sobbed in the rain, as the procession trudged between the rows of palms to the little cemetery where the whites were laid to rest. After the burial, the mourners pleaded to return to the convent with the nuns to keen, as they were used to doing with their own dead. But Augustina told them that the sisters wanted to be alone in their grief, and slowly, sadly, the crowd melted away.

CHAPTER 4

In Yandongi, dawn filtered through the printed material drawn across the small window of the back room. Nza pushed herself up and stretched after the long night. The curtain rippled in the morning breeze; she pulled it to one side to let in the fresh air. A narrow cot, a baby's crib made from a wooden beer crate, and a three-legged stool took shape in the gray light. Ngasa Moke was curled up on the cot, her head cushioned on her hands. The smell of her fetid exhalations and the rasp of her rapid breathing filled the cramped room. Nza's hope of getting her sister to their *nganga* in Bongolu had faded. Ngasa moaned, and Nza bent over and saw the suffering in her face.

"Oh, my little sister," she whispered, *"zela moke."* Hold on. "I will get you some water." She pushed aside the coarse sheet that separated the sleeping room from the main room and stepped quietly to the water crock in the corner. Her husband, snoring peacefully on the plastic sofa, was working double shifts to pay for their needs. Nza filled a small pot from the crock. Kneeling by the cot, she carefully placed her arm around her sister's neck and shoulder and lifted her upper body. Ngasa made a feeble effort to drink, but water ran down her chin; swallowing was too painful. Nza put down the pot and lowered her slowly to the bed. With a wet towel, Nza washed the putrid crusts from her sister's eyes and the corners of her mouth. She cleaned around Ngasa's teeth and bleeding gums and wiped her sister's face. Then she picked up a wide fan she had made from braided fronds and moved the air rhythmically over the cot.

Nza had sat with old mamas at the end of their lives. That had been different. When the old died, they moved to the village of the ancestors and were served by the living. In Bongolu her forefathers inhabited a sacred ficus that had towered over the forest for as long as memory, immune to lightning and storms. Infants who died before undergoing initiation ceremonies that made them full members of the clan went into limbo and were forgotten. Such losses were difficult, but other children could be created. Far more devastating was the death of a young man or a young woman in their most reproductive and energetic years. Those deaths were a threat to the survival of the family. Their lives had not yet been filled by experience. Those who died before they had played their part in the perpetuation of the clan could be denied a place with the ancestors.

Gradually the reds and blues of the cloth by the window emerged from the grayness. Isolated fronds of the palm tree between her house and the neighbors' vibrated in the soft morning air. Soon the sun would rise and the morning coolness would be replaced by searing heat that slowed life to a crawl. By noon nobody would be outside, and goats would squeeze against the huts in whatever slivers of shade they could find.

Nza heard the muttering of Molangi's family, sitting outside their house next door. Molangi, the mother of two, had been killed by the fever the day before. Her body had been buried the same afternoon; none of the usual ceremonies or contacts with the dead woman had been allowed by the elders. Some of the old uncles had objected to this intrusion into their customs; but the *matanga*—mourning—had been retained and would go on for another day with friends coming to pay their respects and to eat and drink. For a family to run out of beer or food during *matanga* would cast dishonor on the dead; thus the bereaved often became debtors. Molangi's week-old baby and her eighteen-year-old sister were both now dying too.

Molangi and Nza had been friends for a long time. Only a few weeks ago they had accompanied Ngasa Moke to the Yambuku hospital. The two young mothers had waited in line for their prenatal check, dreading the sting of the injections. Nza had teased them and made them laugh by tiptoeing around, pantomiming their fears.

"What a couple of wilting flowers you are. What is a little suffering if the shots give you a strong baby."

"We are not as robust as you," Ngasa Moke had replied.

"What counts is not the muscle in your body, but the vital force inside you. If you want your son to be a hunter like his father, you must give him your inner toughness."

"I want my baby to be a politician like you," Molangi had declared.

"Then he, or even she—especially if it is a she—will need very thick skin," Nza had replied, laughing.

That evening Molangi's children died within minutes of each other. The talk next door was rapid and urgent. The bodies were carried to graves dug outside the village. As the mourners returned from the burial, the evening storm hit. Afterward, chairs and mats were again moved outside, and the fire was stoked. Nza heard the mourners sitting in front of the house talking about those who had been killed by the fever in Yandongi and Yambuku, and the sinister power of the *ndokies* that had been unleashed. The *ngangas* would have to intervene.

In the early hours of September 20, Nza, who had

dropped off to sleep on a mat next to her sister, was awakened by the whimpering of Ngasa's baby. She picked him up, sat on the stool, and put him to her breast. The noise of the infant's sucking was loud in the little room. Nza stared at the shapeless form of her sister outlined by the faint light from the window. Suddenly she realized that something was different. Leaning over, she saw that Ngasa had stopped breathing. Quickly she felt her forehead; it was damp and cold. Ngasa Moke was dead.

Nza cried out in anguish, pulled the baby from her breast, and laid him, screaming, in his box. She walked unsteadily into the front room and sat at the table, pouring out her torment in uncontrollable sobs. Her husband awakened and came to stand next to her, his hand on her shoulder. Gradually her crying subsided. After a few moments, carrying her own infant son on her hip, she went back to the bedroom. She picked up Ngasa's baby and sat on the stool next to her dead sister, a child in each arm. She rocked them slowly. The infants, oblivious of everything except their hunger, pulled at her breasts.

Nza's husband returned shortly with two friends to take the body, which they had wrapped in a sheet, to the burial ground outside the village. A truck driver would try to get word to Ngasa Moke's husband in Bongalenza and her mother in Bongolu.

Friends and family walked slowly through the opening in the thornbush fence and joined others sitting on borrowed chairs arranged in a circle under the palm tree. Some of the party officials came, and the local political chief gave Nza ten zaires for beer. There had been so many *matangas* that each family's ration was limited to one case of Skol and two of Primus. Nza's husband went in search of more beer; none was available. He bought a demijohn of fresh palm wine and poured a little of the cloudy liquid into the empty glasses. With no corpse to keen over, and with their emotions drained by all the other deaths in the village, the visitors sat and drank in silence.

Toward evening, when Nza lifted Ngasa Moke's baby to wash him, his little body felt hot. After pulling him up by one arm and splashing cold water over his head, she laid him on a mat to dry in the shade. She added wood to the fire next to the house to cook for her husband and the visitors who remained. She was stirring a pot of simmering rice and plantains when unexpectedly her mother walked into the yard.

"Mama, you are here! How did you know . . . ? When . . . ?"

The old woman leaned forward, frowning at her daughter and those sitting under the palm tree, puzzled by their behavior.

"Mbote, mwana ngai." Greetings, my child. "Why such sadness? I came to see my youngest daughter and my new grandchild. Where are they?"

"Oh, Mama," cried Nza, throwing her arms around the old woman, "Ngasa Moke died this morning." Conversation ceased and, for a moment, life seemed suspended. Then the mama tore the shirt from her withered breasts and, with a piercing shriek, threw herself to the ground and rolled from side to side, covering her head and chest with dust. Still wailing loudly, she stumbled around the yard, beating the air with the cloth, shouting her grief to the ancestors. Nza watched her and wept. The visitors sat quietly and looked down at their feet. A gust of wind kicked up dust devils in the yard and rattled the fronds overhead. The emotion drained from the old mama, and she collapsed. Nza half carried her into the house.

After dark, Nza and her mother sat together in the glow of the fire. Nza had her child on her lap, and her mama cradled Ngasa's newborn to her bony chest. They spoke in short sentences. The guilt they felt about Ngasa's death was softened by their decision to leave at dawn for Bongolu and their own *nganga*. The mama said that Ngasa Moke had given life to a baby boy; she would be remembered for this and respected.

At dawn, Nza and her mama, each carrying a baby, set out for Bongolu. Nza's husband had arranged for them to ride in a plantation truck, sitting on the rice sacks piled high in the back. Normally the trip would have taken three hours, but news of the deaths at the Yambuku hospital and nearby villages had spread fast. The truck was stopped at barriers set up by villagers to prevent anyone from passing. At each roadblock, the driver turned off the engine, and a long palaver took place. Sometimes there was cursing and threats, but after an exchange of information and a few cigarettes, the truck was allowed through.

The fever in Ngasa Moke's baby was now very high; his eyes were dry and sunk deep in their sockets. The mama wiped the bloodstained discharge that oozed from his nose and handed him to Nza who tried to feed him, holding him tight against the pitching of the heavy truck, as it plowed through deep holes and gashes left by the rains. The baby cried weakly and would not suck. She returned him to the mama, then lifted her own child and anxiously put her cheek to his forehead. Her son felt cool and cried only when he was hungry.

In Yasoku Moke, the truck was surrounded by villagers shouting and waving sticks. The driver explained over and over that the truck was from a plantation, not the mission, and that they came from Yandongi, not Yambuku. He made his way to the chief, who was sitting in the shade of a tree, and after much discussion, the driver finally agreed to haul two sacks of the chief's manioc to Bongalenza in return for passage through the village. The mama hid the sick infant under her cotton shawl when men climbed up the side of the truck and dropped the sacks on top of the bags of rice. The driver started the engine, yelling at the others to get out of his way. With a grinding of gears, he let out the clutch, and the truck lurched forward, sending the women and their babies sprawling.

The further from Yambuku they traveled, the more normal the villages appeared. As the sun was setting over the forest, the two women left the truck at Yamuha, a small village of a dozen mud-and-wattle huts where the road coming down from Bongolu joined the main route to the east. The mama was well known in the village, and a room was offered for the night. A gourd of water, peanuts, and *kwanga*, a long roll of fermented manioc wrapped in banana leaves, were brought to the women. The mama was asked about her trip and how things were in Yandongi. The old woman told them she had brought back Ngasa Moke's child after her daughter had died. When it became clear that the mama did not want to say more, they were left alone.

As Nza and her mother spread their *elambas* on the smooth dirt floor, lightning flashed across the sky, strobe-lighting the trees, houses, and the corners of the little room. Thunderbolts seared down from the heavens and crashed into the ground. The deluge poured off thatched roofs, and instant rivulets cascaded toward the road, now a boiling stream of muddy water. Nza and her mother huddled together with the two infants between them. The fury of the storm passed. The night air cooled, and Nza felt her mother shiver beside her. She took the shawl off her own shoulders and tucked it around the old woman who held the hot little body of Ngasa Moke's child in her thin arms. They slept.

The next morning, Nza splashed water from a gourd on the babies, wiping them off with her hand, while the mama walked over to the chief's house to thank him for the shelter and food. After tying the infants to their backs, they proceeded down the road. An old goat was munching leaves on the smooth mound of a grave in front of a hut. He watched the women start down the lane to Bongolu.

Approaching their village, they met a young boy hunting with a slingshot; they asked him to run ahead and announce that Mama Basombe was returning with her daughter Nza. Within minutes their *nganga*, the aunts, and several of their old friends were walking toward them. There were exclamations of joy at seeing Nza again and her baby. The mama told them about Ngasa Moke and held up the baby to show what her dead daughter had produced. The women were escorted to their house, and throughout the day, friends came to greet them, bringing packages of peanuts and manioc and smoked monkey meat. Nza sat by the entrance, welcoming the visitors and sprinkling water over Ngasa Moke's baby who lay next to her on a mat. The infant's crying weakened, and he still would not suckle. As the shadows lengthened, he became comatose, and Nża could arouse him only by pinching his little body.

The day after Lucie's funeral on September 20, Dr. Amene and Masangaya made rounds on their handful of patients. Afterward, they sat in the medical assistant's office over some reheated coffee. They were working long hours, but it was clear to both of them that all their efforts had yet to save a life.

"Frankly, I do not think it is much use for me to stay," said Amene. "I may as well go back to Bumba."

"Maybe you can persuade the authorities to send an infectious disease specialist to help," replied Masangaya. "If Sister Lucie had lived long enough to be flown to Belgium, we might be nearer to knowing what is causing the deaths."

"There are bacteriologists at the university, but it will take a government order to have them travel up here," said the doctor.

"Perhaps you could stop in and see Dr. Zayemba at the Lever Brother plantation in Ebonda. It's on your way."

"I will. Zayemba is an experienced doctor, and the Lever plantations are in radio contact with their head office in Kinshasa. It is certainly in their interest to stop this thing."

"And they have the power to shake the bureaucrats in the capital out of their comfortable chairs," added Masangaya. "The sooner you can get down there, the better. We cannot do more here without help."

That same evening, Amene met with the Lever Brothers' doctors, Kalisa and Zayemba, as well as the doctor from the Bumba hospital and the zone *commissaire*. The next morning, Dr. Kalisa wrote to Dr. J. Busquet, the Lever plantation medical director, giving him the facts about the situation in Yambuku. The letter was put in the hands of the pilot of an Air Zaire plane that landed in Bumba at noon, and it was delivered to the Lever Brothers office in Kinshasa that evening. It was the first official report of the epidemic to reach the capital. Dr. Busquet immediately called the home of Dr. Tambwe, the minister of health, and read him the message.

On Wednesday, September 22, Sukato hurried into the dispensary to prepare for the day. He glanced at Fermina and sensed immediately that something was wrong, but he knew not to ask questions. Without looking at him, she said, "Tata Embu is going to die. He has been sick for over five days. I thought he might improve." Fermina's assistant nurse had been with her ever since she had come to the mission. She had taught him some pediatrics, and he had taught her a little about Africa.

Sukato paused awkwardly, then stepped over to the instrument table. He, too, would miss Tata Embu. The old man had tutored him in how to work for the sisters without surrendering his own values: "Never say no out loud. Rather say, 'Yes, I agree, in principle—unless the unforeseen intervenes.' " This had been Embu's way of keeping the peace; "unforeseens" were always at hand when needed.

"What are you doing?" asked Fermina.

"Thinking about Tata Embu." With his back to her, he slipped some instruments out of his pocket into a kidney basin, then gathered up the two syringes and needles, the metal tongue depressor, and an old Kelly clamp from the tray on the table. "I will take these over to the operating room and sterilize them. I did not have time to do it earlier."

"Let me see," said Fermina, as he passed her. He showed her the basin, and after glancing at its contents, she waved him off. "I will wait, but hurry." He left quickly. She was sure that he was seeing patients for a fee in his house—something she had expressly forbidden—but she had never been able to prove it. There was something about him she didn't trust. He reminded her of a fox, with his eyes close together and his nose thinner than most blacks'. He did his work well but was less eager to please than the other nurses. The routine of sterilizing the syringes and instruments first thing in the morning was almost sacred, and there was no excuse for his being late. She would have to speak to him again, but later. She closed her eyes and sighed. She could not get rid of the picture of Embu lying unconscious, surrounded by his frail wife and half a dozen younger members of the family.

The old man had been like an African *tata* to her. Her real father had been mayor of Niedergraat, a Flemish hamlet, most of his life. He had instilled in her from the moment she could walk that doing one's duty was the noblest virtue—to be accomplished at whatever cost. Tata Embu's devotion to duty, however, was not imposed upon him by others; it followed simply because his work was his life. He was well over sixty but had continued to bicycle the twenty kilometers from his village to work until he came down with the fever. At six every morning, he had been there; she could set her watch by his arrival. He never went home until all the children had been fed and tucked in for the night. He often rode back in the dark; if it was raining, he would curl up on a mat in the ward and sleep with his charges. He had a sharp wit and, like Lucie, could imitate a politician or a pompous visitor from the city with accuracy and humor. Fermina had even heard him do takeoffs on the president's speeches and theatrical declarations that were broadcast to the county from the capital's enormous football stadium; but that had its dangers and she had persuaded him to desist. With the patience and gentleness common in older Africans, he had taught her that the passivity of some of the young mothers with sick children was not caused by a lack of feeling but by an acceptance of the inevitable. He could pick up a screaming child with his large knobby hands and caress away its misery. He could feed the most recalcitrant child, sparing the need for needles and tubes. His expression of hope was always, *"Ça ira."* It will be all right. During very bad times, such as the rebellion or the measles epidemic that killed so many children, he would say, *"Ça ira, peut-être"*—It will be all right, maybe. To him, comfort was as important as cure.

Only a handful of patients waited to be seen. Fermina, consciously suppressing her despair, attended to them efficiently and rapidly. Sukato returned with the sterilized instruments.

"I am going back to the convent. Come and get me if you need help."

"Yes, Sister. I hope you can rest a little."

"I do have a little headache—a nap will help," she replied.

"I will get you some aspirin," said Sukato. He had taken some himself before coming to work. He had awakened with aching in his head and back.

"That will not be necessary, thank you."

Fermina slept until the afternoon. Then, feeling stronger, she made rounds on the handful of children in her pavilion and later stopped in to see Mabalo's widow in her house. Mbunzu seemed no worse, but her child was whimpering with each breath. Fermina put her hand on his head and felt his fever. "Let me take him and give him some fluids. I will have him back in an hour," she coaxed. Mbunzu shook her head. Fermina bit her lip and fought to hide her irritation. "Very well. I will come and see you in the morning." Mbunzu raised her hand in acknowledgment, then hugged the infant to her. The pounding in Fermina's head had returned. She would lie down again before supper.

In the refectory Veronica and Augustina were writing letters, Matilda was thumbing through a medical book, and Antonie was setting the table for the next day. The lights would be on for another hour. The sisters were still numbed by Lucie's death and, although exhausted, none of them wanted to be alone. Veronica had agreed to let Antonie move a cot into her room. Fermina walked in.

"I am sorry to be late," she said.

"More sick children?" asked Augustina.

"No. I lay down for a minute and overslept."

"Sit down, Fermina. I will get you some warm food," said Veronica, getting up.

"Very little. I'm not hungry."

"Hungry or not, you have to eat," replied Veronica, heading for the kitchen. Fermina sat down opposite Matilda.

"You look washed out," observed Matilda.

"Just tired," replied Fermina. "The last few days without Embu to help have been very hard. And Lucie—" Her eyes filled with tears.

"I know," said Matilda. "There is a big hole in our community." There was a knock at the door. It was Sukato. Fermina wiped her eyes with a napkin.

"Yes, Sukato. What is it?"

"Embu just died."

"Oh, no. No," whispered Fermina. Sukato turned and left.

Matilda came around the table, sat next to Fermina, and held her as she cried.

"He was such a good man . . . so unlike the others," said Fermina. "Why does God take people like Lucie and Tata Embu?"

Veronica returned carrying a plate piled high with rice surrounded by watery chicken stew. Antonie went to her and whispered Sukato's news. Veronica moved to the table and put the plate in front of Fermina. "I'm sorry about Tata Embu."

Fermina looked at the food with disgust. "How do you think I can eat when so many are dying?"

"We have to eat to live and stay strong. Weeping won't bring them back."

"Sister!" said Augustina severely. "Gently, please."

Veronica sat down. A small piece of sausage from her uncle in Schilde stuck out of the mound of rice like a flag. "I'm sorry, but she has to eat. Fermina, you must eat. . . ." She raised her eyebrows at the Mother Superior, who frowned at her. "Well, you know what I mean."

Fermina wiped her face and forced a smile. "Vero, you are really too much."

Antonie approached the table with a bottle of wine and a glass. "I think this might help," she said hesitantly. She poured the wine and set it in front of Fermina. When it was left untouched, Antonie again raised the bottle, "Anyone else?" The other sisters nodded, gulped down what was left of their water, and held up their glasses.

CHAPTER 5

The phones in the university were not working. Nothing political this time, just the normal breakdown of service. Dr. Tambwe looked at his watch; he would have to drive all the way out to the "Sacred Hill" on which, just before independence, the Belgians had founded Louvain University's little sister, Louvanium. There was no guarantee that Ilunga would be there. As a senior clinical pathologist and dean of the School of Public Health, Ilunga often traveled to Europe, especially to Belgium, where he was treated with some regard. Since he had become minister of health, Tambwe generally sent his deputy with messages to any other member of the faculty, but Ilunga was not the sort of man who accepted requests from deputies, especially when an unpleasant trip to the interior was involved.

Tambwe, a small round man from the Mayombe region, had worked his way through Montreal's School of Public Health, washing dishes and pumping gas. When he taught at Louvanium, his Canadian education made him an outcast among the Belgian-trained faculty. Still, he knew his subject, and the students appreciated his clarity and humility.

Fortunately, Ilunga was in his lab. Tambwe briefed him on the events unfolding in Yambuku and showed him the letter from the Lever Brothers Plantations' medical director.

"Where is this place?" asked Ilunga.

"Up in Budja country, about ninety kilometers north of Bumba," the minister replied.

"The forest people. I suppose almost anything could be going on up there," said the professor. He was Baluba, the master race of the savannahs from the great center of the country.

"As the letter indicates, many people are dying from what appears to be a particularly virulent form of typhoid," said the minister. "And now that one of the Belgian sisters has died, the Europeans will be agitating for more help to be sent to the area."

"Do they have a doctor in Yambuku?"

"No, just one medical assistant."

"Oh, well . . . when do you want me to go?"

"As soon as possible. The Lever plantations are important to the president; he has assigned an Air Force C-130 to take you up there."

"The president knows about this situation?"

"Yes. I called him as soon as I received the information from Dr. Busquet. I am sending Dr. Omba with you. You know him; he is a Tetela—from the same village as Lumumba. He runs public health in Kinshasa. I asked him to requisition some supplies to bring, including typhoid vaccine. You should be able to leave tomorrow morning."

"Naturally, I will go," said Ilunga. "And when I return, we can talk about the needs of my research program."

"Of course." The minister inclined his head. No service was rendered without a cost.

On September 23 at 9 A.M., Drs. Ilunga and Omba climbed over the cargo strapped down in the main cabin of the large transport and made their way up to the flight deck.

"Welcome aboard the Bumba express," said the Zairian Air Force colonel. He was the commanding officer of the Air Force and the only Zairian pilot qualified to fly the C-130.

"Is all that freight ours?" asked Ilunga.

"No," said the colonel, laughing. "Most of it is merchandise for General Bumba's shops in Bumba. We carry his stuff whenever we fly north." Ilunga understood. Using official means to accomplish personal gain was known as applying Article 15. The fictitious regulation was defined as *"débrouillez vous"*—work it out any way you can—and covered most imaginative and illegal profitable initiatives. Article 15 was the basis of most Zairian entrepreneurship.

The doctors strapped themselves into webbed canvas seats along the side of the aircraft, and the supplies Omba had brought were stuffed into the rear of the hold, just before the doors were closed. As the plane lumbered down the runway for takeoff, Omba began a mental count of his collection of cardboard boxes; some had already been pilfered.

Arriving in Bumba at 2 P.M., the doctors and pilot were driven to the office of the *commissaire* to pay their respects. After drinks were served, the *commissaire* stood up, poured a little of his whiskey into an ashtray for the ancestors, and lifted his glass to his distinguished visitors.

"Welcome to the Zone of Bumba. I thank the president, the guide of our great country and founder of the party, for sending you." They all drank to that. The meeting was short and pleasant. Now that the two medical authorities had arrived, the situation in Yambuku would be brought under control. The *commissaire* gave orders to requisition a Land Rover and a truck for the supplies, and after another round of drinks, the doctors were on their way north to Yambuku.

They arrived at the mission around midnight and were escorted to Masangaya's house by the night watchman. The medical assistant greeted the doctors, then walked them across the road to the spartan rooms that the sisters had prepared in the guest house.

Masangaya reviewed the details of the epidemic with the two doctors over breakfast, then concluded, "Our most urgent need is a diagnosis. We have no idea what we are dealing with."

"I brought the necessary equipment to draw blood to take back to my laboratory at the university," said Ilunga.

"Since we are sent by the president and the minister of health, it is equally important that the people see that we are taking action to stop the deaths," said Omba.

"How do you propose doing that?" asked Masangaya.

"Use the typhoid vaccine we brought with us. After all, we may be dealing with a virulent form of typhoid," replied Omba.

"This epidemic does not resemble any typhoid I've ever seen," said Masangaya, looking at Ilunga.

"I have to agree with you," replied the professor. "But vaccinating the population won't hurt."

Masangaya shrugged and slipped into a white coat. He handed each of the doctors a green operating gown. Masangaya and Ilunga led the way, reviewing again the clinical picture of the disease and its inexorable course toward death. Omba followed, raising his hand and nodding acknowledgment to the handful of workers who stood aside and bowed in respect.

In front of the medical pavilion, an emaciated woman

called out desperately, "*Monganga, monganga,* come quickly and look at my child."

As the doctors surrounded the bed, the infant convulsed and died, a bloody froth slowly bubbling out of its gaping mouth. The mother pressed the baby to her breasts and wept. Masangaya put his arm around her shoulders.

"Where is your man?"

She spoke between sobs. "Burying our other child . . . who died during the night."

A worker nudged Masangaya's elbow. "Tata Ipasa just died," he said, nodding in the direction of an old man lying several beds away.

"We will come." The medical assistant turned to the two doctors, who stood aghast next to the bed. "It has been like this day and night. This woman is the wife of our school prefect, who is himself sick. As you can see, she also has the fever."

Omba took a step back. "What have you done for her?"

"IVs and antibiotics; that's all we have." He looked at Omba. "Would you like to go over her? Maybe you could suggest something different."

"No, no, not right now. We should look at the old man who just died and get a specimen," replied Omba.

Dr. Ilunga, embarrassed, stepped between his two colleagues and put his hand on the woman's forehead. He pointed to the stethoscope in the medical assistant's pocket. Masangaya handed him the instrument. The professor listened to her chest and, after gently palpating her abdomen and noting that her liver was tender but not enlarged, he rested the diaphragm on her belly to pick up bowel sounds. He looked for rashes on her palms and the soles of her feet. When he was through, he folded the stethoscope, handed it back to Masangaya, and said to the patient, "We will do what we can to make you comfortable." He turned to the others. "There is nothing in the physical exam to make this different from any number of infectious diseases."

They walked to the bed where the man had just died.

"Ipasa was one of our best hospital workers," said Masangaya. "He sent his daughter and grandchildren away a week ago and has been living alone. He was brought in yesterday."

"Could you open his abdomen enough to get a specimen?" asked Ilunga.

"Of course," replied the medical assistant. "I'll get a few instruments and be right back. Then we will have to carry him to the common grave behind the hospital." He walked across to the operating room and returned to the bedside in a moment. He and Ilunga pulled on old, patched rubber gloves. Masangaya made an incision through the skin parallel to the old man's flaring right rib cage. Drops of dark blood oozed out and ran down onto his thin abdomen. A second incision cut through the flat abdominal muscles and the peritoneum. The small liver was tucked high under the ribs.

"I will give you some exposure," said Masangaya, passing the scalpel and forceps to the professor. "See if you can reach in and cut out a piece of the liver." Omba watched from a distance. At the moment when Ilunga retrieved the specimen, the brittle bones of the lower ribs snapped, and the wound came together. Masangaya sewed up the incision, then pulled off his gloves. The sharp ribs had torn through the rubber, and his index finger was bleeding at the knuckle. Masangaya squeezed blood out of the wound as he walked over to the sink in the corner of the ward. He ran water over the laceration and wrapped a handkerchief around the wound, then returned to the bed as Ilunga finished drawing blood from the old man's arm. He looked at the medical assistant's crude bandage and frowned.

"I will put some disinfectant on it after we have buried him," said Masangaya. Omba opened the door, as the two others carried Ipasa out to his final resting place. The stench of the pit was overwhelming, and the medical men walked away swiftly, slapping at voracious flies that sucked at the sweat running down their necks.

Masangaya led the way to his office. While the doctors washed up, he put on water for coffee. Then he unwrapped his hand and scrubbed the knuckle with an old nailbrush whose sparse bristles were flattened by long use.

"Do you have any disinfectant?" asked Ilunga.

"I think there is an old bottle of iodine," replied Masangaya, pointing to the medicine cabinet with his chin.

"Gauze bandage?"

"In the drawer." He held his hand over the sink, and Ilunga poured iodine into the wound.

"Yeow! That stuff gets stronger with age," exclaimed Masangaya, waving his hand in the air to ease the burning.

"Where are your sterile compresses?" asked the professor.

"We have a few old ones in the operating room. We wash them; then our patients recovering from surgery smooth and fold them for reuse." He laughed when he saw the surprise on the professor's face. "We are in the bush here, you know," he added. Slowly and meticulously, Ilunga wound the gauze around the wound.

"I have not done this since I was an intern."

"They had gauze in those days?" asked Masangaya, chuckling.

"Oh, yes, indeed, and sterile four-by-fours too," the professor replied, in mock seriousness.

Masangaya smiled. "My old father used to say that progress does not always move in a forward direction."

"He had foresight," said the professor, tucking the end of

the bandage into itself. "Now let's go to the other wards and take more blood samples."

During the rest of the day, with a short break for lunch, the doctors followed Masangaya into workers' huts and the larger houses where some of the teachers and their families were sick. They took blood from half a dozen patients, using disposable syringes they had brought with them. "There is one more woman we need to see," said Masangaya. "The wife of Mabalo, the first man to die."

He knocked. There was no answer. He opened the door a crack. "Mbunzu, it is me, Masangaya. I have brought doctors from Kinshasa to see you."

"Tell them to go away. I don't want to see them."

"May I come in?" he asked.

"Yes, but not the others. The last doctor hurt my arm with all his needles."

Masangaya turned to the doctors, "I am sorry. But she is a strong-willed woman who has suffered much. I'll see what I can do." He stepped into the house and closed the door behind him.

Mbunzu and her baby were lying on the bed. He was shocked to see how wasted the infant had become. He crouched down and put his hand on the little body. It was dry and hot.

"I don't want any more needles," whimpered Mbunzu.

"I'll see to that," replied Masangaya gravely.

"My baby is dying. Mabalo's mama says he is too young to join his father."

Masangaya hesitated. "She is right. I wish there was something I could do, but . . ." He held her shoulder for a moment, then stood up and walked to the door. "I'll return tomorrow."

After supper, the doctors joined Masangaya on his porch. Omba produced a bottle of whiskey, and the three men sat with their drinks in the twilight, listening to the shrill sound of the katydids and pondering the events of the day. The course of the disease was clear; what it was and where it came from were a mystery.

"It certainly presents like malaria or typhoid or maybe even typhus, but the bloody diarrhea and the ulcerations in the throat and gums would be unusual for these diseases," said Ilunga.

"We have used proven treatments for malaria and typhoid and have had no cures at all," added Masangaya. "What about a virus? I know so little about them, I hesitate to raise the question."

"That is a possibility, but we have no way of culturing viruses at the university. We would have to send specimens to the Institute of Tropical Medicine in Antwerp," said Ilunga.

"In the meantime, we must do something to calm the population," said Omba. "We should go ahead with the typhoid vaccinations in the morning."

"What do you think, Professor?" asked Masangaya.

"I am not sure. I wish we already had the results from our specimens. We do have the vaccine, and there is no proof that the disease is not typhoid. I think inoculations would give people some hope that the epidemic can be stopped."

"False hope can be worse than no hope at all," replied Masangaya.

Omba stood up, yawned, and stretched. "You will have to admit that what you have done so far has not saved a life. The old therapeutic adage, 'If what you are doing is not working, you should do something different,' holds true in this situation. I'm for vaccinating as many as possible tomorrow."

Ilunga shrugged. "Very well. We'll do it in the morning.

We can get back to Kinshasa tomorrow night, plant the cultures, and examine the specimens."

Masangaya walked the doctors back to the guest house, told them that breakfast would be at seven with the sisters, and bade them good night. He was relieved to be alone again. The thought of people herded together for vaccinations, or for any other reason, disturbed him. His instincts told him that, at times like this, dispersion and isolation were wiser than assembly. But the professor had concurred with Omba's politics. There was nothing he could do. He could not stop the throbbing in his hand and spent a sleepless night.

Early the next morning, Masangaya sent the night watchman to the workers' quarters with orders that everyone—men, women, and children—must be at the dispensary in an hour for vaccinations.

From meager reserves sent by their Belgian families, the sisters had spread their favorite foods on the refectory table. The strong smell of coffee blended with the nostalgic fragrance of cured beef, cut in paper-thin slices, and smoked mackerel from the choppy waters of the North Sea off Ostend. The remains of a black blood pudding lay partially collapsed on its plate. Veronica sacrificed some of her uncle's sausage, and Antonie unwrapped a wedge of goat cheese that smelled rancid but was not. The bread was freshly baked; the last tin of margarine had been opened. The doctors helped themselves and ate with enthusiasm, while the sisters sipped their coffee and watched their precious delicacies disappear. When only skins and empty cans remained, Augustina held up the coffeepot.

"More?" she asked.

"Yes, please," both men answered. Omba poured the last few drops of condensed milk into his cup, spooned in sugar, and stirred it. "The sisters eat very well in the bush," he said, raising his cup in a salute.

"I hope you've had enough," said Veronica, eyeing the scanty remains on the table.

"Thank you. We have eaten well," said Ilunga. "Who would have thought that one could taste a real Flemish breakfast in this wilderness." He wiped his mouth and pushed back his chair. "Now"—he nodded warmly to the Mother Superior—"our program for the morning. Yesterday, with the help of our colleague Masangaya, we collected specimens of blood to take back to my laboratory. I feel certain that these specimens will provide a diagnosis for us. We think we may be dealing with a typhoid variant—a virulent and lethal one, of course—and we have decided to inoculate everyone living or working at the mission with the typhoid vaccine we brought from Kinshasa."

"Aren't you making the diagnosis fit your treatment?" Fermina interjected. Matilda looked at her and frowned: nurses did not interrupt doctors. Augustina glanced at Masangaya, who was concentrating on his coffee cup. She thought she saw a flicker of a smile cross his face.

"Would you rather have us do nothing?" demanded Omba. Fermina was silent.

"As I was saying," continued the professor, "we plan to vaccinate all the people at the mission this morning." He turned to Augustina. "Then, we can immunize the sisters."

"You can find us back here before lunch," said Augustina, looking around the table. Fermina was tight-lipped.

During the morning, the doctors, helped by Sister Antonie, vaccinated the handful of patients in the hospital and the workers who came to the dispensary. Many of the families had returned to their villages. Masangaya excused himself and made rounds in the medical and surgical pavilions. Three more people had died during the night: two workers at the mission and the four-year-old daughter of one of the teachers.

The sisters gathered on the back terrace at the end of the morning and waited.

"You do not vaccinate people in the middle of an epidemic," said Fermina heatedly, continuing the argument she was having with Matilda.

"That is an old wives' tale. Where did you hear that?" asked the senior nurse. "The only time you do not vaccinate a person is if he has a fever. I am aware that they don't know for sure what is causing the disease, but it may well be typhoid; and if it is, we may prevent further deaths with the vaccine."

The doctors arrived with Sister Antonie trailing behind them, carrying a large cardboard box filled with disposable syringes.

Ilunga announced, "It went well. The people seem relieved that we are doing something for them. Now we will vaccinate you."

Augustina was the first to be injected, followed by Matilda; but when Dr. Omba turned to Fermina, she backed away, crossing her arms.

"I refuse to be vaccinated," she said, her eyes wide and bright, her face flushed.

"Sister, you are a nurse; you must set a good example for the others. The Mother Superior and Sister Matilda have had their injections; now it is your turn," said Dr. Omba, approaching her with a loaded syringe. Fermina turned away and stepped behind Veronica. The doctor persisted.

"If you do not accept the vaccination, what do you expect the other sisters to do?"

"That is their business," replied Fermina angrily. "I will not be vaccinated, and that is the end of it."

Augustina sent a puzzled look to Matilda, who was embarrassed that her younger colleague was acting so petulantly. Veronica turned to Fermina and started to put her arm around her shoulders, but Fermina pulled away, leaving the circle of nuns to stand behind a chair. Veronica followed her.

"Come on, Fermina, let him give you the shot. What difference does it make?"

Fermina glared at her, and Veronica backed off. After a heavy silence, Fermina looked up and whispered, "It is too late. I have the fever."

Veronica put her hands to her face. Omba fell into a chair with a groan. The nuns were stunned. After a moment, the professor took charge.

"If the sister has the fever, she should be transferred immediately to the Institute of Tropical Medicine in Antwerp."

"I have too much to do here. I do not want to go back to Belgium. I will not go," cried out Fermina, her voice rising in panic. "I cannot leave Yambuku!" She turned and ran from the terrace down the corridor. In a second a door slammed.

Ilunga turned to Augustina. "The sister must go to Kinshasa with us. She will be flown to Belgium this evening."

"That was our plan for Sister Lucie, but she died before we could get her out. I'll speak with Fermina." Augustina looked at Matilda, who nodded and followed her.

The Mother Superior knocked.

"Just go in," said Matilda, opening the door. Fermina was sprawled on her stomach, her face buried in the pillow. Matilda sat on the edge of the bed and placed a hand on Fermina's arm. Augustina stood by the door.

"How long have you been sick?" Matilda asked gently.

"Several days," was the muffled reply. The collar of Fermina's blouse was soaked, and her shoulders and neck were hot under Matilda's hand. The older nurse thought about the last few days. What clues had she missed? They had all been exhausted and less talkative after Lucie's death. She could not think of anything specific that would have warned her that Fermina was not well.

"When did your fever start?"

"A couple of days ago, I think."

"Have you taken your temperature?"

"No, I did not dare."

Matilda stood. "Sister, please sit up. We have to talk."

Fermina slowly put her legs over the side of the bed and pushed herself up. She took the towel Augustina held out to her and wiped her face.

"That's better. Now, let's check your temperature," said Matilda. Fermina pointed to the toilet kit on the sink. Matilda took the thermometer from Augustina, shook it down, and said, "Open." Fermina closed her lips around the thermometer and, like a submissive patient, raised her wrist for Matilda to take her pulse. She looked at her teacher's thin brown face and was comforted by the familiar furrows on her forehead. Fermina's religious commitment and discipline had come from her father, but she had learned her nursing skills from this white-haired nun whose fingers rested gently on her wrist.

"A hundred and twenty," Matilda said, looking up from her watch and reaching for the thermometer. "And a high fever! You must feel much worse than you have let on."

Fermina took a deep breath. "Aspirin has kept my fever down and helped with the pain. But the pills are making me sick to my stomach; I cannot keep them down anymore. I am having the same symptoms Lucie had during the first few days of her illness."

"Have you vomited?" asked Matilda.

"Several times, after the aspirin."

"Any diarrhea or bleeding?"

"No . . . not yet."

Matilda pulled the chair over and sat next to Fermina. "You remember that when Lucie was so sick we all decided that she should go to Antwerp—you agreed to that yourself."

"Yes, I remember."

"Now you must go."

Fermina shook her head. "There is no point in my leaving. I'm going to die anyway."

"You must go, Fermina," said Augustina, stepping nearer the bed. "It is best for you, and it is best for all of us. It's the only way the doctors in Belgium can find out what killed Lucie and the others."

"But what will my father say if I abandon my duty and desert my patients?" cried Fermina, shaking her head. "Tata Embu did not run away. No, I will not leave. I want to die here in Yambuku and lie next to Lucie."

Matilda leaned forward and put her hand on Fermina's knee. "I know your father, Fermina. He would expect you to do your duty as a nurse for the mission and your patients. And your duty now is to leave." Fermina held the towel to her mouth.

Matilda sat back. "Sister Augustina and I know how hard it is, but you are our only hope. Think about it and pray about it. We will be back in a little while."

Augustina and Matilda returned to the others on the terrace. Masangaya had joined the group.

"She does not want to leave. We need to give her a little time to get used to the idea," announced Augustina.

"Maybe she's right," said Masangaya.

"What do you mean by that?" asked Omba sharply.

Masangaya turned to the two doctors. "May I have a word with you?" The three men walked down the steps of the terrace.

"The people in this area have isolated themselves and will not allow movement in or out of the villages. Don't you think that taking Fermina to Kinshasa could spread the disease to the capital?" asked the medical assistant.

"That is a risk, of course," replied Ilunga. "But be realistic. We must find out what sort of organism we are dealing with, and that will take more sophisticated studies and cultures than I can do at the university, let alone here in the middle of the forest. And, besides, if Belgian nuns are being killed by an African bug, Brussels will soon be on our backs, and wild stories will be circulating in their press. The sister must be flown to Belgium as soon as possible. I will talk to her."

Masangaya shrugged. He knew that further argument would be useless. Fermina was not just a patient with a disease, she was a Belgian missionary with an African infection. They walked back to the others.

"Would you take me to Sister Fermina's room?" Ilunga asked Augustina. She nodded and led the way. Fermina was still sitting on the bed.

"Dr. Ilunga wants to talk to you," said Augustina.

The doctor spoke from the doorway. "Sister, you are a nun and have taken the vow of obedience. Your superior and I both request you to get your things ready so we can take you to Bumba with us. We will fly down to Kinshasa together and see that you are on a plane to Belgium this evening." Fermina did not answer; her head was pounding, and she felt she might vomit. The professor, seeing that it would take more than simple authority to move this nun, stepped into the room and softened his approach.

"Sister, you came to Zaire for what?" There was no answer. "Didn't you come here to help the Africans? Do you think I can send a sick Zairian all the way to Belgium? He has no family there, he does not know the language, he has nowhere to stay. It is your country. If you really want to do something during this time of crisis, then make the sacrifice of going back to your country so the experts at the institute in Antwerp can find out what is devastating the people of Yambuku. You will receive the care you need, then you can come back here to resume your duties and your calling." He stopped and looked at Augustina, who nodded in agreement.

"It makes sense," said the Mother Superior.

Fermina looked at them for a moment. "Can you give me something for my headache? I can hardly think straight," she said.

"Of course," replied the professor, relieved that she seemed to be coming around. "I will have the medical assistant give you a shot of Dolantine."

Veronica and Matilda helped Fermina get ready for the trip. In less than an hour, the mission vehicle was loaded with her bag. She refused to lie in the back on a mattress. The Dolantine had relieved most of her headache but had aggravated her nausea. When the moment came to leave, Fermina crawled into the front of the Land Rover with Luc. She looked toward the terrace, framed by bougainvillaea and saw her Sisters in Christ standing on the steps, holding handkerchiefs to their faces. She set her jaw and straightened her back. The doctors' Jeep started down the road, and Luc followed. Fermina raised her hand and forced a smile as she drove past her best friends; she knew that she would never see them again. She glanced down the rows of palms as the Land Rover carried her past the little cemetery. Tears rolled down her cheeks.

Adieu, my sister. You can rest where we have lived and worked and lost our hearts. Pray for me, my most beloved friend.

By the time they arrived, the Air Force plane had left Bumba. The Air Zaire agent told them the colonel had flown off because the Yambuku disease had spread into the sky over the forest. Apparently, an excited airport worker told the pilot that crows near the mission had actually been seen to crumple in the air and plummet to the ground. Omba and Ilunga tried to explain that this story was idiotic and impossible.

The Air Zaire plane from Kisangani was late and booked solid. They would need the help of the zone *commissaire* to get seats. They told no one that the sister with them was ill, and they sent word to Luc that she was not to leave the vehicle.

Fermina sat in the Land Rover during the two hot hours they waited at the airport. Luc fanned her with a towel and fetched water, but her fever and the heat in the vehicle soon took their toll: she vomited and became more and more dehydrated. When the plane finally arrived, she staggered up the steps on her own and slumped into a seat in the back next to a window. After the plane took off and gained altitude, the air in the cabin cooled, and she shook with chills. The turbulence aggravated her nausea, and although her stomach was empty, she retched miserably. The flight attendant handed her a musty blanket, which she draped around her shoulders. She dug into her pocket and pulled out her rosary. Between her Hail Mary's, she heaved small amounts of bitter phlegm into the waxed paper bag provided courtesy of Air Zaire.

Ilunga walked back along the aisle once and tried to en

courage her. "We will have you tucked into a nice bed at the Ngaliema Clinic before long. My sports car will be too cramped for me to drive you into the city. As soon as we land, I will go to the university and have an ambulance dispatched to pick you up. I am sure the telephones are still out, so it may take a little while."

They arrived around 10 P.M. at Kinshasa's Ndjili Airport. After all the passengers had left, Ilunga helped Fermina down the steps; Omba carried her bags. They walked slowly into the terminal and settled Fermina into a corner of the large waiting room. Ilunga excused himself and returned shortly with one of the ticket agents from the Sabena counter, a Belgian woman with red lips and a tight blue skirt.

"This young lady is here if you need anything. The ambulance should come for you before long." The two women shook hands.

"Can I bring some tea or anything, Sister?" asked the agent.

"No, thank you."

"It will take me a half hour to drive to the campus," said Ilunga. "I will go right to the hospital and send the ambulance. Tomorrow I will make arrangements to have you flown to Belgium. So, for now, Sister, it is good-bye."

"*Adieu, docteur,*" replied Fermina.

Omba said, "Keep up your courage, Sister."

"I will," she replied.

After the doctors left, Fermina stretched out on the waiting room seats, using her shoulder bag as a pillow. The young woman brought over a blanket and tucked it around her.

"If you need anything, just raise your hand. I will be over at the counter until our midnight flight leaves for

Brussels," said the ticket agent. Fermina nodded. Exhaustion overrode her pain and nausea, and she slept.

When Fermina awoke, she was confused and lost for a moment. Then she focused on a pair of dark blue trousers, and she heard, *"Ma soeur."* She sat up, and her head reeled as a wave of nausea surged up to her throat. She reached down for the paper bag, and the hammering in her head made her cry out with pain. A middle-aged European wearing the uniform of Sabena Airlines stood in front of her.

"Can I help you, Sister?" he asked, alarmed by her behavior. He turned toward the counter and waved for the ticket agent to come over. Fermina heard the staccato clicking of high heels echoing under the dome of the empty terminal. The young woman spoke as she approached.

"A Zairian who said he was a professor at the university left the sister here and asked me to watch her until an ambulance came," she said. She glanced at her watch, "That was over an hour ago."

"Son of a—" exclaimed the Belgian. "Oh. Sorry, Sister."

The ticket agent cut in, "This is Mr. Robinet, our station manager, Sister . . . ?"

"Fermina. From the Yambuku Mission, north of Bumba. If you could find me a taxi . . ."

"A cab driver would rob you silly," said Robinet. "I will drive you in myself." He looked at his watch. "There is a cot in my office behind the counter. It is more private there, and you will be more comfortable. We'll go as soon as the midnight flight leaves; it won't be long now." The two Belgians helped Fermina into the office.

"They brought you down from Bumba and just abandoned you?" asked Robinet, incensed at her treatment.

"They did not abandon me," answered Fermina. "The university phones are out, and the doctor went in search of an ambulance. Maybe he couldn't find a driver; maybe the ambulance had a flat tire. You know how things are."

"Oh, yes," replied the Belgian. "I know how *they* are. That's why I work for Sabena and not Air Zaire." He went out to the counter, and Fermina lay back on the cot. She slept, and the next thing she knew the Belgians were helping her into the back of a car, cradling her head on pillows.

"Where do I take you?" asked Robinet, turning onto the four-lane highway into the capital, thirty kilometers away.

"I suppose to the Franciscan sisters at the Ngaliema Hospital," replied Fermina, swallowing another wave of bile.

"I'll take you to Sister Théofila. Do you know her?"

"Of course, we all know her. I am glad she is still there." She took some deep breaths and prayed that they would arrive before she vomited in the car. Robinet drove fast and with the same resolve as most of his compatriots, swerving only to avoid deep potholes. Fermina clutched the armrest on the door, knowing that the faster he went, the sooner she would find relief. At that time of night there was little traffic, and soon they drove up to the iron gates of the hospital.

After washing her face and sponging off her hot, aching body, Fermina slipped into the nightshirt and crawled between cool white sheets. She looked at the crucifix above the door. *Thank You for getting me here, and thank You for having Sister Théofila on duty.* The Sabena manager had been right: she could not have fallen into better hands.

The Mother of P5, as Théofila was known, had nursed here since the hospital had opened for Europeans years before independence. At that time, it had been dedicated by the Belgian queen, and named La Clinique Reine Elizabeth. Théofila's steady good humor in spite of a clubfoot, and her ability to cope with all sorts of medical problems, from drunken soldiers to stuffy colonial administrators and rigid Jesuits, had brought renown to her service.

Sister Théofila limped back into the room carrying a stethoscope and blood-pressure cuff. Fermina noticed that she was wearing rubber gloves. Théofila stuck a thermometer under Fermina's dry tongue and reached for her wrist. When she had counted her pulse and checked her blood pressure, she pulled the thermometer out, glanced at it, and shook it down.

"You certainly have a high fever. How do you feel right now?"

"My head feels like it's in a vise, and my abdomen hurts from vomiting all day," whispered Fermina.

"I will give you a shot of Dolantine, and we'll get some fluid into you; then you can tell me what has been going on."

Théofila left the room and returned in a moment with a bag of saline and a syringe. After giving Fermina the shot and starting the IV, she pulled up a chair and sat down next to the bed. "Now, you are a nurse; tell me what you know about your illness."

Fermina gave her an account of the events in Yambuku and the symptoms of the people who were dying. She told about Sister Lucie's death and about the onset and progression of her own symptoms.

"I'm supposed to be sent to the institute in Antwerp tomorrow, so the experts can make a diagnosis." She paused, then added, "Frankly, I doubt anything can be done for me—no one has recovered yet once the symptoms have started."

"Come now, Sister. When we find out what is making you sick, I'm sure we can help you. But right now, we must get your fever down and have you feeling better, or

Sabena won't let you on the plane." Théofila stood up. "I will telephone Dr. Edmond; he is on call tonight." She went into the bathroom and ran some cold water into a glass.

"Just take small sips to wet your mouth. Then rest. I'll be back as soon as the doctor arrives." Fermina pulled the sheet up under her chin and closed her eyes. Her head swam pleasantly from the injection.

Half an hour later, the doctor walked into Théofila's office. "She must be terribly sick for you to call me in the middle of the night," said the doctor, scratching the stubble on his chin.

"She is very sick indeed." As Théofila led him slowly to the new patient's room, she outlined Fermina's story and her own findings, ending with the treatment she had initiated. She knocked on the door, and they walked in.

"Sister, this is Dr. Edmond." The doctor approached the bed with his hand out.

"You should wear gloves if you have to touch me," said Fermina. The doctor stopped and lowered his hand.

"Really? Why do you say that?" he asked.

"I am a nurse. I have been taking care of people with the same symptoms in our mission hospital in Yambuku. We have no idea what is causing the illness, but I can tell you that tomorrow I will have a sore throat and diarrhea, and the next day I will bleed from my stomach and intestines."

"Is that so?" said the doctor, taken aback. "How do you feel now?"

"Better, thanks to the injection Sister Théofila gave me. But I have a high fever and I am dehydrated. I've been vomiting all day."

"And you think that what you have is contagious, Sister?" asked the doctor.

"That is certain."

The doctor turned to Théofila. "We'll take all the usual precautions."

Then, very quietly, Fermina said, "Doctor, I'm going to die."

He did not take her seriously.

CHAPTER 6

In Bongolu at first light on the morning of September 23, the mama was awakened by Nza's moaning. She bent over her daughter and felt the fever in her body.

"Oh, my mother," whispered Nza. "Pain is crushing my head, and my throat is on fire."

The mama stood and rewrapped her *elamba* tightly around her flat, pendulous breasts.

"I will go find the *nganga* and return with him."

"Tell him he must stop the pain in my head." Nza pulled at her hair and rolled onto her side.

The mama walked rapidly between the houses of the village where people were starting the morning fires. She continued through the farm bush into the trees. In the dim light filtering through the canopy, she picked her way along a narrow track, pushing aside leaves and branches which came together in a never-ending effort to obliterate the path. The forest floor dipped, and she splashed through the narrow end of a stagnant pond. Slimy mud oozed between her toes, cooling her feet. A pig, startled in his rooting, squealed in alarm and fled through the underbrush. Invisible birds twittered in the dense green cover, and the bark and howl of colobus monkeys echoed through the trees.

Fifteen minutes later she arrived at the edge of a clearing. A sluggish stream meandered between towering boles

whose roots fanned away from the trunks to suck water out
of the rotting soil. A small dwelling under a thick roof of
coarse leaves stood on a rise. Lazy smoke rose in a thin
plume from a fire smoldering in front of the hut. The
throaty chorus of tree frogs, silenced when the woman entered the clearing, resumed. An old man came out of the
hut and stood before her, a loincloth around his narrow
waist.

The mama lifted her hand in greeting. *"Mbote, tata-
nkoko."* Greetings, esteemed old father.

"Greetings to you, Mama Basombe."

"I had to come."

"I expected you." He picked up a black iron pot as she
approached. "Stoke the fire; I will make tea." He walked
down to the stream for water.

The mama reached under the thatch overhang for a handful of sticks and laid them carefully on the fire, then, bending over straight backed, she blew life into the coals. Sitting
on a low stool, she watched her old friend pluck leaves
from a bush near the stream and, picking up the pot, walk
up the well-worn path toward her. His lean body showed
more sinew than in past years, and age and the sun had
wrinkled the skin around his deep-set eyes.

The mother of Nza and Ngasa Moke had profound respect for the *nganga*. He was the brother of her husband,
who had been killed along with three other men during the
rebellion ten years ago. They had tried, with spears and
bows and arrows, to keep a band of a dozen *simbas* from
passing through their village. The rebels—a scruffy bunch,
wild-eyed on hashish—shot their way into the dwellings.
They had skewered the local teacher and his wife to a tree
with rusty spears. They stole what pigs and chickens they
could catch, set fire to the huts, and disappeared into the
forest. The *nganga's* own wife had been killed, but he had

escaped with his brother's family and had gone into hiding with them in the forest, providing them with food and shelter until the brutality moved south, toward Bumba and Lisala. Since then, he had been a reliable friend and adviser to the family.

The *nganga* lowered the iron pot into the fire and sat on the ground. Neither spoke until the water boiled and the leaves had been added to steep. He poured a little of the infusion into a tin mug and handed it to the mama; she sipped cautiously, then looked up at the specks of blue sky shimmering beyond the leafy dome.

"It will be a long, hot day," she said. The old man glanced at her. Without looking at him, she slowly recited the events on her heart.

"Nza left Bongolu because her husband found work in Yandongi's rice plantation. The death of the unborn child inside her belly was caused by her husband's family."

The *nganga* nodded. "That was my conclusion." The mama drank from the cup.

"Her next child was born healthy because you interceded with the ancestors."

"Yes. They understood Nza's need to leave Bongolu." After a long pause she continued. "Ngasa Moke was married here in our village to the hunter from Bongalenza and produced a dead child." The *nganga* looked straight into the mama's eyes. Quietly, firmly, he said, "There were no eligible men here, and the hunter's ancestors met my entreaties with silence."

"Of course," said the mama. She put the cup on the ground, then wrapped her arms across her flat breasts. "Ngasa Moke received injections from the Catholic sisters in Yambuku to make her strong. She produced a healthy baby, but now she is dead. Her infant is very sick, and Nza has fever and pain in her head. Many are dead in Yambuku.

That is why I brought Nza and the children back here to you."

The *nganga* looked away. Like most healers with special skills in the treatment of their fellow human beings, he felt a twinge of relief that the deaths were not occurring in his own village. He had a fleeting sense of vindication knowing that the white man's medicine had not worked and that this family—really his family—had returned to him for care. His gaze returned to the mama. He saw the pleading in her eyes, and pity replaced pride.

"There is much we cannot explain—much we cannot understand. My powers of healing were born in the teachings passed down by my master and grew as I practiced. Sometimes the ancestors are helpful in revealing new truths, but often they guard their history and let me see only their victories. Memory erases defeat, our most painful lesson but our most successful teacher."

The mama was lost in his abstractions. "Will you come?"

The shrill rasp of cicadas vibrated in the still, moist air. After what seemed to her like a long time, he stood up and spread the sticks in the fire to reduce the flames and spare the fuel.

"Of course." After gathering different leaves from his bushes and retrieving his pouch from inside the hut, he joined the mama. Together they made their way along the forest path to the village.

Mama Basombe's house was divided into two rooms by a mud wall. She led the *nganga* to where Nza lay on a bamboo cot. She was on her back, her hands covering her face. Her two young half-sisters sat cross-legged on mats, each cradling an infant in her lap. The healer shook hands with the girls and squatted on his haunches next to Nza.

The mama sat at the foot of the bed and squeezed Nza's foot.

"Our *nganga* is here." Nza uncovered her face and looked up at her mother, then turned slowly toward the old man, whose head was at the same level as hers.

"Nini," he asked softly. What?

"Fever, pain in my head and throat, and heaving in my stomach," whispered Nza. He rested a hand gently on her abdomen, and with the fingers of his other hand, he explored the tender places in her temples and forehead. His hands had a life of their own, calming, soothing. After a while, Nza's pain seemed less intense, the nausea eased, and she slept. The healer stood and looked down at her strong, well-nourished body; he must support Nza's own vital force in its fight to overpower whatever was causing her illness. The oldest treatments, purging and bleeding, might help. Behind him, Ngasa Moke's child whimpered. He turned and, bending over, saw the infant's flaring nostrils and labored breathing; he recognized death's familiar features in the sunken sockets of the little face. He straightened up and walked out into the yard; the mama followed.

"All the women must be purged," he announced. The mama called one of the girls to come out and took Ngasa's infant from her.

"Water," she commanded, pointing to a large enamel basin next to the door. The girl balanced it on her head and set off for the stream that ran behind the village. The mama walked over to the woodpile under the roof. An old aunt, skeletal and toothless, poked her head out and blinked up at the *nganga*. Another aunt muttered something behind her.

"It is our *motumolo*, who lives alone in the forest with the frogs and makes concoctions to drink or put between your *masoko*."

"You will be purged with the others," said the *nganga* firmly.

"Haa!" replied the aunt, pulling her head back into the house like an old turtle.

The girl walked carefully into the yard, steadying the heavy load on her head with one hand. Keeping her back and neck ramrod straight, she knelt, one leg at a time, in front of her mother and the *nganga*. They lifted the basin off her head, poured the water into a pot, and carried it to the fire. When the water boiled, the old man threw in his leaves. After a few minutes, he set the pot aside to cool, then pulled a short bamboo tube out of his pouch and twisted a banana leaf into a funnel. The mama and the girl helped Nza to her feet, and the three women walked into the bush behind the house, followed by the healer carrying a gourd filled with the concoction from the pot. These he handed to the women, leaving them to administer the lavage to one another. When they were through, the mama dragged the thin aunt, shouting obscenities, out of her room and, with the help of the two girls, poured as much of the infusion into her as she could, then pulled the tube out and stood back. The aunt screamed and emptied her colon into the grasses, then scurried back to her room, calling down curses on the *nganga* as she passed him. The mama followed slowly, exhausted from her efforts and her own purging.

"We have all been cleansed except for the fat aunt," she said, approaching the healer.

"Don't bother with her," he said. "No *ndoki* could invade her blighted body." Relieved, the mama tossed the banana leaf funnel into the fire and handed the bamboo tube back to the old man, who shook it dry and returned it to his pouch.

During the next hour, the *nganga* sat and smoked the mama's strong pipe tobacco, and from time to time, one of the women made a dash to the back of the house to relieve herself. Nza's nausea and headache were better, or at least masked by the cramps and burning in her lower belly.

The mama boiled plantains and *mpondu*, the heavy green leaf of manioc. She caught a scrawny chicken, cut off its head with a machete, and as the wings slowed in their beating and the claws went limp, she pushed it into the boiling water before plucking the feathers. Soon the smell of roasting chicken brought the others out of the house. The thin aunt carried a battered tin cup of liquor to her brother as a peace offering. The fat aunt remained inside. The chicken was divided into seven pieces and eaten hungrily, the bones sucked dry by everyone but Nza. She could not eat; the pain in her throat and head turned even the slightest movement into agony.

After the meal, feeling that the women had recovered sufficiently from the first treatment, the *nganga* announced that he would scarify them to relieve and prevent headaches. Slowly, keeping her body stiff and straight, Nza fetched a wooden headrest from inside the house and lay down next to the *nganga*, eager for the pounding in her temples to be released. The healer knelt beside her, then sat on his heels. He rummaged through his pouch and pulled out a small, flat bundle. Carefully he unfolded the cloth protecting a double-edged Gillette blade. Cautiously, using the same cloth, he wiped the film of palm oil from his "scalpel." Nza closed her eyes tightly and braced for the pain. The *nganga* cradled her chin between the thumb and fingers of his left hand and, bending forward, brought the blade over her forehead. Tightening his grip, he slowly and deliberately made four superficial incisions in the skin over her temples. The short lines were of equal length and spaced close together. Little beads of blood oozed from the wounds and ran down into her ears where they puddled before dripping to the ground. The operation done, the healer sat back on his feet and held the blade delicately between his thumb and index finger to keep it clean. He looked down at Nza, satisfied with his work; she sat up carefully. The pain still hammered in her head, but she was sure it would be replaced by the stinging in her temples. She stood, steadying her head with her hands. The mama took her place, lying in front of the old man, her head resting in the concavity of the wooden pillow. One by one the women were scarified—even the fat aunt, although the *nganga* worked on her inside the house where poor light made it difficult to see her black skin. Her incisions had been a little too deep, and he had to rub ashes into the wounds to stop the bleeding. In her stupor she did not seem to mind. He stepped out of the hut, wiped his blade with the cloth, rewrapped it, and stuffed it back into the pouch.

The hot noonday sun beat down; all movement slowed to a crawl. The women were resting after the rigors of treatment. Nza had fed her baby, but she had been unable to awaken Ngasa Moke's child. She squeezed milk out of her breast into a cup and tried to spoon it between the infant's dry, retracted lips, but he would not swallow. Nza lay the child on the mat next to one of the girls, then stretched out on the cot. Outside, the *nganga* looked up at the sun; it was time to return to the forest and sleep.

At dusk the rains came and washed away the feathers and blood in front of the house. Thunder echoed through the trees. During the night Ngasa Moke's infant son stopped struggling for air and died, too weak to cry. It was not until first light, when the mama arose to relieve herself, that she noticed the child was dead. She awoke the girls but let Nza sleep. Quietly they washed the withered little body and used an old piece of cloth as a shroud. Afterward, the mama sat cross-legged under the overhang just outside the doorway, the little bundle in her lap. She looked up into the trees silhouetted against the cloudless pink sky and, swaying gently to its rhythm, softly sang the Budja song for a dead child.

The girls stoked the fire and fetched water and, after a while, Nza awoke and came to sit next to her mother. In spite of the pain in her head and her throat, she forced herself to eat so she could feed her own child, who was still vigorous and hungry. The mama sent one of the girls to notify the *nganga* of the death; the other had already begun digging a shallow little grave. As the sun climbed into the sky, the *nganga* arrived; a young woman trailed shyly behind him.

After burying Ngasa Moke's child near the hut, the *nganga* addressed Nza. "The woman I brought with me just had a healthy child. She has plenty of milk. You must give her your infant to feed until you are better."

Nza hugged her baby tightly. "No, my son stays with me. I will feed him myself."

The *nganga* frowned at the mama, who shrugged a shoulder.

During the three days following the purging and scarification, Mama Basombe and all the women of her family became ill with high fevers, headaches, sore throats, and increasingly severe vomiting and diarrhea. It was clear to the *nganga* that his treatments had failed, but each day he carried them food and water, which he left on a tree stump away from the house. He called out to the mama so she or one of the girls, whoever was strongest that day, would fetch the supplies before they were devoured by animals or birds.

* * *

By the fourth day of the sickness Nza was unable to move off her pallet. Her infant son was crying next to her on a mat. She called feebly for her mother, who came and knelt beside her.

"I cannot feed him anymore," she said, her voice trembling.

"I will ask the *nganga* to give him to the woman with all the milk," said the mama.

Nza raised herself up on her elbow and caressed her baby gently; his crying stopped. She sat up slowly and cradled him in her arms. Then, rocking gently, she looked down at him, tears rolling down her cheeks. "He must live, he must live," she whispered.

The men came to prepare a grave for the family. When they were through, the mama told them to find the *nganga* and ask him to come to her. Then the old woman and her two young daughters dragged the fat aunt to the edge of the grave and rolled her in. They threw dirt onto the body to discourage the flies. At sundown they heard the *nganga* call out to them. The mama picked up Nza's son and, without a word, placed him in the arms of her old friend.

After sunset, the *nganga* hovered over the fire, chewing leaves that eased him into the stupor from which he could call to the ancestors. His petitions for help echoed through the tops of the trees. No answer came. Bitterly he cried out, "It is easy for you to turn away; you do not see them every day." His friends, the frogs, were silent for a moment then, one by one, they added their careless croaking to the whine of mosquitoes; a bush baby wailed in the darkness.

That night Nza vomited dark brown liquid all over the cot and died.

* * *

At first light the old man trudged through the forest toward the Basombe house, a gourd of water in one hand and a cake of boiled rice and *mpondu* in the other. He felt worn out and used; sleep had refused to come after his fruitless trance. His feet dragged along the path, and leaves slapped his face; he was filled with despair. Approaching the dwelling, he saw the mama lying on a mat in front of her door. The fire was out. He sat on his haunches and waited, brushing away the flies that arose from behind the hut. A proprietary crow circled in the gray sky and flapped onto the bare branch of a gnarled tree. He cocked his yellow eye down on the scene and screeched his delight. The mama rolled onto her side.

"Mama Basombe," the *nganga* called out.

She sat up with a groan and wiped the sleep from her eyes with the heels of her hands. *"Ezali pamba, Nza akufi."* It is no use. Nza is dead. "At dawn, we carried her to the hole. The thin one does not hear or speak anymore."

"And you?" he asked, standing up.

"The girls and I are very sick."

"Can you come this far to fetch the food and water I brought?"

"I can," replied the old woman, lying back down.

"Until tomorrow then," said the healer. He turned away and, with feet as heavy as his heart, headed back to his hut.

He knew something was different as soon as he stepped into his clearing. A man was sitting next to the opening in the hut, his legs stretched out, and his back against a log. He seemed to be sleeping. Moving forward cautiously, the *nganga* recognized Sukato.

"Is it all of you together or only your shadow that I see?" asked the old man sternly.

"It is me in flesh and bone, my teacher. I am ill," said Sukato, slowly and stiffly getting to his feet.

"You came straight from the whites of Yambuku?"

"I did. People are dying there. Even one of the sisters died. The whites can do nothing."

The old man poked around the fire. "Are you too sick to carry water?" Sukato bent over, and wincing from the pain in his head, picked up the black pot and headed to the stream.

The *nganga* watched the young man make his way slowly to the bank and carefully lower the pot into the water so as not to disturb the mud. He had taught Sukato when the boy came to the clearing to learn the ways and skills of a healer. Sukato had presented himself right after his initiation ceremonies and circumcision and had walked then with as much pain as he did now. A quick learner and capable assistant, he progressed well until a priest from Yambuku showed up in Bongolu. Several months later a message arrived that the mission was prepared to give Sukato a proper education, and make him into a nursing assistant if he studied well. The *nganga* had let him go without an argument. Returning with the water, Sukato sat and squeezed his throbbing head between his hands.

So you have come back to me, the healer thought. "The voyage may be long, but the bird returns to his nest." The old man smiled and straightened up. He accepted the challenge; he had no other choice. Down by the stream he gathered analgesic leaves, and, scooping mud from the water's edge onto a banana leaf, he carried these remedies back to the fire. Sukato lay on his side, his head resting on his arm. The *nganga* took the pot off the embers and threw in the leaves. He scraped glowing coals into the mud and wrapped the hot pack in an old cloth.

"Lie on your back. This will draw the pain from your head." Sukato obeyed, then flinched from the heat of the poultice. But, after a moment, he relaxed, and the deep, throbbing ache was replaced by the burning in his brow. The old man let the leaves steep for a long time and dozed on his stool by the fire. Sukato slept.

Fat raindrops smacked onto the thatched roof and hissed into the flames. Light from the gray sky above the canopy was fading and, under the trees, forms receded into darkness. The old man carried the smoldering spokes of his fire into the hut and added sticks. He placed the pot with its pungent concoction against the coals. Sukato crawled in, holding the mud pack to his forehead. The *nganga* dipped an enamel mug into the pot and poured the liquid into a drinking gourd. After swallowing some himself, he handed it to Sukato. Smoke hovered under the shallow dome and escaped through a small opening in the thatch. The flames lit up the rough interior of the hut and danced among the shadows on the walls to the drumming of the rain on the roof. When the storm had passed, and the birds and the frogs could be heard again, the old man filled the cup once more.

"What did you learn with the whites?"

"To do what I was told."

"You would have learned that here."

"It is different with the sisters. You do what you are told in their world. You follow their rules in their houses. When you are not with them, they do not control you." He drank from the cup and handed it to the *nganga*, who swallowed what was left and filled it again.

"I learned other things as well. I wore one of their white coats. They have powerful medicines that cure high fevers and the flux. They taught me to set a broken bone and sew a gaping wound. Most of the time their treatments work."

"And when they do not?"

"Then the sick die as they do here."

"And their dead, what becomes of them?"

"They are buried and what they call their souls—our *molimo*—either fly around as people with wings or fry in demon fires."

"Nicely put," said the *nganga*. "So their death is oblivion."

"It would seem to be."

"No wonder they fear dying and avoid it even at the cost of killing others." He struggled to his feet. "That concoction goes straight to my bladder." He walked around to the back of the house. In a moment he returned to the fire.

"I have been unable to prevent the deaths of those in Mama Basombe's house. Nza died last night, and the house is in isolation. If you have the same affliction, there may be little I can do."

"You can intercede with the ancestors before I die so they will receive me."

"I have been unable to reach the ancestors since Mama Basombe brought the Yambuku disease here."

"Nkoko na ngai." Respected father of mine. Sukato bowed his head and held out his hands toward the old man, "Do what you can for me. I am home." The rain had stopped, and the old man thought he heard his spotted civet in the old ficus tree above his hut shake the water from his fur.

The next morning, as the dawn breeze caressed the upper branches and dim light reached the forest floor, Sukato opened his eyes. His clothes were drenched from the night fever; he drank from the pot, and another poultice decreased his headache. The infusion once more brought sleep, and he dreamed of hunting a colobus monkey and wearing its black-and-white pelt on his head, the tail reaching to his waist.

* * *

The *nganga* dropped the *liputa* from around his waist and pulled on an old pair of khaki pants cut off just below the knees. He lowered a torn T-shirt over his head and picked up his pouch. Trudging silently between the huts to the Basombe house, he stood by the stump where he had left the food and water the day before; they were still there. He called out in a businesslike way, "Mama Basombe, Mama Basombe. If you are alive, wake up and answer." The house stood silent before him.

"Anyone. My thin sister. You young unmarried women. Answer me, if you are alive." The crow flew over and landed on an upper branch of the dead tree. The old man threw a stick at it.

"Not your time yet, you black carrion eater." The bird preened his wings, then shook and settled down. The *nganga* walked to the side of the house and called out again several times. Still no answer. He skirted around the grave and glanced in; the flies rose up and covered him. He staggered back, waving his hands around his head, and the flies returned to the hole. He shouted again, but the only response was the buzzing of the flies. Walking gingerly, as if the earth would swallow him, he came around to the front. The stench from inside turned his stomach. He held his nose as he leaned in and counted four still bodies. He turned and moved away rapidly. When he reached the stump, he stopped and faced the house. He sat on his haunches and put his head between his hands.

All that day Sukato burned with fever. His head pounded and his throat was parched. The poultices had lost their effect and had left his forehead blistered. The *nganga's* infusion dulled his senses, which brought him some relief, and although his stomach rebelled at the smell, he drank as much of it as he could keep down. In the evening the old man cooked some rice, but Sukato could not eat.

As dusk crept into the forest and the distant roll of thunder announced the evening storm, Sukato dragged himself into the hut and curled up in a corner. He thought of the people in Yambuku who had died in the hospital with IVs in their arms and their bellies full of the white man's medicines. Death held no fear for him as long as he would be admitted to the ancestral village. He felt a cloth cover his body and saw the healer leaning over him in the fading light.

"The storm approaches. Try to sleep."

"Can you reach our elders? I am ready to go to them."

"I will try, my son."

Sukato relaxed and dozed. The *nganga* gulped down two cupfuls of the infusion and went outside to pray.

The first thunderclap brought Sukato to his senses and increased the agony in his body. He curled up tighter and, covering his ears with his hands, pulled his head down to his knees. His body shook and stiffened. Each bolt of lightning seemed to split open his head, and only the thatch above kept the rain from washing him away. His mouth opened to let out a scream muffled by the hammering of the storm. He slipped into a coma and slept.

The *nganga*, overcome by helplessness, crouched outside the hut, shivering as the rain stung his face and body. He implored the ancestors to speak and threatened them with desertion if they failed to intervene. He strained to hear their response, but only the hissing of rain and the booming of thunder came to him. As the storm passed, its roar was muffled by the forest, and the lightning became a glimmer in the trees. Still nothing. The old man crawled into his hut and collapsed.

* * *

A patter of sticks and nuts on the roof marked the passage of a troop of spot-nose monkeys. The *nganga* awoke. The frogs were in full chorus, accompanied by the repetitive call of a hornbill, and the piccolo tweets of smaller birds flitting among the large waxy leaves of the understory. Above the hut the civet chuckled and yawned. The old man propped himself up on his elbow and looked at Sukato, who was lying on his back snoring gently.

"Sukato," he called. "Sukato, wake up, the night is over."

The young man stirred and gazed up at the rough ceiling. He rubbed his face with his hands and smacked his lips, then ran his tongue over dry teeth. He moved his head to test for pain.

"*Tata*, I feel better!" he said, sitting up.

The old man smiled, then cleared his throat. "Well enough to carry water from the stream so an old man can have his tea?" Sukato stood and steadied himself for a moment against the wall. He was light-headed but free of pain and fever.

The *nganga* had a fire going and was sitting next to the entrance, contentedly puffing on his pipe, when Sukato returned. They drank their tea in silence, and basked in the healing. Questions were not asked, answers not required. After a while the old man knocked the dottle out of his pipe and stood up. "I must go to Mama Basombe's."

"I will come with you."

As the men approached, the crow waddled out of the house and flapped up into his tree. The old man handed a torch to Sukato and pulled a box of matches from his pouch. He lit the thick end which was soaked in kerosene. Sukato let the greasy flame take hold, then flung the firebrand onto the roof. In seconds the thatch was ablaze, and thick smoke rose to the sky, chasing the flies before it. The crow circled overhead, shrieking in anger, then flew off to find another place to feed. An oily smoke escaped from the charred entrances. The old *nganga* and the young African nurse stood together as the remains of the roof collapsed between the blackened walls.

CHAPTER 7

Veronica fueled the old jeep and checked the oil; Antonie made sandwiches and filled a Thermos with coffee for the trip. Augustina was finishing a letter to Adeline, the superior of their main convent in 's Gravenwezel, who had just arrived in Lisala, when Matilda and Veronica walked into her office, followed by Masangaya.

"The Mother Adeline will want to come here, but you must dissuade her from doing so," said Augustina. "I have typed a *laissez-passer* which will help at the barriers," she added, handing Matilda an official-looking document covered with rubber stamps. It was a joke among the missionaries that almost anything with enough rubber stamps on it could be used as a pass, since few of the villagers could read.

"I will insist they send us more nurses and a doctor," said Matilda. "Masangaya has written a letter to Dr. Miatamba, the regional doctor in Lisala, asking for his help as well."

"I worked with him in Kinshasa. He is the best man we have in the north," said the medical assistant.

"You're right," agreed Matilda. "But then I'm prejudiced; I helped train him."

"Better than the two doctors who just left?" asked Veronica.

136

"Different," replied Masangaya. "Quiet and effective. I hope he can come."

Augustina stood up and walked out to the driveway with Matilda. She opened the door of the vehicle and said, "Spend the night in Yalo if you're too tired to drive all the way back."

Veronica shouted above the racket of the engine, "And don't let the big cheeses in Lisala tell you no."

As Matilda drove, the places where she and Luc had been stuck before were fresh in her mind, and she was careful to navigate through the mire, keeping her wheels on the center ridge below the muddy water. At village barriers, she waved the *laissez-passer* at those standing guard; the document worked everywhere except in Yalitaku, where she had seen the dying child on her way up. There, the people would not lower the bamboo poles; they would not even let her get out of the jeep to speak with the chief. She cut the ignition and sat fuming for fifteen long minutes before the old man appeared.

"You said yourself only a few days ago that the village should be isolated after you drove through. Now you want to pass," said the chief.

"I must fetch more help and more medicines for Yambuku. I am well, and there is no danger to you or your people," replied Matilda firmly.

"How can I be sure?"

"I am a nurse: I know. I am a nun: I do not lie."

"Will you bring us medicine on your way back?"

"Of course, if I return this way," replied Matilda, looking down the road and starting the engine.

At the edge of the next village, she was again forced to stop; the place looked deserted. She blew the horn, and a man in a shabby army tunic, whose epaulets hung off the shoulders like clipped wings, crawled out from behind a banana tree. He weaved unsteadily on his feet, clutching a bottle of milky liquor in one hand and a large cudgel in the other.

"Longwa, longwa," he shouted drunkenly, waving the club above his head. Go away.

"Kitisa motema!" ordered Matilda, sticking her head out of the window. Calm yourself! He took a few tottering steps toward her, trying to focus his bloodshot eyes. She flung open the door and towered over him, her hands on her hips.

"Nsoni!" Shame on you! "Drunk, and threatening a sister!" He froze, goggle-eyed before this tall white apparition. "I am on an urgent mission for your people. Take down the barrier and be prepared to do the same thing this evening." She turned her back on him and climbed into the vehicle.

He dropped his club, took a swig from the bottle, and opened the barrier. As she started forward, he shouted, "Cigarettes?"

She held her head high and, with a tight grip on the steering wheel, drove on. There was no barricade at the other end of the village. The road veered to the right, and the huts disappeared in the rearview mirror. Matilda's heart was still pounding; she wiped her eyes with the back of her hand. When she returned at the end of the day, she would take the other road.

A half hour later, she was driving into Yalosemba, leaning on the horn. Sister Marie-Janne came running out of the convent.

"You are back!" She opened the door of the car.

"Only for five minutes," said Matilda, jumping out. "We must not have any contact." She held up her hand to stop Marie-Janne from giving her a hug. "I am on my way to Lisala to see our Mother Superior and the Monseigneur.

The situation in Yambuku is very bad, and they need more help. I just stopped by to see how you are doing."

"We miss you, but we're getting along well," replied the sister.

"I'm happy to hear that, because as soon as I take a shower and pick up some fresh clothes, I'll be off again, and I can't tell you when I'll be back." Several mission workers had gathered to greet Matilda, but she excused herself and walked quickly into the convent.

Matilda stripped, dropping her clothes in a pile in the middle of the room. She stepped into the shower, washed off the grime from the road, and let the cool water splash on her face. After dressing in fresh linens and a crisp white uniform, she opened the door and called to Marie-Janne, who came in and bent down to pick up the dirty clothes.

"Don't touch those, and do not use this shower," said Matilda. "These are precautions we must take. In Yambuku, Sister Lucie is dead and Sister Fermina left for Belgium today, very sick with the fever."

"What about you?"

"A little tired before the shower, but now fine and ready to go. I'll feel even better if I can steal a couple of nurses from Lisala." Matilda covered the pile of clothes with the wet towel, picked up the bundle, and carried it into the grass next to the laundry.

"Be sure you burn these right away," she ordered, walking back to her car, smiling and nodding as she passed the staff who were still waiting.

Matilda pushed the old Jeep as hard as it would go. She thought of the workers' perplexed faces when she had turned away from their outstretched hands. She had never realized how ingrained was the habit of shaking hands with everybody when you said hello or good-bye.

Jules, the radio father, was surprised to see Matilda stride past his desk and greet him with a salute, as she walked into the bishop's anteroom.

A young Zairian priest looked up from behind a pile of papers on his desk. "Sister Matilda, what a pleasure to see you. How are things in Yalosemba?"

"Nice to see you, too. Is Monseigneur in?"

"Yes. He is with the Reverend Mother Adeline."

"Oh, that is good. I have a note for her."

"Do you want me to announce you?"

"If you please. I need to see them both."

The priest walked over to the door and knocked lightly, straining to hear a reply. In a moment the door was opened by a small bald man with heavy glasses resting on the end of his wide nose.

"Excellency, Sister Matilda is here to see you and the Reverend Mother," said the priest. The bishop looked up at Matilda with a smile.

"Providence has sent you. Your Mother Superior arrived from Belgium last night. We are talking about a difficult situation up north—not your hospital, I know—but your opinion as a nurse will be of value to us." He lifted his hand; she genuflected and bowed her head over his ring.

"Matilda! What a wonderful surprise," said Mother Adeline, dark eyes shining from her aristocratic face.

"Please sit down," said the bishop, returning to his elaborately carved African chair. "I was just telling the Mother Superior about the events in Yambuku."

"Everyone at home is devastated by Lucie's death," said Mother Adeline. "I carried the sad news to her family myself. But now we have a radio message that Sister Fermina is sick and on her way to Kinshasa and Antwerp."

"That is correct. I just came from Yambuku," said Matilda.

"You did?" exclaimed the bishop. "I was not told you

had left Yalosemba." He took off his glasses and wiped them to hide his irritation.

"I went only a few days ago, in response to Sister Augustina's request for help."

"Are you all right?" asked the Mother Superior.

"Of course," replied Matilda.

"Then please tell us all you know about the situation," said the bishop.

Matilda reviewed the details of Lucie's death, Fermina's sudden sickness, the rising toll the fever was taking among the Zairians, and the visit of the doctors from Kinshasa.

She continued, "Our most immediate problem is that three out of the six nursing aides are down with the disease, and the number of patients coming to the hospital has increased since the doctors were there. Everyone is exhausted."

"And it is not known what is killing the people?" asked Adeline.

"The doctors from Kinshasa thought it might be typhoid, and they vaccinated the mission workers and us. In fact," she said, feeling her upper arm, "I am still sore from the shot. But the latest thinking is that the disease may be caused by a virus."

"Like the influenza epidemic?" asked Adeline.

"Not quite. This disease causes bleeding."

"How is it spread?" asked the bishop.

"We don't know," said Matilda. "We don't know if it is spread by dust, insects, or by direct contact, and that makes it more frightening." Adeline and the bishop looked at her anxiously.

"I came here for a quick visit to underline the seriousness of the crisis at Yambuku. I also need two nurses to help us, and I have a list of supplies that Sister Augustina wants me to bring back tonight."

"You will have to ask Dr. Miatamba about nurses," said the bishop.

"Of course. I will see him as soon as we are through."

"You had better brief the zone *commissaire* as well." Matilda nodded.

Adeline asked, "Will you be spending the night with us at the convent?"

"No. I wish I could, but I must return to Yambuku this evening."

"Do you think that is wise?"

"My dear mother, all I know is that it is necessary. Sister Antonie is the only medical nun left, and she is a nursing aide."

The Mother Superior sat forward in her chair. "It is also necessary to think of the future," she said. "We have not been able to recruit a nurse for Zaire for over ten years. We must consider the evacuation of the sisters from Yambuku."

"But that would create a panic," said the bishop, cutting in.

"I suppose it might, but if more of my sisters die, there will be no mission at all. Then what would the people do?"

The bishop looked over his glasses at the photograph of Cardinal Malula, the first prelate of Central Africa to be chosen a prince of the church.

"Survive, Reverend Mother—at a cost for the moment, to be sure—but the people and the Holy Church will survive," he replied, smiling. Adeline looked at him and raised her eyebrows.

Matilda cut in. "With your permission, Monseigneur, I would like to finish what I came here to do."

"By all means," said the bishop, standing.

She pulled an envelope out of her pocket. "This is from Augustina. It includes a list of supplies she wants me to bring back."

"The father of the depot will have them ready within a few hours," said the bishop.

Hesitating for a moment, Adeline asked, "Do you think I should come up with you?"

"That would not be wise," answered Matilda. "You are a wonderful, warmhearted Mother Superior, but you are not a nurse. I know we can count on your prayers."

"Then, for the moment, I will stay here and keep in touch by radio," said the older woman, anxious in the face of so many unknowns and impatient at being at the periphery.

Matilda drove to the zone *commissaire*'s office. She informed him of the situation in Yambuku. He listened politely, offering no suggestions or help: Yambuku was not in his zone. She then proceeded to the hospital to look for Dr. Miatamba.

A dozen patients were lined up along the terrace that ran the length of the building. Most sat against the wall; a few lay on mats. These patients had medical problems critical enough to warrant the expense of transportation to the hospital—and the added bribes needed to get through the gates. Each time a patient came out of the examining room, another went in; and those along the wall edged up a little closer to the door and waited again. Time was not a factor—being in line was.

In government hospitals, there was a dearth of doctors. Once the pride of the Belgian colony, these institutions were now lacking supplies and equipment. Patients who needed medicines had to find them on their own. The families of those who required an operation had to scavenge or steal the gauze and sutures—and sometimes even the injectables for anesthesia—before the surgery could be scheduled. Few of the doctors assigned to the wards and outpatient departments spent much time in the hospital. Most had private offices and even small clinics elsewhere in town, where they plied their trade and charged what the traffic would bear. The handful of national doctors who did devote their lives to hospital practice were dedicated and patriotic professionals who seldom reaped the financial benefits or privileges of political appointments. Matilda had worked with Miatamba and had trained two of his nurses. She would have gladly used him as a physician for her own family.

Some of the patients along the wall recognized her and stood up to greet her. "Do not disturb yourselves," she told them. "I am only here for a moment to see the doctor." She slipped into the office without knocking. Miatamba, tall and well built, wearing a white short-sleeved lab coat and khaki trousers, was leaning over an old man on the examining table, listening to his heart and lungs. A nurse assistant looked up; Matilda put a finger to her lips. Miatamba curled an arm around the patient's bony shoulders and helped him sit.

"*Sikoyo, pema makasi, tata.*" Now, breathe hard, father.

The patient's chest heaved in and out. Catching sight of Matilda, he smiled. "*Mbote, ma soeur.*"

"*Sango nini, Tata Biwa?*" she asked, stepping up to the examining table. He had been in charge of the sterilizer when she was head nurse at the hospital. That had been seventeen years ago, after independence.

The doctor looked around. "Sister Matilda! Sneaking into my office without being announced! Are you checking up on me again?"

"You are one of the few doctors I have never had to keep an eye on, and you know it," said the nun. "I need to have a word with you about the situation in Yambuku."

"I have heard rumors," said the doctor. He turned to his assistant, "Be sure Tata Biwa has enough antibiotic for another week. I want to see him in ten days—sooner if he coughs up more green phlegm or his fever returns."

The nurse nodded, helped the patient off the table, and led him over to the desk.

"I'm ready for a cup of coffee," said Miatamba, opening the door of the office. He saw that the next patient was standing, ready to come in. "I am sorry to keep you waiting. I'll send my assistant down right away," he said. Stoically the patient sat back down on the floor.

In the doctors' call room, a young man slept on a swaybacked sofa, his head resting on the stained armrest. Ancient medical journals, provided by a missionary organization in Contentment, Illinois, were scattered over a table covered by an oilcloth patterned with faded red squares. The room was sparsely furnished with straight-backed chairs and a hamper in a corner overflowing with soiled green scrub suits. On an electric burner stood a chipped enamel kettle. The small sink was filled with dirty spoons and mugs. With apologies, Miatamba awoke the young man and asked him to work through the line of patients—he needed to talk with Sister Matilda for a few minutes. The intern stood up, yawned, stretched, and left.

"Not quite as neat and clean as when you were here," said the doctor. "I hope you don't take sugar." He handed her a lukewarm cup of Nescafé. "It's only available on the black market, and that is beyond my salary." She shook her head. "Now, tell me about Yambuku," he said, as they sat at the table.

"I have been there for the past week trying to help the sisters and Masangaya deal with something that has killed dozens of people, including Sister Lucie." Matilda outlined the events ending with the brief visit of the two doctors from Kinshasa.

"What do you want me to do?"

"Come and help us."

"You know Yambuku's not in my district." She shrugged a shoulder without comment. He went on. "Surely after the professor runs his tests or, more likely, after Sister Fermina reaches Antwerp, you will know what is causing the fever and be able to do what is necessary."

"That will not happen in time to avoid losing more lives," said Matilda.

"Sister, if you and Masangaya cannot prevent more dying, what more could I do?"

"Your presence would calm much of the fear in the people."

"In the people or in the sisters?"

"Both, of course."

Miatamba drained his cup and stood up. "More coffee?"

"No, thanks." He walked over to the sink and rinsed out his mug. He knew that the Africans would be more passive than panicked. They knew the sun would shine after the storm. He returned to the table.

After a while Matilda said, almost to herself, "I have a premonition that the worst awaits us."

The doctor looked at her closely. "Sister, are you sick?"

"No, not really. But I am tired and my back aches after the drive," she replied, sitting up a little straighter.

"Give me your hand." He reached across the table and wrapped his long, gentle fingers around her wrist and felt her pulse; it was fast, and her hand was hot and damp.

"You have a fever."

"I may have a slight fever. My arm's sore where they gave me the typhoid shot. I think that's all it is," said Matilda, pulling her hand away.

"Where are you going from here?" he asked.

"To the convent to pick up a few supplies, then refuel the jeep and drive back to Yambuku."

"This evening?"

"Yes. I told you, they are very shorthanded and have more patients than ever." They both stood.

"Be sure and eat something at the convent."

"I will, but I'm not really hungry."

"I know—more like a lioness than a jackal."

For a moment their eyes met in silence. *She is sick and will not admit it,* he thought.

Matilda looked away. *I wish I could just take him with me now.* Miatamba stepped forward, putting his hands on her shoulders. She relaxed for an instant, then pushed him back and fixed him with her gaze. "Will you come?"

"As soon as I can. I wouldn't dare not to," he replied, with a chuckle.

"Can you lend us two of your nurses?"

"That also I will try to do."

Matilda drove back to the convent. Adeline, reluctant to let her go, fussed and scurried around like a mother hen. Finally, she handed Matilda a bag of sandwiches and two bottles of water.

"The water has been boiled and filtered, so it should be safe. Has Augustina talked to you about evacuating the sisters?" she asked.

"No. I think she feels we can handle the situation until the results of the professor's tests or news of Fermina clarify the picture."

"I wish there was more I could do," said the Mother Superior. "I will pray, of course, very hard for all of you. Monseigneur said he would offer a special Mass of benediction to give all of you strength to endure these terrible times."

"You could keep after the authorities to send more Zairian nurses to Yambuku," said Matilda. "Was Monseigneur able to pry the supplies away from the fathers?"

"You will find them all in your vehicle." The two women walked out to the jeep, and Matilda climbed in and started the engine.

"Bless you, Matilda. God goes with you."

Matilda waved. "I will stay in touch by radio."

She took the shorter, more deserted route north to Yambuku. Truck drivers, who relied on village trade to supplement their pay, seldom used it, so there were fewer deep wheel gouges in the road. The sun's last rays escaped from behind thunderheads forming in a darkening sky, but the rain held off. Matilda's foot was heavy on the gas pedal, and the racket of the old vehicle's engine hammered her ears. After an hour of jolting along the road, her neck was stiff, and she had a headache. In the twilight she stopped and, without switching off the engine, drank from the water bottle and nibbled on a sandwich. Her eyelids stung from fatigue, and her left shoulder throbbed. She found aspirin in her medical bag and took three with a swallow of water. The dusty headlights cast a dull yellow beam into the tunnel of darkness. Thick vegetation bordered the sides of the road and blocked out all but a strip of indigo sky. She stepped out, pulled a rag out from under the seat, and wiped off the lights. Climbing back into the Jeep, she shifted into gear and pushed on into the night. "Blessed Mother, be with me," she whispered. Then she less formally addressed her guardian angel, a hardworking spirit who had trouble keeping up with her: *I count on you to show me where the ridges lie in the mud holes so I can guide the wheels along them; let the villagers sleep, so I can pass through without discussion; and keep this faithful vehicle going for another couple of hours, then I will let you rest, and I will rest, too.*

The headlights hypnotized the nightjars nestling in the warm dust on the road; they flew up at the last moment, just clearing the hood, the white spots on their wings flashing by the windshield. The first village she came to had a barrier—a single bamboo pole—which she removed, replacing it when she had driven through. An old man and a woman were caught for a moment in the headlights. Behind the cone of light, jouncing between the walls of vegetation, she drove on and on. Dreamily she thought of the road overarched by maples that ran from between her family's farm, past Veronica's home, into the village of Schilde. She rolled down the window and the blast of wind, smelling of wet sand, somehow revived her. She closed one eye at a time, to relieve the stinging. The aspirin was working. Her headache was less severe; she felt better. To keep awake, she sang loudly, alternating between praise to the Virgin Mother and nursery ditties about farm animals. The second village looked deserted and had no barriers.

In Yambuku, the day had been heavy with work and apprehension. Antonie was still in the hospital, tending the sick. Veronica sat in the refectory writing:

26 September 1976
Dear Gabrielle,

Fermina is on her way to Kinshasa, then to Belgium because she is also stricken by the same illness that killed Lucie. I am waiting for Sister Matilda to return from Lisala with medicines and a doctor. In the meantime, let me tell you what happened this afternoon.

Right after lunch, some twenty blacks appeared. Their faces and bodies were smeared with red and white paint.

They ran and shouted around the mission buildings, waving their spears and muzzle loaders. Then they shot off their poopoo guns and charged the entrance of the medical pavilion where those sick with the fever lie dying. They hurled their spears and left them quivering in the earth, then retreated. They regrouped and charged forward again to retrieve their lances, then ran shouting to the next pavilion. After repeating the same exercise in front of each pavilion, they marched to the house of the fathers and danced, drumming wildly on small drums tied to their waists. We watched from a distance as Father Gérard sat calmly on his terrace. After the ceremony their chief announced that they had now exorcised the evil spirits causing the deaths and that following two rains sent by the ancestors, the disease would be ended.

As you know, it is now the rainy season so two deluges are bound to come anyway. Well, as I have often said, they have their ways and we have ours.

I hear the Jeep, so will quickly close and welcome Matilda. She is a source of great strength and comfort.

With all my love,

Your Sister in Christ

The headlights swept across the refectory. She picked up the kerosene lantern and walked out to meet Matilda.

"Veronica! You shouldn't have waited up for me."

"I was worried about you after such a long drive." She grabbed the bag out of the car and, with the lantern, led the way to Matilda's room. Matilda went to the sink, ran water on a towel, then collapsed gratefully in her chair and wiped her face. Veronica lit the candle on the bed table.

"I will make you a cup of tea."

"One cup, then I will take a shower."

After ten minutes, Veronica returned with the tea to find

Matilda asleep. She left the cup on the table, blew out the candle, and went to bed.

At 2 A.M. Veronica was dreaming that she was helping pick apples in her orchard at home and Matilda was calling, "Veronica, come over here and hold the ladder or I will fall. Veronica! Veronica!" She awoke with a start.

"Vero, help me!" Matilda cried out from the door of her room. Veronica jumped out of bed and ran down the hall as Augustina and Antonie came out of their rooms and followed. By the dim light of the candle, Veronica saw that Matilda's cotton nightdress was stuck to her thin body, and her anxious face was covered with sweat.

CHAPTER 8

After matins, Veronica checked on Matilda: she was asleep on her side. Veronica backed out of the room quietly, walked across the road to the medical assistant's house, and knocked on the door. It opened, and Masangaya stood on the threshold.

"Sorry to disturb you this early," said Veronica.

"It's all right, Sister. I haven't been to bed yet. More people died during the night."

"*Ô mon Dieu, mon Dieu,* when will it stop! I hope we hear from Fermina's doctors soon."

"So do I."

"Could you come over and see Sister Matilda? She returned from Lisala, then called for me during the night. I am worried about her." Veronica tried to peek around him into the house, but his body blocked the doorway. "I heard you sent your wife and children to Ebonda. Would you like me to bring you some breakfast?"

"No, thank you, Sister. I have somebody taking care of me. I will come over as soon as I've cleaned up."

Veronica turned and walked down the steps. The door closed behind her. *Another woman . . . an easy solution for him. A woman in the secular world was expected to feed her man, bear his children, and satisfy him in bed. St. Paul had passed on his chauvinist views to Timothy: women*

*were not to teach but to learn, listening quietly and sub-
missively to men.* Veronica was glad she was a nun. Her
marriage to Christ was demanding, but serving Him was el-
evating and made her feel good, and her vows did away
with some of the more persistent complications of woman-
hood—most of the time. She was also relieved that it was
Antonie who cleaned and did the laundry in the house of
the fathers except, of course, for Father Dubonnet, who
never took a real bath or washed his clothes. But then
Antonie seemed to thrive on menial service. Veronica
walked up the steps and along the corridor to the refectory
where the sisters were having breakfast.

"Did Matilda sleep the rest of the night?" asked
Augustina. Antonie poured coffee for Veronica and pushed
the bread and cheese over to her.

"She's still asleep," replied Veronica. "I asked
Masangaya to see her. She blames her fever and night
sweats on the typhoid shot. I hope she is right."

The three nuns ended their meal in silence.

"I'll be in my office," said Augustina, pushing back her
chair. "You will let me know what he says, won't you?"

"Of course," answered Veronica.

Antonie started stacking the dishes, but Veronica stopped
her. "I'll do that; you have your hands full at the hospital."

Antonie stepped back, a little surprised. Veronica finished
clearing the table, then stacked the dishes in the kitchen
sink. Afterward, she walked down the corridor and sat on
the front steps to wait for the medical assistant.

In the distance, she heard the choir practicing for Mass.
She wondered how full the church would be with so many
of the mission workers sick or away with their families in
their own villages. Listening more carefully, she noticed
there was none of the high-pitched drumming that went

with the deeper beat that set the rhythm. Could Bienvenu, the young man who kept the rice-decorticating machine running, have left as well? What would happen to the harvest? The agricultural cooperative depended on a handful of men who had been trained to keep the trucks and other machinery operating. The coffee growers and paddy workers would have to return to subsistence farming if the machines rusted in the fields and the harvests rotted on the ground. The women would again do the backbreaking work while the men sat under shade trees and drank and smoked *bangi*. The singing stopped. Would the faithful continue to be faithful, or would they return to their animistic beliefs?— the skin of a leopard imbued the man who wore it with the power and stealth of the animal. Masangaya walked up to her and she stood, brushing the dust off her seat.

"I will just go in and tell her you're here," said Veronica. The medical assistant nodded. He carried a scuffed leather bag with a broken clasp. Veronica knocked lightly and walked in. Matilda's chin and nose seemed more prominent, or it may have been that the hollows in her cheeks and the darkness around her lids were more conspicuous. She smiled as Veronica stepped up to the bed.

"You're awake."

"I was just dozing, and relieved to be feeling better. Thank you for your help last night. Were you able to go back to sleep?"

"Of course," said Veronica. "Matilda, Masangaya is here to see you."

"He doesn't need to see me," protested the nurse, sitting up in bed. "He should be taking care of the patients that are really sick."

"I asked him to come."

"Vero . . . !"

"Here's a comb. I'll straighten your sheets and let him

in." Matilda combed her hair and lay back on the pillows. Even that small effort reawakened the pain in her head. Veronica stepped to the door and opened it.

"Come in, Masangaya. Sister Matilda is delighted and grateful that you have come." The medical assistant walked in and put his bag on the chair.

"Sister Veronica should not have bothered you. I'm sure you have more than enough to do."

"Good morning, Sister," said Masangaya. "That is true enough, but we need you well to carry the load with us." Veronica put his bag on the bed, and pushed the chair behind him.

"Thank you," he said, sitting down. "I understand you came in late last night after a very long day. How were things in Lisala? Will they be able to send some reinforcements?"

"I saw Dr. Miatamba, who sends you his regards. He will try to come and is doing what he can to recruit two nurses."

"Good. Now, *ma soeur*, tell me what is going on with you."

"Very well," she said patiently. "Yesterday, on the way back from Lisala, I developed a headache and a little fever. My arm, where I was inoculated, was hot and painful. I took some aspirin and felt better until the middle of the night when I awoke soaking wet with another headache and pain in my back, probably from all the bouncing on the road. Veronica gave me more aspirin and changed the bedclothes, and I slept until you came in."

"And how do you feel now?"

"Not too bad," replied the nurse, with a quick look at Veronica.

"What does that mean?" asked Masangaya.

Matilda paused and looked at him. "Actually, I still feel

tired and slightly achy. Yesterday was a long, exhausting day." The medical assistant nodded and waited for more. "Aspirin and a little more rest is all I need."

"Fever?" he asked.

She felt her brow with the back of her hand. "Probably, but not much."

He pulled a thermometer from his bag and handed it to her. She stuck it under her tongue and pursed her lips.

After checking her pulse and blood pressure, he read the thermometer. "Half a degree of fever. As you say, a couple of aspirin should take care of that." He put a stethoscope around his neck. "I would like to examine you, if I may."

"Yes, I suppose you should," replied Matilda.

Masangaya thumped her back and listened to her chest. He ran his hands over her shoulders, feeling some heat and eliciting some tenderness where she had been vaccinated. After examining her abdomen, he folded his stethoscope and stuffed it into the bag. Matilda smoothed out the sheet that covered her and lay back looking at him expectantly.

"I think you must be right, Sister. The effect of the aspirin has worn off. If you take two every three or four hours, with a little food and drink, and rest in bed today, you should recover quickly."

"Just what I thought," said Matilda.

"I'll give Veronica some chloramphenicol and nivaquine for you, then we will have covered the causes of your fever from several directions." For an instant, each tried to read behind the gaze of the other and concluded: *no questions—no lies*.

"That makes sense," said the nurse. "Thank you for coming. I'm sure I'll be back on my feet tomorrow." They shook hands and Masangaya left.

"I'll be right back with the medicine," said Veronica, following him out of the room. She caught up to him.

"What do you think?"

"Sister, I have stopped thinking. I only take one step at a time, without knowing where the path leads." In silence, they walked to the operating pavilion and into his office. He handed her the antibiotic and the malaria pills.

"I will report back to you this evening," said Veronica.

"Fine," said Masangaya, closing the door behind her. He stretched out on his cot, hoping for sleep. Death was crowding death, and nothing would stop this disease until all who were destined to die were in their graves.

Veronica pushed her way through the Africans as soon as the Mass and its dramatic moments were over. She opened Matilda's door and was relieved to see her sitting up in bed, reading her breviary.

"You will never guess what happened," said Veronica, trying to catch her breath. "Father Gérard collapsed during his sermon!" She sat in the chair by Matilda's bed and wiped her face with the end of her veil.

"Is he all right?" asked Matilda.

"I don't know. Two of the Zairian curates had to help him into the sacristy. Dubonnet had to finish the Mass."

"Calm yourself and slow down, Veronica, then tell me what happened," said Matilda.

"Well, just as I thought, the church was less than half full because most of the teachers and workers sent their wives and children away after Lucie died. The men who are still here have been with the mission for years. They will stay as long as the sisters and fathers remain. Anyway, Father Gérard was delivering one of his hellfire and brimstone sermons. He believes the epidemic is a punishment inflicted upon Yambuku by a righteous God because of 'the immoral and dissolute behavior of the people.' He worked himself up into a storm of indignation. He can be terrifying, you know."

"Yes, I know," said Matilda, "but that is nothing new. What happened?"

Veronica pulled the chair closer to the bed, and continued her story.

After communion, as the choir was singing, Father Gérard had suddenly stood and stopped the music with an imperative wave of his hand. A tense silence fell over the congregation, as he stepped into the pulpit. He wore the green chasuble with its yellow cross and green stole embroidered with golden thread. His gray beard with its white streak under his prominent lower lip gave him the look of Moses on the mountain.

"I have before me the prophesy of Isaiah when Jerusalem was overwhelmed with iniquity. Today these words apply to all of you here Yambuku: 'And it shall come to pass, that instead of sweet smell, there shall be stink; and instead of a girdle, a rope; and instead of well set hair, baldness; and instead of a rich robe, a girding of sackcloth; and instead of beauty, shame.' "

Behind the choir a drummer beat the rhythm of a dirge. A deep-throated *da-doom, da-doom* echoed under the metal roof, and the people's heads and shoulders swayed to the somber beat. Father Gérard's large hands emerged from the lace cuffs of his alb, as he clutched the Bible and raised it up before him like the stone tablet on which God's laws had been chiseled.

A whisper of "Libela, libela," raced through the congregation, as the people repeated Gérard's African byname, "Forever, forever."

"This is—the word—of God," thundered the priest, shaking the book in time with the drumbeat. "A God—who tolerates—no affront—from His children. A God with whom you will not trifle. This epidemic is God's punishment because you have not lived according to His laws. You have frequented the brothels of Bumba and used mistresses to satisfy your lust. You have disobeyed God's commands, and He has sent this pestilence to purge and punish you."

In the front row, Antonie looked anxiously at Augustina, who pursed her lips, nodding her reassurance. The drumbeat and the priest's resounding voice reverberated among the dusty hardwood beams and fell like crashing waves on the people who cringed and huddled together. They were awestruck by the fury of his passion. Their heads, shaved in mourning, nodded with each stroke of the drum. They were already crushed by death and now Libela's God wanted more.

Gérard paused and leaned on the pulpit to catch his breath. He wiped his face on his sleeve. Bracing himself against the pulpit rail, he continued—now pleading. The drumming dropped to a throb in the background.

"My children, my poor children, God wants you pure so you can ascend to His heavenly throne. You must atone for the filth in your souls, or perish and burn in the fires of hell." He paused, his gaze fixed on the cross over the entrance to the church; color drained from his face, his eyes rolled up in their sockets, and he sank to the floor. Antonie stood and started toward him, but Augustina pulled her back. The drumming stopped. A murmur arose as two curates rushed to him and dragged him out of the pulpit toward the sacristy door. Recovering quickly, Father Gérard tore himself free and staggered to his feet. He stepped back into the pulpit, clutching the rail. The *da-doom, da-doom* started again.

"I exhort you, my sons and daughters in Christ, to stop your womanizing and drinking and smoking of hemp so that, in His infinite love, He will lift this scourge from Yambuku and welcome you back in the sheepfold of His church." He stood straight, his hand thrust out over the congregation, and boomed, "In the name of the Father and of the Son and of the Holy Ghost." He turned and walked slowly into the sacristy, slamming the door behind him. The drumming stopped, and a sigh of relief spread through the church. Then Father Maas stepped in front of the altar, and the people lifted their heads and smiled and whispered, "Dubonnet, Dubonnet."

The priest raised his hands and spoke softly: "My brothers and sisters in Christ, the laws of God and nature are unyielding and hard like rocks that direct the flow of forest streams. But unlike the laws of nature, we have an advocate before the bar of justice in Heaven—Jesus Christ. If we live like Him, our sins are forgiven over and over again. We live like Him if, in the midst of our grief, we love and comfort one another. Those who have died are released from earthly pain and are at peace. We who remain still struggle with our own natures. I will stick with the trees that claim the abandoned gardens and send their roots deep for water; they do not die quickly. The caterpillars eat their leaves, but they cannot eat them all. Some of them, like some of us, remain standing. Some will die, but not all will die. Now go in peace and care for one another."

Vero finished her narrative with, "So I came right over to tell you."

"Do you think Father Gérard is all right now?"

"I think so," replied Veronica, topping off Matilda's glass. "He walked into the sacristy without help and slammed the door. His pride was probably wounded by fainting in front of the Africans. Do you need anything? I will come back with your lunch in a little while."

"Thank you for the report. I will take two more aspirins and sleep. I have to obey orders," said Matilda.

Father Gérard, as was the custom after Sunday Mas was sharing a bottle of wine with the sisters on the convent terrace when Veronica walked up the steps.

"Father, I am relieved to see you up and around. To your health," she said, raising her glass.

"Thank you, Sister. To yours," replied Gérard, returning the salute. "I am fully recovered. I have been fasting for two days to atone for the sins of the natives, and the heat during Mass got to me."

"You still do not look very good to me," said Veronica.

"You would not look your best either, Sister, if—"

Augustina cut in. "That was a powerful sermon, Father. I'm sure your confessional will be crowded this evening before vespers."

"I agree that the sermon was powerful, but I do not believe that the behavior of our Africans is the cause of the epidemic," said Veronica.

"Read the Old Testament," said the priest.

"I read the New Testament," said Veronica with conviction. "I just do not think God would punish the people of Yambuku in such a way. Anyway, some of the teachers and workers who have died were good, honest people who did not carouse around and smoke *chanvre*. And what about Lucie?"

"It is often the wicked that cause the death of the innocent," snapped Father Gérard.

Augustina put her hand on Veronica's arm, but Veronica pulled away and said, "Father, the people of this region have smoked pot and drunk *lotoko* for years. Killing off a few with a disease is not going to change their habits. It is their custom. It's their way of dealing with a hard, isolated life."

"It is God's punishment because they do not obey His commandments," shouted the priest.

"Their *ngangas* say that the disease is caused by ancestral spirits of a tribe that used to live here and was displaced by the present occupants," said Veronica, unabashed by Gérard.

"Where did you hear that?"

"In the villages when I was making my rounds a couple of days ago."

"You should spend more time on your knees in the chapel and less listening to the gibberish of the natives," said the priest severely. He turned on his heel and went down the steps of the veranda, out into the noonday heat.

"There is nothing as simple or as stubborn as a Flemish nun," he muttered to himself. He walked with his head high, his heels kicking up little puffs of dust as he marched toward the house of the fathers. In a moment the sisters heard a loud crash.

"He's taking it out on that poor table," said Antonie, hiding a grin behind her hand. "I think you made him angry."

"Lately he's always angry about something. He would do better to think about getting us more help instead of blaming the disease on God," said Veronica. "Why would God pick on Yambuku? The people here are no worse than anywhere else in this region."

"Maybe he doesn't feel well," said Antonie.

"Well, I hope he stays healthy. He would be a very difficult patient."

Antonie added, "Too bad Father Dubonnet isn't here. He understands the people better than any of us."

"He left on the mission bicycle right after Mass to make

his rounds in the villages," said Veronica. "Come on, let's fix Matilda her lunch."

Father Dubonnet was at that moment eight kilometers west of Yandongi in the village of Bombanga. He was preparing to baptize two children and say Mass for the handful of villagers who were members of the church. After these ceremonies he sat with the elders under a purple bougainvillaea whose branches had been spread out and supported with stakes to make shade.

The priest learned that a man called Liwagu Masombo had died during the early hours of the morning. The family had immediately buried him behind the house, according to the instructions of the chief. Two days previously, the man's twenty-five-year-old wife had died, followed by her baby. During the last three months of her pregnancy, the young mother had been a patient in the Yambuku hospital's prenatal clinic. She had delivered her baby in the maternity pavilion.

Masanga ya mbila, fresh palm wine, only faintly fermented, was passed around to the elders and the priest by the small, leathery man who climbed palm trees to draw off their milky sap. After the plastic cups and mugs were filled, each man poured a little onto the ground for the ancestors, then raised their tumblers, said *"Santé"* like Europeans, and drank. Then, when the chief's pipe was pulling well, the priest had passed his pack of Belgas to the others, and all the cigarettes were lit, the conversation turned to the disease that had cost Bombanga two adults and a child. These three were the only villagers who had traveled to the mission hospital over the last few months.

After a long discussion, with several men raising their voices at the same time, the consensus focused to a *ndoki* present in the hospital. Neither the origin of this destructive spirit was known, nor why it was there. The *ngangas* would find those answers after they had communed with the ancestors. But it was clear that a vicious, deadly force was loose in the hospital and that something had to be done to appease it. The talk turned to which counterforces would have the power to be effective.

In the evening, riding back to Yambuku, Dubonnet thought about the elders' talk of appeasing the lethal spirit in the hospital. After putting the bike away, he picked up an old cassock from his room and walked over to the church. He folded the robe into the shape of a club, poured holy water into the baptismal font, and soaked the end of his crude aspergillum. Then, throwing the soggy vestment over his shoulder, he marched out into the twilight and headed to the hospital: his goal, exorcism—not appeasement. The few people he met along the way stepped to the side of the road and gaped as Dubonnet strode past with unusual intensity and speed. His first target was the medical pavilion.

He stepped into the building and paused. The handful of visitors who sat watching over the three patients at the far end of the ward looked up and gasped, startled by the shaggy, ghostly figure standing by the door in the dim light.

"In the name of Jesus," shouted Dubonnet, waving the cassock over his head, "I cast you into the deepest recesses of hell. . . ." The visitors jumped to their feet as holy water sprayed the empty beds and windows. Dubonnet advanced toward the sick, his voice booming out, "And chain you there forever, never to seek the ruin of souls again." The visitors fled, and the patients, frozen on their mattresses, watched in terror as the priest slammed the wet club on their bed frames, showering them with water. Next, he walked out of the building and into the pediatric pavilion. Repeating the same ritual with the same intensity, but this time more softly, he tiptoed between the rows of beds.

Some of the children were awake and waved to him, accustomed to any behavior from this father. He waved back and admonished them, "Sleep, sleep." As soon as he left the ward, four of the people attending the children crawled out from under their beds and followed at a safe distance, expecting the walls to fall down and the heavens to open up, as he continued to march through all the pavilions exorcising the *ndoki*.

Yambuku had been spared a storm that evening. As night took over, a silver glimmer appeared in the western sky, heralding a full moon, which slowly climbed out of the trees and cast its glow over the hospital buildings. Somewhere, beyond the boundaries of the mission, the rhythmic beat of drums could be heard. Around the drums, people danced in the moonbeams that filtered through the trees and threw money in the river to appease the spirits.

CHAPTER 9

"I've not been this lazy for as long as I can remember," said Matilda as Veronica walked into her room later that evening.

"You look better, though. You should try taking Sunday off more often." Veronica put the tray she was carrying on the table.

Matilda moved to the edge of the bed and ran her fingers through her hair. "Arrange for the sick to be well on the Sabbath, and I will be glad to take the day off." She reached for her sandals and, after banging them on the floor to dislodge overnight spiders or scorpions, slipped them on and stood. She rolled her head back and forth to work the stiffness out of her neck, then stepped over to the table.

"Rice pudding, buggy bread, bananas, and tea. Back to normal meals. I'm glad I'm not hungry."

"Those Kinshasa doctors liquidated our supplies from home," said Veronica. "They are probably telling everyone that we eat like *fÿnproevers* all the time."

"A small price to have them take Fermina to Kinshasa. I can see her being tucked into a hospital bed in Antwerp as we speak," replied Matilda.

Antonie knocked on the door and walked in. "I have just seen Father Gérard. He refused the food I took to him."

"He probably feels sick because he behaved like an idiot," said Veronica.

"Yes, losing one's temper can certainly ruin a good appetite," said Matilda. "How is he otherwise?"

"Silent and short. When I asked him how he felt, he just scowled at me," replied Antonie.

"But he let you fuss over him. He probably likes that," said Veronica.

"Maybe. But I get along with him better than you do. I do what he wants without challenging his views. He let me take his temperature and count his pulse and gather up his soiled clothes for the laundry."

"If he really gets sick he'll be like a leopard with a broken fang," said Veronica.

"I have heard that Father Dubonnet won't let the sisters do anything for him," said Matilda.

"That's right," answered Veronica. "And won't even let Casimir wash his linen. He swims with his clothes on and rubs soap into his cassock, then rinses it as he paddles around the pond next to the pump house."

"A little eccentric, isn't he?" asked Matilda.

"He is different," said Veronica. "But did you know that he gives money to the hospital? He told Augustina that if anyone found out he would stop doing it; so we have to keep that to ourselves."

Matilda sat at the table, took two spoonfuls of pudding, and pushed the food away.

The next morning she was up for matins and coffee. Although her suntanned face was a little pasty and dark circles remained under her eyes, she seemed almost back to normal. After breakfast Augustina went to her office, while Matilda walked to the radio room where Veronica was waiting for Lisala. A worker, raking the flower beds around the bougainvillaea next to the corridor's low wall, bowed from the waist as she passed, *"Mbote, ma mère."*

"Mbote," she replied, with a wave of her hand.

"Yambuku, Yambuku, Lisala here," came over the radio in Father Jules's toneless voice.

"Go ahead, Lisala. This is Yambuku," replied Veronica.

"A message from the Catholic Communications Center in Kinshasa for you." Veronica had her Bic poised over the paper.

"Go ahead, Lisala."

"Message reads: 'SISTER FERMINA STATUS STATIONARY. FEVER PERSISTS. HOPING FOR IMPROVEMENT. SHE IS AT NGALIEMA CLINIC.' Did you copy?"

Veronica's hand tightened on the microphone. "Fermina is not in Belgium?"

"The father at CCC reported that she is at the Ngaliema Clinic in Kinshasa," repeated Jules, impatience giving his voice a little modulation.

"Did Kinshasa say she will be going to the institute in Antwerp?" Veronica persisted.

"No, Sister. The message only states what I read to you. Do you have anything for Lisala?"

"Nothing," said Veronica. Then she added quickly, "We may need to call you later today. Please be listening this evening."

Father Jules's voice came back with a long-suffering sigh. "Very well. If you think it necessary, I will be tuned to you. Over and out."

Veronica snapped off the radio and spat into the microphone, "You heartless old goat, the only thing you are tuned into is—" Matilda's hand on her shoulder stopped her. She looked up at her friend.

"Sorry. But he's like a machine." She put down the microphone and stood up. " 'Hoping for improvement' means that she is worse."

"Or too sick to travel," said Matilda. They headed for the Mother Superior's office where Veronica repeated the radio message.

"No, that cannot be!" Augustina exclaimed as Masangaya walked in. "Fermina is still in Kinshasa."

"I knew we could not trust those Zairian doctors," said Veronica bitterly.

"But if Sister Fermina is in Ngaliema," offered Masangaya, "she is already in the care of Belgians."

Augustina cut in, "I am sure the doctors and nurses at the clinic know what they are doing, and Fermina will certainly let them know what she thinks. Anyway, she is in God's hands, and we can do nothing but pray for her now." She turned to Masangaya. "What *is* our situation this morning?"

He thought for a minute. "The news of the doctors giving injections spread fast, and more patients are coming back to the hospital, hoping to be cured. We now have nineteen patients with symptoms of the fever, and although no one died last night, I expect most of them will be dead before the week is over. Mandu, our last nurse, is sick. I was just told that he left sometime after dark. The patients had to take care of themselves during the night."

"We should hear from Dr. Miatamba very soon," said Matilda.

"We can only hope so," replied Masangaya. "I am also worried about Ambwa and his family." He turned to Matilda. "He is the head of the girls' boarding school. Two of his children have died, and I gather from one of the school cooks that he and his wife talk of leaving to save their two-year-old."

"If Ambwa leaves, who will supervise the girls? And where would he go?" asked Veronica.

"Bumba, probably. He has friends among the teachers there."

"The roads are barricaded along the way; they won't be able to get through," said Matilda.

"He has a motorbike and knows the tracks around the villages," said Masangaya. He paused and looked directly at Augustina. "There are still seventy girls in the boarding school. I have given orders that those who live within twenty kilometers are to return to their villages in the morning. We have already kept them with us too long. Escorts or not, they will be safer away from here."

"As you wish," said Augustina.

"Now, if you will excuse me."

Before she could say more, he was gone.

Augustina was in her office all day receiving reports from the outside and comforting bereaved families. She handed out rice and salt and even cotton sheets to all who needed help. An air of heavy anxiety hung over the mission; people avoided one another. The weaverbirds had flown off, leaving a skeletal palm tree festooned with empty hanging nests.

Over supper, there was little conversation. Matilda had gone to bed without eating. Antonie came in from the house of the fathers and sat with her hands folded on the table as Augustina and Veronica were finishing the meal.

"Father Gérard's fever is up to forty degrees Celsius, and he has hiccups. It's awful; every time one hits him, he groans with pain, as if he is being beaten from inside."

"There is no way to stop them?" asked Veronica.

"I tried to have him hold his breath, but he cannot do it

for very long. His respirations are rapid, and his feet are puffy. I wish we had a doctor who could look at him."

"What about the medical assistant?" asked Augustina.

"I suggested Masangaya, but Gérard said no, that he was good with a knife but not much else."

"Have something to eat," said Veronica, pushing a half-empty bowl of soggy rice across the table.

"No, I'll just have coffee and maybe a little wine, if we have any. I want to ask Matilda what to do with the father." Veronica poured the coffee and fetched the last bottle of St. Emilion, sent by a friend in Antwerp, off the sideboard. There was just enough left for a glassful.

In a few minutes Antonie was tiptoeing into Matilda's room as Veronica watched from the doorway. Antonie made out Matilda's form under the sheet; she stepped up to the bed and turned around, signaling Veronica to come in. In the dim light, both nuns saw the lurid, wet face and dark, sunken eyes. Matilda's mouth was open, her features slack jawed and ugly. They gasped.

"Oh, dear Lord, no!" said Veronica, shrinking back into the corridor.

"Go tell Augustina. I'll sit with her," whispered Antonie. Veronica held a handkerchief to her mouth and nodded, tears running down her cheeks.

The flame in the kerosene lantern was turned down as low as possible; it cast a feeble glow in the room. Matilda moaned, and Antonie moved closer to the bedside. Matilda looked up, then fixed her eyes on Antonie's gloved hands. A heavy gray moth fluttered noisily out of the blackness beyond the open window and landed on the lamp, disturbing the mosquitoes on the warm glass chimney. Veronica returned to the room with Augustina. They approached the bed.

Matilda's lips moved; Antonie bent over to hear her whisper, "I would like the sacrament."

"Shall I call Father Dubonnet now?" asked Antonie softly.

With a little shake of her head, Matilda said, "In the morning." She turned on her side and closed her eyes. Antonie made a sign that she would stay, and the other sisters left.

Two roosters crowed in turn from opposite ends of the mission, like buglers echoing each other's call. Matilda awoke as the flapping of loose leather sandals reached her ears. Father Dubonnet's shaggy head peeked around the door.

"Come in, Father. I am waiting for you. Thank you for coming so early."

"Veronica ordered me here." He put his small leather kit for Mass on the bed table. "I would have come anyway." Antonie gave her chair to the priest.

Matilda tried to sit up but fell back on her pillow. "Would you give me last rites?" With some effort, she pushed the pillows behind her back. "I received the grace to accept death during the night. I hope I will not have to spend too long in purgatory. You will pray for me, won't you?"

"Of course. But I think you will breeze through purgatory. It is easier to be a good Christian if one has the skills to teach or cure, like you. Some of us, who just talk religion, may not get through as fast. I almost went into medicine, but I could not see spending all those years under gray skies among our inflexible *Flamands*."

She smiled at him. "The people here love you—Veronica told me—and you love them, although you like to hide it under that big beard."

"Come now, Sister, I am supposed to be ministering to you, not the other way around. Are you having any pain?"

"Some—in my head and in my stomach. But it is not unbearable."

"Do you have anything important to confess?"

"Oh, yes." She looked away and thought for a moment. "Pride. I was very puffed up when the Mother Superior briefed me and asked for my advice. I want to be needed."

"False humility is a far greater sin than pride, Sister. Have you ever seen a good worker who is not proud of what he produces? Pride catapults us out of mediocrity."

"You are different, Father." Matilda looked at him closely. "Veronica said you were different." Dubonnet raised his bushy eyebrows quizzically.

"She meant 'different' in a good way, an unexpected and comforting way," she added quickly.

"We are all a little different after we have lived in Africa for a while. I feel like a stranger when I go back to Europe." He ran his fingers through his beard and brushed the stray hairs off his cassock. "I will give you a general absolution that will cover the big sins and all the little ones."

He made a perfunctory sign of the cross over her and recited, "May Almighty God have mercy on you and forgive you all your sins and bring you to life everlasting. Amen." He rummaged around in a deep pocket. Matilda noticed there were smudges of dried red mud on his cassock and one of the buttons was missing. He pulled out a small stole, its simple embroidery threadbare, most of the tassels gone, gave it a shake, and after touching it to his lips, he hung it around his neck. Then he retrieved a test tube with a rubber stopper containing holy oil.

"I borrowed this from the hospital years ago," he explained, putting it on the bed table.

From his other pocket he extracted a wad of cotton and two broken cigarettes. He stuffed the cigarettes back, and after picking out the flecks of tobacco, he poured holy oil onto the cotton. Matilda closed her eyes and folded her hands in prayer. Dubonnet held the oil-soaked cotton delicately between his nicotine-stained thumb and forefinger. He made the two strokes of the cross on her forehead.

"Through this holy anointing may the Lord in His love and mercy help you with the grace of the Holy Spirit." Then he asked, "Where else do you hurt?"

"My throat," she said, putting her hand under her chin, "the back of my neck, and my stomach."

Dubonnet made the sign of the cross with his gentle instrument under her chin. "Mother of Jesus, give your servant strength and ease the pain. Lean forward just a little," he said, anointing her neck. "Ease the pain." With his hand, he made the sign of the cross over her body and knelt beside the bed.

"Our Father which art in heaven, hallowed be Thy name. . . ." The priest and the nun recited the familiar, comforting words in unison. He gave her the viaticum, placing the Host between her lips, and touching the tip of her tongue with a cotton ball dipped in his small flask of wine. He blessed her and stood.

"There. I hope you feel better. Death will bring you relief from the suffering that remains the lot of those of us still living. I will pray for you as you cross through purgatory. But you must intercede for us who remain here, hot and sweating, living in this world of microbes and weeds and sucking mud. For atonement, pray that we will be more understanding and impose our own rigid views and ambitions less on those we have come to help."

"Thank you, Father. I will pray for that and for you."

* * *

Dubonnet opened the door a crack. Gérard was lying on his side, his knees drawn up and his head propped on two pillows. He was breathing deeply, but every ten or twelve breaths, his body was convulsed in a loud hiccup followed by a moan, as the air left his chest. Dubonnet looked over his shoulder at Antonie. She held up a syringe with medicine in the barrel.

"The medical assistant suggested I give him this," she whispered.

"What is it?" asked Dubonnet.

"Dolantine, a sedative."

From the room came a rustle of sheets and a muted cry. "My God, how long do I have to—*huuckk . . . oohhh*—suffer this torture!" The priest and the nun walked into the room.

"Sister Antonie is here with an injection for you. It'll relieve your hiccups," said Dubonnet.

"No injections! Is there nothing else?" asked Gérard between convulsions.

Dubonnet looked at Antonie, who shook her head. "No," he said. Then he added, "Unless you want to try my own concoction. It'll stop a train."

"I will try anything except a shot."

Dubonnet went out of the room and returned a few minutes later with a glass of murky liquid. "Here. Take three big swallows while you are holding your breath."

"I already tried that."

"But you did not have my concoction to drink."

Gérard pushed himself up slowly and sat, bracing his head with one hand, reaching for the glass with the other.

"One, two, three, go!" said Dubonnet.

Gérard took three large swallows and spewed out what remained in his mouth. His eyes bulged and he gasped, "Holy Mother of God, are you trying to kill me?" His mouth was wide open, sucking air in and blowing it out. He held the glass up. "What the devil is this?"

"An eye-opener. I drink one every morning to keep from getting sick. It is one third whiskey, a third Pernod, topped off with gin. For nutrition I add an egg yolk."

Gérard handed Dubonnet the glass and lay back, his hands trying to squeeze the pain out of his skull.

"I do not want any more of your treatments," muttered Gérard from behind his hands.

"I have no more to offer," replied Dubonnet.

Silence reigned for a few moments. Then Gérard lowered his hands and wiped his face with the corner of the sheet. "The hiccups are gone!"

"Naturally. What else can I do for you?"

Gérard smoothed the wrinkles out of his undershirt, folded the sheet at his waist, and slid his legs over the side of the bed.

"I want to go to the church. You must celebrate Mass and give me the sacrament for the sick in front of everyone." He leaned over, reaching for his sandals, but the intensification of the pain in his head and a wave of vertigo and nausea forced him back into bed.

"You are in no shape to go anywhere," said Dubonnet. "Anyway, if you have the fever, which seems likely, you risk giving it to others. The Africans avoid speaking about death until it has happened, but we can be more realistic. I just gave last rites to Sister Matilda. Yesterday she was better and even worked. Now, I doubt she will last through the night. I would bet that both you and she have been sick for longer than you admit."

"That is possible. It is not our habit to complain," replied Gérard.

Antonie collected the priest's underwear and the cassock folded neatly on his chair. "I will take these to the laundry and return in an hour to take your temperature and give you some medicine."

"And I will be back this evening to take care of your spiritual needs," said Dubonnet, as they headed for the door.

Gérard pushed himself up on an elbow. "Do you have to leave?"

Dubonnet stopped and turned. "No, I have nothing to do that cannot wait." He sat back in the chair as Antonie closed the door.

Gérard spoke slowly and deliberately. "I know I am dying. I want you to hear my confession when you return this evening. After I make an act of contrition, you shall, of course, absolve me of my sins, and we will celebrate Mass together. My soul will be prepared to depart . . . neatly scrubbed and wrapped in our well-regulated dogma."

Dubonnet leaned forward. "That is what we have done over and over again for the people," he said gently.

Gérard paused, uncertain whether to continue. After a moment he looked up, searching the face of his brother priest. "It seems different when the focus is on a representative of the Redeemer." He paused. "I have always heard that doctors make bad patients. It must be difficult for them to die well of a disease whose fatal, inexorable course is familiar to them. I suppose a physician devoted to his patients, who has seen them through suffering and up to death's door, might better accept his own end, his own mortality. But a surgeon, a man who subjects his patients to death-defying operations, who fights death as a personal adversary, to him death is defeat—his defeat—and his patient's demise."

"And you think you have been more of a surgeon than a physician to the congregation," said Dubonnet.

Gérard shrugged a shoulder.

"That is one way of looking at what we do," said Dubonnet, leaning back in his chair. "To me, we are like shepherds—or even sheepdogs, driving the flock through purifying troughs and into pens constructed by generations of herders. We are like our shaggy Flemish Bouviers with dirty beards, guarding our charges from predators. Sometimes we live in the fold and become part of it. We comfort a little here and there but have scant influence on where the sheep graze or where they hide when they are frightened."

"So what is a good priest?"

"One who follows the dictates of his conscience and does nothing with evil intent."

Gérard sighed and lay back on his pillows. "Do you think I have been too ... surgical?"

"Maybe a little too colonial at times," said Dubonnet, laughing. "I do not know; only God will grade our ministries. Many of our charges find security in being told what to think; some need support or a big shoulder to cry on; others need a kick in the rear end. I have always respected your discipline and certainty about things. The Africans call you libela—definitely, forever—however you want to translate it."

Dubonnet looked at the carved masks mounted on geometric Bakuba mats nailed to the wall. Nearby were ceremonial daggers and blooded spears. Gérard had not collected these trophies; they had been given to him. "You have achieved a level of respect and prominence with the people rare for us Belgians."

"Is that a good thing?" asked Gérard, hoping for reassurance.

"You will find out soon enough. Your stand against the rebels was courageous; you saved the mission from their pillaging. After the rebels fled, events followed their natural course: the mercenaries came hunting kaffirs. Do you remember the one who collected African heads for a white medical school in the south?"

"Who could ever forget him," replied Gérard.

"After the mercenaries, nothing happened for a while. The villagers kept to themselves, silent and afraid, minding their own business. Then the Army, who were supposed to protect the people, crept in at night and took what the others had left and raped the women. Thanks to you, our sisters were not there and, thanks to a merciful God, I was on leave in Belgium and spared the horror of martyrdom." Dubonnet reached into his pocket and pulled out a battered pack of Belgas. He concentrated on tamping a cigarette on his stained thumbnail, then lit it with a wooden match and sucked in a deep chestful of smoke. As he blew it out, he remembered where he was.

"Oh! I am sorry. Do you mind?"

"Not at all, Jef. Why haven't we talked like this before?"

"Death was not around the corner to free us from our inhibitions. Even a turtle would try crawling out of his shell when he is on his back and cannot turn over," replied Dubonnet, standing. "I hope you can rest." Gérard folded his hands and smiled.

The *commissaire*'s receptionist in Bumba, her hair done up in cornrows tight on her scalp, sat at a table, carefully stroking scarlet polish on her long fingernails. A snug bodice, made from a political cotton print, only just contained her bulging breasts. She looked up, annoyed at the interruption, as a man and woman walked in tentatively and stood before her. They were hollow-eyed, and the dust on their faces was streaked with sweat.

"Yes?" she asked, waving her hands to dry the nails.

The man leaned on the table for support; behind him, his

wife pulled the child off her back and sat on the floor. The man cleared his throat. It was parched and cruelly sore.

"We have just come from Yambuku. I am the director of the girl's boarding school. I need to see the zone *commissaire*."

"From Yambuku!" The receptionist stood up, knocking over her chair.

He stepped back alarmed. "Yes. We have just arrived. We need help."

She turned and yelled over her shoulder, "Get away from the table and wait outside." She banged on a door, opened it, and announced in alarm, "People from Yambuku are here to see you, *Commissaire*."

"Yambuku! No! That is impossible. All the roads are blocked."

The *commissaire* stepped into the doorway and glared at the couple. "How did you get here? Who are you? What do you want?"

"I traveled along the paths that skirt the villages. I am Ambwa, a teacher at Yambuku. Two of our children died. We came to Bumba so that our last child would be safe."

"You should not be here. Yambuku is dangerous. Leave this office immediately—go away, go to the hospital. They will take care of you."

"But, *Commissaire*—"

"Go! Go now, or I will call the police," he shouted, slamming his door.

Ambwa helped his wife slowly to her feet and lifted the child onto her back. He held her steady as they left the building, climbed onto their motorcycle, and headed for the hospital. On the way he stopped at a friend's house. The man was also a teacher and agreed to take the child while the parents received treatment. Afterward they admitted themselves to an empty pavilion. No one would go near them.

On September 28, the following cable was received at World Health Organization Headquarters in Geneva from the Medical Service of Unilever in Brussels.

A SERIOUS EPIDEMIC OF A NATURE STILL UNKNOWN IS GOING ON IN THE REGION OF TWO OF OUR PLANTATIONS IN BUMBA ZONE, YAMBUKU COLLECTIVITY. WE THINK IT POSSIBLE A FULMINATING TYPHOID OR YELLOW FEVER. SAMPLES HAVE BEEN TAKEN BY UNAZA (NATIONAL UNIVERSITY OF ZAIRE) FOR WHO (WORLD HEALTH ORGANIZATION) AND HAVE BEEN SENT TO ITM (INSTITUTE OF TROPICAL MEDICINE) IN ANTWERP TO BE ANALYZED. WE WOULD BE INTERESTED TO KNOW THE DIAGNOSIS BY TELEX AS QUICKLY AS POSSIBLE. IN THIS WAY, WE WILL BE ABLE TO ORGANIZE A CAMPAIGN OF VACCINATION FOR OUR EMPLOYEES. SIGNED/DR. J. BUSQUET, KINSHASA.

This was the first information to come out of Zaire regarding the epidemic.

CHAPTER 10

"Matilda cannot keep anything in her stomach, and Father Gérard's breathing is worse," said Augustina, looking at the medical assistant across her desk. "Is there anything more we can do for them?"

Masangaya replied, "In the hospital, five people died this morning; others are unconscious, ready to die. The wards smell like a charnel house." He leaned forward and put his hands on Augustina's desk. "Mandu is too weak to work; I have no one left to help on the wards." His voice rose in anger. "Nobody buries the cadavers. I chased a child away from her dead mother on the way over here. One of the teachers has been dragging bodies to the pit with a loop of rope tied to a bamboo pole." He fixed Augustina with his eyes and asked in a slow, hard voice: "Will we get help?"

An early evening breeze, gentle enough to cool without raising the dust, stole through the open door, touching the Mother Superior's veil, and ruffling the curtain at the open window behind her.

"I wish I could give you an answer." She looked at her watch. "I asked Lisala to be listening this evening. I'll make my request again."

The medical assistant sat back. "I do not understand why we are being ignored even after Sister Matilda went to

Lisala. The only thing they say is 'Keep up your courage. We are praying for you.' " He continued, his voice calmer but firm. "Whatever kills these people is hiding in the mission and the hospital."

"I have suspected that myself. But we have no proof," said Augustina.

"Proof or not, everyone must be evacuated," Masangaya replied bluntly.

"That will be difficult. Obviously, we cannot leave Matilda and Father Gérard and they're too ill to move." Augustina pushed her chair back and stood. "You look exhausted. Let me get you some coffee."

As she left for the kitchen, Masangaya rubbed his forehead to try and ease the dull ache in his head. He stretched and gazed out the window. The flame tree next to his house had lost most of its scarlet flowers; the pods hung heavy and dry. One more evening storm and the tree would be bare.

Augustina spoke as she reentered the room. "I thought that Dr. Omba and Professor Ilunga would be back with medicines and vaccines by now. It is disturbing that we have heard nothing from them or from the authorities in Kinshasa."

"Judging by the speed with which they left, I doubt we'll see them again soon," said Masangaya. After a pause he added, "Maybe the authorities have decided to let nature take its course and not intervene. Maybe the disease will just stop after it has killed all it can reach." While he drank the coffee, Augustina wrote her message for Lisala, then handed it to him. He passed it back with a nod, stood up, and left.

At the threshold of Matilda's room, he greeted Antonie, then walked to the foot of the bed. Matilda was asleep. He observed her quietly. What a change from the energetic, straight-standing woman that had come a week ago. Now her face, even in sleep, showed her suffering. Her breathing was rapid and short. Thick beads of moisture formed on her pale, putty-colored forehead. Perhaps feeling his presence, she opened her eyes and smiled feebly. He held up the bag of saline.

"I think it will help the pain and the dryness in your throat."

She pulled her arm slowly from under the sheet and turned it palm up, then taking a deep breath, tried to relax.

Masangaya put on rubber gloves. He poured alcohol onto cotton, then, preparing the tubing to go into the bag, hung it on an IV stand and brought the whole setup to Matilda's bedside. After gently tightening a soft rubber tourniquet above her elbow, he wiped off her forearm with the cotton. Matilda had not bled from her stomach or her bowel, but everywhere she had been stuck with a needle, there was a livid bruise. Masangaya thought he could feel a vein under her elbow crease and, pushing the needle through the skin, tried to thread it into the vessel. For a moment he thought he was in, but in seconds, a blue swelling surrounded the puncture. He released the tourniquet, pulled the needle out, and put pressure on the bleeding hole with a wad of cotton. Once more he tried. His head swam, and his back ached from leaning over the bed. He had to rest, but first the sister needed the fluid. He reapplied the tourniquet below the elbow and, turning her arm over, saw a good dilated vein on the back of her hand. In a second, the needle was in. He taped it to her hand and the hand to an arm board.

"Good work," she whispered.

"*Pardon, ma soeur,*" he said and quickly turned away.

Stripping off his bloody gloves, he dropped them in a paper bag by the door and walked out.

At 8 A.M. on Wednesday, September 29, in Kinshasa, Dr. Alain Collard had just sat down at his desk in the Belgian Embassy when the telephone rang.

"*Merde,*" he said, picking up. "*Allo, oui?*"

"Father Bertrand from Catholic Communications here. I have a Sister Clarysse in my office. You need to talk to her. She just arrived from Lisala with reports of a serious medical situation north of Bumba."

"My dear father, there is a 'serious medical situation' all over the bloody country," said Collard, cradling the phone between his shoulder and neck as he lit a cigarette.

"I think you should see her," insisted Bertrand.

"All right, send her over." Although the morning was still cool and the asphalt on the streets had not yet turned to glue, beads of perspiration formed on his red face. He was chief of the Belgian Medical Cooperation, but at times like this, he longed to be back in the bush. He went over to a side table and put water on to boil for coffee. The noise of the morning traffic on the Boulevard 30 Juin struck him as less raucous than usual, then he remembered the recurrent gas shortage. A faint odor of wet vegetation off the river mixed with wood smoke from the docks floated in on the morning breeze. Zaire was his home, and he loved it.

Collard had been born and raised in the Congo. At the time of independence his father was chief doctor for the colony and an internationally recognized expert in the fight against sleeping sickness and leprosy. After Collard finished his medical training at Belgium's Louvain University, he had returned to the Congo and run a rural hospital in Bas-Congo country near the Angolan border. During the internecine fighting between the various Angolan factions before independence, Collard took care of many of Holden Roberto's wounded Angolese fighters. In spite of backing from the United States and Zaire, Holden's men had been outgunned and outmaneuvered by the Cuban-supported Angolans. Collard was as near to being a Zairian as was possible for a white man; and Brussels, in a moment of wisdom, had made him head of its extensive medical program in the country. There was a knock on the door.

"Entrez," he said over his shoulder, as he dumped a spoonful of Nescafé into a mug. A short, square nun walked in.

"I am Sister Clarysse."

"Please sit down," said the doctor, taking his place at the desk. He raised his mug. "Coffee?"

"Not yet," replied the sister. "I have been all over town trying to find someone who can help us. They finally sent me here."

"So I'm your last resort, Sister?"

"Yes. It would seem that way." Clarysse explained that she had arrived from Lisala, sent by the Reverend Mother Adeline, to inform the authorities—"I suppose that is you"—of the epidemic raging in the mission of Yambuku.

"What epidemic?" asked Collard.

"That is just it. Nobody knows what is killing so many. One sister is dead. Another one, as well as a priest, are gravely ill, and hundreds of people have died in the villages. Surely you've heard about the Yambuku sister who is here in your Ngaliema Clinic?"

"I have heard nothing," said Collard, grabbing the telephone. He dialed the clinic, the telephone rang, then went dead.

"Merde! The damn phones are impossible. Excuse me,

Sister, but it is getting harder every day to call anyone. Tell me all you know."

"I have not been in Yambuku myself. My information came by radio messages from the Mother Superior to Lisala. Why don't we go to the communications center, and you can call Lisala yourself. Maybe they have more news from this morning."

"Father, you were right again," said Collard, as he walked into the radio room. "Can you try and reach Lisala?" Bertrand fiddled with the dials; Father Jules's tired voice pushed its way through the *weeepp*s and *wooo*s and crackles of the single sideband. Bertrand handed Collard the microphone. After identifying himself, the doctor asked for all the information available about the disease in Yambuku. The Lisala priest gave him the main symptoms, confirming everything Clarysse had reported.

"Thank you, Father. I would appreciate it if you would keep me abreast of any further developments," said Collard.

Afterward, Collard drove Sister Clarysse to St. Anne's, a convent where transient sisters were accommodated, and reassured her that every effort would be made to deal with the situation in Yambuku. Returning to the embassy, he quickly called together a handful of Belgian colleagues, dispatching his assistant to the clinic to find out what was going on with Sister Fermina. One of the doctors raised the possibility that Lassa fever, an African hemorrhagic disease that had hit Nigeria several years ago, might have broken out in the north. But those assembled had been trained in tropical medicine and knew little about viruses.

Collard called Dr. Tambwe, who had been a friend long before he was appointed minister.

"Collard here, *confrère*. I am glad your phone is working. I just heard about an epidemic north of Bumba. I would like your backing to fly up there."

"By all means," replied Tambwe. "I sent Omba and Ilunga up a week ago. I am waiting for their written report, but Omba did advise me that they thought it was a virulent form of typhoid."

"Apparently one of the sisters from the Yambuku mission is at Ngaliema," said Collard.

"Don't rub my nose in it! I had a call from the president's office; the director blames me for exposing the city to the disease, whatever it is. Ilunga brought back some blood specimens. The results are not out yet. I would like you to take Dr. Maréchal with you when you go." Collard frowned into the phone and thought: *Goddammit! The French are up to their old tricks. I wonder what they have promised Tambwe.* Although the French Medical Cooperation was minute compared to the Belgian effort, the courtly French were experts at squeezing maximum credit from small investments of money and personnel. Still, Maréchal was a good man.

Collard added, "I would like to radio Lisala and tell them I'm flying to Yambuku. Instructions for the area will follow."

"Excellent," replied Tambwe. "Do what you think is necessary, but please keep me informed."

Next Collard called Army HQ—their phones always worked—and was put through to General Bumba, who approved, happily, another C-130 for Bumba the following day, and even offered to have a helicopter ready to facilitate the doctors' travel north. Collard's last call went to Brussels via satellite. He requested protective gear and disinfectant be sent to him on Sabena's evening flight to Kinshasa. After signing the usual bureaucratic letters a secretary had left on his desk and writing out a radio message, he drove back to the Catholic Communications Center.

Lisala responded immediately when Father Bertrand called.

"Ready to copy," said Jules.

"This is an urgent message for you to pass on to Yambuku. 11:30 A.M. KINSHASA TO YAMBUKU VIA LISALA: AREA OF YAMBUKU IS DECLARED HIGHLY DANGEROUS. ALL MOVEMENT IN OR OUT OF YAMBUKU IS FORBIDDEN. KINSHASA WILL DO ALL IN ITS POWER TO HELP. DR. COLLARD WILL COME UP AS SOON AS POSSIBLE. WE REALIZE YOUR FRUSTRATION AND THE SEVERITY OF THE PROBLEM. HAVE CONFIDENCE IN US."

In Yambuku on the morning of September 30, Augustina, Veronica, and Antonie lingered over their coffee, listening to the shortwave news from Brussels. The speaker had just announced that a record $3.25 million had been paid for a Rembrandt in New York. "And now the news from Africa," intoned the announcer. "We are sorry to report the death of Sister Fermina Breck, at the Ngaliema Hospital in Kinshasa. Sister Fermina was born on the seventh of January, 1934, in Schilde. She served as a missionary and nurse in the Yambuku Catholic Mission from—" Augustina turned off the radio.

"Fermina dead! Dead in Kinshasa, and we hear about it on the Belgian radio," she exclaimed.

"It makes me feel that we are cut off from the whole world," said Veronica.

"How awful that Fermina died in a strange place far from her family and from us," said Augustina.

"Maybe Masangaya is right," murmured Antonie. "The authorities have decided that there is nothing to be done, and we are best left alone."

Veronica asked angrily, "Why didn't Kinshasa tell us over the radio last night?"

"They may not have had the courage," replied Antonie.

"Or they did not know themselves," said Augustina, getting up. She walked out, and in a moment they heard the door to her office close.

"We shall all die," said Veronica.

Matilda watched in silence, her glassy eyes following every move that Antonie made. Antonie avoided those eyes; she could not bear the desolation behind them. All the words of comfort had worn thin; talk was hollow, empty, even embarrassing. Matilda had hardly spoken since Father Dubonnet had given her last rites. Antonie picked up the water pitcher, walked to the door, then hesitated and turned back toward Matilda.

"We heard on the radio that Fermina's suffering is over; she has joined Lucie in Heaven. What a reunion all of you will have." Matilda stared up at the cross on the wall, and her lips started to move.

Veronica was reading her breviary on the terrace, where Antonie came to sit beside her. "I told Matilda about Fermina," Antonie said. "I think it helped." Veronica closed the book and watched the gardener as he swept away the leaves that had fallen during the night. Neither rebellion nor plague interrupted his appointed duties. She looked at Antonie.

"I'm not afraid of death, but I am terrified by physical suffering and pain. Lucie and Fermina were so much braver than I will be . . . and now Matilda."

Antonie, with a rare show of affection, put her hand on Veronica's shoulder. "The truth to me is that if we suffer enough in this life, we will spend less time in purgatory.

The punishments of purgatory frighten me more than suffering here," she said.

"I do not know what to say to her," said Veronica, laying the prayer book on the table.

"Maybe we should just sit with her like the Zairians would do with one of theirs."

Antonie got up and walked into the refectory; she filled the pitcher with cool water from the icebox, then returned to Matilda's room. Veronica followed after a moment but at the door stopped, glanced in at Matilda, and quickly pulled back to lean against the wall. Matilda had been staring at the door as if in a trance. Veronica turned back toward the terrace, and picking up her breviary, fled to the chapel.

For a long time she knelt, repeating Hail Mary's over and over to fill her mind with anything that would erase the memory of Matilda's eyes. She heard movement behind her, and the Mother Superior passed by, genuflected, and knelt at her prie-dieu. *How can she continue to hide behind that shell of calmness?* thought Veronica, knowing full well that inside Augustina a layer of passive denial blocked out the smells and sounds of disease: she rarely had any personal contact with the sick in the hospital. To the Mother Superior, the sun followed the rain, and the mysteries of life were not meant to be explored. Her security was anchored to her simple, incurious faith, and a daily routine that seldom varied—like that of the gardener.

Veronica sat back and opened her book. She tried to read the lessons of the day, but thought instead about her guardian angel and spoke to him. *When my time comes I want to go quickly—an accident or an explosion would be best—but only after I have done all I can down here.* She knelt and prayed to Matilda's angel. *If you want to do something to help us, make it possible for her to die today.* She felt uncomfortable and knew that staying in the chapel was escaping sitting with Matilda. Standing, she stepped into the aisle and genuflected. Then, making the sign of the cross, she walked out, leaving Augustina alone on her knees.

Veronica waited just inside the door of Matilda's room. After only a few minutes, Matilda stopped breathing and died peacefully. Antonie stood and leaned over the bed.

"Do not touch her," said Veronica in alarm. But Antonie was already closing Matilda's eyelids with gloved fingers.

Father Dubonnet and a few Zairians—also wearing gloves, masks, and gowns—took the corners of the sheet and lifted Matilda's body into the coffin they had nailed together outside her room. She was lowered into the ground just as the two grave diggers finished their work—less than one hour after her death. There was no ceremony, no Mass. Father Dubonnet recited prayers for the dead to the hollow notes of dirt hitting the wooden box.

Afterward Dubonnet walked to the house of the fathers. Gérard was in a deep sleep. Dubonnet pulled a chair over and sat by the bed. His eyes were drawn to the glowering masks with their grotesque features which covered the wall. Feathered fetishes and rattles lived on the top of one of the bookshelves. All these were mementos given to Gérard in the course of his battle to eliminate the fears and superstitions of the *ndokies*. Now, they seemed to stare down at the dying priest.

"My brother, can you hear me?" Dubonnet spoke into Gérard's ear. "Sister Matilda just died. I am on my way to church for the evening Mass, which I will dedicate to Fermina and Matilda; I will include you as well." Gérard nodded and closed his eyes.

A thunder squall hit the mission during the Mass. The voices of the celebrants were drowned out by the roar of the rain on the tin roof; the service proceeded like a pantomime. Just before the blessing, the rain stopped as suddenly as it had started, and Dubonnet's "In the name of the Father, and the Son . . ." was loud in the unexpected silence. As the people were filing out of the church, a mission worker ran up.

"Come quick. It is the father," he shouted. Dubonnet ran to the priest's house. Gérard was lying on his back. His face and forehead had turned a dusky blue, and a thin white foam trickled out of the corner of his mouth. Dubonnet pulled the sheet over the priest's head and sent a worker to find the coffin makers. The storm was returning. The wind picked up and shook the trees; the palms bent, and their fronds thrashed the air. After a few minutes, one of the carpenters arrived and stood unsteadily, red-eyed and petulant before the priest. "The box cannot be made for this father. He is a *nkumu*; he cannot be buried in silence at night. Other *nkumus* have been called. They will decide."

A wet moon glow seeped through the crack in the curtains. The room's stillness was broken only by the persistent whine of mosquitoes. Veronica sat at her table, the kerosene lamp turned down low. She had tried to sleep, but every time she closed her eyes, Matilda stared at her out of the storm, and she heard again the shrieking of the mourners at her grave. She began a letter to Gabrielle.

Yambuku, 30 September 1976
Dearest Little Sister,

We have lived through a day in Hell. With Lucie and Fermina dead, and now Matilda released from her torment at midday, I feel strange, almost guilty, because I am still living. We have asked for help, but we are abandoned. Antonie has been an angel of mercy to Matilda and Father Gérard. Who would have thought it? I have been useless—unless it was my prayers to Matilda's guardian angel that cut short her suffering. But we buried her like a stranger, with no Mass.

Gérard died as the evening service ended. There were very few people in the church. After Matilda's burial, most of them had returned to their houses to drink *mbondo*, the poison they mix with their banana liquor to prove their innocence by defying death. Augustina, Antonie, and I walked over to the house of the fathers. A crowd had already gathered, an ugly crowd, crazy from drink—*primitif*. They were frenzied animals. Their eyes were wild, and spit ran out of their mouths. Around their bellies, some wore only strings with pods and leaves or feathers. Dubonnet drove up in the Jeep. He left the engine running and the headlights on and, carrying planks for the coffin, laid them out on the terrace. He ordered the carpenter to nail them together, but the man refused and even lifted his hammer, threatening the father, shouting that the other *nkumus* would dictate the ritual, not he. When Dubonnet went inside for Gérard's body, I asked the secretary of my cooperative and his brother to come with us and help. Dubonnet had them put on gloves and gowns before going into the room, but it was no use. When they saw Gérard's terrible purple face, they shouted: "You and your gloves and all your beliefs in microbes . . . it is not that, it is not that at all." They threw the gloves and gowns onto the cadaver. "You whites always say there are germs and viruses, but we know differently." They ran out, and the noise of the crowd increased, and the rain started again, and lightning—it was infernal. I have never been so frightened in my life. But Dubonnet was calm. "Take the tablecloth, and we will cover the body and roll him in it like the Zairians do." So we carried Gérard out into the noise of the people and the storm. It was hard to see because the headlights were shining in our eyes, but we laid him across the back of the jeep and climbed in as Dubonnet raced the engine and stood on the horn to clear the way. Two men climbed onto the hood and clung to the windshield, pressing their grotesque faces against the wet glass; but Dubonnet moved forward slowly, and the rain hammered us. I was crying with fear, but Antonie sat in the back like a statue, her arm around the body to keep it from falling off. When we started down the path between the palms, Dubonnet went faster, and the people fell away and disappeared in the rain. The tablecloth flapped away from Gérard's feet; they stuck out and shone each time the lightning flashed. Dubonnet stopped at the picket gate, so the headlights would show the way into our little cemetery. We carried the body slumped between us to the open grave next to Matilda's mound. We pushed it into a hole and were splashed by the foaming mud.

The storm was a real one, with a howling wind thrashing the trees. Afterward, everyone converged on the convent. They had all turned against us, and we three nuns were there, not knowing what to do. Father Dubonnet had disappeared. We had nothing prepared, so we had to boil up some rice and hunt for other food; we were completely exhausted. There were so many to feed. Everybody was drunk, and they were not tired. And we knew that if they ate, they would start dancing. We begged a few who were our friends, and still not too drunk, to take the others to the workers' quarters, so that they would not stay in the convent all night. We just could not have taken that.

Now we are alone, and I cannot sleep. Our families and friends are miles away. We have no more to say to each other. We know that each is thinking about her own death, which must come soon. We are completely crushed.

CHAPTER 11

The old man squatted listlessly by the small fire, elbows resting on bony knees, arms limp in front of him. Sukato bent over and wrapped his fingers around the *nganga's* hand.

"I must return to Yambuku now."

"Who waits for you there?" asked the healer, pulling his hand free. He watched a leaf floating carelessly down the stream hang up on a snag.

"My work and my pay."

"I asked *who*, not what." The old man looked at him directly.

"I have a woman that cost me much money. She is the one thing I have earned that I do not have to share with my dead father's brother and his people."

The old man's gaze returned to the stream. The leaf rotated slowly and broke free in the sluggish current.

"So you return to the whites for your pay and your woman."

"I must earn money for more schooling."

"So you can make more money?"

"Yes."

"Always more. It will not last." The leaf had disappeared from view; another followed and missed the snag.

"Tata na ngai," said Sukato. I do not understand.

197

"Someday, when your bones cannot carry you, you will understand. Now fill the pot with water, then go."

Sukato walked through the forest and out to the rain-gouged road that ran through the village. The setting sun cast long shafts through the trees and dappled the dusty track. He walked along slowly, aware of his weakness and the heaviness in his legs. But there was no hurry. He would reach Akete in a couple of hours; darkness would hide his passage through the village, then he would sleep by the road.

Hours later he awoke to the chatter of monkeys and bird calls overhead. Chickens squawked in the village, and nearby someone was chopping wood. Bamboo poles had been placed across the path at both ends of Akete, but no fires smoldered in front of the huts; his passage went un-challenged. He walked down to a stream that ran under a rough plank bridge and knelt on a log used by women to pound their wash. He splashed water on his face, cooling the rawness that lingered on his forehead. Then he set out with more purpose, eager for his woman's cooking and the feel of her body under him. In the half light of dawn, he came to Yandongi. The dogs were barking, goats nuzzled the garbage, and a man swayed drunkenly across the road. All seemed normal. He quickened his pace and before long was walking up the steps of the medical assistant's house to report back for work.

Masangaya sat on the edge of the bed, and rubbed his eyes. "You have lost a little weight, and your forehead looks blistered,"

Sukato followed Masangaya to the sink. "The *nganga* of Bongolu cured my fever."

The medical assistant glanced back at him but made no comment. He turned on the faucet. "It is good you are

back; all the other nurses are gone or dead." Masangaya
filled a pot and carried it to the stove to heat, and as he
dressed told Sukato about those who died—Matilda,
Fermina in Kinshasa, Father Gérard, and the village people
and the mission workers who kept coming into the hospital.

"I will meet you in half an hour, after I have gone home
to clean up and get my white coat," said Sukato, heading
for the door. "It will probably be more like an hour," he
added as he left.

At noon on September 30, Collard and Maréchal left Kinshasa in a C-130 for Bumba. Cartons of protective gear had
arrived on Sabena's morning flight from Brussels. After
threats and the transfer of money into eager palms, they persuaded the customs officials to let workers load the boxes
into the transport just as the turboprops came to life. Arriving in Bumba at 5 P.M., they were met by Dr. Amene. Over
a beer on the terrace of the Catholic mission, Amene told
them what he knew, passing on the latest rumor that six hundred people had died in the forest. Afterward, the three doctors walked to the administrative offices of the zone.

The *commissaire*, a small round man with no neck, was
dressed in a finely tailored dark blue *abacos*. His head
seemed cushioned in the folds of the bright green cravat
worn by the party faithful. He was a successful plantation
owner, a member of the president's clan, and was accustomed to power and privilege. Coming out from behind his
desk, he shook hands warmly and invited them to sit down.
A decorative young woman, with breasts and buttocks
wrapped snugly in green cotton, minced into the room,
carrying a tray with bottles of Skol and glasses. Two Army
officers and the police chief followed her, shook hands all
around, and sat. The hostess, with great concentration,
popped the bottle tops off with her teeth and poured beer

slowly down the side of each glass. On the wall behind the *commissaire* hung the ubiquitous portrait of the president, his expression resolute under his leopard-skin hat. The woman passed the glasses around and left.

Collard then broached the reason for their visit. "The minister wants an estimate of the number of sick and dead. As soon as possible, we shall helicopter to Yambuku to collect blood specimens from patients. These will be sent to Europe, so that the organism responsible for the disease can be identified. Until we know more about the cause of the epidemic, the Zone of Bumba is in the strictest quarantine."

The heavy silence that followed was broken by the *commissaire*. "We thought you were bringing medicines and vaccines. Ten days ago, Dr. Omba of the Ministry of Health and Professor Ilunga from the university stopped in here on their way to Yambuku. What became of their investigations? What happened to the sister they took back with them?"

"Their investigations continue, and the sister died in Kinshasa," said Maréchal.

Alarmed, the Army officers and police chief put their heads together and conferred in whispers. Then one of the officers asked, "Do you mean that no supplies will come to us?"

"That is correct," replied Collard.

"Did General Bumba send instructions?"

"No."

"And no one and nothing is supposed to leave Bumba?" gasped the incredulous *commissaire*.

"That is also correct," stressed Collard. "The major will receive a directive from group headquarters to set up roadblocks to stop all movement in and out of the zone. The soldiers will be ordered to shoot those that cross the barriers."

"What about the riverboats?" asked the *commissaire*.

"They will not be allowed to dock."

"How will our supplies come in . . . and the crops go out?" He wiped his face with a big white handkerchief.

"They won't," replied Collard. Then he added, "We hope this quarantine will not last long. We will work hard to find the cause of the disease and stop it."

"This will ruin our commerce," moaned the *commissaire*, slumping in his chair. The Army officers and the police chief rose to their feet, hoping to be released.

Then Dr. Amene volunteered, "There is a teacher from Yambuku in the Bumba hospital with his wife. They are alone in the pavilion."

"How did they get here?" asked Collard.

"On a motorcycle," said the *commissaire*, sitting straighter. "The man came to see me. He was terribly sick; his wife could hardly walk. I sent them immediately to the hospital."

Amene continued, "There are also forty-three girl students from Yambuku who were brought down by truck and are camped in the empty Army base. The older ones told me their parents might come and get them. Right now they are sleeping on concrete floors and have very little food. What should we do with them? And what should we do with the teacher and his wife?"

Collard leaned forward. "They will have to be completely isolated where they are. If any of the students or the teacher and his wife have been in contact with others in Bumba, then the whole town is at risk, and those contacts will have to be found and also isolated."

"Yes, the girls must return to their villages. I have been nowhere near them, and I only saw the couple from the doorway of this office. I told them to get out . . . to go away," stammered the *commissaire*, waving his arms to show how he chased them out. "Neither I nor my secretary went near them."

"Then you should be all right," said Collard. "But it would be prudent for the major to post troops around the pavilion where the couple is hospitalized. One of us will check on them in the morning."

Later, when they were clear of the building. Maréchal remarked to Collard, "You certainly shook up the *commissaire* with the severity of the quarantine."

"Yes," added Amene. "He has his fingers in every commercial enterprise in the zone."

"And an entourage of cousins and uncles and little brothers to provide for," added Collard.

Collard and Maréchal said good night to Amene and then walked past thornbush enclosures where families squatted around cooking fires. The haze of wood smoke that hung in the trees reflected gentle light from kerosene lanterns.

"Can the Army be trusted to control the quarantine?" asked Maréchal.

"If the soldiers are frightened enough, they will keep people from passing the barriers," replied Collard. They returned the greetings of a family as they walked by their hut. "What scares me is that we do not know how the disease is spread. Is it carried by mosquitoes or flies, or by dust or water?"

"Or by the body fluids and blood of those who die," said the Frenchman. "We will have to mobilize the epidemiologists from the Pasteur Institute."

"Or from Antwerp," added Collard.

"Of course," said Maréchal diplomatically.

Overhead the moon glowed on the edges of clouds. They reached the guest house, took cold showers, and crawled into sagging cots under patched mosquito nets that were heavy enough to keep out air as well as insects.

* * *

It was 6 P.M. in Lansing, Michigan. Aaron Hoffman reached into the refrigerator and retrieved a can of Budweiser from behind the 2 percent milk and orange juice.

"Last can," he announced, popping it open.

"That's your department," said Rachel, pouring an onion soup mix into boiling water. "Remember? You do booze and garbage, I cook, and the kids study."

"Right," said Aaron, lowering himself into an armchair in front of the TV and clicking on the news—more about the swine flu epidemic. The cool beer tasted good.

Rachel turned to Anna, their four-year-old, who was coloring pictures at the table. "Go wash up, little one, and tell Mark supper is almost ready. He's in his room."

Earlier in the day, Aaron had vaccinated hundreds of people and made two trips to the hospital autopsy room to take blood from the cadavers of patients who had just died. His job was to determine whether the swine flu had contributed to or had been the direct cause of death. He had returned home tired, wondering whether this epidemic would be as bad as projected ... or worse. People were getting pretty squirrely about it.

Dr. Aaron Hoffman was an officer in the Epidemiology Intelligence Service of Atlanta's Centers for Disease Control. He had been sent to Lansing to set up, with the Michigan Health Authorities, a surveillance program to detect cases in the impending swine flu epidemic. At that moment the U.S. government was committed to vaccinating the whole population against a virus that CDC thought would sweep across the country with as many deaths as in the great influenza epidemic of 1918.

The telephone rang. "Hello? Oh, hello, Eric. Yes, he just came in," said Rachel. "Hang on. I'll get him."

She put her hand over the mouthpiece. "Don't talk too long."

Aaron got up from the chair, muted the TV, and went into the kitchen.

"Hello, Eric. What's up? More bad news on the flu?"

"No. Just called to see how you were doing and to touch base with you about some sort of hemorrhagic fever that has hit Africa."

"Where in Africa?" asked Aaron, aware of Rachel glancing at him from the stove. "What's going on?"

"We've had unconfirmed reports that something ominous is happening in Zaire and the Sudan. There are rumors of hundreds of people dying. We are waiting for official word from World Health." Eric Robinson was coordinator of field epidemiologists of CDC and Aaron's immediate superior.

"Why are you calling me?" Aaron gave a short laugh. "I'm up to my neck in swine flu." His mind was racing: he had only recently returned from four years in Africa.

"Just thought you might be interested," said Eric.

"Well, I am, but you know the bosses thought I needed a domestic post for a while, and Rachel has just started back to school, and the kids are settling in, and . . ." Rachel had stopped dishing out the soup and was looking steadily at Aaron. He raised his eyebrows and shook his head defensively.

"Well, just keeping you posted, Aaron. Nothing sure yet. We'll stay in touch. Good-bye."

Aaron hung up the phone and, pulling a chair up to the table, concentrated on eating.

"You make the best soup," he said. Her silence demanded an answer. "Okay, Rachel, there are rumors of some sort of epidemic in Zaire and the Sudan."

"I suppose they want you to go."

"He just asked me if I was interested."

"And you said, 'No way. I can't stand Africa. I love it here with good old swine flu and the Michigan state health people,' " said Rachel, with a bite to her voice.

"I didn't tell him anything. You heard me. We have a serious epidemic of our own right here. If anyone needs help, I do. People are getting pretty scared."

The meal was a quiet one. As they cleared the table and were washing up, Rachel's anger boiled over.

"Aaron, if you decide to go, have you thought at all about anyone besides yourself? What about me? What about my law career? What about your promise to help with the kids while I'm in school?" She slammed a pan into the sink. "Don't you think that a good lawyer can make as much difference in the world as you can?"

He let her talk, knowing that his answers would not be what she wanted. She scrubbed the inside of the pan. "When we bought this house it was fine with CDC. We had their blessing, remember? But you know damn well if Eric wonders if you're interested in some bloody, mysterious epidemic in Africa, they're thinking of sending you there." She wiped her hands on her apron, turned her back on Aaron, and followed her children upstairs.

Aaron turned on a football game but could not concentrate and switched off the TV. After recording the events of the day in his notebook and writing a list of the things to do in the morning, he went upstairs to bed; Rachel was already asleep. Aaron closed his eyes and saw slow-flowing, mud-colored streams and naked kids jumping up and down, family groups sitting outside wattle huts, bright cotton prints drying on thatched roofs, small log spokes around a fire, sweet-smelling smoke curling up and fading into blue sky, muscular cumulus clouds flexing and writhing before the evening storm. He could smell the hot earth and hear the whine of mosquitoes, the barks of dogs, the clucking of scrawny chickens around the manioc bushes scratching for grubs, and the laughter of children—happy, round faced and round bellied. . . .

On October 1, in Bumba, Collard and Maréchal were awakened at 5 A.M. by the loud clanging of the mission bell, calling the faithful to Mass. After another cold shower, they walked over to the mission terrace for breakfast. As they were finishing their coffee, Amene arrived and agreed to check on the Yambuku schoolgirls in the quarantine camp while they went to the hospital.

Collard carried a small medical kit; Maréchal brought a bundle of protective clothing. The soldiers who were lounging around the entrance of the hospital recognized them as doctors and let them through. They approached the pavilion where the teacher and his wife had been secluded. The place was deserted. In the open doorway at the end of the ward, several enamel dishes of untouched food were covered with flies, their irreverent buzzing loud in the heavy silence. Inside, the woman was lying in the bed nearest the door. Her husband sat in a chair next to her. Both were dead.

The soldiers shook their heads when Collard asked them for help with the grave digging. Their sergeant pointed to a group of men dressed in prison blues working on the road; he shouted for them to come over.

"I need a couple of men to dig a grave and carry the bodies of two patients who have died in the pavilion," repeated Collard to the prisoners. No one stepped forward.

"You will have the rest of the day off after the grave is dug." No one moved. Collard whispered to the sergeant, who nodded his agreement.

"The two men who help me will have their sentence excused," said the doctor.

One man stepped forward. "We know of this sickness. We would rather be prisoners and alive, than go in there and die like they did." The sergeant shrugged and waved them away.

The doctors dug a grave twenty meters from the entrance of the pavilion. Collard haggled with the sergeant for a little gasoline to burn the bodies. The soldiers lounged in the shade of a mango tree, watching from a distance. Stripping down to their underpants, Collard and Maréchal donned paper gowns and hats, covered their faces with masks, and pulled on booties and plastic gloves. A soldier left a jerry can of gasoline next to the hole, then hurried away.

The doctors walked to the pavilion, scarcely daring to breathe. Collard pushed the dirty dishes away with his foot and kicked the door wide open. Hordes of flies were feasting on the blood and excreta which had come from the mouth and bowels of the dead woman. Some of the filth had overflowed the red mattress and dripped onto the floor. The stench was overwhelming. The man had died in a wooden school chair with his right arm resting on the writing table. His head was thrown back, his mouth gaping. His eyeballs were hidden by big iridescent flies, sucking out the last drops of exudate.

Collard swallowed the bile that rose from his stomach and blinked the sweat out of his eyes. He took small breaths to avoid the stink and shook the flies off his mask. The paper gown was already soggy around his shoulders.

"We have to try for a specimen," he said to Maréchal, who stood staring at the bodies.

Collard walked back out to their pile of clothes and took a syringe and needle and a rubber-stoppered test tube out of his medical kit. Returning to the dead woman, he pushed her over onto her back. Willing himself not to vomit, he stuck the needle through the skin above her pubis and pulled back on the plunger. No urine. He did the same thing with the man and was able to withdraw a few drops of liquid, which he squirted into the test tube.

Maréchal helped him pick up the woman's body, carry it out to the hole, and drop it in. Their sodden paper gowns were disintegrating; flies settled on their bare shoulders. Shutting their mouths tight behind their masks, they went back into the ward for the man. Rigor mortis had fixed his body in the sitting position with his right arm flexed at the elbow. The doctors grabbed him by his shoulders and feet and carried him out, then lowered him onto his wife. The grave was too shallow for both bodies, and the man's right arm stuck out. Collard poured gasoline over them. He struck a match and threw it into the grave as he backed away. The fuel flamed up, and the couple burned. Greasy smoke rose slowly in the sultry morning sky, carrying the stink of burning flesh.

After the fire subsided, the doctors shoveled dirt onto the blackened remains. Until the last shovelful, the man's charred hand thrust out of the mound—a final, silent plea for help.

By midmorning Masangaya had sewn up two men from Yandongi who had hacked at each other with machetes. Luckily, they were both drunk enough not to need local anesthesia, since none was left in the pharmacy. During the afternoon he tried to catch quick naps on the cot in his office, but his head hurt more when he lay down. In the evening he returned to his empty house: the woman he had paid to cook and sweep after his wife left had disappeared several days ago. He opened the icebox and pulled out a plate of cold rice pudding, walked out onto the terrace, and sat on the steps to eat. The first mouthful lay heavy on his tongue; he gagged and spit it out. Even the bland smell of rice made him queasy. He got up and walked slowly back to his office; he might not have the strength to go there later if he was called in the night. He was sitting on the cot, his back against the wall, when Sukato came in.

"*Mbote, tata*. How are you?"

"Tired. Exhausted."

"Have you eaten?"

"Yes, a little."

Sukato sat on the stool. He had spent the day doing what he could for the few people in the hospital. He was worried by the emptiness of Masangaya's expression, but he knew better than to pry.

"I heard you had a busy afternoon in the OR."

"Yes." Masangaya rubbed at the stiffness in his neck. "Even in the midst of tragedy the Budja still drink and fight. Did you see the two drunks I sewed up?"

"No, but one of the workers told me they were pummeling each other again on the road."

"And, you, how does it go with you?" asked the older man, changing the subject.

"I am fine, but I have more bad news. Mandu is too weak to respond." Masangaya pushed himself off the cot.

"So, now we are down to you and me." He leaned on the windowsill. The sun was setting behind a bank of clouds. A woman ran toward the children's pavilion carrying an infant bundled in a sheet. He turned around and faced Sukato.

"Why do they keep coming?" whispered Masangaya in exasperation.

"Because we are here, they still have hope," replied Sukato.

"Everybody should have been evacuated long ago." The

medical assistant sat on the cot. "You get some sleep; I will try and do the same."

"Good night, *tata*. I will come by in the morning."

As dawn lightened the eastern sky, Sukato quietly opened the door to Masangaya's office. The medical assistant was asleep on his side, breathing rapidly. The room smelled of vomit and stale, rancid air. Sukato took the slop bucket out and tossed the contents into weeds behind the building. Leaving the door open, he sat on the steps to wait. Before long, the sun climbed out of the trees; a ray shone through the window and onto Masangaya. He stirred, tried to roll over on his back, but groaned and resumed the fetal position. Sukato approached the bed and put his hand on his friend's shoulder.

Masangaya whispered, *"Mbote, petit."*

"Mbote, tata. Sango nini?"

"Not well."

"I will make you coffee."

"My throat is too sore."

Sukato walked over to the sink and filled a glass of water. "Try to drink."

Masangaya took several painful sips and handed the glass back. Sukato pulled the stool over and sat down.

"Tata, there is no time left for delay. You must go to the *nganga* in Bongolu. He cured me when I had the fever."

The medical assistant wiped his face with a towel and sat up stiffly. "I don't know," he said, shaking his head. "I am not connected to Bongolu. My people are Lubas from the Kasai. I only know that I have the fever. The European medicines won't work any better on me than they have on all the others."

"So the *nganga* is your only choice," said Sukato, pressing his point.

Masangaya took a deep breath and let it out slowly. "I wish I could see my own village *nganga* in Tshuapa, but that is too far away."

"My *nganga* knows about you," said Sukato. "I told him how much you have done for our people. I am sure he can help. We could use the mission Land Rover. It is only thirty kilometers to Bongolu."

Masangaya thought for a moment. "Very well. I will ask Sister Augustina." He eased himself out of bed and washed his face in the sink, then put on a clean white coat and stepped out of the office. Sukato was at his side. Masangaya walked carefully so as not to jar his aching head and back. Within a few minutes he stood in the Mother Superior's doorway.

"Good morning, Masangaya. Come in. I will be through in a minute."

"I must not come in, Sister."

"But why . . . ?" She looked up, then dropped her pen. "Oh, no! Not you!" She stood and came toward him. He backed away.

"I have come to ask you if I can use the Land Rover to drive to Bongolu and see the *nganga* who cured Sukato."

"I doubt Sukato had the fever," snapped Augustina.

"He had the fever, Sister."

"But, Masangaya, I am sure we will be sent more medical help."

"It will come too late for me." They looked at each other for a moment.

"This is unbelievable! Do you really think a *féticheur* will help?" asked Augustina, shaking her head.

"I cannot say. All I know is that Sukato had the fever, and now he is well. *Ma soeur,* he is the only one I know that hasn't died from it. If our medicines worked I would stay, but we have not saved a single life." He paused, leaning heavily against the doorway. "May we use the Land Rover?"

Augustina retreated behind her desk and looked down at her papers. She sighed and answered flatly, "I will have Luc drive you." She looked up at him. "Will you come back tonight?"

"I will do what the *nganga* orders."

The Mother Superior gathered stray pieces of paper and placed them methodically in the register she kept like a ship's log, then closed the book. She stood and looked straight at the medical assistant.

"So, we do not know when we will see each other again."

"That is right, Sister."

"I will pray for you."

"It will help knowing that you are praying for me. You have been a mother to many of us."

"*Adieu,* my friend," she said.

"*Adieu, ma mère,*" he answered, and turned away.

Augustina slumped into her chair and stared at the empty doorway for a few moments, then sat up and scribbled a note for Lisala. She walked to the radio room and turned on the machine and put in her call. Father Jules answered, "Go ahead, Yambuku."

"Please transmit to Sister Adeline and the monseigneur the following message: '10/2/76 LAST NIGHT NURSE MANDU DIED. MEDICAL ASSISTANT HAS FEVER AND GOES THIS MORNING TO THE *FÉTICHEUR* OF BONGOLU SINCE NO DOCTOR COMES HERE. WE ARE ABANDONED AT THE MISSION. FRIGHTENED. ALONE.' That is all."

"Message received. I will pass it on to the authorities immediately. And, Sister . . . keep up your courage."

Without a reply, Augustina turned off the radio, walked

back to her office, and asked one of the workers to fetch Veronica and Antonie.

Augustina told the sisters about Masangaya and interrupted their comments and questions with, "There is nothing else I could do. Now, I sent for you because we must decide a course of action for ourselves. Veronica?"

"Well, we cannot just sit here and wait for death. Before Matilda and Gérard died, Lisala wanted us to go to Yasoku and isolate ourselves until a solution could be found. Maybe now is the time to go."

Augustina nodded. "Antonie?"

She looked at the other sisters. "Shouldn't we ask Father Dubonnet what he thinks?"

"He went to check on the villagers early this morning. We can speak to him when he returns," replied Veronica.

Augustina nodded. "I will notify Lisala of our intent. Antonie, please see that the Land Rover is filled with fuel when Luc returns from Bongolu. Veronica, see to it that we have some food and kitchen things, then go to the laundry and tell Evariste to come to my office. We will give him the keys when we leave. I will help you as soon as I can."

Just before 10 A.M. Veronica joined Augustina in her office.

"Maybe it would be better if you did not check with Lisala. They might not allow us to leave," said Veronica.

"I told them I would be on the air at ten, so I must do it," replied Augustina, walking out of her office. Behind her, Veronica followed in silence. She saw Augustina's hands shaking as she picked up the microphone.

"Lisala, this is Yambuku. Do you receive?"

"Lisala here. Go ahead, Yambuku."

"Do we have approval from the authorities to leave and drive to Yasoku?"

"A moment." There was a long pause filled with crackles. Augustina adjusted the dials, and the static waned.

"Yambuku, Lisala here."

"Go ahead, Lisala; we are listening," said Augustina.

"I have a message from Kinshasa for you. Are you ready to copy?"

Behind her, Augustina heard Veronica mumble, "Holy Mother of God."

"Yes, Lisala," replied the Mother Superior, with forced patience. "We hear you very well. Please go ahead."

"The message is from the minister of health in Kinshasa and the Belgian Embassy. They request you not leave Yambuku. Do you receive?"

Augustina heard a noise behind her, turned, and saw Veronica run from the room.

"I understand. I understand the instructions, Lisala. We are forbidden to leave. We must stay here."

"That is correct," came the precise voice of Jules. "There is more."

"I am taking note."

Jules' read: " 'RELIGIOUS PERSONNEL MUST STAY AND AWAIT ARRIVAL, AT NOON, OF HELICOPTER WITH DOCTORS, MEDICINES, AND SUPPLIES ON BOARD. SISTERS ARE REQUESTED TO MAKE LANDING SITE HIGHLY VISIBLE WITH WHITE SHEET PLACED ON GRASS, NOT SAND. REPEAT, NOT SAND.'

"Did you receive?"

"Yes. Helicopter arriving at noon," repeated Augustina, with relief. "Thank you very much. We are encouraged. We will await the arrival of the doctors. Over to you."

"That is all from Lisala."

"Please thank the authorities. Over and out." Augustina put down the microphone and turned off the radio. She squeezed the wooden cross that hung from her neck. *Thank you, Blessed Virgin, for your intervention and mercy.* She stood up, walked down the corridor to Veronica's room, and knocked on the door.

Veronica was in her chair, hugging her pillow, trying to control her shaking and tears.

"Veronica, doctors are coming at noon in a helicopter."

"A helicopter? Are they coming to get us?"

"Lisala only said they were coming. We are to spread a sheet on a grassy place to show them where to land." Veronica threw the pillow onto the bed.

"I will get one from the laundry. Where shall I put it?"

"On the soccer field."

At noon, Augustina, Veronica, and Antonie stood next to the sheet and watched the sky. A light breeze discouraged the flies. Twelve-thirty came and went. One o'clock—and still no sign of the helicopter.

"I'm going back to the convent and listen for any radio messages. They must have been held up somewhere," said Augustina.

Finally at 3:30, Augustina heard Lisala calling Yambuku. She was given the following message: "10/2/76 LISALA TO YAMBUKU: DO NOT LEAVE YAMBUKU. ISOLATE YOURSELVES IN A NONCONTAMINATED LOCALE. WAIT FOR HELICOPTER. COMMUNIQUE FROM ANTWERP: ILLNESS OF EXCEPTIONAL CONTAGION, MAY BE YELLOW FEVER. TRANSMITTED BY CONTACT WITH BLOOD, URINE, SALIVA, EXCRETA. DO NOT GO INTO PLACES WHERE SICK WERE IN BED. BURN ALL LINEN IN CONTACT WITH THE SICK. VISITS OR MEETINGS ARE ABSOLUTELY FORBIDDEN."

"End of message. Did you receive?"

"Message received. Thank you," replied Augustina.

Jules continued, "Everybody here prays for you, Yambuku. Keep up your courage. Stay in touch with us. Take the radio with you."

"Thank you, Lisala. Over and out."

Augustina sat at the radio for a long time, absently fingering her rosary. They would not be flown out. It would be hard to tell Veronica and Antonie. They had all touched the bodies and linen of the sick and dying. There was no hope for them.

CHAPTER 12

As the helicopter climbed away from the town, cool fresh air blew through the vents, replacing the smell of stale beer and sweat in the cabin. It had taken most of the morning for Collard and Maréchal to locate the pilots, who had spent the night in a Bumba bar dancing with prostitutes to a new song called *"Épidémie."* In the small hours of the morning, the major commanding the local troops drove the pilots to his house where Collard found them in their underpants drinking coffee. Sullen and hungover, the men came out with tales of horror they had heard during the night of bloated bodies from the Yambuku mission, rotting in the sun. They took an hour to dress and drive to the airport. Miatamba, who had just arrived from Lisala, was there to meet them. Then another hour was wasted rounding up workers to roll out barrels of fuel and hand-pump it into the chopper. Now, at last they were airborne.

The pilot looked over his shoulder at the doctors, and shouting above the noise of the machine, announced: "I will fly you over Yambuku, but I will not land."

"You have orders to take us to Yambuku," yelled Collard, his red face inches from the pilot's head. Miatamba pulled him back and cupped his hands around Collard's ear.

"Let him get there first, then we can see about landing," he said.

They headed west along the river, then at Ebonda picked up the road that cut north through the forest. At Yamisolo, the road forked northwest to Yambuku and northeast to Yasoku. They turned east, and moments later a cluster of red brick houses next to the sheds of a coffee plantation came into view. The grass around the buildings was overgrown, and the paths between the empty houses were choked with weeds. On the other side of the coffee fields, figures poured out of the mud huts along a rough dirt track and waved.

"This is Yasoku. I am landing here," shouted the pilot over his shoulder.

"Goddammit . . . ," said Collard, half out of his seat.

"Yambuku is only thirty kilometers north," said the pilot. "You can requisition a vehicle and drive." He headed into the wind and lowered the chopper slowly onto the road. Squawking chickens ran for their lives, and the people rushed into their huts to escape the downdraft; some of the thatched roofs were blown away in a cloud of dust. The pilot switched off the engine, and as the rotors slowed, the villagers reappeared and surrounded the machine. Two older men emerged from the crowd. Collard stood and opened the door as the men approached. They shouted at him, pointing to the huts without roofs. He pulled the door shut and turned to the pilot. "They don't seem very happy about what you've done to their houses."

The pilot swore and switched on the engines. "It will cost us a fortune if we stay here," he said to the copilot, as the whine of the turbines increased in volume. The old men backed away, still yelling and shaking their fists at the machine as the blades sliced through the air and dust.

As they cleared the ground, Miatamba reached forward and, lifting the headset a little off the pilot's ear, said, "Yambuku is only a short flight from here. You will be ridiculed if you return to Bumba without having accomplished your mission."

"All right," snapped the pilot, "I will take you there, but I will not stay."

Miatamba leaned back in his seat and gave Collard a thumbs-up.

In a few minutes, they were circling Yambuku's large mission and farm. As they started their descent, three nuns ran out of a building, waving up at them; a few Zairians followed at a distance. Collard looked down at the circle of fine dirt that blew up from the flattened grass next to the sheet below. He felt his stomach tighten with fear. Was the disease really yellow fever? Or was it something else that clung to the dust or hid in the bellies of insects? As the wheels touched and the engine was cut, the sisters clutched their veils and skirts.

"We will be on the ground for less than an hour. All of you stay in the machine until I have talked with the sisters," he ordered.

Collard stripped and dressed in a protective gown, booties, hat, and gloves, then struggled into an ultrafilter mask which covered his head and face. Picking up a bullhorn, he opened the door and stepped carefully onto the turf. The others remained strapped in their seats. The three nuns ran toward him. Collard raised his hand in a sign for them to stop.

"Do not approach." His muffled voice was amplified by the loudspeaker. The women halted.

"My sisters, I am Dr. Collard of the Belgian Medical Co-operation. We have come to help you and to learn as much about the disease as possible so we can prevent more deaths." He stopped to catch his breath. "Since we are not sure how the disease is spread, I must ask you to come no closer than ten meters." Sweat ran off his forehead under the rubber headpiece and stung his eyes. He felt a little foolish in his long paper gown and "gas mask" in front of the women and Zairians, but fear triumphed over pride. He forged ahead.

"I have brought letters from your superiors and from your families. I will get them from the helicopter and put them on a post over there," he said, pointing to a fence with his gloved hand. "Then you can come forward and take them." As Collard walked back to the chopper, the sisters huddled together.

"They have not come to take us away," said Veronica tightly.

"They cannot; we may be contaminated," replied Augustina.

Behind her, Antonie put her hands to her face and started to cry.

Collard returned and balanced a bundle of papers on top of a fence post, then retreated nearer the helicopter. Augustina retrieved the packet and walked back toward the others.

"He can at least take the letters we have written," said Veronica, turning toward the convent.

"Wait," ordered Augustina. She took a couple of steps nearer the doctor and called out. "We have written letters to our families and to our mission sisters. May we fetch them for you to mail in Kinshasa?"

"That is not possible," replied Collard. "The risk is too great."

They all stood in embarrassed silence until the doctor spoke through the bullhorn once more. "We have the description of the disease from Dr. Amene, but could you tell me what you have seen?"

Augustina raised her voice again and outlined the course of the disease they all knew so well.

"Has anyone recovered?" asked the doctor.

"Mbunzu, the wife of Mabalo, the first man to die. She had symptoms of the disease, yet is improving," replied Augustina. "She lives in the third house over in the workers' huts." She pointed off to the left. "There are eight others who are sick over there."

"Thank you, Sister," said Collard. "We will get blood samples from those who have the fever."

He walked back to the helicopter, and in a moment, Maréchal and Miatamba, dressed in protective clothes and masks, joined him on the ground. Collard carried a bag with syringes, test tubes, and a box of matches; Maréchal had a bundle of extra protective clothes tucked under his arm. The sisters watched.

A woman stood in front of the first hut, her left hand cradling her forearm as she extended her right hand in greeting. Collard hesitated, then offered her his gloved fingers. She opened the door, and the doctors entered the small front room where a young woman and a man, lying on mats, hid their faces from these specters, as they would have done from the masked fiends that danced around the fire in dark ceremonies. Their bodies stiffened with fear when Collard raised his hand in greeting; a stifled *"Mbote"* issued from his mask; they responded with a passive *"Ehhhh."* He knelt between them, and Maréchal handed him a tourniquet and syringe. Miatamba talked quietly with the woman by the door. Collard told the couple he had to draw their blood to find a treatment that would cure them. Each lay rigid as he tightened the soft rubber tube around an arm and then stuck the needle into an elbow vein. Maréchal filled the test tubes. When they were through, the doctors nodded their thanks and left.

Outside, Maréchal and Collard stripped off their gowns and gloves, avoiding contact with the outer surfaces. Miatamba had touched no one in the house, so remained gowned. At a distance, the three astonished nuns caught sight of the naked doctors and turned away as Collard set fire to the pile of protective clothes.

"The sun's ultraviolet rays will kill viruses we might have picked up," said Maréchal.

"I hope so," replied Collard, seeing the nuns and quickly pulling on a fresh gown.

Veronica peeked over her shoulder. "They are decent now," she announced.

"Would you like something to drink?" shouted Sister Augustina. The men looked at each other; they were parched but did not trust the water.

Collard shouted back, "Thank you, no. We are not thirsty."

The doctors followed the same routine in the next hut but this time burned their gowns and redressed out of the sisters' sight. They moved on to Mbunzu's house, knocked on the door, and walked in. An old woman sitting by the bed shouted in alarm and scurried to the back of the hut. Mbunzu sat up, glaring at the intruders.

"*Sik'oyo nini*," she snapped. Now what!

"*Malembe, mama. Kobanga te,*" answered Miatamba. Easy, mama. Do not be frightened. "We are doctors who have come to try and stop whatever is killing so many people."

Mbunzu relaxed a little, but the old woman cringed in the corner, her eyes wide and frightened.

"Sister Augustina told us your husband was the first to die of the fever. She said you have been sick yourself but are now getting better."

Mbunzu looked down at her hands clasped between her knees. "My husband died, and my baby died."

"I would like to take a little blood from your arm, so we can send it to experts in Europe and find out what killed your man and your child," said Miatamba gently.

"No!" she snarled, turning away from him. "Needles have been jabbed into me, and nothing has changed."

He looked down at her for a moment then, taking off his mask, squatted next to the bed. "Do you know of others who have had the fever and are better?" he asked.

"The nurse Sukato is that way," she answered. Then turning to look at him directly, she added, "He was cured by the *nganga* of Bongolu. No white men's needles were stuck into him."

"Good. I will certainly see Sukato and ask him for a little of his blood." Miatamba wiped his forehead with his sleeve. He paused before speaking again. "My sister, it is very necessary to have some of your blood as well." After a long moment, Mbunzu lay back down on the bed, and held out her arm. Miatamba placed the tourniquet and looked carefully, but even the veins on the back of her hand were flat and difficult to see. Collard opened the door to let in more light.

"It's always the way," he said. "Terrible veins in the patient you need to stick the most."

After some searching, Miatamba felt the slight bulge and resilience of a vein in the crease of her elbow. He reached back, and Collard put a syringe in his hand. A quick swab with alcohol, and he pushed the needle through the skin, carefully advancing it, until he felt the soft yield as the beveled tip pierced the vessel wall. Pulling back the plunger, he filled the barrel with blood.

"Come and hold this now," said Miatamba, looking at the old woman. She crept out of the corner and sat cross-legged next to the bed, pressing her bony finger into Mbunzu's elbow.

"I will let you know what happens, Mbunzu," said Miatamba, as Collard emptied the blood into a test tube. "Now we must leave."

"Tikala malamu, mama," said Collard.

"Kende malamu, monganga," replied Mbunzu, looking up at Miatamba.

The doctors walked back to the helicopter. They transferred the test tubes into thermos jugs and added dry ice made from the carbon dioxide tank they had brought with them. While the others stripped away what was left of their soggy gowns, Collard took off his mask and threw it in the helicopter, then carried a bundle of protective clothes and several large containers of Decaris to the fence post. He turned to the sisters.

"I will be back soon. Here are some protective gowns and pills which may improve your immune system. I must insist on the strictest quarantine. No one is allowed to come into or go out of Yambuku or the mission. On the roads just north of Bumba, the military have orders to shoot anyone who tries to leave the area. As soon as we know what is causing the epidemic, we can take more specific measures to prevent its spread and cure those who are sick. Until then, you are not allowed to leave. That is an order."

"We understand," said Augustina.

"We understand, but we think it is going a little far not taking our letters," muttered Veronica. Augustina silenced her with a look.

"You have done much by coming, Doctor. We do not feel so abandoned now," said Augustina.

"Many here in Zaire and in Europe are working full-time on this epidemic, and I am sure we will have some answers soon," said Collard. "In the meantime you should move out of the convent. Do you have an empty house where no one has been sick or died?"

"The guest house, over there," said Augustina, indicating a brick building next to the convent.

"Good. I was told in Kinshasa that Father Jef Maas is with you. Where is he now?"

"In the villages, comforting those who have lost family."

"Does he take precautions?"

"Yes," replied Veronica. "He does not touch the people."

"Will he move into the guest house with you and stay in quarantine?"

"I will ask him, but I have little control over what he does," replied the Mother Superior, walking over to retrieve the protective clothing and the medicine.

"He must be in quarantine with you," insisted Collard.

"I know," replied Augustina, looking at him over the bundle.

"Sister, I wish there was more I could do," said Collard. "Thank you for your help. I will keep in touch." He walked back to the chopper, stripped off his gown and gloves, and added them to the pile beside the machine. He threw a match onto the clothes. The rotors started to move as the engines were turned on. Jumping into the cabin, he tossed his booties and cap into the flames. The blades *whoosh*ed, gaining in momentum, and blew the burning paper across the field. In a moment, the helicopter lifted off the grass. The sisters waved and their veils fluttered as the rotor breeze swept over them; then all was suddenly still, and they stood downcast, avoiding one another's eyes.

Augustina broke the silence. "We have much to do," she

said. Veronica took the bottles of pills from her as they started back to the convent.

"Decaris! That is for filaria," she said in disgust. "Is that the best they can do?"

Late that afternoon, the sisters moved into the guest house. Veronica surrounded the building with a cordon sanitaire made of white gauze bandage supported by sticks pushed into the ground. Antonie followed her but was of little help. Augustina wrote a warning in Lingala and pinned it to the gauze. It read:

DO NOT CROSS THIS BARRIER OR YOU WILL DIE.
TO CALL SISTERS RING BELL.

She put the small handbell from the chapel below the sign. The three nuns sat on the covered stoop of the guest house.

At dusk, Dubonnet rode up on his bicycle, stopping in front of the stretched bandage; the sisters stepped off the terrace to meet him.

"I heard along the road that a helicopter landed here this afternoon," he said.

"That's right," replied Augustina.

"Is this bandage supposed to prevent your escape or keep the rest of us out?" He leaned the bike against a papaya tree.

"Both," said Veronica. Dubonnet stepped over the gauze, and they all walked back to the porch.

Augustina reviewed the events of the afternoon and finished by telling him that they had prepared a room for him in the guest house.

"So the four of us will await our fates together," said

Dubonnet with a chuckle. "But I will continue to make my rounds. Now is when the people need me the most."

"Dr. Collard asked after you," said Veronica. "I told him you did not touch the people in the villages. But it would be safer for us if you changed into a different cassock before coming into the guest house."

"I can do that, if you think it is necessary," said the priest. "Is there anything to eat?"

"There is bread and cheese in your room," said Antonie.

Veronica cut in. "How will we know if you have on a different cassock? I have never seen you wearing what I would call a clean one."

Dubonnet scowled at her. "I will draw a skull and crossbones on the cassock I wear in the villages and exchange it for one I shall wear only in the presence of our pristine nuns." He bowed deeply and swept his hand flamboyantly toward the women. The sisters laughed.

After dropping off Miatamba in Bumba, Collard and Maréchal landed in Kinshasa at 10:30 P.M. Collard took the thermos containing the blood samples to a small laboratory in FOMETRO (Fonds Médicale Tropicale) headquarters, which had been formerly used for the sleeping sickness prevention program. For the last time that day, he stripped off his clothes and put on protective gear. He opened the thermos and, with great care, separated the specimens into two lots: one for the Pasteur Institute from Maréchal, and one for the Institute of Tropical Medicine in Antwerp from him. The two thermos flasks were stored in the refrigerator and would be turned over to the pilot of a UTA plane scheduled to leave for Paris in the early hours of the morning.

Collard stood under the cool jet of a shower in the guest bathroom of FOMETRO, scrubbing off the grime and smells of the trip. Afterward, he phoned his wife to tell her that he thought it prudent to have no contact with her or the children for a few days: he was not sure how many. He ate a sandwich of cold cuts and cheese and fell asleep as soon as he went to bed.

CHAPTER 13

Miatamba heard the door squeak open. He rolled over on his back and stretched. Opening his eyes he saw the black tribal lines and chevrons on her forehead. She was scrutinizing him as she would a fat, black-headed grub about to be popped into her mouth and cracked between her teeth. She pushed her lower lip out over her sharp chin and waggled a finger in his face.

"You have visited a place where people, including the *mindele*, are being killed. You are the head of the family since your father, my own brother, died. Your first responsibility is to us." Miat swung his feet off the couch and sat up. The old woman backed off a step but continued to glare at him.

"My duty is to go where people are sick and dying," replied Miatamba. He looked around the aunt and called out, "Is there any bread and coffee?" His wife brought in a steaming mug and a plate of food and set them on the low table in front of him.

The aunt returned to the attack. "It is the priests who are making you desert your family for some white missionaries in the north."

He turned to face her. "That is not true. Four whites have been killed, but hundreds of our brothers and sisters

229

have died, and more are dying every day. There is no doctor there. I must go."

The old woman squatted in front of him and, with her hands clasped, rocked gently on her heels, muttering and moaning in her misery. As he was finishing his breakfast, she spoke again, pleadingly. "I know this is expected of you because you are a doctor, but if you were to disappear ... I can hide you in the pirogue and ferry you across the river to where you cannot be found."

"More doctors—white and Zairian—will be going to Yambuku soon. I will return home when they arrive," he said.

The aunt stood up and, dismissing him with a wave of her hand, left the room in disgust. His wife returned with their two children. She refilled his cup. "Would you like more to eat before you leave?"

He shook his head and looked up at her. "Do you have enough money for the next few days?"

"We have all we need. You will be careful, won't you?"

"Of course." He stood and gathered up his medical bag and small suitcase. "I will not be away long."

He walked out to his Jeep. His wife and children waved from the gate, but it was easier for him not to look back.

By late evening he had reached Modjamboli, forty kilometers from Yambuku. After talking to the villagers, he sat with the elders and listened to their news. They talked of the epidemic until darkness had fallen. He gratefully accepted the chief's offer of a hut, and women brought him food and *sese*. He was about to lie down when a boy ran up, out of breath.

"Could you come and see my mother, *monganga*? She is very sick."

"Where is she?"

"In a house at the end of the village."

"I will follow you."

In a moment they arrived at a small hut where the yellow glimmer from a kerosene lamp showed a woman lying asleep on a mat. Miatamba knelt beside her and put his hand on her hot dry forehead.

"Banda mikolo boni ozali na mpasi?" Since when have you been sick, mama?

"Mikolo sambo." Seven days.

Her story came out haltingly, in whispers. She had taken her pregnant daughter to the Yambuku hospital; the young woman died after delivering a stillborn. She returned alone. A few days later the fever struck her. Miatamba brought the lamp closer to the woman's face and saw that her eyes were red and thick bloodstained spittle ran from the corners of her mouth.

"You must stay in the hut and not go out. Food and water will be brought to the door." He paused. "No one, not even your son, is allowed to come in here." She looked at him for a moment, then turned her face to the wall. He stood and left, feeling empty and useless. Outside, the boy was waiting, sitting on an upturned bucket.

"Where is your father?" he asked.

"Dead," replied the boy.

"Who is with you and your mother?"

"The chief's wife is my mother's sister. But—" He shook his head. Miatamba squatted next to him.

"But she never comes around?" The boy nodded, and tears fell off his cheeks.

"If your mother joins your father in the village of the ancestors, the chief's wife will take you into her house." Miat stretched forward to hear the boy's whispered yes. He had also been raised by an aunt—the old woman who had scolded him this same day. He put his arm around the child's shoulders and waited while he wept. There was nothing he could say: life would never be the same for this little one. After a while, Miat wiped the boy's face with a handkerchief.

"Tell me your name, *mwana*."

The child whispered again.

"Try to listen to me, Ipo. Now is the time to be strong. You must sleep across the door of your mother's hut and make sure that no one enters, including you. You must lay food and water each morning by the entrance for her, but you must not go in for any reason." Miat stood and looked down at the boy.

"Ipo, how old are you?" Only a year older than his own son. He put his hand under the boy's chin and lifted it.

"With your father gone and your mother sick, you must be the man in the family."

The boy looked up at the doctor. "I understand," he said.

Although exhausted, Miat slept poorly, and dawn found him weary and stiff. He repeated to the chief the instructions he had given the boy, and after thanking him for the hospitality, continued on his way. By mid-morning he was climbing the long hill to Yandongi and Yambuku. He drove past the empty house of the fathers and the deserted convent to the guest house that Augustina had indicated to Collard as their place of isolation. He stopped at the white gauze barrier and climbed out of the Jeep.

"Thank God!" exclaimed Augustina, running toward him. Antonie stayed in the shadows of the porch, and, covering her face with her hands, she wept.

"I have come to be with you until others arrive," he said.

Veronica joined Augustina. "O Blessed Mother, thank you for bringing him back," she exclaimed. "Welcome, Doctor Miatamba! What a relief to see you. I will fetch clean sheets and a pillow, and you can stay in the girl's dormitory across the road."

"That will be fine," said the doctor. He raised his hand in greeting as several workers dragging rakes and pushing a cart filled with leaves and dead flowers walked up slowly and stood to watch. Three potbellied children stopped their shuffling across the road and waved at him shyly. He waved back.

On October 3, Collard was awakened by a call from Antwerp. The World Health Organization in Geneva had ordered Dr. Thys, chief of the virology division, not to accept more specimens from the fever patients in Zaire and to send any he already had to England's Porton Down.

"My God, why?" Collard demanded. "And what do you mean 'more' specimens? Ours should be just reaching you now."

"Too dangerous to be handled except in maximum containment labs like Porton or the Centers for Disease Control in Atlanta," replied Guido van Eck, one of Thys's young assistants and a friend of Collard. He explained further. "We did receive some specimens from Louvanium about a week ago; they seem to be growing out something, but since they arrived lukewarm we are not sure of their significance."

"So Ilunga did send specimens," said Collard.

"For what they are worth," added Guido. "I assume your specimens were taken properly and will arrive packed in dry ice."

"Of course, *monsieur le prof*," replied Collard with mock seriousness. "In the meantime, WHO thinks we can play with it in the bush, but it is too risky for you in Belgium? What a waste of effort!"

"Nothing will be wasted," replied Guido. "Our material is on its way to England; they have the serum from the Sudan as well. And we'll continue to watch a few of the tissue cultures Thys wants to keep. But that is between us. Do not forget that with the Marburg virus there were accidents even in specialized labs in Germany. The truth is that the fat cats in WHO do not want your virus loose in Europe."

In Paris, on the morning of October 5, Dr. Pierre Burine arrived at the arbovirus laboratory of the Pasteur Institute. He was a small, wiry man with thinning gray hair and a deeply lined face that showed the effects of his years in those deserts and tropics of interest to "*la grande France*." A Gauloise hung from his lower lip. A yellow Urgent slip lay on his desk. He dialed the number for the chief of overseas operations. "Good morning. Burine here."

"Ah, Burine, thanks for calling back. I received a message from Kinshasa that there is a package sent by Dr. Maréchal of the French Medical Aid Mission in Zaire to our institute. Apparently the daughter of the French military attaché put it in the hands of the UTA pilot just before he took off from Kinshasa."

"Right, I'll bring it in myself," replied Burine.

Within the hour he was at the De Gaulle-Roissy Airport. He checked at the airline and at customs, but no one knew anything about a package from Zaire. He telephoned the pilot, who was at home.

"Oh, yes, I brought a package from Kinshasa. The Army people met the plane when we arrived in Paris. I turned it over to them."

After calling around, Burine finally located someone at a large military hospital south of Paris who knew about the package. He drove over and retrieved the parcel from the cold room of the blood transfusion center.

Back in his laboratory Burine opened the package. A letter was taped to the internal wrapping. He skimmed through Maréchal's medical outline, then unscrewed the top of a wide-mouth insulated container. Test tubes wrapped in cotton nestled in what remained of the dry ice. At that moment Burine's telephone rang.

Claude Guimain, virology chief of the World Health Organization, came on the line. After greeting his old friend, Guimain told him that he would be receiving a package from Zaire.

"I have it," said Burine, watching the vapor hover at the rim of the thermos, then float slowly down its sides like foam from a tankard of beer.

"Do not open it," warned Guimain.

"I already have.'"

"Pierre, that package contains dangerous material. It can be handled only in a maximum containment lab."

"What disease are we dealing with?" He heard a light snapping noise.

"We don't know. It comes from people in Zaire who are dying from some sort of hemorrhagic fever. Antwerp has received some specimens, and we have instructed them to send what they could to Porton Down and destroy the rest. I think—"

"Just a moment, Claude." He set the phone down and, with a notepad, fanned away the vapor at the mouth of the thermos. Carefully he pushed the cotton away from several of the test tubes with a glass rod. Quickly he stepped back and grabbed the phone.

"Claude, one of the tubes just cracked!" There was a moment of silence on the other end of the line.

"Pierre, as carefully as you can, taking full sterile precautions, repack the contents in a secure, sterile container and send it straight on to CDC in Atlanta."

"It will be on the next plane," said Burine, staring at the table.

"And, Pierre, I would like you to go to Kinshasa as soon as possible as a WHO consultant to see what is going on there."

The sisters were down to their last bolt of cotton sheeting for shrouds, but fewer people seemed to be dying, and the reports from the villages of new sick had become a trickle. With Dr. Miatamba's arrival, patients stood in line once more for routine examinations and illnesses. The cordon sanitaire remained up but more as a symbol of uncertainty than a barrier.

After a few days, Miatamba persuaded Veronica to dress in protective paraphernalia and help him clean up Masangaya's house. She jumped at the chance to work with him. Always thorough, she insisted that all the furniture be moved outside and washed off with disinfectant. He objected and teased her about being compulsive; she, with her hands on her hips, scolded him for being lazy, and they both laughed without restraint. From the porch of the guest house, Augustina folded her arms firmly across her chest and frowned: there was something wrong with the sound of their laughter. She watched them come and go as they carried the furniture into the house. Then Miat helped Veronica pull off the gown and untie the mask from around her neck, and as she turned and looked up to thank him, her veil slipped off.

"Veronica," shouted Augustina, "that's enough. I need you here."

Miatamba looked up, surprised. Veronica walked toward her Mother Superior, pinning her veil back where it belonged.

After a shower, Veronica sat at the table in her room and started a letter to her sister. She resolved to add to it every day until someone came to take it to the mail.

Yambuku, 4 October 1976

My Dearest Gabrielle,

Something exciting has happened. Dr. Miatamba, who was with Dr. Collard when the helicopter came, has returned to stay with us and help out. It was one of those things I wanted to tell you about right away because it lifts such a heaviness from our hearts.

Already word has spread that a doctor is here, and patients are presenting themselves for treatment of malaria, boils, diarrhea—you know—all the usual things. Dr. Miat, who seems to have no fear of the fever, sees the patients in the dispensary with Sukato. This evening a few men came to the medical assistant's house, where he saw them on the terrace. Later he hopped across the cordon sanitaire, reassuring us that he was quite well, and that if we were not sick by now it is very unlikely that we are infected. Wouldn't that be wonderful. I almost hesitate to believe it, but Miat elicits confidence, and I daresay he knows what he is talking about. I will pray that he is right.

5 October 1976

This afternoon a woman was brought to the doctor in labor. Dr. Miat examined her on the terrace and sent for me. He pulled the table out, and we helped her lie on it. We did not dare go to the hospital, where the source of the fever might still be lurking. Using up all the local anesthetic he carried in his bag, Dr. Miat did a cesarean section right there by the fading light on the porch. He had me keep the wound edges apart with two bent spoons, so he could open the uterus.

It was only after everything was over that my knees started to wobble, and I felt a little seasick. This was my first operation.

Last Saturday I tried to send you and our dear parents letters by the helicopter, but Dr. Collard would not take them for fear of contamination. I tell you quickly that I have washed my hands in strong soap and water before touching these pages, so you have not to worry. Dr. Miat will see that they are posted when he does leave us, so I will not repeat the news that I have already written. As you know, diaries are not allowed in our congregation, but a letter to you every day, if there is something to report, is different.

Most of our days are long and dull. We have nothing to do but wait. It reminds me of the times when you and I were sent to the potato cellar behind the barn as punishment. I do not know whether staying in the guest house is to isolate us from others or others from us. As I write this, it occurs to me that Father Dubonnet and Dr. Miat come and go as they wish; maybe the cordon is only to protect us "weaker" sisters, until, of course, one of the men needs our help.

During the time before Dr. Miat came, we hardly spoke or looked at one another. We prayed like machines. Although the doctor has tried to reassure us, we are still too frightened to take our temperatures. Yesterday, we spread DDT all over the convent, throwing cupfuls in the rooms where Lucie and Matilda died. We sprinkled some down the corridors and on the terrace, so the floors are all white. When we have to walk over to the convent to get food from the icebox, we wear aprons and touch nothing. When we return, we hang the aprons on nails in the brick posts that support the roof over the terrace, and leave our shoes on the steps. The convent which used to be such a happy home is empty now, and dead. Antonie is too frightened to ever go there alone.

Augustina brought the hospital records over here, so

she has no need of her office. We have carried the radio and the batteries into the end room of the guest house. Augustina is in the laundry every day to supervise Casimir. The few workers who are still here do their normal jobs of trimming the bushes, sweeping in front of the terrace, and raking leaves out of the flower beds. Augustina works with them all day. I stay on the terrace and do what I can for the Zairians who walk up to the cordon sanitaire and ask for help. I have set up a table where I work on a big jigsaw puzzle to pass the time. Today there was nothing to do except wait for people to come with notes from the villages, announcing who is sick and who has died, or requesting salt or white cloth to wrap the dead. I send them to Sukato and the doctor if they are sick or need medicine. Did you know that in the old days the villagers brought messages to the whites stuck into the split ends of sticks because the first Belgians did not want to take something directly from the hand of a black? Well, some of the older men are doing the same thing now.

Augustina gave the keys to the dispensary to Sukato, and he continues to work, only stopping by to say good morning or good night. We are giving out salt, sugar, sheeting, and other supplies freely; I hope Sukato is doing the same thing. He is a smart one, like a fox, and always out for himself. I hope he is not selling what he should give freely. I wish Masangaya was here, but I am afraid that he might be dead. A few days ago he became ill and left to see the *féticheur* who Sukato says cured him of the fever.

6 October 1976

Last night I did not close my eyes once!

When the helicopter came and left without taking us

away, something snapped in Antonie. She does not dare to be alone and has moved her cot into my room. All day long she follows me like a whipped dog. She talks very little and always seems on the verge of tears. At night she is restless and moans in her sleep. The beds in the guest house are old, and the springs squeak with the slightest movement—it is impossible to sleep two in a room. I moved my bed to where we stack the bags of rice for the workers. Tonight will be better.

For the past few days Casimir has been sick. Yesterday, he sent word that he was too weak to leave his bed and come to the laundry, and last night he died. We all knew he stole from us, but he did it in such a polite, kindly way that we were almost glad we never caught him at it. Augustina had tears in her eyes but did not weep. She will do the laundry herself now. I copied the radio message she sent out this morning. These are the statistics from her tally sheet:

Number of dead from the beginning Sept. 8 up to Oct. 6: Men 99. Women 97. Youths (5–15 yrs.) 24. Children (0–5 yrs.) 33. Total of 253 deaths that we know about.

Augustina has stopped trying to lead us in prayer and seldom utters a word. She did ask me to cook rice for the workers, since their women are either dead or have been sent back to their villages. At least it is something to do. Today a few more people came for cloth to roll up cadavers.

7 October 1976

Last night I slept with rats. Really! In the middle of the night I heard noises, so I lit a candle and saw rats chewing through rice sacks next to my bed. I was horrified and thought of all the diseases they carry. I clapped my hands, then covered myself with two sheets, head and all. But I could still hear them squealing and scampering around my head. And it was too hot; I had to throw off the sheets and sit up and clap my hands to try and scare them away—filthy creatures. What a night! Dr. Miat was over for coffee this morning and said he would set traps if he could find some.

This evening, after supper, Dubonnet lingered on the step of the terrace and smoked and stared into the dusk. I sat next to him. The mission buildings were silent and empty like a ghost village abandoned in a war. The smell and smoke of the few cooking fires among the workers' huts hung heavy. I hope a storm will wash the air tonight. The father seemed withdrawn and more quiet than usual. *"Nini?"* I asked him. "What?"

He looked at me, frowned, and, flicking away his cigarette, told me about a Budja peasant he had met earlier in the day who had questioned him about poverty. This man told Dubonnet that above anything else in the world he wanted a radio.

"What are you talking about?" Dubonnet asked him. "I have no radio. I do not need one."

The Budja replied, "That is different. You have chosen to be poor; I have not. You are content to be poor; I am not. Tomorrow you could be rich and possess a radio, if you want. But even if I hope all my life, I have no choice; a radio will never be mine, unless I steal it. My poverty is real—yours is not."

Dubonnet looked at me and shrugged. "I had no answer for him." Then, with that rascal smile, he asked, "Did I ever tell you the story of the Protestant missionary who lived in the Kasai for many, many years in a simple mud hut with his simply dressed wife?"

"No, I haven't heard that story," said I.

He lit another cigarette. "This is a true one."

"Yes, Father. If you say so." (You can never tell with him.)

"This old, thin missionary and his old, thin wife in her flowered cotton dress with long sleeves were given a feast by the chief of the clan a few days before they were to leave for America and retirement. All the villagers came and brought them gifts: chickens, smoked monkey meat, gourd cups, little carved fetishes . . . you know the things they give. Then the chief stood up and made a speech, reviewing all the good things that the old couple's white church had done: the school with its rows of benches and chalkboard, the church with its pictures of the bearded white Christ and His white mother, the dispensary, Bibles, etc. . . . and ended with, 'These old friends have become part of our village, and *mama* and *tata* to many of our young people. We all hope they will live long and happily in the big house they must have built in America with all the money they did not spend while they were here with us.' "

"There you are," said I to him, as we both laughed. "They knew the missionaries had a choice."

Dubonnet is so good for us. Although he is the only ascetic I have ever known, I doubt that the others have his sense of humor. I do wonder, though, whether they are all so allergic to soap.

Later, Dr. Miat walked over from Masangaya's house and regaled us with stories of his life in Russia, where he went to medical school.

Apparently, in spite of their Lumumba Institute in Moscow, the Russians—the real ones—are more racist

than we Belgians ever were! He squatted down, fold
his arms across his chest, and, bouncing on his hee.
shot his legs out like the Cossack dancers he admires.
But after a few jumps, he toppled over. He, too, makes
us laugh and forget ourselves. It is now very late, and my
candle is starting to sputter. But I am still afraid each
time I go to bed that I may wake up in the morning with
fever.

8 October 1976

Another day has passed, and I continue with my letter
to you. I hope something will change soon before it becomes a book.

This morning Augustina decided to clean the girls'
dormitory. I watched her from my post on the terrace. I
had offered to help, but she ordered me to stay in the
guest house with Antonie. I did as I was told (for once)
to make things easier for her.

First, she had the workers drag out all the mattresses
onto the grass, then she sprinkled our "holy dust"—
DDT—on them, next, wearing her rubber boots and a
pith helmet, she stamped her feet on each mattress to
drive out the microbes. I have never seen her so active.

This evening Miatamba, who had seen patients in the
dispensary with Sukato most of the day, showed a
Mickey Mouse film for the few children still around the
mission. These little ones, some of whom are orphans,
stand looking at us beyond the cordon for a good part of
the day. The doctor had them sit on the terrace of the
house of the fathers and projected the film onto a sheet.
We heard their shrieks of joy and hands clapping in the
distance. Miat is with the people all day. Those who
don't need to be treated by him come simply to talk. He
avoids no one, but he still does surgery on the terrace.

When the show was over, Miatamba stepped back into our area of quarantine and sat with us. He brought the news that Adika, one of the midwives trained by Lucie, died in a coma in Bombanga, not far from here, where her parents lived—and where they also died. Their *nganga* fled, and the cadavers rotted in the house for several days before Adolo, another midwife, and two workers from the hospital buried them.

After the doctor leaves us, the nights are long and filled with fear, and if fear alone could kill, Antonie would be dead. She pulls her chair next to mine and sits with her legs tucked under her, waiting, waiting, and waiting. I know she cannot help it, but her behavior stirs my imagination and feeds my own dread. Augustina is just as silent but keeps physically active, making copies of her reports when she is not in a frenzy of laundry, raking, sweeping, or clipping bushes with the workers. I miss talking to Augustina. I am lonely for Matilda and Fermina, and especially dear Lucie. How different this vigil would be if we were all together. I thank God for Miat and Dubonnet, and for you, my little sister. As this letter grows in length, I feel so close to you. Good night for now.

9 October 1976

It is morning after another horrible night. A deluge woke me. Over the roar of the storm, I heard Antonie screaming through the wall. She hammered at my door, rushed in, and tried to hide among the rice sacks. She called out to Matilda and Father Gérard to protect her, then suddenly stopped. I lit my candle and saw her wide eyes, fixed on me like a cornered animal. Stringy hair clung to her wet temples.

"I am so sick," she panted, her voice scarcely audible above the hissing rain.

I asked if she had taken her temperature. She cringed and shook her head. I grabbed the candle and, going to her room, found a thermometer.

The rain stopped as if a faucet had been turned off; the lightning flashed, but the thunder was off in the distance. After a moment Antonie sat up, took the thermometer out of her mouth, and leaned toward my candle to read it.

"Normal!" she whispered.

"It was only a nightmare," I told her harshly, covering my own fright. "Go back to bed."

For the rest of the night I couldn't sleep. I felt guilty for having been so curt with her. This morning I encouraged her to help me with the puzzle, but after a few minutes she returned to her room.

Not knowing whether we have been contaminated or not is terrible. Yesterday evening we recited the chaplet, following Father Dubonnet. Then he led us in prayers of intention, and we discovered who was sick and who had died in the villages, as he called out the names of families in need. Praying for others seems easier than praying for myself.

Gabrielle, I have to write this and I hope you will understand why. This morning I passed a black stool. I know that a week from today I will be dead, but somehow I am less afraid than I was. Now the timing is set; the doubt and waiting are over. I am sad at the thought of leaving you and our blessed parents, but I will be waiting for all of you and helping to prepare your way. The agricultural cooperative will have to be rebuilt from zero again because most of those who ran it are dead, but I would just as soon leave that to someone else.

Soon I will be with my dear friends in Christ. My heart warms at the thought. Do not be sad for me, little sister. I am ready and at peace, and I can pray again. I write this to you because I cannot tell Antonie, and I do not want to tell Augustina. Dr. Miatamba is on a tour of the villages, so I will speak to Father Dubonnet this evening.

My dear little sister, pray a lot and live fully in the beauty of our faith. Life is very short. Adieu.

CHAPTER 14

Howard Fields rushed through the air lock of the maximum containment lab. Peeling off his scrub suit, he quickly showered, then threw on his shirt and pants and ran upstairs to the paneled conference room for a meeting with Dr. Doug Chambers, director of CDC, and Senator Horace Healy of the Armed Services Committee.

"Sorry I'm late, sir," he said, trying to catch his breath. His undisciplined gray hair was still wet. The director introduced him, adding, "Dr. Fields came to us from the National Institutes of Health. He is a rare combination of research scientist and field epidemiologist. He solved the riddle of Machupo fever in Bolivia in 1962 but almost died of the disease. We chose him to put together a special unit to study and develop diagnostic tests for some of the most lethal diseases we know about—the hemorrhagic fevers like Machupo, Lassa, and Marburg." He then asked Howard to brief the senator on the situation in the Sudan and Zaire.

"About a month ago, a phone call came through from a German physician at the Institute of Tropical Medicine in Hamburg." Howard summarized the call and added that to date CDC had not been contacted officially by the Germans or anyone else.

He continued. "It wasn't until the end of September that we found out that WHO was involved in the Sudan through the British and Porton Down, their maximum containment lab. We also heard rumors that something similar was breaking out in Zaire. I called Charlie Street—he's an old friend at Porton's in charge of their lab work—and asked him to brief me on developments and send me some specimens. Charlie airmailed some sera he had received from Antwerp but only after I sent him some of our diagnostic reagents.

"Yesterday, Ken Scott, our electronmicroscopist, came to my office sheet-white, and told me that he had just seen a horrible-looking arbovirus under his scope grown out of the stuff Charlie sent from Zaire. He told me it *looked* like Marburg, a real killer African fever. Margaret Leatherford and I checked the virus against Marburg antibody; it is *not* the same."

He took a swallow of water. "Yesterday, we got word from the Pasteur Institute in Paris that serum from a woman who had apparently recovered from the disease in Zaire was on its way. As we speak, Dr. Leatherford is testing this serum against the virus from a Belgian nun who died from the disease. That's why I was a little late for this meeting."

The door into the conference room opened, and Margaret peeked in. She caught Howard's eye and signaled him to come out.

"It's absolutely, unequivocally positive. The virus from the dead nun in Zaire and the convalescent serum light up like a Christmas tree when I put them together under the fluorescent microscope." Margaret's usual British reserve was overridden by her excitement. "The stuff from the Sudan was also positive, but the reaction is weaker," she added.

"God Almighty, it's a new bug," said Howard. "I'll go back in and tell them."

The two senior men looked up as Howard returned to the

conference room. "Dr. Leatherford just told me that the virus is definitely a brand-new bug. It resembles Marburg, so we know how lethal it is. If it's spread like the flu, then the world may be in for Andromeda."

The senator left in a few minutes, with assurances of his assistance, and Chambers put in a call to Claude Guimain in Geneva. He told him that CDC had just proven that the disease was being caused by a new Marburg-like virus and that it was time to get moving. Guimain thanked him politely and replied that they were doing everything possible, but that they were having trouble with the government of Zaire, which did not seem to want others in. Chambers asked Guimain about the Sudan. The Frenchman replied that they were working on a plan. Frustrated, the CDC director said, "I am sending a team to Geneva with all the material they might need. It is up to you to get them in somewhere to help. I do not care whether it is the Sudan or Zaire. Tomorrow you will have my two top people, Aaron Hoffman and Howard Fields; that should tell you how serious we think this is."

While Chambers was talking to Switzerland, Howard called Aaron and briefed him on the latest developments. "I will be going with you. Margaret needs to stay and coordinate the work at the lab. My major effort will be to find convalescent patients, so we can harvest serum with antibodies to treat the sick. Your job will be to see how far this thing has spread and where it comes from."

"Sounds like a worthy challenge," replied Aaron.

Howard and Aaron were in a conference room at the WHO in Geneva. With them around the table were Guimain; his boss, David Cockburne, chief of infectious diseases; a scientist from Porton Down; doctors from South Africa and the Sudan; and a WHO staffer. Howard and

Aaron had just rushed in from the airport. All they had been told so far was that Porton Down had dozens of dead guinea pigs and some negative tests for a few of the known hemorrhagic viruses, and that Antwerp had a photograph from their electronmicroscope of a Marburg-like virus.

Howard reviewed his most recent findings, then asked for a summary of the clinical and epidemiological information from Zaire. The chief of the British Sudan team responded by avoiding his request and launching into a presentation of the organization and aims of his program. The Englishman sat down, and Howard stood.

"Okay. Now what about Zaire? What's going on there?" he asked.

Guimain and the others looked a little embarrassed. "We cannot tell you too much yet." answered Guimain. "I sent Pierre Burine from the Pasteur Institute to Kinshasa four days ago. When you arrive there, you will be working with the representative of the French Medical Aid Mission, Dr. Maréchal, and with Dr. Collard of the Belgian Medical Mission. Of course, our World Health representative, Dr. Adrien, is there. I can't tell you—"

Howard interrupted. "Just a minute, Claude. We have to know the background of this epidemic if we are going there. What measures are being taken? Do they have any idea of how it is spread?"

"Howard, I'm sorry," cut in Guimain testily. "I cannot reveal to you confidential information until the host government has invited you officially."

Howard paced to the board and back to his chair, struggling to keep his cool. "Claude, you know Chambers will get us in. We have only one day for briefing—maps, lists of people involved, and all the rest. Come on, we're on our way to Zaire, and we have to know what we're facing."

Guimain looked at Cockburne, who picked out a paper from the pile in front of him and pushed it across to Aaron.

"This is the private letter from the Lever Brothers' plantations' medical director."

"Thank you," replied Aaron, showing the letter to Howard. "What about the other stuff—maps, clinical descriptions, and the rest of it?"

"Sorry," replied Guimain, lifting his shoulders and hands as all good Frenchman do when they surrender to the inevitable.

"I'm sorry too," snapped Howard.

Guimain pushed back his chair and stepped around the table to the Americans. "You gentlemen must be tired from your trip. Why don't you go to the hotel and rest. We will get together again for dinner."

He arranged for a car. A secretary took the Lever plantation letter from Howard, photocopied it, and brought it back to him. Guimain escorted the CDC men downstairs, asking them news of their families, promising them a relaxing dinner by the lake in a restaurant that specialized in fresh perch and passable Swiss wines.

In the car, Howard slouched in the backseat, exhausted. "They want our necks out there; we have the bug and what they need, and they stick to their bloody bureaucratic rules."

"It'll work out. Chambers will come through. He always has," said Aaron.

In Bongolu, the dawn of October 7 came with the rain, a steady rain that continued after the night storm. The *nganga* sat under the dripping overhang at the entrance to his hut, nursing the embers of a fire. In a black pot, leaves and roots bubbled slowly. As the gruel thickened, it released puffs of pungent steam. The old man was pessimistic about Masangaya's chances of surviving the fever. Sukato lived on, but the *nganga* had known his family and was able to draw on the strength of the young man's dead grandfather, a skillful hunter. By means the old man did not seek to understand, Sukato's vital force had stiffened, and he had lived. The ancestor required the entrails of two goats, but the healer was allowed to eat the meat and even feed some of the broth to his young patient. Nothing was working for the medical assistant: he was unable to retain even a small enema infusion and had vomited the goat broth. During the night, the *nganga* had put himself into a deep trance with his pipe and its sweet, heavy smoke. He demanded that his own ancestors intercede with this stranger's forefathers in the Kasai, who were savannah people and spoke languages unknown in the Budja forest. He received no answer.

The old man took the pot off the fire and placed it in a puddle of rainwater that had formed at his feet. When it cooled sufficiently, he scooped out the glutinous mass and carried it into Masangaya, who was lying naked on a woodslatted cot. The old man molded the poultice around the top of Masangaya's head and sat on his haunches to wait for an effect. By the time the rain had stopped and the sun was reaching its zenith, it was clear that the cataplasm was ineffective. Masangaya fought for breath through an open mouth, his lips pulled away from dry teeth in a grimace of suffering. His spirit would leave the body soon. It would be a lonely passage with no family or friends to console him and lament his leaving.

A heavy mist arose from the ground to meet the scorching sun; hoards of insects swarmed around the dying man and feasted on the thick sweat that covered his body. All day long the healer sat crouched in the corner of the hut, his forehead resting on his knees, listening to the rhythm of the dying man's struggle for air. At times Masangaya's breathing was inaudible, then it resumed and increased in volume, becoming deep with chest-filling inspirations, only to fade again into silence—a silence broken by the croaking of frogs and the drip of water off the roof and trees. From time to time the *nganga* covered the man's sunken eyes with a rag wetted in the rain bucket outside the door. He did not try to clean up the mess from Masangaya's bowels, which had dripped through the slats and lay in a stinking pool, soaking into the dirt floor. The day dragged on as the healer, dozing much of the time, kept his vigil; finally, he struggled to his feet to relieve himself behind the hut.

He looked up. Black clouds were massing again; more rain would keep the track to Bongolu closed. Except for the wind's whisper in the upper boughs and the croaking of his friends, the forest was quiet. He reached for the rough hoe he used to cultivate his plants and stiffly set to work scooping a grave out of the soggy forest floor. By the time he had finished, the first fat raindrops splattered on his thin shoulders and bald head.

After their first night's sleep in forty-eight hours, Howard and Aaron met in the coffee shop off the hotel lobby.

"You've been in Africa before; why is it so hard to get us into Zaire?" asked Howard. "We never had this much trouble in Latin America."

"Could be all sorts of things," replied Aaron. "Maybe Zaire isn't ready to admit that they have a problem which could affect their reputation and their economy. Maybe the Belgians don't want anyone else in their old backyard. But the most likely reason is simple snafus. Things may be a little chaotic. Ministry of Health telephones in Kinshasa may be on the fritz, or papers and telexes could be stuck at the bottom of a functionary's basket at the World Health regional office across the river in Brazzaville. Maybe the clerk with the rubber stamp had to take his mother to the hospital or go sit through a family funeral. Who knows?"

After breakfast the two doctors taxied to the WHO building. In the brisk autumn morning the trees were shedding their leaves, and as they climbed up from the city, they saw a new mantle of snow had covered the mountains on the far side of the lake. They were ushered right into Claude Guimain's office.

"Good morning, gentlemen." Guimain greeted them, all smiles. "I just received a cable confirming your invitation to Zaire."

"Great," replied Howard. "Now we can get down to work."

The meeting was short. The information Guimain reviewed from a folder was meager and spotty. He had no maps. Howard arranged to have their seventeen boxes of material transferred to the midnight Swiss Air flight to Kinshasa, and the two Americans took their leave of Guimain and walked down the hall to the Monkey Pox Office.

Sporadic outbreaks of the disease had occurred in the Bumba area over the last several years; maybe they could spare some maps. Aaron was pleased to find an old colleague, David Anderson, at his desk. Aaron filled him in on why they were there and what they needed. Anderson went to a large file and pulled out maps of Africa, Zaire, and detailed maps of the Equateur Province and the Bumba area. In half an hour the CDC men had a better idea of the territory and people around Bumba. Anderson invited them to his home for dinner, saying that he would get them to the airport in time for their flight.

* * *

Inside the *nganga's* hut, Masangaya's jaw jerked open
with each reflex gasp of air. Then, after a deep sigh, his
breathing ceased; his body shuddered briefly and relaxed.
The old man reached into the dead one's mouth and with
a piece of cloth wiped out the saliva and removed the soft
crusts from the teeth and lips. He balled up the rag and
threw it into the fire, mumbling to Masangaya's spirit,
"When this has burned, nothing of you will remain with the
body."

After the flame subsided, he tied a liane rope around the
dead man's feet and, easing the other end over his shoulder,
pulled the body off the bed, out of the house, and into the
rain and mud. At the grave, he untied the rope and pushed
the body into the hole with his foot. Then he straightened
up, breathing heavily. He curled the rope and dropped it at
his feet. The rain splashed his face and ran down his chest.
Raising his arms above his head, he shouted over the noise
of the storm:

"O bino bankoko, bakolo ba mabele,
Boyebi motu oyo awuti kotika biso.
Alingaki bana ba bino mingi.
Nayebi azali mompaya,
Kasi nasengi bino, bankoko ba ngai,
Bofungolela ye nzela akende na boboto,
O mboka ya bankoko ba ye."

O you ancestors, who possess this land,
You know the man who has just left us.
He loved greatly your children.
I know he is a stranger,
But I request you, my ancestors,

To open the way, so he can go in peace,
To the village of his own ancestors.

He lowered his arms, took up the hoe, and covered the
body with wet earth.

CHAPTER 15

Yambuku, 10 October 1976

Dearest Gabrielle,

I would be frantic if the letter I finished yesterday was already on its way to you; luckily it will not be until Dr. Miatamba leaves. I was very frightened when I wrote it, but now I am almost surely back to normal. After supper last night, I said to Father Dubonnet, "It is my turn now." I told him what I had seen in the toilet. He asked me if the other sisters knew, and when I replied no, he told me to wait three days before saying anything. What a wise man. This morning when I awakened, I was fine. I felt the back of my neck and knew I had no fever. I went to the WC and saw that what I passed was normal. So I sat right there on the toilet thanking God that I was still all right.

This morning we stepped over the cordon and, for the first time, walked to church. Father Dubonnet, who has been saying Mass for the few people still here, told us we should join him and not just sit around brooding or working on the puzzle. A teacher called Jaba, who lost his wife to the disease, sang during the praying. His songs were in Lingala and about death. They would translate something like:

If we die, it is a crossing of a threshold.
As we cross this threshold, we are welcomed by
God, if we have lived well.
If we have not lived well, there is someone else
who awaits.

I know he has suffered, but he was gloomy before all this. So after the service I said to him, "Listen, Jaba, stop singing that way! Heaven knows, there are many happier songs you could sing."

It was right after this that Sukato walked up to us very soberly and announced that Masangaya had died in Bongolu. Again, our spirits were thrown to the ground. What a waste of our best people! I saw Augustina start to cry, but she quickly walked away toward the guest house. Sukato seemed embarrassed, almost humbled. I think he really believed that his *féticheur* would work a cure. I had been so happy after Mass, happy enough to get after Jaba. I was so sure I knew what God wanted from us. The rest of the day I sat at the puzzle but only found two pieces that fit, then helped Augustina cook.

After supper, Dubonnet asked us to pray together for our friend Abia, who had died a few hours earlier. Relief and despair, when will this roller coaster end?

Abia was in his mid-forties, I guess—anyway, one of our older teachers. Two days ago Augustina and I were cleaning out the rats' nests in the supply room when we heard the bell ringing at the cordon sanitaire, and there was Abia, surrounded by children. He looked done in; the children were dazed and caked with mud and clung to him. I quickly fetched a chair and set it on the other side of the cordon. He slumped onto it, and the children lay in the grass. He told us what had happened.

Early on in the epidemic, he had sent his wife and

eight children to their own village. He stayed on here to
help run the primary school. After Amongo, the director
of the school for teachers, and his wife died, Abia took
charge of Amongo's seven healthy children; their ages
ranged from a three-month-old to twins who were about
eleven. With so many people dying, Abia decided to take
the children as well as their teenaged aunt, Bernadette, to
his village. He began by carrying three of them: the
youngest in his arms, one on his shoulders, and the other
wrapped to his back. Bernadette tied a child to her back
and balanced a bundle of extra clothes on her head. The
twins and their nine-year-old brother walked. Abia
stuffed all the money he had in his pocket to bribe their
way through the barriers. They progressed well during
most of the first day, the guards letting them through for
a fee but escorting them with shouts and threats of beat-
ings with long sticks if they strayed from the narrow center of the road through the villages. Abia told us he was
struck and jabbed several times when he stopped to try
to buy food for his charges. A woman did throw a roll
of *chikwangue* into the road for them.

He told us that during the middle of the second day he
sheltered the children under a hedge of coffee bushes
next to the road. They ate a little of the food and drank
from a muddy puddle. Flies tormented them, and rest
was impossible; but they stayed in their shelter until the
worst of the heat passed. Resuming their journey, they
came to Yoputa, where the people would not let them
through, even for all the money Abia had left in his
pocket. It was here that a steady rain began, soaking
through their scanty clothes. So Abia and the children
huddled together through the night. Before dawn they
started back to Yambuku. You would not believe the
children's condition—it was terrible to see them. Some

whimpered with hunger. Augustina sent Antonie after Dr. Miatamba. Our poor Abia—we knew what the hollowness around his eyes might mean. The doctor was able to get him to his feet and supported him as they walked back to his house. Then he returned for the children. Augustina and I loaded a basket with rice and bananas and a few cans of pilchards and walked to Amongo's house with the doctor and the children. We left them in the care of Bernadette. Abia was a good man, faithful, a hero in a way. We prayed for him together. Father Dubonnet said that he was another one of the lucky ones: his suffering was over.

I have been writing to our parents, but not with as much frankness or detail as I have put in letters to you. This evening we were listening to the news from Belgium when the announcer said, "We have a message for Jeanne de Vleck, Sister Veronica, from her mother." And Mother's voice came over the air, very calm: "We are all praying for you. Everything is being done to help. We love you very much." She did not tell me to be careful or ask me to come home.

You will not believe what has been going on. At sunset a couple of days ago the drums in the workers' quarters started to beat. We thought they must be celebrating something or that another of them had died. But the drumming continued past midnight and into the early hours of the dawn. The same thing happened last night: again the drums kept us all awake. Antonie became hysterical with fright. She imagined the blacks were about to attack us because we have not been able to control the epidemic. Augustina and I sat with her until first light when the drums finally stopped, and she dropped off into an exhausted sleep. I asked one of the gardeners what was going on down there; he told me that it was the

mwembu—voodoo man—exorcising the *ndokies* to bring
an end to the epidemic. Augustina asked Dr. Miatamba
to investigate. And I told him to be sure they did not cast
any spells on him. He assured us that his character is
strong enough to withstand that sort of influence. Can
you image—voodoo in a Catholic Mission!

Miatamba walked slowly past the deserted house of the
fathers, past the empty church, which reared up splotchy
white in the glow of the half moon. He followed the path
behind the rows of workers' huts, carefully skirting piles of
putrid rubbish. The drumming grew louder. In a moment
he stood on the dark side of a termite mound and took in
the scene.

A roaring fire, cracking like a whip, shot sparks into the
air, illuminating a dozen men and women dancing around a
giant fig tree. They advanced one foot at a time, waving
their arms wildly toward the tree, their naked torsos and
heads rotating lasciviously to the frenetic, staccato flailing
of a high-pitched drum. Suddenly the drumming stopped;
the dancers collapsed. Then, slowly the beat resumed, and
the people stirred, rhythmically arising to continue the sat-
urnalia toward another frenzy. An animal scream focused
the doctor's attention on a woman who lay on her back,
writhing like a wounded snake; he recognized her as one of
the mission's young teachers. A man with a scrotal basket
and phallus hanging at his groin hovered over the woman
and beat a copper bell with a stick as she dug her heels in
the dust and pushed her glistening body up a path leading
to the house at the end of the row. Wood was thrown on the
fire and in the explosion of sparks, Miatamba saw in the
doorway the gleam of the voodoo man's eyes and teeth
staring at the body slithering toward him. He called out to
her, and she grasped her breasts and rubbed them with

juices from between her legs. In a moment the woman reached the hut, and she was pulled inside and the door slammed shut. The man with the copper bell walked down the hill and selected another initiate from a group of young women huddled together staring, stunned by hashish, into the fire. Miatamba shook his head and turned his back on the spectacle.

Later in the day, the bell beside the cordon rang, and Augustina and Veronica were surprised by the tall thin form of the Protestant pastor of Yahombo. He greeted the sisters effusively, the wide, studied smile of the illuminati splitting his face. A horseshoe of white curly hair framed his glistening black pate. He mopped his face on the shiny lapel of an old black suit coat, and, clasping a Bible to his chest, he intoned, "Thank you, Most Reverend Sisters, for coming out to see me. I bring the greetings of my congregation, who have been praying that the Lord Jesus would look down upon your mission and bring to an end the ravages among your followers." He bowed his head and, with a finger, steadied his gold-rimmed spectacles.

"You are kind to think of us," replied the Mother Superior. "How are the people of Yahombo?"

"We are healthy and thriving, thanks to the Blessed Son, our Savior," replied the pastor, his smile firmly fixed.

"I am glad to hear that," said Augustina.

"And to what do we owe the honor of your visit?" asked Veronica, keeping up the civilities. The cleric pulled at his collar and looked away.

"What can we do for you?" asked Augustina.

"It is what we can do for you, Sister, that brings me here," replied the preacher, holding the Bible before him in both hands.

"You have a missionary doctor that can come and help us?" ventured Veronica.

"No, no. Nothing like that." He paused. "I think it would be better if I spoke with Father Jef Maas. He knows our village."

"Very well. He should be back soon," said Veronica brusquely. "We will tell him of your visit and your request when he returns."

Dubonnet borrowed Veronica's Vespa and went to the Protestant village that evening. An hour after nightfall the sisters heard the *putt-putt* of the scooter as its light bounced off the trees and the walls of the guest house. Ceremoniously, Dubonnet removed his visiting cassock with the death's-head insignia across the chest and stepped into his house cassock.

"Most interesting," he said, as he sat on the terrace step. Veronica brought over a kerosene lantern.

"What did he want? What did he say?"

"Patience is not one of your virtues, Sister. Have you a little something for me to eat? A piece of papaya is all I could get out of the Protestants."

After he had eaten, carefully measured the sugar into his coffee, stirred it, and lit a cigarette, he was ready to tell the sisters about his visit to Yahombo.

"I learned that a week ago a woman dreamed that God was punishing the Catholics. The reasons for our chastisement had not been disclosed to her. However, many believe the woman has insight into these things. I recognized a number of Yambuku people who have moved over there because of her dream. One thing is certain: no one in Yahombo has died of the fever. The pastor told me that a few days ago he had a dream similar to that of the woman but with the clear revelation from God that the Catholics were being punished because they did not know how to worship. He believes that God has charged him to march over here with his flock to enlighten us in prayer, so that the epidemic will cease to exist."

"Of all the nerve," exclaimed Veronica. "I bet that in spite of his plastic dog collar he isn't even ordained."

"Veronica, let the father finish," said Antonie, with more gumption than she had shown since they had been behind the cordon.

"He is ordained in their church. He was trained by the Americans," said Dubonnet.

"That explains his conceit," replied Veronica.

"Sister, Sister." Dubonnet laughed. "He is really a very humble man who wants to help us."

"And what does he propose?" asked Augustina.

"That he and his congregation come tomorrow and hold a service in our church."

12 October 1976
Dear Gabrielle,

I just have time for a quick note. In an hour I must rehearse the choir and congregation. The Protestants are coming over this afternoon to pray (after their fashion) in our church. Then, supposedly, our people will no longer die from the fever. Can you believe that? Although I might not admit it to them, I think we pray to the same God. Dubonnet says that none of them have died. Is it because their converts are more prudish than ours? Who knows? Anyway, they will be here in a couple of hours, and I want to be sure that we are ready to show them that at least we can sing. Even that will be hard enough because several of our drummers and most of the choir are dead.

* * *

What a day this has been, my little sister. People who have not been in church for months came this afternoon. They were curious to see what the Protestants would do. At 2 P.M., the hour set for the confrontation, we Catholics were all assembled. We waited. After half an hour, still no Protestants. We waited an hour. By that time, most of the children were screaming and running around in spite of the scoldings and struggles of the mamas to keep them quiet. Augustina took two of the little ones on her lap, and I retrieved a toddler who was trying to crawl up on the altar. You know how hard it is for children to behave in church, especially in the middle of the day when the whole building is an oven. I was exasperated at the thoughtless delay. Then I saw Father Dubonnet leaning against the front portal—on the lookout. I told the choir to rehearse one more time and walked down the aisle to join him. Still no visitors. He looked at me with that half smile, half frown he wears sometimes.

"Your choir sounds a little puny—a little frail, I would say."

"You would be frail too if you had been through what they have," I snapped at him. Honestly! He can be so annoying. What a time to be critical when we are all doing our best. But he went on.

"You have been through much yourself, Sister, but you are anything but frail," he said and laughed. I was ready to bite his head off, but looking at him I just couldn't help myself; I had to laugh too. I asked if he thought the Protestants might have had second thoughts. He said no, that they had probably taken extra time "to strap on their spiritual armor before challenging the sisters"! Then, off in the distance, we heard singing. In a moment all our people had poured out of the church to stare at a long procession of Protestants, chanting as they waved palm leaves and books over their heads. You would think that after being late they would come straight to the church. But no, they paraded all over the mission, their great cortège winding among the buildings, then circling the church, and finally marching in right through our Catholic faithful, who stood openmouthed. They took over the part of the church nearest the altar; their pastor beamed down on us from behind the lectern. Dubonnet and I watched it all from the doorway.

As soon as the chatter died to whispers and the people had adjusted themselves on the benches for a better view, the preacher led them in the vigorous singing of psalms and hymns. The words were known to all of us, and the melodies were African, so we Catholics joined in, our drummer picking up the beat. For twenty minutes everyone sang and swayed together; the volume rattled the rafters. The singing ended when the preacher raised his Bible before him and waved everyone to their seats. Then he launched into a commentary that lasted well over an hour. Every time he paused for breath or to wipe his face, his Protestants shouted hallelujah and nodded their heads. His preachment, unfortunately for us, was given in a mixture of dialects and languages; the words shot out of his mouth like bullets from a machine gun. Did he even speak from the Bible? There was no way of knowing. Our faithful became restless and some even slept until he brought the whole congregation to their feet for a final thundering rendition of their version of "Onward, Christian Soldiers." Next, he announced that God was now satisfied, and there would be no more epidemic. All the people in the church clapped—Dubonnet loudest of all. Where is his loyalty! He shook hands warmly with the pastor and cheered as we watched him lead his people out of the church and down the road toward their village.

Now we have both the Protestants and the voodoo man using the epidemic for their own ends. I wonder what Father Gérard would have done, God rest his soul.

My prayers are with you. I will end this letter and have it ready for anyone who is heading south in the next few days. Please keep my letters. If I come through and when this is all over, I would like to read them again.

Your own sister and Sister in Christ,
Veronica

CHAPTER 16

Dr. Burine landed in Kinshasa as the sun was coming up over the Bateke Hills on the morning of October 6. Maréchal was at the airport to meet him. After retrieving luggage and supplies and paying off porters and minor officials, Maréchal's driver led them to the car. The two medical men had been friends since the days of French Equatorial Africa with its pith helmets and khaki shorts. After a minute of pleasantries and catching up on family news, Burine lit a cigarette and asked, "Any fresh information from Yambuku?"

"Not much," replied his colleague. "The last message came from our social service volunteers in Lisala. They asked if they would be evacuated like the Americans in the Peace Corps."

"Lisala? I gathered that the epidemic was north of Bumba. Is it spreading?"

"No, it may even be subsiding. The authorities are furious that the Americans hauled out most of the Peace Corps people in the embassy plane without even notifying the locals, let alone getting their permission."

"And ours will stay?"

"Of course. Lisala isn't even in quarantine. What worries us more is the Belgian nun who was flown down here and hospitalized in the Ngaliema Clinic. She died a couple of days after her arrival; that was a week ago. The personnel in the pavilion are in strict quarantine. Soldiers are posted in the hospital grounds to keep people from entering or leaving. But the troops are as terrified as everyone else and would probably run if anyone from the pavilion tried to sneak out during the night. Then the whole city would be threatened."

"And all the whites would head for the airport or cross over to Brazzaville," added Burine.

Maréchal nodded and said, "And the capital would have to be quarantined—a political impossibility." The driver slammed on the brakes while a bus festooned with people swerved to avoid a bicyclist. *"Zoba!"* shouted the driver, as he leaned on the horn and raced past the bus. "Idiot!" He slowed next to the long column of men pedaling to work from the outlying slums. Maréchal continued, "A health department technician told me his minister was fired by Mobutu's office for allowing the sister to be brought to Kinshasa."

"Is it generally known that the infection is, or was, in Kinshasa?" asked Burine.

"Local newspapers have carried reports from the north, but the sister's death has mostly been kept out of the press—although many people know about it, especially the embassies."

"And the embassies' reactions?"

"Ours is wait and see. The Belgians are hammering on the minister's door for more action, and the Americans are wondering if their dependents should be sent home. The AID director, an aggressive mulatto, has ordered cases of condoms. Someone told him that in South Africa an American couple hiking through the country apparently contracted the disease because vervet monkeys lived in the tree under which they were copulating."

"The monkeys or the couple?" asked Burine, laughing.

"Probably both," said Maréchal. "You know how monkeys are."

Burine flicked his cigarette out of the window. "What about the locals?" he asked. "Are there any signs of panic?" They were driving past the factories next to the river docks and the sweet, heavy smell of a palm oil factory stirred Burine's memories of Africa.

"No panic," replied Maréchal. "Yambuku could be on another planet as far as most people in Kinshasa are concerned. The only reaction from the presidency is a determined effort to keep any threat out of the capital or any really bad news out of the press; but there is nothing new in that."

The driver pulled up in front of Maréchal's house, and a watchman swung open the gates. "Take a shower, if you'd like, Pierre. I'll see about coffee," said Maréchal as they walked into the house. "Then we can drop in on the local WHO office for a courtesy call and afterward drive to the clinic."

The meeting at WHO had been polite but unproductive. When they pulled up to the entrance of the Ngaliema Clinic, they found the gates chained shut. The guard and the sergeant in charge were chatting in the gatehouse. They recognized Maréchal, did a phone check with P5, and allowed the car through. Sister Théofila stood waiting for them at the door. Following introductions, she ushered them into her office and offered them seats around her small desk.

"Dr. Maréchal has told me a little about the circumstances of Sister Fermina's death," said Burine. "It must have been a very difficult time for you." Théofila nodded and pulled a chart out of her desk. She reviewed the clinical details and treatments received by her recent patient and handed the record to Burine.

After a moment to scan the pages, Burine said, "Her serum was among those I forwarded to the United States before I left Paris yesterday. We should have a better idea of the nature of the disease soon."

"I hope so," said Théofila. "She died horribly. I have never seen anything like it."

"Before Fermina's death, the other patients under the sister's care were discharged or transferred, and the pavilion personnel have been isolated," added Maréchal.

The nun glanced at Burine, who handed her back the chart. She replaced it carefully in the drawer and, fiddling with paper clips and pencils, said, "All the nurses, the aides, and I have been living in the empty rooms. The convent sends food."

"And none of your team show signs of the fever?" asked Burine. The sister shook her head, then looked up at him, distress and fatigue etched around her eyes.

"I should not actually say, 'all my nurses.' Mayinga, who took care of Sister Fermina, was supposed to return to work yesterday but didn't. She has never done that before."

"You allowed her to leave the pavilion?" exclaimed Maréchal.

"Yes, and I have not slept since." Théofila was close to tears. "I know it was wrong, but she needed to prepare for her trip to the United States. We had used the same precautions we take with hepatitis and typhoid patients, and she talked me into letting her out for a few days." She wiped her eyes. "Mayinga won a scholarship to study advanced nursing and had to pick up an exit visa and go to the American Embassy." Burine and Maréchal stared at her. She looked down at her hands, which were clasped tightly in her lap and added, "Yesterday afternoon, I asked the convent to send a Zairian sister to Mayinga's house. Her family had not seen her. I hope nothing has happened to her."

"Do you think she might be ill?" asked Burine.

"I hope not, but it is possible."

"We have to find her," said Maréchal, standing up.

The doctors took their leave of Sister Théofila. Standing in the doorway of her pavilion, she watched them drive off. She whispered, "Dear God, please let them find her well."

Maréchal told his driver to take them to Mama Yemo Hospital. After pushing their way through the people outside the emergency room, they bullied a clerk into showing them the patient register. Mayinga had been seen two days previously for a high fever, malaise, and abdominal pain. Apparently, after a negative malaria smear, she had been sent to Kintambo, the hospital for infectious diseases.

Twenty minutes later, the doctors, now thoroughly alarmed, were leaning over the outpatient records at Kintambo. Mayinga had not been admitted but sent by taxi to the University Clinic "because she was a nurse." By now it was noon, and everything in the city closed down until 2 P.M.

"We'll go back to FOMECO for lunch—Collard will be there—and then drive out to the campus on the Sacred Hill," said Maréchal.

As they sat down to eat, Collard handed Burine a message he had just received from Professor Thys in Antwerp. It was a week old.

We have tentatively identified the cause of the Yambuku hemorrhagic fever. It may be the first big epidemic of Marburg virus, until now only a lab workers' disease. The Germans have destroyed their old supplies of convalescent serum. A few units with Marburg antibody may still be in South Africa.

"We must call Johannesburg," said Collard.

"Can that be done from here?" asked Burine.

"There are no official channels. But if anyone can contact them, it will be Abirama, the director of the president's office," replied Collard, dialing. "Dr. Collard here. I need to update the director on an urgent situation."

After a moment, Abirama came on the line. "Yes, Doctor, what can I do for you?"

"We have received word that the virus which is killing so many in Yambuku is probably the same one that killed scientists exposed to vervet monkeys in German labs—it's called Marburg. The only supply of Marburg serum seems to be in South Africa. Is it possible to be in touch with Pretoria and ask them to send up what they can spare?"

"For the presidency, nothing is impossible, Doctor," replied the director. "I will call you back." Collard put the telephone down, and it rang immediately. It was Sister Théofila.

"Mayinga just returned. She is very sick."

"Thank God she's back," said Collard. He passed the message to Burine, who rose. "Tell her I'll be right there."

A few minutes later Abirama was back on the line. He told Collard that Dr. M. Sierakowski of the South African Institute of Medical Research in Jo'burg would send whatever they had of convalescent Marburg serum obtained from two survivors of the disease in 1975. Dr. Sarah Suzman, chief of the department of epidemiology, would hand-carry the container to Kinshasa herself. No airline was allowed to bring passengers from Johannesburg to Kinshasa, of course. But he had spoken to a former Zairian foreign minister turned entrepreneur who imported meat from South Africa and operated an aircraft winked at by both governments. Transportation of the serum and the South

African doctor was, therefore, "no problem." The doctor would be met at the airport by presidential protocol.

Sister Théofila handed Burine a gown and gloves and the rest of the protective gear. "Mayinga has all of Fermina's symptoms. Her temperature is a little over forty degrees Celsius, her tongue and throat are covered with ulcers, and she cannot keep anything in her stomach. I have started an IV," she said, as the doctor turned his back to her so she could tie the tabs on the gown. "Everything you need to draw blood is there," she continued, pointing to a tray. "The other syringe has Dolantine in it—her pain is severe." She hesitated, then added, "You know she has been all over town?"

"Yes. We will need to mobilize the authorities. Her contacts must be found and isolated," said Burine, opening the door and walking into the room.

Although it was hot, Mayinga had the sheet pulled up over her shoulder, and her face was pressed into the pillow.

"*Mademoiselle* Mayinga, I'm sorry to see you so ill," said Burine. He put the tray on the bed table. "The sister tells me you are one of her best nurses and that you took care of Sister Fermina." The Zairian nurse acknowledged this with a nod.

"Tell me where you hurt," said the doctor. Mayinga turned her head slightly, then, opening her eyes wide, faced him directly.

"My throat and head . . . Why was I only given an apron when I was with Fermina?" she asked hoarsely.

"Perhaps the gravity of Sister Fermina's illness was not yet appreciated." He touched her lightly on the shoulder. "We will do all we can to help you." He told her about the serum that was on its way from South Africa.

Mayinga turned her head away from him and mumbled, "Just give me something for the pain."

"I have some Dolantine for you. I will inject it into the IV as soon as I have withdrawn a little blood for testing. Have you been given any medicine elsewhere?"

"Nivaquine at Mama Yemo," she replied, and pulled the sheet away from the needle taped to her forearm.

"Were you given anything at the University Clinic?"

"No. I was told they had no beds for infectious diseases and that I should go home."

Burine clamped the IV tubing and wiped off the injection port with alcohol. He reached for the syringe, then pushed the needle through the rubber, pulling out enough blood to fill two test tubes. After releasing the clamp, he slowly injected the Dolantine into Mayinga's vein. In a moment her eyes closed, she sighed deeply, and let go.

The sisters washed down their breakfast of cold rice pudding with extra cups of coffee. Father Dubonnet swallowed his morning eye-opener and wiped his whiskers with the back of his hand. He peered at the bottle of whiskey and shook it.

"Enough for two more days."

"Then what?" asked Veronica, getting up to help Antonie clear the table.

The priest stood and returned the bottle to the sideboard. "Then He will provide."

Antonie gave him his leather bag containing holy water and priestly tools. He looked at her, pursed his lips, and frowned. "Still long faced, Sister?"

"Nightmares keep me awake," she whispered.

"Do not lose hope, Antonie," he said softly but firmly. He put his hand on her head. "You are blessed with a soul of service. Our Holy Mother walks beside you in the dark

tunnel of your fears. She will strengthen your spirit."
Antonie raised a handkerchief to her eyes. "And do not
cry," ordered Dubonnet, lowering his hand. "Only the good
die before their time." He walked out and strapped his bag
to the bicycle. Veronica laughed as she watched him ride
off, head high and beard flowing around his neck. As the
nuns turned back to the table, the bell rang near the cordon
sanitaire. Three *ngangas* from villages near the mission
stood waiting.

The oldest, who had worked with Veronica in her agricultural cooperative, was their spokesman.

"Sisters, we know that you whites do not believe in
ndokies. To you the epidemic is caused by invisible germs,
but for us *ndokies* provoked the tragedy. Although there
have been no new deaths in our villages during the last few
days, we must satisfy the ancestors; otherwise the killings
will start again, and this time everyone will die."

"And what do you want from us?" asked Augustina.

"We do not expect you to participate in the ceremonies.
Your presence would not be well accepted," replied the elder. The others nodded their agreement. "But everyone
must contribute. First money, then a personal possession."

Augustina thought for a moment, then said, "We will
think about your request and give our reply tomorrow."

"Today," said the spokesman, in the direct way of the
Budja. "Preparations are underway to hold the ceremony
tonight."

Veronica cut in. "All right, all right, *tata*. Return this afternoon." The men nodded and left.

Augustina turned on Veronica, her face tight with anger.
"It is not for you to answer them. I must speak to Father
Dubonnet first."

"Dubonnet will have us do what they ask," snapped Veronica. "If you will remember, he believes in exorcising

ndokies himself." She waved her hand impatiently and stomped off.

Antonie followed, pleading to her back. "But, if we give them money, we confirm them in their beliefs," she whined.

"If we *don't* give them money as well as something from each of us and the people die like flies, they will blame us," retorted Veronica, sitting at the table with the jigsaw puzzle. Augustina joined them and stood leaning against the post. After a moment Veronica looked up at her Mother Superior.

"I'm sorry. We've been cooped up together too long. But don't you remember the time Dubonnet reproached Fermina for scolding a Zairian mama who had taken her child to a *nganga*? He said that if the mama was convinced her child would be cured, she was morally bound to act upon her belief."

"Unorthodox, just like Dubonnet," replied Augustina.

"I also remember years ago," continued Veronica, "when Matilda was here as a nurse and she had water on the knee. She treated herself, but nothing worked. A *nganga*, who happened to be in the dispensary, saw her limping and asked if he could help. After examining her knee, he offered to cure it. You were against the idea, but she persuaded you to accompany her after she assured all of us that she would not drink anything he gave her. You saw what happened."

"Yes, I certainly did. He smeared stinking muck on her knee and wrapped it with a filthy strip he ripped off an old undershirt."

"And in a couple of days, you'll recall, the swelling subsided."

"Very well, Veronica," said Augustina. "You always seem to have the last word. It exhausts me to argue with you. We can give them a few zaires, but what do you suggest for personal belongings? We have few possessions of our own."

"We can each contribute one of these," said Veronica, pulling a crumpled hankie out of her pocket. Augustina shrugged a shoulder and walked back to her room. Antonie looked at Veronica's handkerchief then her own. "I will wash and iron them before we hand them over," she said.

Mbunzu sat with Sukato behind the *nganga* of Bongolu. Her husband, Mabalo, had been born in Yalikonde. It was there, only a kilometer from Yambuku, that healers and their acolytes waited for the sun to set. The *nganga* of Yalikonde and the old man of Bongolu sat on stools facing each other in a circle of their juniors. During most of the afternoon, they had presided over a growing heap of old bicycle tires, broken gourds, clothes so torn they defied mending, cracked wooden cups—whatever the people could spare. Latecomers from more distant villages hurried forward to throw their contributions onto the pile, then, approaching the circle with deference, extracted from a pocket or waistband a soggy zaire and dropped the currency into a basket by the feet of the *nganga* of Yalikonde. They sat with the others waiting for the ceremonies to start. A child cried, then suckled. A motorbike coughed its way into the clearing; the son of a chief parked it behind a tree and made the rounds, respectfully greeting his elders. One of the healers began tapping out rhythms on his drum, then stopped to throw a stick at a mangy, skeletal bitch sniffing at the pile of offerings. She scurried away, her rows of swollen tits swinging from side to side. The *nganga* of Bongolu looked up as a flight of black kites screeched on their way to night perches. He spat in the dust between his feet and spoke deliberately.

"Only the appeasement and help of ancestors will ensure the end of this epidemic."

The wisdom he had gleaned through his encounters with Sukato and Masangaya gave authority to his views. Sukato leaned forward to refill his *nganga's* cup with the *sese* Mbunzu had provided for the occasion. The old man swallowed a mouthful of the strong, bitter palm wine, his eyes fixed on what had been added to the mound at the center of the clearing. Tied to a bamboo pole planted in the middle of the sacrificial pyre, three white handkerchiefs fluttered in the evening breeze.

A thin, bespectacled woman was the first to march down the steps pushed up to the door of the unmarked DC-8. She carried a cold box, such as one would take on a picnic, marked Heineken. A protocol officer from the presidency stepped up to meet her.

"You are *la doctoresse* from Johannesburg, Madame Suzman?" he asked. Sarah nodded.

"Please, madame, let me help you," he said, reaching for the box.

"No, no. I must keep it with me," she replied in a clipped, precise South African accent. The officer acquiesced and led her to the VIP lounge. He indicated that she should sit in one of the overstuffed chairs. A willowy Zairian woman glided in with a tray of soft drinks and beer. The officer requested Sarah's passport, and when he had it in hand, informed her that the authorities would hold it "for safekeeping." Sarah objected, but he told her not to worry, the document would be returned when she left the country. Moments later she was escorted out of the lounge to the street where Burine and Collard were waiting. After depositing her suitcase in the trunk, she climbed into the back of the car, placing the Heineken box carefully next to her on the seat.

"That is the fastest I have ever come into any country, especially one that thinks South Africans eat blacks for breakfast," said Sarah.

Collard laughed. "One of the advantages of the friendly chaos that exists in Zaire. Normal procedures don't operate anymore, but if you know the right people, everything is possible."

Traffic was scanty, but the road was in such disrepair that it took them almost an hour to reach the city. During the drive Burine summarized the facts of the epidemic in the north. He outlined the clinical picture of Sister Fermina's death and Mayinga's illness and her movements through Kinshasa.

"Since yesterday, the health authorities are rounding up as many of her primary contacts as they can find and isolating them in Pavilion 2 at the clinic. The fact is the people in this city of one and a half million are at great risk."

"I brought all the Marburg serum we could spare," said Sarah. "I'm afraid it is only enough for four patients with the disease, and as you probably know, we are a long way from developing a vaccine. What evidence points to Marburg?"

Collard told her about Thys's message, and Burine added that they would soon have confirmation from CDC in Atlanta.

Sarah said, "I also stuffed some vials of heparin in my bag to deal with the intravascular clotting, which seems to be the basis of bleeding in these fevers." The doctors discussed the dangers of heparin, the priorities for the patient, and decided to drive directly to Ngaliema.

Burine parked the car in front of Pavilion 5. Sister Théofila led them to her office. She briefed Sarah on

Mayinga's status and answered the doctor's questions. The two women, speaking Flemish and Afrikaans, chatted away like cousins. Sarah reached into the box and pulled out one of the units. She explained to Théofila that the antibodies in the plastic container were probably the only hope they had of saving the Zairian nurse's life.

"Then let us go to her," replied the nun, adding that Mayinga's sister, a student nurse, was watching over her. The heavy boot on Théofila's clubfoot echoed down the tiled hall. The two doctors followed. She paused in front of a closed door.

"This was Sister Fermina's room. I keep the door locked. Before she died she made it clear to all of us that the disease was contagious and deadly. Since then, the cleaners refuse to enter the room, and I am not much good with a mop anymore." She hobbled across the hall to another room. Disposable gowns, hats, and masks were stacked on a table next to a box of rubber gloves. A large white apron hung from an IV stand. She unfolded a gown and held it open for Sarah; Burine also put on the protective gear. Collard said he would wait in the hall with the sister.

When they were ready, Burine knocked and opened the door. A woman walked briskly toward them, her finger held in front of her mask.

"Mayinga sleeps," she whispered. Théofila motioned her out to the hall and closed the door.

"This is Mabia," she said. "Dr. Burine from France, and *la doctoresse* Sarah Suzman from South Africa have come to see your sister." The tall young woman nodded to the doctors. She had on a long apron and rubber gloves.

"I am grateful you are here," she said. "When she is awake she is in agony. She cannot swallow or move in bed because of the pain."

"We will give her more medicine, Mabia," said Burine, as they walked in.

He was shocked to see the change in Mayinga. Her face was swollen, and dark blotches covered her neck and upper chest. Thick, blood-tinged saliva oozed from the side of her mouth. Mabia gently wiped the secretions away with damp gauze which she dropped in a waste bucket next to the bed. She put her hand on her sister's forehead.

"Mayinga, doctors are here to see you. One is from South Africa." Mayinga groaned, blinked open her eyes, and looked up at Sarah. She worked her tongue over cracked lips.

"You are . . . from South Africa?" she asked in English.

"From the Institute of Infectious Diseases in Johannesburg," replied Dr. Suzman. "Where did you learn to speak English?"

"In school. I have scholarship"—she spoke very softly—"for nursing studies in America." A spike of pain distorted her face.

Sarah put the cold box onto a side table and opened it. "Well, in that case, we had better stop talking and get to work."

Burine stepped up to the bed. "Mayinga, we received word from Europe that the cause of the Yambuku epidemic and Sister Fermina's death is the Marburg virus. Dr. Sarah has brought with her serum containing antibodies to the virus. We will give you a unit now." He touched her hand. "Do you understand?"

"Yes."

Sarah added a bag of serum to the hook on the IV stand, pulled down the tubing, and, after removing the needle from its sheath, stuck it into the injection port. She stared up at the drops of straw-colored serum that joined the column of fluid to battle for Mayinga's life. Her faith in a merciful God had vanished in the smoke from Nazi ovens, which had incinerated her Dutch family, but she willed that the treatment would be effective. They all watched silently as the bag of serum emptied.

"Now," said Sarah, "I will start a series of heparin injections to control the bleeding in your tissues."

"Heparin!" Mayinga gasped. "But I am already bleeding; heparin will make me bleed more."

Burine stepped forward again. "We think that your bleeding is caused by the bursting of small vessels plugged with clots: the heparin will help dissolve those clots."

Mayinga shook her head. "No heparin."

"It is all right, my sister," said Mabia. "These doctors know what they are doing."

Sarah pulled back the sheet. "This has to be given under the skin and repeated every six hours."

Mayinga shook her head and tried to cover herself, but the movement increased her pain and she gave up. Sarah injected the anticoagulant into her abdominal wall.

Burine held her hand. "We will give you some more Dolantine so you can sleep. You'll see, Mayinga; tomorrow you will feel better."

She turned her face into the pillow. "I will die like Sister Fermina."

"Nonsense," said Sarah. "I did not come all the way from South Africa to see you die."

In the hall Mabia, trying to control her tears, thanked the doctors again and added, "The regular clinic doctor refuses to enter the room."

"Do not be too hard on him," said Théofila. "He is afraid because he has a wife and children."

The morning sunlight filtered through the palm tree beyond the window, casting zebra-striped shadows that

danced slowly on the wall. Mayinga's heart cried for home
and family and those she loved. She had ordered Mabia to
keep them away, even though their presence would have
been a comfort. Tears blurred her vision. The serum, the
IVs, the heparin meant nothing. The scholarship for which
she had worked so hard meant nothing. She was twenty-
two years old and dying. She wanted her mother.

At the periphery of the large circle of packed earth, the
nganga of Bongolu sat on his haunches, elbows resting on
his knees, head hung forward, moving slightly with each
deep respiration. Sukato let him sleep and dream and the
others—there were eight now—bypassed him as they
handed around a pipe, each drawing in a lungful of its
heavy, rich mixture. A small, smokey fire kept the mosquitoes away now that twilight yielded to darkness. A few
people still hurried forward to throw an offering under the
triple white banner, then joined the growing crowd of villagers sitting in quiet expectation at the edge of the clearing. Three men added armfuls of sticks and bark, then sat
behind the healers. The sacrificial pyre stood ready.

The *nganga* of Bongolu raised his head and opened his
eyes, and, gazing up at the trees, he intoned: "O venerable
ancestors, witness our sacrifices to you. Strengthen us to
withstand the attacks of others, that we may continue to
honor you and increase the force of your descendants."

He stood, and the *nganga* of Yalikonde picked a branch
from the fire, blew embers into flame, and passed it to the
old man. Waving the torch above his head, he walked
slowly around the circle of people, who raised their arms as
he passed and let out a long murmur of approval. Then,
standing before the pyre, he hurled the brand with a shout
of defiance. In a moment flames leapt out and climbed the
stake, engulfing the sisters' handkerchiefs. The *ngangas*

formed a line behind the old man and, beating a tattoo on small drums tied to their waists, wound around the circle, adding the rhythmic stamping of their feet to the roar of the blaze. The cadence quickened as together they charged toward the fire, shouting, then retreating from the heat to charge again and again. Puffs of dust arose from the ground like phalanxes of ghostly warriors awakened by the hammering of feet and drums. Firelight caught the gleam of sweating, straining muscles, swaying and jerking as one, and the crowd, spellbound, joined the column as it weaved around the fire. Suddenly, three apparitions with large wooden heads, white-rimmed hollows for eyes, and jagged teeth carved in mouth slits charged into the circle, shaking rattles and roaring like beasts. The crowd fell back in terror, but the *ngangas* rushed to block the demons from the fire. Screaming and drumming fiercely, they backed the intruders away. The villagers shouted their victory, and the dancing became tumultuous until the fire burned low, the liquor sapped energy, and the people slept where they lay.

The aircraft's rear door swung open, and the blast of hot, humid air hit Howard and Aaron like a sauna. American embassy people were at the foot of the stairs to meet them. Aaron made sure that the cartons of equipment and supplies were properly handled and kept together. Eventually, money passed between hands, and everything was accounted for and loaded onto a truck. In Kinshasa, they were assigned rooms in the embassy guest house and fed breakfast.

At 9 A.M. on Sunday, October 10, they were driven to FOMETRO, where a meeting was already underway, chaired by the minister of health. Thirty people were seated around the table, and more stood behind them. The CDC men were introduced and places vacated for them to the right of the minister. After welcoming them officially to

Zaire, Dr. Tambwe gave a résumé of the epidemic in the north and told them about the nun who had been brought down to Kinshasa. Aaron translated the French for Howard.

"Sounds like they have things pretty well organized," said Howard in an aside to Aaron.

The minister invited Howard to give the gathering his latest information, so referring to his notes, he stood and made the following points.

"Scientifically we are dealing with a new virus—something like Marburg, but a new bug.

"This virus struck simultaneously in south Sudan where, since September, there have been one hundred thirty-seven cases with thirty-nine deaths in the villages of Maridi and Nzara. In northern Zaire the outbreak of the disease, as you know, is in a zone which WHO considers contiguous to south Sudan because the two populations are apparently in contact.

"It would be too much of a coincidence for the epidemic to have started in each area independently. The index case in Sudan has not been identified for the moment and will have to be found.

"If our investigations are to succeed, it is important that all medical personnel in the infected zone avoid contamination, both for their own safety and that of others.

"Right now, the strictest quarantine of suspected or possible cases must be enforced to prevent an extension of the epidemic into the city of Kinshasa.

"At present there is no treatment for those with the disease. But we think that the bleeding associated with the fever is caused by clotting in vessels and that treatment with heparin must be initiated as a priority.

"If we can find convalescents, we should be able to detect the presence of antibodies in their serum. We will do this using indirect immunofluorescence on slides prepared by CDC from cells infected by this new virus.

"We will need a competent team as soon as possible to collect serum from convalescents using plasmapheresis.

"We still do not know how long the virus persists in the blood of the sick, even in the presence of antibodies. It takes two weeks for CDC to detect the virus in a positive serum, but how long the inoculated cellular cultures must be kept before we are sure of a negative result, we cannot say.

"A faster technique might be direct detection of viral antigens from the blood drawn from the sick.

"Facilities must be established in the epidemic zone to allow biological follow-up of the sick, serologic and virologic work, and epidemiologic studies."

Howard looked at the gathering over the top of his glasses; they seemed to be paying attention.

"Where does the virus come from? Even though any virologist would like to know the answer to that question, for now ecological research must be considered a luxury compared to the medical problem. The means at CDC's disposal are not enough to study a large number of specimens taken from rodents, monkeys, insects, etc. The research needed to discover the source must take second place, and the ecological work will be done after completing epidemiological studies."

Howard's eyes swept over those sitting around the table. He continued, "This virus has a great power of transmission from one human to another. We consider it the most serious risk in public health in the last twenty-five years." As he sat down and was stuffing the notes back into his briefcase he added, "So, Mr. Minister and friends, we have our work cut out for us."

Thin, scattered applause came from around the table. Dr.

Tambwe stood up, expressed his gratitude for the report, and addressed the two CDC men. "There is a plane waiting at the airport to take a team up to Bumba."

"That's great," said Aaron. "Who's going?"

"You are," replied the minister. He pointed out that the president and the people of Zaire were expecting prompt action on the disease. A lively discussion followed; it became clear that there was no real plan of action. Thus the immediate flight was postponed, and the official meeting broke up into smaller working groups.

Later Howard and Sarah talked about precautions needed at Ngaliema Clinic. They had met before at a conference on Lassa fever in Atlanta in 1975. Howard went over the details of information that unfortunately proved the Marburg serum Sarah had given the Zairian nurse would have no effect against the new disease.

"That is sad news for Mayinga," said Sarah wistfully. "I hope I have not harmed her." She stood and looked down at Howard. "But now that I'm here—and I am, after all, a clinical virologist—I want to stay. Is that clear?"

"Very clear, Sarah, and very helpful. Maybe you and Burine can get the quarantine straightened out at the clinic while the rest of us work out logistics and administrative details for the trip to Yambuku."

The situation at Ngaliema and the possible spread of the disease into the city was an immediate concern. News reports from Brussels and, that same day, from *The New York Times* had been circulated throughout the city's expatriates. People of all nationalities were frantically contacting the authorities for information about the epidemic and asking whether they should put their families on the next plane, what they should do about their pregnant wives, and whether the schools would be closed.

Sarah returned to Ngaliema to start work on quarantine

procedures, while Aaron and Howard were driven to their quarters where they showered and put on fresh clothes for a working lunch with Drs. Tambwe and Collard.

After the meal, they went over the official documents Tambwe had drafted to set up the international commission to be inaugurated at a 5 P.M. meeting that same day. They confirmed the need for representatives of the commission to fly north as sóon as possible. Drs. Hoffman, Collard, and Burine were chosen for the trip. They would determine whether a laboratory and treatment center were practical possibilities and draw blood from any convalescing patients they might find.

Later that day in his embassy office, Collard tried to enlist one of the Belgian public health doctors to accompany him to Yambuku. After the lengthy briefing, the doctor turned pale and stood to take his leave. "Really, Alain, you must be joking."

CHAPTER 17

Dinner over, Augustina led the way out to the terrace. The meal in the refectory was a happy one, with exchanges of information between the doctors and the nuns. Burine had contributed money to buy meat, and the tender flesh of a young goat, rice, and *pondu* had been washed down by two bottles of communion wine provided by Father Dubonnet. Now they all sat on the terrace around a table dimly lit by a single bulb hanging from the ceiling. No one spoke for a while. It was as if the first rush of meeting, the excitement and tears, had drained them of words. The shrill of mosquitoes accentuated the silent darkness. Aaron looked at the three exhausted nuns and shaggy, comfortable priest and pulled a bottle of Johnnie Walker from his briefcase and held it up; Veronica went for glasses. As the whiskey was being served, Collard excused himself and hurried off in the direction of the guest house. In a moment he returned carrying a ball of gauze. Grabbing a glass, he raised it and toasted the end of the sisters' isolation. He put a match to the bandage that had been the cordon sanitaire and threw it into the dirt beyond the terrace. Veronica applauded, Antonie stood with tears rolling down her cheeks, and Augustina bowed her head in prayer.

Later Aaron lay on his back listening to the snores of his colleagues reverberating in the long room. The trip up had been a magnificent adventure; their reception in Bumba was friendly, catalyzed by the bag of money Collard had dumped on the *commissaire's* desk. When Aaron had questioned the wisdom of bribery, Collard had replied that cooperation required compensation, adding that Belgium had been corrupting the country for decades.

Plans for the day were finalized at breakfast. Collard and Miatamba in the FOMETRO Land Rover were to cover the communities along the northern road to Abumombazi; Burine, with Sukato to interpret, would be driven west by Luc. Aaron and Veronica would head east on the Vespa. They had only three days to gather what preliminary information they could about the epidemic; the definitive work would be done when the big team arrived from Kinshasa. Aaron outlined the methodology of epidemiological surveillance as he would to medical students. Referring to notes he had made flying across the Atlantic, he listed questions to be asked and proposed a form on which the answers be tabulated.

"All good suggestions, *confrère*," said Burine, lighting a cigarette to hide his irritation. *Les Americains,* he thought, *si didactique.* He stood. "Now we go to work. Yes?"

Aaron and Veronica helped load the Jeeps with water, sandwiches, and medical supplies. Collard put in bottles of vitamins and nivaquine.

"What are those for?" asked Aaron.

"Pills are like currency in most of the villages."

"Should I follow your custom of paying off the chiefs?"

"Not necessarily. But they might welcome a few cigarettes."

Veronica and Aaron waved as the two vehicles drove off.

"Now us," she announced. Aaron looked skeptically at the red motor scooter. Veronica tied the box of medical gear to the rack in front of the handlebars and stuffed a water bottle and food under their paper gowns. She climbed on and wedged Aaron's briefcase between her legs and the seat, then kicked the Vespa into life. Still without a muffler, the little machine roared like a racing bike.

"Hop on," she shouted, tucking her gray skirt under her thighs. Aaron looked at the few inches of seat left for him, and his doubts increased.

"I don't think it'll work," he yelled.

Father Dubonnet rode up on his bicycle and dismounted to watch from the steps of the terrace with the other sisters. Augustina raised her hand like a *gendarme* halting traffic. Veronica throttled down.

"Use Matilda's Jeep," ordered the Mother Superior.

"It is *kaput*," shouted Veronica, running a finger across her neck. Aaron straddled the back of the seat and, unsure of where to put his hands, hooked his thumbs in his belt. Veronica gunned the engine, and the scooter lurched forward. Aaron toppled off and lay on his back in the dust. Dubonnet guffawed and clapped his hands. "Like *les cowboys du far West cinéma!*" Veronica, a good fifty yards away, slammed on the brakes and looked over her shoulder. Antonie laughed for the first time in weeks but quickly covered her mouth. Augustina ran down the steps to Aaron as he struggled to his feet.

"Are you all right?" she asked.

"Of course," replied Aaron, brushing himself off. Veronica returned and wheeled up next to him.

"This time, put your arms around my waist and hold on," she directed. Aaron swung a leg over the saddle again and gingerly clasped his hands around the nun's waist. He turned his toes in, resting them next to her feet.

"Now hang on," she commanded. He tightened his grip, and they took off slowly and with more dignity. Augustina, for a second, tried to look severe, then laughed and hugged Antonie. Dubonnet pedaled off, swinging his bike from side to side to the rhythm of a Flemish ballad which he sang raucously and off key.

Once on the road to Yandongi, Veronica twisted the throttle as far as it would go. Aaron leaned against her back and felt her softness in his arms. As the little machine hit its stride, Veronica's veil blew into his face. He cocked his head to the side and let it flow past him. The wind in his hair and the exhilaration of racing down a dirt road glued to a nun struck him with force, and he yelled, *"Formidable! Formidable!"* Veronica nodded and slowed as they reached the tunnel through the bamboo that led to Yandongi.

This was the first time since the epidemic that Veronica had left the mission, and as they approached the barrier of the first village, the guard recognized her, jumped up, and snatched away the pole across the road. He saluted as she rode by. Laughing and clapping their hands, children and women poured out of their huts and followed the Vespa to the center of the village; Veronica and Aaron climbed off. Some of the children stared at Aaron and shook hands shyly when he stooped down to greet them. Others crowded around Veronica with their potbellies pushed out until she greeted them with a pat on the head and a *"Mwana kitoko"*—good child. Mothers with infants on their backs and a machete or a leaf-wrapped "sausage" of food balanced on their heads crowded around Veronica, gesticulating as they chattered away. They spoke without shyness, slapping their thighs or nodding with grunts of *"iyo"*—all jabbering at the same time. Aaron watched Veronica as she laughed with the women or scolded them and saw that they loved her. Suddenly the women stopped talking. Veronica looked at one of them and shook her head. "She would not leave like that," she said.

The woman answered, "We did not think she would, but we hoped that reports of her death were wrong." Veronica stepped away from the group and turned her back to them, and cried. Aaron went to her.

"They asked me if it was true that Sister Lucie was dead, or whether she had left them without saying good-bye and returned to Belgium." She looked up at Aaron and saw the question on his face.

"Lucie was the first nun killed by the fever," she said brusquely, wiping her eyes, then added more gently, "I'm sorry, I thought you knew. She was my closest friend—like a real sister, and these women loved her."

They were led into the shade of a thatched roof supported by poles under which the elders were sitting on stools or carved V-shaped chairs. Veronica introduced the doctor, and he was received with restraint as he walked around to shake hands. A ring of children, quiet in the presence of their fathers, stood goggle-eyed, fingers in their mouths. Thin dogs with tails curled tightly over their backs sniffed and scratched. The hot smell of red earth, whiffs of wood smoke, and ripe vegetation were as Aaron had remembered them in his dreams of the African interior: he felt at home. From a gourd, the chief poured pale liquid into a small tin tumbler which looked like a measuring cup, and passed it to Veronica. She held it up toward Aaron.

"*Lotoko*. It will light a fire in your throat and burn all the way down to your stomach. Father Dubonnet drinks it to prevent disease when he is on his village rounds." She sipped and passed the drink to Aaron, who followed her example and handed back the mug.

"I see what you mean," he said, sucking air in and out of his mouth to cool his tongue.

The ritual over, Veronica launched into the reasons for their visit, then told Aaron to speak. He outlined the information he needed, and she translated, freely adding her own comments and questions.

The chiefs had a list of the people who had been sick and who had died. It was difficult and sometimes impossible to be certain that death had come from the Yambuku fever; many other diseases killed the forest people. But when fever, bleeding from the gut, headaches, and body pains came together and lasted a week or less, Aaron had to assume that a hemorrhagic fever was the cause of death. He listed the information on the form he carried on his clipboard. All this took a good bit of time, but Veronica was in her element, focusing on the task at hand, aware that Aaron was watching her with clear admiration. When she posed the question of whether anyone was currently sick, the meeting broke up, and they were shown houses at the edge of the village where people lay ill. Veronica walked back to the Vespa and rode it down to the huts. From the box on the front rack she pulled out what Aaron would need. He stripped down to his underpants. She helped him into the gown and handed him the rest of the gear, item by item. The villagers watched and whispered from a safe distance, wondering what sort of magic ceremony was about to happen. Children peeked around their mothers' long skirts. Aaron felt a little silly and terribly hot. Sterile procedures were a pain. He had never been at home in a laboratory or operating room. Again, with Veronica translating, he walked up to the first man, who sat slumped over on a stool. He started down his list of questions.

"How long have you been sick?"

"Mikolo minso," was the reply.

"Forever," interpreted Veronica.

"Do you have fever?" The man was sweating but less than Aaron, who felt the patient's cool forehead with his gloved hand.

"Iyo," with a nod.

"Do you hurt?"

"Iyo."

"Where?"

"Nyonso." He waved a hand over his body from head to toes.

"Diarrhea?"

"Iyo."

"Vomiting?"

"Iyo."

"Blood?"

"Iyo."

Aaron documented the responses carefully on his form and moved over to the second patient, a woman resting on a log next to an unlit cooking fire. She also answered affirmatively to all his questions. He paused and turned to Veronica, who was trying to hide her amusement.

"They've learned that a negative answer will deny them treatment," she said. Aaron looked down at his questionnaire: its value took a nosedive.

"But we have no treatment to offer them," he said.

"I know that," Veronica replied. "But they will be satisfied if we give them pills in exchange for their blood."

The sick wanted injections rather than pills, and a long palaver ensued. Veronica handed out nivaquine and vitamins to the patients' families and the elders in attendance, before permission to draw blood was obtained.

The routine was repeated at a second hut. Then the doctor and the sister approached the last two patients, a man and a woman stretched out on mats under a lean-to extending from the thatch roof. They lay in foul-smelling, black stool. Aaron backed out of range of the flies and, for the first time, fear grabbed his belly. He looked over his shoulder and saw Veronica pulling a gown over her blouse and skirt and stuffing her veil under the elastic of a blue paper hat. They walked over to the patients together and saw their glassy, fixed eyes and the bubbles of fresh blood on their lips.

Aaron turned to Veronica. "This is the sort of gaunt, absent look of terminal disease described in Siegert's book *Marburg Virus*, I read on the plane from Kinshasa."

"It is the look of the fever," said Veronica. She leaned forward and addressed the couple. "The doctor must take blood from your arm, then—"

Aaron held up his hand. "They can't hear you; they're too far gone." He knelt down and quickly applied a tourniquet to the woman's arm. As he pulled back on the plunger and blood spurted into the barrel, a gurgle came from the man's throat. He coughed red foam and died. Aaron removed the tourniquet, emptied the blood into a vacuum tube, and backed away. He and Veronica stood staring at the couple on the ground. The woman groaned and gasped for air; a trickle of blood oozed from the needle hole in her arm. The man lay still; flies explored his nostrils and open mouth.

"There is nothing we can do," said Aaron. They turned and walked back to the Vespa. Aaron dropped the test tube into one plastic bag and the syringe into another. They stripped off the gowns and threw them on the ground with the gloves and masks. Aaron quickly pulled on his pants and shirt, then looked at Veronica. Her shoulders and neckline showed through her sweat-soaked blouse as she straightened her veil on her head. He struck a wooden match and dropped it on the pile of protective clothes. He stepped away from the smoke and felt light-headed.

"Would I have been blamed if the woman had died while I was drawing her blood?"

"Yes," replied Veronica. "Of course."

* * *

Over the evening meal, the doctors and nuns reported on their day's work. Aaron and Veronica had visited five more villages and found only two more sick people; both were feverish but had no other symptoms. Burine and Sukato brought in blood samples from a dozen people in ten villages. Collard and Miatamba had covered twelve villages and found only three sick. The other doctors handed their data to Aaron, happy to have him gather all the bits and pieces and enter them onto his form.

After dinner they moved to the terrace and planned for the following day. Aaron asked the sisters if Mbunzu was still at the mission, saying that Howard considered it important for them to confirm the level of antibodies in both her and Sukato.

Sukato had already willingly given blood, he reported, adding that he had even offered to escort them to Bongolu to meet the *nganga*.

"Mbunzu left the mission after her parents and child died," replied Veronica. "She is in her uncle's village taking care of his children."

"How far is that?"

"About eighty kilometers on the road to Yalosemba. We can go there in the morning."

"On the Vespa?" asked Aaron.

"No," cut in Augustina. "I had one of the mechanics check Sister Matilda's jeep. It is fueled and ready for you."

"If you came with us we could move through the villages faster," said Veronica, turning to Miat.

"Fine. I would like to see Mbunzu again," he replied.

Collard and Burine were studying a local map. "We will pick up where you left off and continue east," said Collard to Aaron.

"Could you inquire in—" Aaron checked his notes

"—Ya ... mon ... zua, the village where the couple were dying, and make sure they buried the bodies right away?"

"Yamonzua?" Burine found it on the map. "Thirteen kilometers from here. Of course; no problem." He turned to Collard. "Do we have plenty of gowns and gloves?"

"Yes. Now, the preservation of the samples—"

Augustina interrupted, "Maybe other details can be worked out in the morning." She looked at her watch. "The generator will be turned off in half an hour."

At three in the morning, Veronica, in a long white nightshirt, banged on the door of the girls' dormitory and called to Collard. "A man just brought his wife to the convent in a handcart. She has been in labor for two days and looks terrible—she may even have the fever." Collard came to the door in his shorts, rubbing his eyes. "Her husband says the village midwife sent them because the baby's head is blocked and cannot come out," added Veronica.

"Head blocked?" repeated the doctor, shivering in the early morning cool.

Veronica nodded. "You'd better get some clothes on before you catch cold."

"I'll be right there," he said, closing the door. He dressed in the dark, then walked across the road to wake up Miat. They covered the options. With the operating room and delivery room still contaminated and anesthesia a problem, Collard ruled out a cesarean.

"I had to do one under local when I first came, but I used up most of the Xylocaine," said Miat.

They walked to the convent. Augustina was waiting for them at the foot of the steps with a lantern.

"Where's Veronica?" asked Collard.

"I sent her back to bed," said the Mother Superior, holding up the lamp.

A man sat staring at a thin woman lying jackknifed on her back in a small handcart. Her legs hung over the side. She was moaning. Her eyeballs were rolled up, the whites visible in the dim light. Collard pulled away the cloth covering her thighs and saw the bulging between the woman's legs.

"We will have to do a Zarat."

"What is that?" asked Miat.

"It is a procedure I learned from a missionary doctor in the early sixties. You split the pubic bone, and the pelvis spreads and allows more room for the delivery."

"I was never taught that," said Miat.

"Of course not—much too simple and effective to be taught by a university professor, but I can tell you that it really works and is sometimes less traumatic than a cesarean."

Veronica reappeared, dressed. "Couldn't sleep," she said to Augustina.

Collard turned to Miat. "Get what local anesthetic we have left, some Dolantine from the dispensary, and a sharp scalpel." To Augustina and Veronica he said, "We need gowns and gloves and towels for the baby—a little more light would help, too." He put his hand on the man's shoulder. "Help me carry her up the steps to the table."

Ten minutes later, the woman was laid out. Miat and Collard were in gowns and masks. Augustina and Veronica stood holding a lantern in each hand. Antonie, who had joined them, was ready with linen for the baby. Miat squeezed the woman's upper arm in his gloved hands, and Collard slipped a needle in a vein bulging in her elbow crease and injected a syringeful of Dolantine.

"Quickly now. We don't have much time." Collard pushed two fingers under the woman's symphysis pubis, and his thumb found the midline of the bone in the pubic hair. He infiltrated Xylocaine under the skin. The woman cried out and moved, but Miat held her firmly to the table and handed Collard a scalpel. He incised the skin, and, after locating the junction of the two pubic rami that formed the arch of the pelvis, he curled a finger around the bone, laid the blade on the cartilage and applied pressure. The woman moaned again, but the Dolantine seemed to be working. Sweat ran down Collard's forehead and he shook it off; Veronica turned her head away from the scene but held the lamps steady. Antonie took over for Augustina, who sat on a chair and put her head between her knees. Collard, using his thumbs for added pressure, pressed the knife deeper into the cartilage. Suddenly there was a pop and the arch spread. Collard quickly worked the infant's arm back into the birth canal and, with Miat pushing on the uterus, a baby boy was delivered. Collard turned him upside down, cleared mucus from his mouth, and then slapped him on the back. Still, the baby did not breathe and looked dead.

Collard pulled down his mask and, covering the infant's nose and mouth with his own, blew into the tiny lungs, then compressed the chest. After several cycles, the newborn coughed and sputtered and sucked in air on his own. Collard passed him to Antonie.

"Well done," said Miat, delivering the placenta. "The Dolantine must have suppressed his respiratory center."

Veronica held a lamp in front of Collard's face and exclaimed, "Doctor, you have blood all over your mouth!"

"Oh, my God," he said. *"Quel idiot!"* He looked at his bloody gloves and the blood all over his gown and shoes. He stripped off his gloves and gown. His work as a doctor, the traditions lived out and left to him by his father, his professional ego—all had taken a beating when he had buried the couple he had ordered abandoned in Bumba. The reflex of pulling down his mask to blow air into an apneic infant proved that his professional instincts were back in control.

Veronica handed him a towel. "What can we do, Doctor?"

"There is nothing anyone can do," he replied. "The coin has been tossed. Either I will get the fever or I will not."

Early the next morning Miatamba, Veronica, and Aaron set out in search of Mbunzu. Vero, who was easily carsick, sat in the front seat with the window down. Along the way they did rapid surveys in the villages. Miat examined a dozen sick and took samples of their blood. Sometimes he wore all the gear, other times just gloves. Veronica dispensed nivaquine and vitamins like cowrie shells or currency, and Aaron recorded information. Miat kept things moving.

Eventually, they arrived at the village of Mbunzu's uncle and were directed to his hut. Mbunzu was splashing water from a basin onto a robust little boy, holding him by the arm as he kicked his feet and screamed. As soon as she saw Veronica she plunked the infant down on a towel and ran to her; they hugged. Her uncle was a big man in a clean white shirt and khaki pants. He recognized Miat and shook hands with Aaron, but was clearly suspicious. He called out to Mbunzu, who ran into the house and returned carrying a chair and two stools. The men sat as she pulled a T-shirt over the baby's head and joined them with the child on her lap. Two older children appeared, shook hands, then stood behind Mbunzu. In the middle of the discussion, Mbunzu suddenly stood, and yelled, *"Te! Makila te. Tonga te,"* and rushed into the house with the baby. The uncle shouted and stood blocking the entrance. Veronica interpreted what was going on for Aaron.

"Dr. Miat told them you wanted more of her blood, and

you saw what happened. She has a horror of needles, and I cannot say I blame her, after all she has been through." Veronica turned to the uncle and spoke in rapid, staccato Lingala.

Miat translated quietly for Aaron. "She is telling him that all the people who were sick and did not die could become sick again and that we need her blood to give her the right medicine." Aaron started to object to the lie, but Miat shook his head to silence him, explaining that all of Mbunzu's family, including her child, had perished during the epidemic. Her uncle's wife had also died, and now she was the mother to his small ones. She wanted to take them back to the mission school but had no money, and the uncle wanted her to stay.

Mbunzu appeared in the doorway with the infant balanced on her hip. Miat had a quick word with Veronica, then stepped over to the uncle. The men walked to the end of the yard. Veronica leaned toward Aaron. "Dr. Miat is negotiating the price for her uncle to allow Mbunzu to return to the mission for a visit. Once she is there, we can do what is necessary about her blood."

During the drive back to Yambuku, Miat announced that Mbunzu would be permitted to visit Yambuku if the uncle received two sacks of rice, a goat, and batteries for his transistor radio. He thought the batteries might be a problem: they were in short supply.

Collard and Burine returned to the mission less than an hour after the others. Aaron and Collard decided to quickly inspect the hospital before darkness. They dressed in protective gear, including the antiviral "gas masks," and Aaron carried his camera. Collard was feeling fine and made light of his possible exposure to the fever the night before.

In the delivery room, large splotches of blood and feces on the floor and on the table had long since been sucked dry; only a few heavy flies still buzzed noisily in the small airless room. The stench was overwhelming, and Collard opened a window as Aaron aimed his camera at a Mayo stand, focusing on a blood-caked vaginal speculum and one of those medieval sharp-pronged cervical clamps. A fly rose from the metal tray and landed on the lens.

CHAPTER 18

Aaron soaped his head and body for the third time, then pulled the chain on the brass shower head. He rinsed off in tepid water that sprayed out from a drum sitting on the roof beams. The fresh smells of soap and wet bricks were a comfort after a day in the villages. He scrubbed and scratched the sand fly bites that covered his lower legs above the sock line. What diseases did they or that obscene, glutted bluebottle carry? he wondered as he toweled off. Leishmaniasis, kala-azar, relapsing fever, ran through his mind.

Back in the dormitory he sat on his bed, took out a Wipette left over from the flight from Switzerland, and carefully cleaned his camera. He could not reach every little cleft and groove on the lens piece. A virus had to be in living cells to survive, and flies carried all sorts of filth, living and dead, on their legs. The convent bell rang for supper; he slipped into a fresh shirt and khaki pants, resolving not to let his imagination run wild.

The dinner was quiet; even Veronica said little as she bustled around making sure the doctors had enough to eat.

"When do you think the others will come up here?" asked Miatamba.

"As soon as Howard can organize the move and get the supplies for plasmapheresis," replied Aaron. He turned to the sisters. "We withdraw whole blood from a person who we think may have antibodies, then we separate the serum from the cells, and reinject the cells into the donor. Teams will have to survey every village in the zone to find the few people who have recovered and, at the same time, establish that the epidemic has burnt itself out. And, of course, we will want to try to reconstruct the details of what happened; most epidemiological fact-finding is done after the event."

"Are all of you leaving in the morning?" asked Augustina.

Collard answered. "The specimens must be repacked and sent off as soon as possible, and I have my other jobs with the embassy and the Presidential Medical Services waiting for me."

"I fly back to Paris in two days," said Burine.

"What about you, Dr. Miat?" asked Veronica.

"I can stay another day or so, then I should return to my responsibilities in Lisala," he replied.

"That leaves you," said Veronica, leaning over Aaron's shoulder to pour coffee into his cup.

"Howard Fields expects me in Kinshasa tomorrow," he replied.

"For what?"

"To report on our findings and help him plan, I suppose."

During a lull in the conversation that followed, they heard the wind gusting in the trees; a window slammed in the kitchen.

"Do you think we could move back to our rooms in the convent?" asked Augustina.

"If they are scrubbed and disinfected with *eau de Javel* or Lysol," replied Burine. "The same applies to the hospital buildings." The other doctors nodded their agreement. Another blast of wind carried dust into the room. Augustina closed the window and suggested that the doctors retire to the dormitory before the storm hit.

Aaron, Burine, and Collard lay on their backs, mulling over their experiences of the last few days as the lights dimmed and went out.

"What do you think about the situation here, Burine?" asked Aaron, turning toward the Frenchman's indistinct form under the mosquito netting.

"It seems clear that the epidemic came from the hospital and that it will be over when the last poor souls who fled to their villages are buried."

"And you, Collard?"

"I agree with Burine. The main question the authorities will want answered is whether the zone is safe and free of disease. Your surveys will determine that. I think my work is finished here."

"What about the sisters?" asked Aaron.

Collard yawned and stretched. "The sisters? What about them?"

"They seem depressed at being left alone again," replied Aaron.

"They did seem a little subdued at supper, but maybe they are just tired," said Burine.

"I wouldn't worry about them," said Collard. "The sisters are a tough breed."

"Still, they concern me," persisted Aaron. "And I'm curious to know what goes on in those women. Antonie seems almost like a recluse. Augustina is stoic and solid—"

"Like a rock," added Burine.

"And Veronica?" asked Aaron.

"Ah," replied the Frenchman. "There is a woman."

Collard sat up in bed. "Before you become too poetic, let me tell you that it is impossible to see into the heart of a

Flemish nun. I was brought up by them. Just when you think you know what they're thinking, and how to get around them, they wallop you with a ruler."

They laughed. Then, after a moment, Burine propped himself up on an elbow. "Why don't you stay, Aaron? I'll tell Howard you are needed here."

"I was thinking the same thing," replied the American. "I'll sleep on it." They said good night. Putting his hands behind his head, Aaron looked through the window. Lightning streaked across the sky, and the wind whipped the fronds of a palm tree. Deep thunder rumbled close enough to vibrate his cot. He turned on his side and covered his head with the wafer-thin pillow, but flashes reached through his eyelids. Rain, driven by gusts, beat against the windows and shook the door on its hinges. Stifling under the pillow and coarse sheet, Aaron threw them off and sat on the edge of the bed. The next thunderbolt lit up a crucifix over the door, its image remaining in relief as he lay down again and closed his eyes. A Jew trying to sleep in a Catholic mission lying on a cot in a girls' dormitory.

He thought about Veronica. . . . Although she had cried when the village women asked about Lucie, she seemed the most resilient of the nuns. He was impressed by her energy, by the way she tackled work and the way she moved. She did not fit his picture of a Catholic nun—acquiescent, eyes to the ground, hands folded into the long, loose sleeves of their gowns, gliding down cloistered halls to kneel in silent prayer. Veronica would have made a hell of a wife, unless crossed. Rachel had some of the same traits in her makeup. Her strength came from ambition, Veronica's from . . . He rolled over on his side again. The storm had passed, and the night was silent except for the drips off the roof and the snores of the others. He closed his eyes and saw Veronica pinning her veil back on, the curves of her neck and shoulders showing through her damp blouse.

The next morning, as the men were dressing, Aaron announced his decision to stay. He would include a note to Howard with their data and write a letter to Rachel which Burine could mail from Paris. As the doctors walked over to the convent for breakfast, Aaron asked, "What if they want you quarantined in Kinshasa?"

"I'll be on my way to Paris before they can make up their minds," said Burine with a chuckle.

Collard waved the question aside. "After delivering the specimens, I will be lost in the well-guarded bowels of the Belgian Embassy."

As soon as Burine and Collard left for Bumba, Augustina assembled the half-dozen workers and gardeners who had continued to perform their regular duties throughout the epidemic. She organized them into two cleaning parties and with Veronica's help dressed them in paper gowns and hats and tied masks across their faces. Fingers were coaxed into rubber gloves, and soapy water and Lysol handed out. The men chattered nervously and stood like mannequins in *mindele* costumes which covered their khaki shorts and aprons. Augustina, herself dressed in blue, led two men into the convent to scrub down and disinfect the nuns' rooms and chapel. Miat volunteered to supervise the rites of purification in the operating and delivery rooms and in the wards. Tucking his gear under his arm, he led his squad to the hospital. Veronica and Aaron swept and tidied the guest house, made up Aaron's bed in the room next to Dubonnet's, and carried the table with the jigsaw puzzle back to the convent. At midmorning the work parties came together around a small bonfire which was consuming the protective clothes. After lunch, Miat walked to the dispensary with

Aaron and saw a handful of patients Sukato had kept over for him. He reviewed the dispensary routines with Aaron and the nurse.

"I'll do my best," said Aaron, "but I have been away from patient care too long to be of any real help."

"Don't worry," Miat assured him. "There is very little that Sukato cannot handle."

"What about surgery?"

"I'll return in a week or ten days. Hang on to the patients that need elective operations. For emergencies, apply Article 15."

"What's that?"

"Work it out as best you can; there's a surgical atlas next to the sterilizer," replied Miat with a smile. "Cookbook surgery, I think you Americans call it." They laughed—Aaron nervously.

Luc had washed and fueled Miat's Land Rover. He helped the doctor with his bags as Dubonnet joined them to say good-bye. Everyone shook hands and a moment later the vehicle disappeared around the corner. Aaron and the priest followed the sisters back into the convent and sat at the refectory table.

"I will warm up coffee, then we can plan for the next few days," said Augustina, heading for the kitchen.

Veronica opened a cabinet under the sideboard and pulled out an old Victrola, wound it up, and selected a record from a well-worn album. Dubonnet tipped his chair back, pulled a dark cheroot from his pocket, lit it, and blew a thick pungent cloud across the table. Antonie coughed and waved the smoke away from her face. The needle scratched out the strains of Strauss's "Voices of Spring," and Veronica, resting her hands lightly on the sideboard, let her feet move in time to the music. Then, as the melody soared, she turned and, with her body and skirt swaying,

waltzed around the table, oblivious of Antonie's openmouthed amazement and Aaron's smile. Augustina paused
in the doorway, frowning. Veronica twirled onto a chair in
front of Aaron, and they laughed. The priest blew a smoke
ring toward the bulb in the ceiling as the Mother Superior
carried the coffeepot to the sideboard and stood staring at
the Victrola. The tone arm head rode the bumps in the
warped disk as it made its way toward the clear ring at the
center. Augustina stood with her back to them, closed her
eyes tight, and leaned against the sideboard for support. She
heard laughter again but did not stop the music.

Aaron was awakened before sunrise by the sisters chanting their prayers. Folding the pillow behind his head, he lay
back, surrounded by the pale, amorphous cocoon of mosquito netting. Veronica's voice rose above the others in
strong, pure tones. He pictured her kneeling, her back
straight and strong. He covered his nakedness with a corner
of the sheet. A vehicle chugged down the road behind the
mission. Men called out to each other as they met, and in
the distance he heard Zairians singing to a drumbeat. Sitting
up, he pushed away the netting and dressed. Once outside,
he leaned against a brick post, watching the faint glow in
the eastern sky, a prelude before the sun colored the grays
of dawn. Pure, undusty air carried the fragrance of flowers
whose shape and color hid close to the earth. He walked
slowly toward the church. The singing grew louder, a
rhythmic, unrepressed melody working with the drums. He
stepped inside; the place was packed. People standing in
the back welcomed him shyly and made room for him
along the wall. He squeezed in between a man and a
woman, feeling the heat and firmness of their shoulders.

In the candlelight, dark wood beams cast dancing shadows on the peaked roof. On either side of the altar, a tall

man stood at attention. Each held a spear at his side and wore a leopard-skin robe draped across one shoulder like a Roman toga. The chorus was grouped in front of the congregation to the right of the nave. The men occupied the first two benches. Behind them, the women, many with infants on their backs, swayed and clapped to the sound of the drums. The singing was full-throated, without vibrato, high-pitched, and nasal. He smelled the mustiness of African bodies. An infant cried. He saw the mother bend, tilting her shoulder so the child slid forward and found her breast; the crying stopped.

Father Dubonnet rested his hands on the altar and gazed upon the congregation from under his bushy eyebrows. His chasuble matched the green and red geometry of the altar cloth, and the vestment's yellow cross peeked out from under his massive beard. He shifted his weight slightly in time to the music and nodded encouragement to a young drummer playing at Mass for the first time. Slowly, moving in cadence to the beat, he spread his hands in an arch over his head, then lowered them in an attitude of prayer. The singing died to a whisper and stopped.

The priest walked to the side of the altar. A boy with a shaved head held a gold-leafed tome against his chest, open for the reading. Skinny legs protruded from baggy shorts, and like a music stand, his hands gripped the leather binding, and his chin steadied the pages. Looking up, his eyes were fixed on the priest. Dubonnet patted the boy's head, then, squinting down at the text, read the lesson, following the lines with his finger. As he turned the pages, the boy's chin went up and down like a well-oiled machine. The reading over, Dubonnet relieved the child of his burden, made the sign of the cross over him, and returned to the altar. The boy hopped down the steps and sat proudly at the feet of an old woman.

Father Dubonnet's sermon in Lingala was short. He cast his words and phrases with gentle authority like a sower who has worked the soil and knows it to be receptive and fertile. He paused frequently in his discourse; the people's *lyo*s filled the church, and the soft pulsing of the smaller drum bounced among the rafters. There was no pounding of the pulpit nor dogma hammered into heads, but rather a conversation between a priest and his people. The sermon over, the congregation stood for the doxology and sang and clapped in rhythm. Father Dubonnet strode down the aisle holding hands with the boy who had supported the Bible for him.

"Up early, Doctor," said the priest, as Aaron greeted him out on the front steps.

"A wonderful way to start the day," replied Aaron.

Dubonnet urged the boy forward. "Shake hands with an American scientist, *mon petit*."

"Bonjour, monsieur le scientiste."

Aaron took his hand. "What is your name?"

"Impanda Elandu," replied the boy. "Father Dubonnet calls me 'Bienvenu.' "

The priest put his hand on the lad's shoulder. "A bright boy and good with a soccer ball. But we need to develop his leg muscles to match his brain. This is his grandmother." Dubonnet indicated an old woman who had joined them. Aaron took her hand. The priest continued. "Both his parents died during the epidemic."

Over the next three days Aaron and Veronica worked in the villages. Every night Aaron went to bed after a good dinner with the sisters, exhausted but satisfied that the surveillance was going well. He was in an exciting place, doing the work he loved, with a woman—a nun—who knew her way around and whose efficiency and humor added to the pleasure of each day. His only worry was the preservation of specimens he gathered from those who were or had been sick. Collard had brought up from Kinshasa two ten-gallon thermos tanks filled with dry ice and liquid nitrogen. He had taken one back with the frozen blood they collected; the other was here and would last until Howard and the others came up with more supplies. In most of the villages, after they finished the medical work, Veronica gathered her agricultural people around her. She introduced them proudly to Aaron, then urged them to produce as much as possible so they would have plenty to sell when the official quarantine was lifted. At the end of the third day, before supper, she wrote again to her sister.

18 October 1976

My Dearest Gabrielle,

We are back to normal—as normal as we can be without our Sisters in Christ. I think of them every day and pray for their souls. I am sure that their transit through purgatory will be brief, then we can count on their prayers from Heaven to help us rebuild.

A team of three doctors led by Dr. Collard has come and gone. Only Dr. Aaron Hoffman remains. He is a gentle soul, this American doctor, and the first Jew I have worked with. And he tells me that he has never had a nun as an assistant before.

Yesterday we were driving along, talking about Africa during the colonial period and the role played by missionaries. Suddenly he stopped the Jeep and turned off the engine. He faced me, looking puzzled. I asked him, "What is it? What is the matter?" "Nothing," said he. "It's just that the way you live seems abnormal to me." He did not understand how I could renounce being a wife and mother.

As you know, Gabrielle, many people think we are out of the ordinary—even a little odd. I told him that I was married to Christ, and my family was His family. He thought for a moment, then, without saying more, we continued down the road.

Later in the day after we had visited several villages, he said, "A real wife is someone you can touch." Then he asked me if women become nuns to avoid taking care of men.

That was funny, don't you think? I told him sometimes we would like very much to get out of domestic chores. I said we do the priests' laundry and cleaning, and those of us who work in hospitals and schools give comfort and tenderness like any other woman.

Then he brought up chastity, which he said was "unnatural." I replied that not everyone can live with the vow of chastity, but that to some it was probably a blessing.

My dear sister, no man has ever spoken to me about these things before. But his questions continued. He wanted to know if chastity precluded fantasy. As I write these words, even to you, I feel my face grow warm. "Do you have problems with fantasies?" he asked me.

I told him, "Certainly, but never to the point of throwing myself onto the thorns of rosebushes like St. Francis." He laughed, and so did I, and again we drove on.

After dinner we sat out on the terrace with Augustina. Dr. Aaron told us that as a child his grandmother, a profound and Orthodox Jewish lady, took him every Sabbath to the synagogue. He remembered old men intoning the dogma of the Talmud and teaching the importance of ceremonies that unite Jews throughout the world. In medical school he came up against the suffering of good and innocent people, and could not accept a God that did not intervene. He told us of the famines in northern Africa, of the poverty in Asian slums, and even of the unjust triumph of selfish, greedy men in the Western world. Apparently, just over the last three months, thousands have been crushed by an earthquake in China; a hurricane killed and maimed thousands more in Mexico. In South Africa, Lebanon, and Argentina, mass murders continue. He could not tolerate that so many were in misery—he was angry that God would allow such a thing. We did not presume to answer. Then he told us that before arriving in a Catholic mission, he thought he would be working with people who considered simple prayer and goodwill the solution to all these tragedies. "But," he said, "you sisters work hard to relieve suffering, and most of your praying is done before the rest of us are up and around."

I replied that, for me, it was very simple. God is a person, not a vague idea. Every man and woman longs for love. I told him that in God I find perfect, uncomplicated love.

I want to try and remember Augustina's exact words to him. She admires this young doctor; I can tell. She said something beautiful, something like: "The God of the Old Testament is a God of rules and vengeance. Ours is more like a father who understands human nature because he created it. Dogma controls through fear; spirituality through love. God gives each of us the freedom to choose how we behave in the face of nature's disasters or even our own defeats."

After a long pause he got up and wished us good

night, but before stepping off the terrace he turned back and said, "What you believe shows in the way you live."

This morning we received a message from Kinshasa, through Lisala radio, saying that Dr. Howard Fields, the head of the international team, agreed that Aaron remain in Yambuku.

I must end this now. I think Sister Augustina plans to send Luc to Lisala for more supplies in the next day or two. He will see that this letter is delivered to you.

That evening Augustina handed an envelope to Aaron. The outside was soggy with the sweat of the man who had come up from Bumba on his pedalo. Aaron ripped open the envelope; the message was scrawled on yellow foolscap.

Aaron:

This note comes with a Dutch pilot we located who has the guts to fly to Bumba. Burine sent a message through Air Zaire that you are staying in Yambuku. Can't say I blame you, you lucky stiff. I wish I was there myself.

The situation at the Ngaliema Clinic is stable for the moment. When the Zairian nurse died, the people in isolation tried to break out of their building. The soldiers, who were supposed to prevent such a catastrophe, ran away, and Sarah single-handedly pushed those quarantined back into their rooms and locked the doors. We have spent an inordinate amount of time on an evacuation plan to be applied if one of us gets sick. South Africa is the only country willing to accept an infected member of the team.

The American Embassy insists I give them a confidential briefing every day, followed by a press briefing.

They are very demanding and have been of no help whatsoever. It has been through the American doctor who runs the Presidential Medical Services that we have obtained a generator and the cryocentrifuge we will need to set up for plasmapheresis in Yambuku. I miss your help. Many of our meetings are held after midnight in an atmosphere that gets happier as the wine flows.

The rest of us should be up in a couple of days, God and the Zairian government willing.

Yours,

Howard

"The international team should be here the day after tomorrow," said Aaron, as he joined Augustina and Veronica at the table. They discussed living arrangements and food needed for the new arrivals, and Aaron explained plasmapheresis.

"I will send Luc for supplies in the morning, and we can prepare the other rooms in the guest house. The *doctoresse* from South Africa can sleep with us in the convent," said Augustina.

"And we can use Masangaya's house," added Veronica. Antonie joined them, slipping into her chair without a word. "Cheer up, Antonie," said Veronica. "More doctors are coming in two days. We are to become a scientific center."

Antonie looked down at her plate and picked at threads in her napkin. Then, with a glance at Augustina, she mumbled, "I found some bloodstained handkerchiefs under Father Dubonnet's pillow when I put fresh linen on his bed this afternoon."

"Did you speak to him about it?" asked Veronica.

"Of course not," said Antonie, glancing at Veronica. "What do you think—"

Augustina cut her off with a movement of her hand and turned to Aaron. "Doctor, would you speak to Father Dubonnet?"

"Certainly," he replied. "Has he been sick before?"

"Not really, but he smokes like a chimney, as you can see from his beard, and when he is tired his voice is hoarse," replied the Mother Superior. "We have all been worried about him, but he does not allow us to mention his health."

After supper, Aaron walked over to the guest house, tapped on Dubonnet's door, and poked his head in. The priest was asleep. Aaron closed the door quietly. He checked the room again shortly after dawn but found Dubonnet's bed empty.

After a morning of preparing for the arrival of the Kinshasa team, Aaron and Veronica headed north to a village that had reported several sick. The road was filled with mud holes, and they had to go slowly, reaching their destination as clouds billowed violently overhead. They worked rapidly, but as Aaron drew blood from the last patient, the storm crashed down on the village. Quickly they gathered up their gear and ran toward a large rectangular hut where a man waved them into an empty room. The lightning came in series of flashes followed by thunder. Shivering in their wet clothes, they stood by the door, watching the trees shake and bow in the wind. Glancing over his shoulder, Aaron saw a low chair with a sloping back which he indicated to Veronica. He lowered himself onto a tattered mat and sat cross-legged next to her. The storm continued unabated, rain gusts pounding the thatch as thunder echoed around them. A flash lit up the form of Veronica, the shape of her breasts and the smooth curves of her thighs under

her rain-soaked blouse and skirt. They cringed together as
a bolt sizzled through the trees and exploded next to the
hut. He reached for her hand and held it. Their eyes met
during the next flash, then she turned her head but left her
hand in his. Slowly the thunder faded into the distance and
the sound of the rain lessened.

The lantern on the refectory table lit Augustina's worried
frown as she waited. The steady rain added to her anxiety
and anger. They had missed supper and were probably
stuck in a mud hole for the night. Henceforth, she would
insist that Luc accompany the doctor and her irrepressible
nun. Better still, when the doctors arrived from Kinshasa
she would assign Veronica duties that would keep her at the
mission. *Holy Mother,* she prayed, *keep them safe, and steer
Veronica away from the precipice of her emotions.* Minutes
later, headlights swept across the room. She grabbed the
lantern and strode out to the terrace as Veronica stepped
down from the Jeep.

"What happened?" asked the Mother Superior tightly.

"Nothing," replied Veronica. "The roads are terrible, and
we had to wait out a storm in a hut." She turned and waved
to Aaron, who waved back and drove on to the guest
house.

Veronica sat in the dark refectory, waiting. Augustina returned from the kitchen with the lantern in one hand and a
plate of cold food in the other.

"Thank you," said Veronica. "I am sorry if we made you
worry."

"I want to trust you, Veronica. But you walk too close to
the edge of temptation with a man like the doctor."

"I can take care of myself," said Veronica.

"I think you probably can, but you could make difficulties for a man with your openness and strong ways. Then your control might be useless."

"I will think about it."

"And pray."

"And pray. Good night, my mother."

CHAPTER 19

4 November 1976
Dear Gabrielle,

The scientists from America and Europe arrived from Kinshasa two weeks ago. They leave tomorrow. The epidemic is over. Only Dr. Aaron will stay on for a few more days to settle accounts and tidy up.

Looking back it all seems to have happened so quickly. First the deaths of so many of our beloved sisters and friends in Yambuku and all the people in the surrounding villages. Then the visiting of all the villages to be sure there were no more sick hidden away somewhere, followed by the search for the few who recovered and might have antibodies. Soon we will be alone again. They still do not know where the virus came from, but we are all sure that the barricading of the villages ordered by the chiefs was the main reason the epidemic was stopped. I wonder who will take credit for this!

Did I tell you we moved back to our bedrooms in the convent? Terrible memories, which I thought time had blurred, returned, with all their sounds and smells. Three of the six rooms talk of our sisters who went to Heaven. We still cannot believe they are dead: the rooms look as if their occupants are on holiday. It is good we have hard work to do. There is little time to think.

Serum can only be made from the few people who have antibodies to the fever, so these survivors are brought to the mission and asked to contribute their blood. Their first reaction is always negative. But after a full explanation and the promise of twenty zaires, they are willing. Blood is collected in half-liter plastic bags which are taken to the centrifuge. After the serum is removed from the top, the red cells are immediately returned to the donor. The serum, which could save other fever victims, is stored in a freezer sent up from Kinshasa. The work has to be done with great care to detail. Although I miss taking the doctors to the villages, I am pleased Augustina assigned me to help with the blood; it is the most important task of the scientists—like decorticating rice so it can be eaten. Dr. Fields, the chief of the team, gives me money for the donors, and I dole out for each of them enough food for a week (to help them produce more serum). I keep track of all expenses.

You should see our hospital! You would recognize the walls but nothing else. The operating room is where we take the blood under the direction of *la doctoresse* Suzman. She speaks Dutch and French. Before going to South Africa, she was a paratrooper in the Israeli army during their war of independence. Can you imagine such a thing? She is tiny, without much muscle, and eats like a bird, but according to Dr. Aaron, she is one of the best doctors for viral diseases in the world.

The new radio transmitter is now in Dubonnet's old room in the guest house—he has moved back to the house of the fathers. Every hour we have direct contact with Kinshasa and Bumba, and the reception is better and clearer than with our old radio.

The doctors use one of the other rooms in the guest house for meetings. Its walls are covered with maps of our zone as in a military campaign. The laboratory is in the dispensary. There are many complicated machines you cannot understand anything about without long explanations.

It is unbelievable—everything that came from Kinshasa. In the dispensary there are even two electric refrigerators, working day and night off a huge new generator. We have light all night if we want it, which is a good thing because, with so much work to be done, it is 11 P.M. before we are in bed. The three of us are up at 5 as usual for morning prayers. The chapel seems so empty. Augustina and I do the reading; Antonie hardly speaks. We are very worried about her.

The doctors brought new mattresses, sheets, and blankets, and also food—a lot of canned food, and cases of whiskey and wine. We cleaned and painted the house where Masangaya used to live and made room for th two young virologists from Antwerp. Dr. Suzman is staying with us in the convent. The cooking is done for some in the kitchen of Masangaya's house. The rest eat with us. Augustina has her hands full feeding all these people, but the food is good, and they pay well for it. Dr. Fields told Augustina that the mission would not lose any money and that all the supplies they had brought from Kinshasa would stay. Dubonnet grumbles about the luxury, but he enjoys their Johnnie Walker and cognac . . . and particularly the California wine they brought in cases.

A stuffy professor from Belgium has been in Yambuku for a few days. He came to collect animal specimens that might give a clue to the source of the virus. He orders us around like servants, with never a please or a thank you. Yesterday he shouted at me, "Bring me a comb and soap." I was so angry, I turned my back on him and complained to the Mother Superior. But all Augustina did was say, "*Tika, tika,* Veronica. He's used to bossing nurses; humor him. He's a fish out of water here." We will all be glad when he leaves.

Yesterday the doctors found three people with antibodies, including a child of fourteen and a pregnant woman. That woman is causing a new problem. There are viruses and diseases (for example, German measles) that are passed from a mother to the infant she is carrying. The doctors do not know yet whether the virus of the epidemic is transmitted the same way. They will need to have the baby examined when it is born in March, so that if it has the fever the necessary precautions can be taken to prevent another epidemic. They tell me that the little bit of serum with antibodies they have been able to collect might help cure the baby or anyone else that shows up with the disease.

There is a possibility we will come to Binga on holiday if we ever have the time. We keep asking the doctors when we may leave, but they always put us off. Nobody dares give written permission. I suppose with all the people here, we could not go anyway. You just cannot close such a big mission for a while, can you? Augustina badly needs a vacation. She should return to 's Gravenwezel as soon as possible, taking Antonie with her for medical treatment.

Dr. Aaron tells me Father Dubonnet must return to Belgium as well. The *doctoresse* Sarah examined him and thinks he may have a cancer in his throat. We are not supposed to know about this. She had to fight with him before he agreed to leave. When he is with us, he is still his old self, but it is sad to see him when he thinks he is alone. I watched him walking up the hill from the spring house. He stopped several times to catch his breath, then sat on the ground, puffing and coughing, with his head in his hands.

At the mission itself, life has become almost normal. People are returning to their fields to gather rice, something you would not have believed a few weeks ago. Our schools will be opening again soon. Yesterday, Dr. Fields gave permission that the lower school may gather the children and start classes. I must find a new director and five teachers. They will have to come from Yambuku itself because nobody else will accept work here. I may have to take over the girls' lessons myself.

What will happen with our hospital? I do not know. We absolutely have to go to Binga to discuss our future. We receive only a few letters, since the usual planes still do not arrive in Bumba or Lisala.

We miss hearing from all of you, but our Lord has His view of our situation and His own solutions for the future. Our duty is to work seriously to increase our love for each other and, of course, for the Zairians. Sometimes that love is not a gift but comes only as we work and pray and remain loyal to our responsibilities.

Such a long rambling letter! I must close now and help Augustina with dinner. She has asked the mission in Lisala to send nurses and teachers, but so far the Monseigneur has replied that no help is available. When she and Antonie leave with Dr. Aaron I'll be the only "*mondele*" here. (God give me strength to carry on.)

Dr. Fields offered to take this letter to Bumba and ask the fathers there to send it on to you, my dear and much loved sister, and Sister in Christ.

Veronica

Dinner had started as a somber affair. When Dubonnet failed to appear, Aaron went to look for him but returned to report that his room was empty and the bicycle was gone. Augustina, sitting at the head of the table, said grace. She remembered in prayer each of the departed sisters, Father Gérard, and the hundreds of Zairians who had perished. She thanked God for the arrival of the scientists and asked that He protect them on their voyage back to Kinshasa. Then the smell of roast goat in rich palm oil and pepper gravy, a mountain of rice, plantains, and *mpondu* uplifted the mood. Aaron filled glasses with wine. Howard proposed a toast to the sisters and the mission. Sarah raised her glass to Augustina and Veronica and thanked them for all their help and hospitality; then they all tucked into the feast with relish. Later, while the nuns cleared the table, the doctors moved out to the terrace to review the details of what Aaron would do over the next few days. After a nightcap they went to their rooms to pack and get ready for an early departure.

Breakfast was hurried with much coming and going as vehicles were loaded with baggage. Finally everyone gathered in front of the convent. As Augustina, Veronica, and Antonie stood on the steps of the terrace shaking hands with the doctors, Dubonnet walked around the corner of the building. He handed Luc a battered suitcase held together with coarse string, then stood in front of the sisters.

"Reverend Sister." He nodded formally to Augustina. "I will call on you in 's Gravenwezel after I am free from the clutches of the doctors." Augustina took his hand and kissed it. He continued, "Veronica, stay with God as his warrior, but remember that people of goodwill fall flat on their faces." He made the sign of the cross on her forehead. "And you, Antonie, my Sister of Service. Thank you for your care. May the Holy Virgin comfort you through dark tunnels and lead you back into the light."

"Bless me, Father," whispered Antonie, kneeling. He did, then pulled her to her feet.

"Courage, Sister. You know my old saying: only the good die before their time. You and I—" He stifled a cough with his handkerchief, then went on. "What I mean is, I have a long road to walk before they can hang that title around my neck." Antonie tried to control her tears. The priest turned, climbed into the back of the Land Rover, and slammed the door. The doctors stuck their heads out of the windows and shouted their good-byes as the vehicles drove off.

Aaron spent the rest of the day making a master copy of the data and going over the accounts with Augustina and Veronica. He had a few more trips to make to specific villages to check out epidemiological details, then he would leave with Augustina and Antonie.

By late afternoon Veronica was sitting in front of Augustina's desk reviewing the mission's supplies of food and fuel, now plentiful with what the scientists had left. Without Augustina and Antonie, new workers would be needed for the laundry and kitchen.

"Lisala confirmed this morning that they can send us no help," said Augustina. Veronica shrugged and seemed to deflate a little. Her fatigue showed in the lines under her eyes and in her rounded shoulders.

"I will manage," she said.

"I am sure you will, Veronica. But I think we should take matters in our own hands. I will send a message to Binga requesting that your sister Gabrielle join you here as soon as possible."

Veronica sat up. "Do you really think they will let her come?"

"Of course, if the request is from me. Adeline is back in

Antwerp, and our beloved Matilda is in Heaven. I am the senior sister for our mission in Zaire."

"Should you radio Lisala?"

"No. This is something we will do ourselves. I'll send Luc with a note to Binga. On the way he can stop in Ebonda and deliver a letter to Sister Nunciata in which I have asked her to come for a few weeks to help you with the schools. He can take a detour to Bangabola with a note for Sister Serafina, your friend, I believe. As you know, she is now the Mother Superior of the Franciscan Missionaries of Mary. I have explained your situation here after we leave, and I—"

"You have already written all the letters?" exclaimed Veronica, jumping up. She ran around the desk and hugged Augustina.

"Of course. Although you have added to my gray hairs, your vitality has helped sustain me." Veronica hugged her again. Augustina pushed her off, straightened her veil, and added, "In an exhausting sort of way."

The following day at dusk Luc returned with the three new sisters. Aaron was introduced and given a seat at the end of the table opposite Augustina. Serafina, a Spanish nursing sister who had taught Sukato, plied Aaron with questions about the epidemic. Gabrielle and Veronica served up a huge meal spiced with cheese and cold cuts and glazed fruit which the sisters had brought with them. Aaron retired to his room early, sure that the nuns had much to talk about and would be more at ease without him.

After breakfast Aaron, Veronica, and Augustina remained at the table while the other sisters left to go about their business. Addressing Augustina, Aaron asked if Veronica could accompany him on his last day in the villages.

"I have three more places to check, including Bongolu,

where Nza and Ngasa Moke and their family died," he said. Then he looked at Veronica. "You knew them. It would be a big help if you came with me."

"I would like to," replied Veronica. She glanced at Augustina. "But Bongolu is seventy kilometers away."

"I know. But we could do it easily if we left right now. Sukato told me about the *nganga* in Bongolu, and I would like to meet him."

"Sukato and his *nganga*! Did he tell you the old man cured him?" asked Veronica derisively.

"He did, and gave me all the details of his treatment."

"And you believe him?"

"I didn't say that. I said I would like to meet the healer."

"You will learn that they have their ways and we have ours, and it is best not to mix them. Anyway, I have called a meeting of the agricultural cooperative this afternoon."

Aaron turned to the Mother Superior. "You have all the help you asked for now. Couldn't one of the other sisters cover for her?"

"Not today, Doctor. She has too much to do here. I will send Luc with you."

Augustina stood, and she and Veronica began gathering up the coffee cups, bringing the conversation to an end. Veronica walked out to the kitchen. Augustina added before following her, "We will wait for your return and have a little farewell dinner tonight." She was dismissing him. Aaron acknowledged this with a nod and walked out to the terrace to await the driver.

He sat on the steps, worried that he had been insensitive in pushing for Veronica to come with him. Was there really an agricultural meeting? In a few minutes Luc drove up. Veronica and Augustina waved from the door of the kitchen. Aaron waved back, missing Veronica more than he would have thought possible. Was it her inaccessibility that made her so attractive? Was his desire fueled by what he could not touch?

Late in the day Aaron joined the sisters on the convent's terrace before supper. He reported a successful day, although he had been unable to locate the *nganga*. He assured them that he would be able to announce to the authorities in Bumba and Kinshasa that the official quarantine for the whole area could be lifted.

"But the quarantine has been over for days," said Veronica. "Gabrielle and I have already made rounds on the Vespa to tell people that the mission is back to normal."

"Yes," said Aaron. "Official pronouncements usually follow the fact."

Dinner was in honor of those traveling the next morning. Veronica had decorated the table with flowers. A pork roast and two bottles of California wine made it into a festive affair. After the meal Veronica carried the Victrola out to the terrace. Music floated on the night air. Antonie excused herself, saying that she had more packing to do. Veronica and Serafina danced, and invited Aaron to join them, to the applause of Nunciata and Gabrielle. Augustina sat watching, happy that Veronica would be surrounded by friends after she left. They all moaned when, like the Mother Superior she was, she looked at her watch and brought the party to an end. Aaron carried the Victrola into the refectory, then Veronica walked down the steps with him. They strolled a little way together in the direction of the guest house and paused to watch the moon come up behind the palm trees. They wandered on and talked more of their day and of the progress made in restoring the mission activities to normal. Then Aaron stopped and, looking down at her, said, "I've learned a lot from you, Veronica."

"What?" she asked, cocking her head.

"That being a missionary is tough work, and that at least

one nun I know is subject to the same feelings and fears as
. . . other women."

"You were about to say, 'normal' women." She laughed.
"You are making progress."

"Yes, indeed, great progress." He laughed with her, then
snapped off a twig of bougainvillaea. He wiggled it under
her nose. "Kidding aside, when we were in the villages together you showed me dedication to a calling."

"You are as dedicated to your profession."

"In some ways I am. But devotion to a profession is less
demanding than devotion to people. I saw the love that
passed between you and the Africans, even when you were
tough with them. If I had a sister, I would want her to be
like you."

"What a nice thing to say. I have a brother who reminds
me of you. He is the only one in the family who is not in
the religious life, but he, too, is a good man."

"I have also learned that you nuns live in the real world
without being part of it."

Veronica thought for a moment. "Our missionary order
works in places where the natives need what we bring them
and teach them. That does not mean we have to accept all
their values and live as they do."

"Of course," said Aaron. The moon was topping the
trees behind Veronica, casting its soft light on her head and
veil. He looked down at her, but her face was in the shadows.

"Do any of you eventually leave your circumscribed religious life?"

"Not many. The weak ones fall by the wayside during
the training years."

"Those allergic to rosebushes?" he asked, chuckling.

"Definitely! Rose thorns are not for everyone." Suddenly

she looked down and slapped her ankle. "Fire ants!" she
shouted, stamping her feet and brushing her legs frantically.

They ran toward the convent, stopping at the terrace to
pull the remaining insects off their legs.

"The ants broke up our conversation, which was getting
so serious," said Veronica, out of breath and laughing.

"I meant every word. But I agree we were getting pretty
heavy," said Aaron. "Good night, Veronica. See you at
breakfast." He walked toward the guest house.

"Good night, Doctor." She watched him go.

Aaron glanced at his watch. He had entered the last data
on his master sheet, his bags were packed, and he still had
almost an hour before departure. He set off slowly down
the path between the two rows of royal palms, past the coffee fields spotted by termite hills as tall as a man, to the
small cemetery where Sister Lucie, Sister Matilda, and Father Gérard were buried. He stood looking at the rough let-
tering on the white crosses. Veronica had shown him
pictures of the two nuns and the priest and had told him
tales that brought them to life. None of the stories had been
sanctimonious. Gérard's stand before the rebels went with
his nature and his resolve. Lucie's devotion to her pregnant
mothers and their babies, and Matilda's intimate care of
Lucie, which led to her own death, were simple matters of
fact in the life of people committed to the service of others.

He strolled over to the empty church and stood leaning
against the doorpost, his eyes drawn to the massive crucifix. Blood streamed from the thorn wounds down Christ's
pale forehead and ran into the gullies of agony next to his
nose and mouth. The metal roof pinged as it expanded
under the sun, and pale lizards scurried to the ends of the
dusty beams in search of shelter from the heat. Aaron saw
again the congregation squeezed together on the bare

benches, row upon row, swaying and singing to the rhythm of the drums.

He walked slowly through the workers' quarters and said, *"Mbote, mama"* or *"Mbote, tata"* to those who raised their hands in greeting. He had yet to meet a Zairian who would not shake his hand or return his smile. They took the time to be polite. Yet he had also seen the vapid stare of men stoned on *chanvre* and the staggering gait of those drunk on banana liquor. Although they recognized that these customs eased the brutal heaviness of the forest and the storms, the missionaries decried these abuses.

Beyond the workers' huts, he walked down the hill to the spring and pump house. He passed the sacred or haunted tree—depending on who told the story of the voodoo man. He walked a hundred yards into the forest along a path that meandered between huge boles of ficus and other hardwoods he did not know. Thick green vegetation seemed to close in on him as he looked around. Quickly he retraced his steps back to the mission.

"I will take your suitcases if they are ready, *mon docteur*."

"Thank you, Luc." He looked around the guest house room where he had felt at home. "It is very hard to leave."

"We hope you will return soon," said the driver, picking up the bags. He followed Aaron out of the room.

Augustina, Veronica, and the other sisters were waiting for him on the convent terrace.

"I packed sandwiches and a bottle of water for the drive down to Bumba," said Veronica, handing him a neatly tied cardboard box.

"Thoughtful and efficient as always, Veronica," said Aaron. He gave the box to Luc. "I shall miss all of you—and this place and its people." He hesitated for a moment, then he wrapped his arms around Veronica and gave her a hug.

"Thank you for everything."

"*Allez, allez,*" she said, as she would to the children. Then, more quietly, "It is we who thank you." She reached up and kissed him on the cheek. "*Bon voyage et bonne continuation.*"

After shaking hands with the others, Aaron walked down the steps to the Land Rover. As they drove off, he twisted the rearview mirror so he could look behind. He saw Veronica waving to him, and his heart ached.

CHAPTER 20

Veronica tugged on the rope, and the clanging of the bell resounded over the mission. The big rains had ended; there was a freshness to the morning as the night mist rose and lingered for a moment in the treetops. She pulled hard, and from every direction children converged on the school, raising puffs of dust and shouting, *"Noki-noki."* Veronica hurried across the road, clapping her hands and shooing them into the classrooms. The morning rituals had resumed.

During the days following Augustina's departure, Veronica, Nunciata, and Gabrielle recruited three young women, past graduates of the mission schools, and gave them the training needed to be teaching assistants. Veronica supervised and helped in the cleaning of workers' houses left empty by the disease. Serafina and Sukato scrubbed out the wards and other hospital buildings one more time, and restocked the pharmacy and dispensary from the supplies left by Dr. Fields's team. Fuel for the generator was still a constant problem, so the mission used it for only two hours each night.

Now, each morning, Veronica led her sisters in prayer, planned the day, issued orders to the workers, and threw herself into the revival of mission activities. As the new Mother Superior, she joined the people flocking to the church at dawn to pray and sing. Her vitality lifted the congregation to fresh hope. The farm flourished, and lines of sick waited patiently by the dispensary.

In the early mornings she was still awakened by the nightmares of Antonie's pounding on the doors or Matilda's eyes glaring at her in the darkness. Unnerved, she would crawl out of bed and pad down the hall to the office with her kerosene lamp to pore over her books and plans, looking for errors or items she might have missed. Before dawn she would check the laundry and recheck the inventory in the supply room, then inspect the garage buildings and maintenance shops to be sure the locks were on the doors. Cleophas, the night watchman, who observed her from a distance, would stay out of her way. Exhausted, she would then climb into bed for a couple of hours sleep before matins. Augustina had done a better job of delegating responsibility.

One evening two weeks after Augustina's departure, Gabrielle and Veronica were drinking coffee in the office after supper. They were finishing an initial report of progress in the mission when Sister Serafina joined them.

"Everyone tucked in for the night?" asked Veronica. She glanced at her watch, then reached for the lantern on the desk, struck a match and lit it just as the lights faded and went out.

"Yes. We had a full morning in the dispensary and have a dozen patients in the medical ward and maternity." Serafina pulled a chair over to Veronica's desk and sat down. "Everyone seems to be doing well except for a man Sukato admitted a couple of hours ago."

"Where did he come from?" asked Veronica.

"Yandongi. His family carried him in on a makeshift stretcher."

"What's the matter with him?"

"I'm not sure. Sukato put him in the little room next to

the dispensary. He will try to find out more about him from the family."

"In the isolation room?" asked Veronica. "Why?"

Serafina looked at her two colleagues. "Sukato thinks this man may have the fever."

"Impossible," said Veronica. "The doctors and scientists searched the whole area and were sure the disease had burned itself out. There has not been a case since the end of October."

"Then Sukato is probably wrong."

"Of course, he's wrong. You have to watch him, Serafina. He made himself very useful to the scientists, and they spoiled him."

"The patient is terribly sick," said the nurse.

"Well, what do you think he has?" asked Veronica.

"I don't know. I have never seen a fever patient. His temperature is over forty degrees Celsius, he has a severe headache, and—"

Veronica interrupted, "That does not make it *the* fever. At the beginning of the epidemic we realized that many diseases start the same way. What about malaria?"

"Sukato is covering that possibility by giving him nivaquine," replied Serafina. "But there is something about this man that is different from most of the patients I have seen with acute malaria—probably just an unscientific impression, Vero, but I think you should come and see him anyway."

"I'm not a nurse. But I wouldn't worry about it too much. Sukato is probably just trying to impress you with his knowledge. Dr. Hoffman was sure that the disease had disappeared."

"Still, Vero, I would be relieved if you looked at him. You and Sukato are the only ones . . ."

Veronica pushed back her chair and threw her napkin on

the table. "All right, if it will make you feel better. But I am sure the man must have something else." She felt her throat tighten and put her hand to her neck.

"Is something the matter with you?" asked Gabrielle.

"Of course not," she replied, swallowing hard and taking a deep breath. *It cannot be the disease! Keep calm, do not spread your fear.* She felt light-headed.

"Why don't you see him in the morning, Vero?" asked Gabrielle, getting up. "It is almost time for bed."

"No," answered Serafina bluntly. "I admit I may be overconcerned, Gabrielle, but he needs to be seen now."

"Very well," replied Veronica, wiping off her face and reaching for the lantern. "I said I would go."

Serafina added quickly, "If he does have the disease, Sukato has antibodies and will be safe. I told him not to let anyone else in the room."

"Good," said Veronica. "Gabrielle, you stay here." Veronica pushed a box of matches toward her. "There is a candle on the bookshelf. We'll be back in a moment."

"I will come with you."

"No!" commanded Veronica. Gabrielle sat down, taken aback by her sister's severity.

In the yellow light of the lantern, Veronica and Serafina's shadows played on the bushes along the path to the hospital. Frogs in the wet grass beside the path fell silent, then resumed their croaking as the women passed. In a moment they came to the brick building and its open window. Sukato, in protective clothes, squatted by a smoky lamp to fill a plastic syringe from a vial. He straightened up, and his shadow rose on the wall like a hovering specter.

"*Tika,*" called out Serafina. "Wait. Where is the family?"

"They ran away," said Sukato.

"What did they say about the patient?" asked Veronica.

"Nothing, Sister. They ran away," repeated the nurse.

Veronica handed the lantern to Serafina and leaned forward. On the bed next to the window a man lay on his back. The frontal ridges of his eye sockets, his flaring nostrils, and stained teeth caught the dim light from the lamp in the room. She heard him suck in air and push it out in shallow, rapid grunts.

"*Tata*, can you hear me?" she asked. There was no response.

Sukato bent over and tapped him on the shoulder. The man let out a groan. "He is awake, *ma soeur.*"

"*Tata*, can you hear me now?" she repeated.

The man's head turned slowly toward the window. "*Iyo.*"

"How long have you been sick?"

"*Poso moko,*" he answered hoarsely. One week.

She asked deliberately, underlining each word, "Were you with a sick person recently?"

"*Nayebi te.*" I do not know.

"Does your head hurt?"

"*Iyo.*"

"Throat and mouth hurt?"

"*Iyo.*"

"Have you vomited and had diarrhea?"

"*Iyo.*"

"Blood?"

"*Te. Makila te.*" No. No blood.

"Good," said Veronica.

"*Ma soeur*, he has the fever," announced Sukato from inside the room.

"That can't be. He has not bled from his stomach or bowel," said Veronica.

"Neither did the last ones who died."

Veronica steadied herself on the windowsill and fixed her eyes on the man's face. Suddenly she turned to Serafina and shrieked in a voice that shattered the stillness of the night, "Did you touch him?"

"No, Vero," replied the nurse, shaken. "I told you—only Sukato has been with him."

Veronica persisted, with urgency in her voice, "You did not examine him? You did not touch him yourself?"

"No, I did not."

Breathing rapidly, Veronica turned away and headed for the dispensary. *Oh, God, what am I going to do? I cannot go through it again.* She closed her eyes and saw the image of Matilda on her deathbed, staring into space. When Serafina approached carrying the lantern, Veronica was sitting on the doorstep with her arms crossed, rocking back and forth. She did not greet the nurse or even acknowledge her presence for some time, then suddenly she struggled to her feet. "We must leave. Get Nunciata out of bed and meet me in the office." In the darkness, she walked away in the direction of the convent.

Within a few minutes, the nuns gathered around Veronica's desk. Her face was ashen, her words flat and measured. "My sisters, we must not panic. The most important thing is that none of us have been exposed to the patient." She looked straight at Serafina.

"That is right, Veronica," replied the nurse. "Sukato is the only person to lay a hand on him and, as you saw for yourself, he wears gloves and a gown and the rest of the protective clothes."

"Yes, yes." Veronica waved her hand to dismiss the point. "Now, listen to me. You will each return to your own community. We cannot, we must not, stay here. At this moment, we know that since none of us have been in contact with the man we will not get the disease. Even so, if the authorities find out that the fever has returned to Yambuku, we will be forbidden to leave." She looked down at her clenched fists. "You will have difficulties in your missions over why you left Yambuku, but that is better than staying here. As for me . . ." She closed her eyes, and her voice dropped to a whisper. "I do not have the courage to stay alone." She looked at each of them. "I am certain the man has the fever. If he dies during the night, it will be eight days from when his symptoms started. For me, that will be the final proof." She waited for their response.

"You are the Mother Superior. We will do what you request," replied Serafina quietly. The other two nodded. They kept their eyes on the flame in the lamp. No one spoke. A faint silver glow from the rising moon filtered through the door.

Veronica pulled a handkerchief out of her pocket and held it to her mouth; her voice was subdued. "There is one more thing I must ask of you." She hesitated. "I need time to get away. If the authorities hear about the disease and find me, I will be forced to return here. My only chance is to catch a plane from Gbadolite. Please say nothing about the patient or about me for two days." She hid her face in her hands. "By that time I will be out of the country." Gabrielle put an arm around her sister's shoulders. Nunciata sat quietly.

After a moment, Serafina reached across the desk and gently pulled Veronica's hands away from her face. "We understand, Vero. You have been through so much. We will do as you ask."

"I am so frightened, so terrified. . . ." gasped Veronica, grasping Serafina's hand. After a moment she straightened up, stuffed her handkerchief back in her pocket, and looked up at Gabrielle. "Wake Luc and Evariste and tell them to prepare for our departure at dawn. When we were about to evacuate during the epidemic, Augustina gave Evariste the keys and money to pay the workers. We will do the same thing now."

The sisters left, but Veronica remained at her desk, staring at the outline of palm trees in the moonlight. They seemed to point to the cemetery where Lucie, Matilda, and Father Gérard were buried. Again she heard the drunken cries of the blacks and saw them staggering around the back of the Jeep. She heard the dull thud over the sound of rain as Gérard's body was pushed into the hole. A knock on the door startled her.

"What do you want?"

Luc approached and stood before her. "For the love of God, Sister, do not say the man has the fever. Tell the people he had tuberculosis and it returned to kill him. Everyone understands that can happen. If they believe the fever has returned, everyone will run away again." He came a step nearer. "You can say you received a message asking the other sisters to return to their own missions. You can tell them your chiefs have called you back to Belgium. That also the people will understand."

"It is wrong to lie, Luc." Veronica thought for a moment, her eyes fixed on the lamp. "But then perhaps you are right." She looked up into this old friend's worried face. "Oh, Tata Luc, I don't know anymore. What if the fever has only been hiding somewhere in the forest or here in the mission buildings? What if the scientists are wrong?"

Luc lifted his shoulders in a little shrug. " 'What if' never helps, *ma soeur*. We can only do what is necessary now. I will be ready at dawn."

Veronica spent the next hour alone in the chapel on her knees. Putting her lantern on the prie-dieu, she read the same passage in the breviary over and over. She tried praying, but the words seemed stilted. Returning to her room, she packed, then lay on the bed. In seconds, she was sound asleep, fully dressed.

Within the hour, there was a loud knock at her door. "What is it? Who is there?" she asked, fright making her shout.

"It is me, Sukato."

She lit a candle, stepped to the door, and opened it.

"I came to tell you that the man died."

"The fever!"

"It is possible, *ma soeur*."

"The sisters will be leaving in the morning," she said curtly.

"I understand your need to be with your own people," replied the nurse.

"You will take care of things here, Sukato?"

"Of course." He turned and disappeared in the darkness.

Veronica closed the door and looked at her watch— 2 A.M. She replaced the candle in its holder, peeled off her wet uniform, ran the water in the sink, and wiped her face and neck. Retrieving a fresh blouse from her suitcase she slipped it over her head, combed her hair, and pinned on her veil. She lit the lantern and opened the window wide. The moon was hidden by clouds: it was pitch-black.

"Cleophas, are you there?" she called out to the watchman.

"Oui, ma soeur," answered the old man from somewhere near the end of the open hallway.

"Quickly, go wake up Luc and tell him to come right away with the Land Rover."

"Oui, ma soeur."

She walked swiftly down the hall, knocking on doors and asking the sisters to meet her on the terrace. Back in her room, she closed her bag and carried it out.

Within minutes the nuns, in their long white nightgowns,

were standing in front of her. The sweat on Veronica's face glistened in the light of her lantern, and the fear they saw in her eyes stunned them.

Her voice was cold, accusatory. "The man just died—akoufi, like all the others." She took a deep breath and continued rapidly. "I have called Luc and will go as soon as he comes. The rest of you, leave at first light. Gabrielle, the keys are in Augustina's desk drawer." The lights of the Land Rover swept over them.

"Put my suitcase in the car, Luc. I will be right there," she called out. She turned back to the sisters, "We will meet again when God wants it." Without further talk, they embraced, and Veronica ran down the steps and climbed in next to Luc. Within minutes the Land Rover disappeared into the night.

They drove through Yandongi, and then north toward Abumombazi. Veronica sat upright, concentrating on the road. The headlights stabbed the gloom, lighting the dense vegetation that flashed by. There had been little rain, and the road was dry and dusty.

Around four in the morning they entered a high tunnel cut through seventy kilometers of primeval forest where no man lived. Veronica looked up and thought of the vaults of the great cathedrals in Europe which, at night, were hidden in darkness, but the warm rows of candles in the chapels around the nave and the sweet smell of incense welcomed the wanderer and the frightened. Here, the forest was black. No moonlight or glow from the stars penetrated to the base of the giant trees. She shuddered and slumped in her seat. Luc drove on steadily. Dawn filtered through the canopy as they passed out of the tunnel into Abumombazi.

"Do you want to stop here at the mission, Sister?"

"No, only at Gbadolite." He slowed to allow people on

the road to step aside. Some waved when they recognized the mission vehicle, but Veronica did not return their greetings. Soon they were beyond the town and back into the forest.

"Why don't you try and sleep, Sister?"

"I cannot."

Veronica was easily carsick, and Luc was used to her not talking. They began passing more villages around which large patches of forest had been hacked away to grow coffee and manioc.

Arriving at Gunde they turned west on the road to Mobayi-Mbongo that runs just south of the Ubangi River and the frontier with the Central African Republic. Near Dondo there was a military roadblock manned by paracommandos from the Kota-Koli (rock men, in the language of the Ngbandi). Luc stopped and turned off the engine. The soldiers sauntered up to the vehicle with their FALs hanging off their shoulders. A sergeant asked for papers, and Luc showed them the registration.

"Where are you going?"

"To the mission in Gbadolite," replied Luc.

"Cigarettes," demanded one of the soldiers.

"We do not smoke."

The soldier snatched open the door next to Veronica. *"Bima."* Get out.

Veronica glanced at Luc, who nodded calmly, opened his door, and stepped out. Veronica squeezed past the soldier to avoid touching him and backed away. He reached inside the vehicle, pulled out her suitcase, and tried to open it as Luc came around the back to stand between her and the sergeant.

"Fungula," demanded the soldier. Key.

"No," said Veronica, clinging to her shoulder bag. Luc spoke into the ear of the sergeant who immediately ordered the soldier to put the suitcase back in the vehicle. Disgruntled, the man rummaged through the glove compartment, then waved them back in. *"Kota, kende."* Get in, go.

"Bring cigarettes when you come back through," ordered the sergeant, as Luc started the engine.

"Animals," snapped Veronica, as they pulled away from the roadblock.

"They are just bored," said Luc.

Veronica frowned at him in disgust. "What did you say to the sergeant?"

"Nothing of great importance," replied the driver.

"Luc, what did you say?" repeated Veronica severely.

"I mentioned that you were on your way to take care of the president's old aunt." His voice was barely audible above the sound of the engine.

"Luc!"

"Oui, ma soeur?"

"Nothing."

They drove through Banzyville and arrived at Gbadolite just before noon. Luc had eaten some bananas and peanuts and had drunk from an old army canteen on the way up. Veronica had taken nothing.

"Where to?" asked Luc.

"The airport."

Ten minutes later they pulled up to the terminal. It was brand-new and modern-looking, built to service the presidential jets. Veronica ran into the building, hoping no one would recognize her. A mass of shouting, shoving people were in front of the Air Zaire counter. She looked at the arrival and departure boards and saw that there was only one plane a day leaving for Kinshasa. It departed at 7 A.M. and stopped at Mbandaka on the way.

"Are these people for tomorrow's flight?" she asked a man standing next to her.

"Yes."

She counted ten people in line ahead of her. The progress forward was desperately slow. Veronica was sure that her only hope lay in the fact that the harassed agent behind the counter was a European and that he might have a soft spot for sisters. For the moment, the agent was embroiled with an enormously fat man who was pounding the desk and shouting. The clerk was refusing to accept three metal footlockers for the morning flight. The police intervened, and after a long, acrimonious argument, the fat man settled for a single crate to go. When Veronica finally reached the head of the line she requested a seat, laying her money on the counter.

"I am sorry, Sister, the plane in the morning is fully booked," said the clerk.

"That cannot be possible. I have to get to Kinshasa."

"If you are here at six in the morning, there might be a cancellation, but I doubt it. Do you want me to put you on for the next day?"

"No, that is out of the question." She felt like screaming at him. "I should be in the capital tonight, but since you only fly once a day I will have to leave in the morning."

The phone rang. The man picked it up and listened, rolling his eyes to the ceiling where a fan pushed hot air onto the people below.

"Tell him to borrow the president's DC-10, for Christ's sake!" He put his hand over the mouthpiece. "Sorry, Sister. The governor's office wants ten seats in the morning." He winked at Veronica and spoke into the telephone. "He can take a *nonnette* who is standing here in front of me." He slammed the phone down, then took a deep breath and let it out slowly.

A man behind Veronica tried to push her aside. She dug

her elbow into his stomach and he retreated. She grabbed the counter with both hands. "Well?"

"Sister, even if you were Saint Mary herself, there is nothing I can do except wait-list you for the morning," said the agent.

Veronica grabbed her money and spun around. The man behind her stepped out of her way. She pushed her way toward the exit. She tried to think, to pull together a plan. The Mission of the Fathers would be able to use their influence to get her a seat. But she did not dare show her face there. She crawled back into the Land Rover. Luc waited for his orders.

"To the French convent," said Veronica. "I know one of the sisters there."

The convent was only ten minutes down the road from the airport. The nuns welcomed Veronica but were worried when they saw how drawn and exhausted she was. They led her into their refectory and offered her lunch. She drank coffee but hardly touched the food.

"Are you sick, Veronica?" asked her friend, Madeleine.

"No. Just tired." Avoiding her friend's eyes, she added, "The other sisters at Yambuku were called back to their missions, and I have been ordered to Belgium. I will be better after a rest." She walked out to the Land Rover where Luc was waiting.

"Good-bye, Luc. I will ask the sisters to let you fill up the vehicle here. You should spend the night and drive back to Yambuku in the morning." She thanked him, and they shook hands. Veronica turned away, then came back. "And, Luc, if three months from now I am not in Yambuku, the Vespa is yours."

"You will return, *ma soeur*."

Veronica walked into the convent, and Madeleine led her to a guest room where she undressed quickly and crawled between the rough cotton sheets. She slept for several hours. When she awoke, for a moment she did not know where she was, and the terror of the previous night returned. She tried to go back to sleep but could not. Would word of the fever leak out of Yambuku? Would she be hunted down and ordered to return? Every footstep in the hall could be someone coming for her, every distant jangle of the telephone a report that Sister Veronica should be held if found. She pictured the snug room under the heavy beams which had been hers in the family farmhouse near Schilde. She longed to climb into the old oak bed and cover her head with the heavy quilt her grandmother had made to celebrate her first communion. How often she had found security in that warm dark nest when storms rattled the gabled windows. Here there was no protection; there was no protection for her in the whole country. Was she really safe in this room? The chapel would be more secure—a sanctuary. Maybe God would come to her rescue, if He could recognize her in her present state. She jumped out of bed, threw on her clothes, and opened the door carefully: the hall was empty. Quietly, she closed the door behind her and, feeling like a fugitive, hurried down the hall to the chapel.

By the time Collard's medical meeting at the Gbadolite hospital ended, it was dusk, and he drove to the house of the fathers for dinner with the district priest. After the meal the two men sat out on the veranda. Over generous glasses of the priest's cognac, they discussed the deteriorating economics in the country and the tightening grip of the security "gorillas" on the people. After a while the father broke the flow of their conversation.

"Before you came I received a call from one of the nuns at the French convent. She is worried about a sister from

Yambuku who has driven all night to get here. She is apparently distraught. You were there during the epidemic. Maybe you should see her; she might need medical attention."

Collard was tired after the long flight from Kinshasa and the medical meeting, but he bade his host good night, climbed into the Jeep he had borrowed from one of the doctors, and drove over to the convent. He introduced himself to the nun at the door, who acknowledged that a Belgian sister from Yambuku had arrived, but had not indicated that she expected a visitor.

"That is normal," said the doctor. "She does not know that I am in Gbadolite. Do you know her name?"

"I am sorry, Doctor—"

"Sister, please find her, and tell her that Dr. Collard is here."

Reluctantly, she showed Collard into the parlor and a few minutes later returned to report that the sister was alone in the chapel and could not be disturbed.

"It is very important that I speak with her." He thought for a moment, gauging the best way through this starchy nun. "She may have a medical problem," he confided.

She hesitated, then replied, "Very well, Doctor. She does look as if she might need help. Please follow me."

Collard stopped at the entrance, allowing his eyes to adjust to the twilight that filtered through the stained glass windows behind the altar. After a moment he saw a nun kneeling at the rail. Which sister was she? He stepped silently into a pew and sat. A painted plaster image of the Holy Mother glowed softly in the faint light of candles at the foot of her pedestal. The town's distant murmur was muted, and only an occasional creaking as the roof cooled with the approach of night interrupted the faint sound of the nun's weeping. The small red lamp over the altar and the candle flames brightened as darkness fell. A bulb in the hallway cast its dim glow a short way up the aisle and over the rear pews. The sister pushed herself up from the rail, made the sign of the cross, and genuflected. She turned and with her head bowed came down the aisle, clutching her breviary to her breast. Collard recognized Veronica and stood as she approached. She looked up and, seeing the silhouette of a man, let out a cry of alarm.

"It's all right, Veronica. It's me, Collard." He put out his hand instinctively.

"You found me! I won't go back with you." Like a feral animal, she shrank back from his touch. He was shocked by the change in her.

"Take you back where? For God's sake, Veronica, why are you so frightened?"

For a moment she looked at him like a cornered animal, then suddenly sobbed out, "Oh, Doctor, I ran away." Collard put his arm around her shoulders and led her to a pew. He pulled a handkerchief from his pocket and wiped her eyes.

"Now, tell me what happened," he said softly.

Her voice was barely audible. "A man came into the hospital yesterday with the fever. I panicked and ran away. I am terrified the authorities will find out and make me go back." She hid her face in his shoulder and cried. He held her, and after a while, her crying eased. Suddenly she pulled away and looked into his face. He had been "the authority" at the beginning of the epidemic.

"You will not report me or make me return to Yambuku? I promise you I did not touch the patient." She paused, then raced on with a new idea. "We could go back to Yambuku together. I would be fine if you were with me; it is just that I cannot be there alone in another outbreak of the fever."

"You shall return to Belgium," said the doctor. "You should have been sent home for a rest after the epidemic."

"But I wanted to stay. Everything was starting to work again until the man came in. If a doctor had been with me, I would not have been so frightened. Luc is still here, we could return to the mission and—"

"Veronica, I cannot go to Yambuku on this trip. I am sorry, but I must be in Kinshasa tomorrow. I will send one of our doctors up as soon as possible to deal with the situation." Veronica reached for his handkerchief, wiped her eyes, blew her nose, and handed it back to him.

She continued. "I would have called you on the radio to ask for help, but then Lisala and everyone else would have known what was going on, and I would have been ordered not to move, like before."

"You are returning to Brussels," said Collard firmly.

"I tried to buy a ticket earlier, but all the seats were taken."

"Don't worry. You can come with me. I have priority orders."

"But I only have money for a ticket to Kinshasa."

"That is also no problem. I will buy your ticket to Brussels; that is the least the Belgian Embassy can do. Now you must go to your room and sleep. I will come for you at six in the morning." Veronica put her arms around his neck and kissed him on the cheek.

"Thank you," she said.

"It is nothing." He felt his face flush and started to say more but retreated into official politeness. "I am glad to help."

It was not until after she was back in bed that she wondered how he had found her in Gbadolite. Her fear returned. Had he already known about the dead patient? Had he, in reality, been sent to take her back? She refused to believe that, and although the echoes of her escape kept her awake for a while, she finally went to sleep. At three in the morning the recurrent nightmare of Fermina pounding on her door, shouting, "She's dying! Come quickly," crashed into her sleep. She awoke drenched in sweat. On her knees beside the bed she recited Hail Mary's until the hammering of her heart slowed.

Habit awakened her again at five. She dressed, wondering how much of what had happened yesterday and during the night had been a dream. She walked down the hall and stepped into the chapel. The French sisters were in the front rows for their morning prayers. Veronica slipped into the rear pew where she had sat with Collard. She thanked her guardian angel for watching over her, but prayed to the Blessed Virgin to remove her lingering doubts about Collard's intentions.

The morning service ended, and the nuns filed out. Sister Madeleine invited her for breakfast, but Veronica declined, saying that she needed to be ready when the doctor came for her. Out on the veranda they sat silently in wicker chairs to wait.

The more Veronica thought about Collard's "miraculous" appearance in the chapel, the more her suspicions told her he had known about the death in Yambuku. His presence was no coincidence, and his refusal to accompany her back to Yambuku meant that he had already acted to isolate the area. Had Gabrielle and the others been intercepted on the road? Had their superiors raised the alarm? Were the Zairians scattering into the forest again to die? A car turned off the road into the mission compound. Collard sat next to the driver—a priest. Veronica clutched her hands to her breast as the vehicle came to a stop in front of her. Collard bounded up the steps of the veranda.

"Are you ready, Veronica?"

"Why did you bring a priest?"

"The father is an old friend." He reached for her suit-case. "He offered to drive us to the airport."

"You told him about Yambuku!"

"No, Veronica. I told him you were one of the sisters who had kept things together during the epidemic and that you were exhausted and on your way back to Belgium for a well-earned rest."

Veronica watched Madeleine approach the car and greet the priest.

"What is she telling him?"

"Veronica, snap out of it. You are acting like a child," said Collard firmly. He took her arm. "Your lack of trust should shame you. Now relax and come along, or we will miss the plane."

As Veronica approached the car, subdued but still wary, Madeleine turned to face her. *"Bon voyage, ma soeur, et bon retour."*

"Please forgive me for being so distracted. I am too tired to be myself," said Veronica. "Could I ask you one more favor? Would you please tell Luc that everything is fine? Tell him a doctor will be in Yambuku very soon. And wish him a safe trip home."

"I certainly will," replied the French nun. Veronica pulled a five-zaire note out of her shoulder bag.

"And give him this. Tell him not to forget cigarettes for the soldiers at Kota-Koli, and tell him I am sorry about . . . sorry to leave this way."

Veronica gazed down the road to the airport. Tears ran down her cheeks, and she missed Madeleine's wave as they drove out of the compound.

CHAPTER 21

Within minutes a muscular Belgian wearing Air Zaire epaulets on his short-sleeved shirt followed Collard to the jeep.

"All set, Veronica. This is Vanderbeck, the station manager. You are traveling on a medical pass." The big man and Veronica shook hands.

"Good morning, Sister. I am sorry to hear you are not well. You and the doctor are in front seats behind the bulkhead. They are not luxurious but a little quieter than in the back with the children and chickens. I'll send someone for your bags and come for you myself when we are ready to board."

"You're a real friend," said Collard.

"No problem," replied Vanderbeck. He turned to Veronica. "Can you imagine, Sister? He comes up here, has lunch with the doctor and dinner with the priest, but forgets his old drinking friend until he needs an extra seat on the plane."

"Don't be too hard on him," said Veronica. "He has been a godsend to me."

"Ah, yes," exclaimed Vanderbeck. "Always the gallant one!"

"Next time. It's a promise," said Collard.

The station manager had them in their seats before the other travelers started up the steps of the Fokker Friendship.

Veronica glanced nervously at the passengers as they struggled through the aircraft's front entrance. Many wrestled with unwieldy bundles or bulging cardboard boxes held together with string. Perspiring mamas shepherded wide-eyed children down the aisle, then wedged themselves into their own narrow seats. Veronica turned her face to the window and stared at the distant forest. Finally the loading was done, the door closed, and the engines started. The plane's air-conditioning blew in through the vents above the passengers' heads, and a fine mist gathered on the ceiling, promising some relief from the stifling heat in the cabin. They taxied for what seemed an interminable time: the runway had been lengthened to handle presidential jumbo jets. As the plane finally gathered speed for takeoff, Veronica reached for Collard's hand and held it tightly.

The flight across the equator to Mbandaka was a short one. The plane landed, then pulled up to the terminal of the provincial capital. Only a handful of passengers disembarked, and new ones were loaded. A small man wearing heavy black-rimmed sunglasses, dressed in the dark blue *abacos* and light green neck cloth de rigueur for party officials, sauntered in and sat across the aisle from Collard. He nodded at the doctor and stared at Veronica while the engines started and then were suddenly switched off. As the whine of the turbo props subsided, the speakers in the cabin announced a slight delay. One of the crew swung open the cabin door, and two men in camouflage uniforms stepped into the aircraft. Veronica grabbed Collard's arm and whispered, "You won't let them take me!"

"Security check," announced one of the men. "Have your tickets out for inspection." They started down the aisle looking at faces rather than boarding passes.

"It's all right, Veronica. They are checking the Zairians, not us," Collard assured her. Moments later the soldiers returned, pushing a man in front of them and out onto the tarmac. The engines were started again, and a few minutes after takeoff, the plane was climbing through the overcast into a cloudless sky. Collard patted her hand, and she released her grip.

"Now you're safe, Veronica. Get some sleep." She nodded and wedged her shoulder bag between the seat and window, then leaned back and closed her eyes.

After a while Collard put down his reading and looked over at Veronica as she slept. She had dark rings under her eyes, and her skin was sallow and dry. She was not the vigorous, sunburned sister he remembered. She frowned in her sleep, mumbled something, then was still. He had never seen a nun so vulnerable. He stared at the back of the seat in front of him. Childhood memories flooded in. *La mère* Gudrun—large, fearsome, and never to be crossed—had run the convent school near the government hospital in the Bas-Kongo where he had been raised. *La mère* and *monsieur le docteur*, his father, represented the two pincers of the colonial claw that had controlled the country—Church and King. Gudrun had been singled-minded in her conviction that *les autochtones* (natives) were to be brought to heel under the Ten Commandments as interpreted, of course, by the Mother Church. The political upheavals of the late fifties were of no more importance to her than the rare episodes of indiscipline in her school. He had suffered under the lash of her rawhide *chicotte* more often than his Congolese schoolmates. The Reverend Mother felt that, because he was the son of a respected Belgian physician, he must be forged into a good example for the others. Thinking of Gudrun brought to mind his father, a gentler influence. The doctor had been a civil servant dedicated to the establishment of medical services in the Congo. The riots in Léopoldville in 1959 had depressed him. With all the *évolués* trained to think and behave like Europeans he could not understand the country's reckless rush toward independence. Collard glanced over at Veronica; she was sleeping soundly. Now King and God, at least Gudrun's God, had lost their grip on the country.

After another three hours, they began their approach to Kinshasa, dropping over the president's Chinese pagoda and estate on the banks of the Congo, and moments later touched down at Ndjili Airport. The central building was a white rotunda decorated with modern African ceramics. Footsteps echoed under the high dome, where paint was peeling and some of the windowpanes were smashed or missing. Collard claimed their bags, shortcutting hassles with a wad of zaires pressed into the palm of a porter. He led Veronica to a corner of the large echoing waiting room and sat her down on a bench.

"Give me your passport. I won't be long." He walked over to the Sabena counter.

As soon as he left, she tried to make herself as inconspicuous as possible. The plane was fully booked, but Collard, who sometimes took care of the airline's personnel, was a good friend of the station manager, and a ticket was finally produced. He returned to stay at Veronica's side, getting up only once to go upstairs to buy her a cup of coffee and a piece of cake, and a bottle of Primus for himself. When the flight was called, he led her to the aircraft and up the steps into the main cabin and helped her settle into a seat in the back next to a window.

"Now, you'll be fine. I will see to the situation in Yambuku, so please don't worry about that. Your main task is to get well."

"Thank you," she said, her eyes filling with tears.

"No more tears now, Veronica. I will see you when you

return. *Bon voyage.*" He put his hand on her shoulder, then turned and walked rapidly out of the plane.

After takeoff, Veronica pushed her seat back, tucked a pillow behind her head, and was soon asleep. Two hours later, she opened her eyes and stretched. She was on her way out of Africa, on her way home, a home she had left over twenty years ago. She wondered which of her eleven brothers and sisters would be there. She pictured them one by one, then she came to Gabrielle . . . and, instantly, guilt, like bitter bile, rose in her throat. *What have I done, what have I done? I ran away and left my own sister. She and Serafina and Nunciata are probably quarantined in dingy rooms . . . and Luc and Evariste and all the others I abandoned. What a coward I have been!* She looked out of the window and saw, thousands of feet below, long shadows cast by the setting sun behind black basalt mountains. She had deserted her mission and would never be allowed back. She would live in shame, her years of devotion and work ruined. How could she face those who had trusted her and thought of her as a capable nun? Her family would be devastated.

The shadows lengthened on the desert below and, in moments, the twilight faded; the wastelands were a black, bottomless void. She was without hope. Her brain was numb and as empty as the night beyond the thin shell of the aircraft. Then she thought of Aaron. She remembered he was probably still in Antwerp at the Institute of Tropical Medicine. She would call him as soon as she reached Brussels. He could come to the airport right away and bring money for a ticket, and she would fly back to Zaire on the same plane before she was really missed. He might even return with her.

* * *

As the big jet taxied to the covered ramp, Veronica was ready. As soon as the seat-belt sign was turned off, she stood, gathered her things, and clambered over the Portuguese businessman. She pushed her way up the aisle as passengers started their slow, weary parade off the plane. Running up the covered corridor into the satellite building where the international flights came in, she rushed to the pay phones. None were free. She hurried down the long hallway, avoiding the slow moving walkways, into the main terminal. She found the number of the institute in Antwerp, darted into an empty booth, stuffed coins into the machine, and dialed.

"Institute of Tropical Medicine," announced a woman's voice.

"May I speak to Dr. Aaron Hoffman, please?"

"Dr. Hoffman?" There was a pause. "Who is he with?"

"I don't know. He was in Zaire for the epidemic in Yambuku." Another pause.

"I will switch you to the office of Dr. Thys's assistant." The phone rang, and Veronica started to count. On the tenth ring it was answered. "This is Melina, Dr. van Eck's secretary. May I help you?"

"I am trying to find Dr. Aaron Hoffman."

"I am sorry, madame; he was here but finished his work yesterday. I don't know if he is still in town. He was staying at the Rubenshof. May I give you the telephone number?"

"Oh, dear . . . yes, please. Wait, let me find a pencil." She wedged the phone between her shoulder and ear, dug into her bag, and pulled out a pencil stub and her ticket. "I'm ready." She jotted down the number, said thank you, and dialed again.

"I will ring the doctor's room," said the switchboard operator at the hotel. A woman answered, "Hello."

"May I speak with Dr. Aaron Hoffman, please?" asked Veronica, in French.

"I'm sorry, but he's not in," replied the woman.

"I must speak to him," insisted Veronica. "It is very important that I reach him."

"He has gone out to do a little shopping before we leave. May I take a message?"

"He's leaving? Oh, no, he can't be," exclaimed Veronica.

"I am Mrs. Hoffman. Is there some way I can help you, mademoiselle, or is it madame?"

"I am Veronica, Sister Veronica from Yambuku. Surely he told you about me and what we did together."

"Yes. He told me what a great help you were in the villages."

"Now there is an emergency. The fever has started again in Yambuku, and I thought he should know, and that maybe he would feel it necessary to return with me."

"I don't think that is possible," Rachel replied. "We are scheduled for a trip throughout Europe for the next two weeks before returning to the United States."

"I am sorry, madame. It was just a thought. Please forgive me for bothering you. . . . It's just that . . ." She slumped against the back of the booth. She tried to continue. "Madame Hoffman, please understand—" but her voice broke as anguish rose in her throat. She hung up and faced the wall to hide her tears. Aaron had been her last hope of salvaging her reputation. She struggled to think through her fatigue. Should she call her family? No, that would only complicate things more. What about Sister Adeline? She was in 's Gravenwezel. She might be persuaded to send her back. Veronica dialed the number and spoke in French rather than Flemish to disguise her voice from the office sister.

"I am sorry, madame. Sister Adeline is not in the house."

"Where is she?"

"Madame, I cannot—"

"I know, I know," blurted out Veronica, "but please understand, it is very important that I reach her."

"She went to Brussels to do some errands. You will have to call back this evening," replied the office sister.

"What about Sister Augustina? Can she come to the phone?" She heard her voice becoming shrill.

"The Mother Superior of our Yambuku mission?"

"Yes. Yes. Is she there?"

"Madame . . ."

Veronica tightened her grip on the phone and, reverting to Flemish, she burst out, "I am Sister Veronica. Please call Augustina to the phone."

"Veronica! Why were you speaking French? This is Ursula. Where are you? Are you all right? You sound frantic."

"Please, I beg you, no questions. I must talk to Augustina."

"She is visiting the Claes."

"Sister Matilda's family?"

"Yes. If you want to call her there, I will give you the number."

Veronica wrote it down, said thank you, and hung up. She hesitated before calling, not wanting Matilda's family to know she was in Belgium. Yet, if Ursula knew, the news would spread in minutes. She dialed and waited for Augustina to come to the phone. A young couple strolled by, their arms wrapped around each other. A child sucking a lollipop trailed behind, watching a half-dozen suntanned youths in shorts and wild shirts under heavy backpacks, laughing their way to new adventures. A bored attendant pushed an old woman in a wheelchair past the telephone booth. Her lap was hidden under a pile of packages and plastic bags. Veronica wished with all her heart that she could melt into the crowd of normal people with simple problems.

"Hello. Sister Augustina here."

"This is Veronica. I am in Brussels."

"Veronica? Sister Veronica?"

"Yes."

"You are in Brussels?"

"Yes. At the airport."

"Why? What happened?"

"The fever returned to Yambuku."

"And you are here? Who gave you permission to leave Zaire?" asked Augustina severely.

"No one. I panicked and fled. I regret it enormously. . . ." Veronica's voice wavered as she struggled for control. "If you can come to the airport with money, I will buy a ticket and return right away." There was silence at the other end. "Augustina, please, what must I do?"

"If you are already in Brussels, you cannot return to Zaire. You may have endangered people in the plane."

"No," shouted Veronica into the phone. "It's not like that. You can be sure that I have not caught the disease."

After a short pause, Augustina gave Veronica her orders. "Wait at the airport, but do not shake hands with anyone or talk to anyone. We have to make certain you are not contagious."

"I am certain," said Veronica frantically.

"I hope you are right, but I must call the Tropical Institute and ask them what to do with you. In the meantime, I will send the mission van for you. Wait where the taxis pull up for passengers and, Veronica . . . do not touch anyone."

"I understand," said Veronica, surrendering. She hung up and leaned against the side of the booth. She had been so sure that she had not been exposed to the disease. Now Augustina had raised doubts, and the doctors of the Institute of Tropical Medicine would force her to unravel the events of the past few days. Could Serafina have been contagious; could she have passed on the infection when they embraced? If so, was Collard now carrying the virus? "It is not possible," she said out loud, shaking her head at the telephone. She walked slowly to the passport control desk. A blond, rosy-cheeked policeman smiled at her and took her papers.

"Welcome home, Sister," he said, stamping her passport and handing it back.

"Thank you." Would he be infected by touching her documents? She walked over to the baggage area. Her suitcase was the only one left; it circled around on the carousel like a lost dog, abandoned by its master. She lifted it and carried it out to the sidewalk where the taxis lined up. Pushing her suitcase against the wall, she sat on it. A car coming from Antwerp would take a while. She watched people coming and going—happy families reunited, sad ones saying good-bye—and she thought of the first time she had left home for Africa. A lifetime ago.

The Mass had been celebrated by the Monseigneur himself. Veronica and Lucie, dressed in new white habits that marked them for missionary service in the tropics, sat in the front row. Behind them knelt the sisters of the congregation in black robes and black veils offset by the flare of their starched white headpieces. The families and friends of the nuns being offered for foreign duty sat behind them.

After the service everyone filed down the hall for a breakfast laid out on long refectory tables. Veronica sat, radiant, between her proud parents. Gabrielle, in her early teens, was across the table, her eyes wide with admiration. Veronica's brothers and sisters joined them. For an instant she felt again the excitement of wearing white among her black-robed sisters. But now, being singled out was the last thing she wanted. She forced her mind back again into memory.

She and Lucie sat behind their fathers in the mission bus on the way to the Antwerp docks. Lucie's father, who dealt in rare Flemish books, was anxious about his young daughter setting off for strange, distant places. Veronica remembered her own father saying, "Do not worry; they go under God's protection." But, to Lucie's father, Africa was still "the dark continent," peopled by primitive tribes with strange and sometime savage customs. As a formal Catholic, he supported the religious convictions of his women, and, as a solid burgher from Antwerp, he appreciated the civilizing role played by Belgian missionary teachers and nurses. But the Congo was a long way off, and there were too many unknowns.

Veronica could still see the S.S. *Elizabethville*, flagship of the Compagnie Maritime du Congo. She could smell the mixture of wet pilings, rope, and salt water that rose from the dock. The families gathered in the Customs shed while papers were checked by officials, then baggage was taken away in handcarts by porters smelling of beer and garlic. Finally the hands of the clock in the tower overlooking the scene moved and its chimes rang out the hour. Ships' officers shouted, "Passengers on board, please," as they moved through the crowd. Veronica gave each member of her family a hug and a kiss. Gabrielle, who was crying, she held for an extra moment, then whispered in her ear, "Your turn will come soon."

She remembered the excitement she felt as she stood looking up at her father, knowing how proud he was of her commitment. He made the sign of the cross on her forehead with his thumb and said, "Go with God." She gave him a hug, then turned quickly to walk through the gate with the other passengers and up the gangway, disappearing into the imposing flank of the ocean liner. A black steward led the two nuns to their tiny cabin. After checking their bags, they ran up the stairs to the lifeboat deck with its great white funnel on which was painted the blue flag and gold stars of *Le Congo Belge*. At the rail they searched the crowd below and waved as a distant cheer came from their families.

Veronica closed her eyes and heard again the steam whistle behind the funnel splutter and hiss to clear its brass tubes before releasing a deep-throated blast that startled the passengers on deck and reverberated around the harbor. She heard the cry of seagulls around the mast tops and saw them swoop to skim the water where bilge had left a patch of refuse on the surface. Then the space between the ship and the dock had slowly widened, and the strip of scum and garbage floating on smooth water was replaced by sun-lit ripples as the liner eased out into the breeze from the estuary of the Scheldt. She and Lucie had glanced at each other and tried to smile, but the reality of the time and distance which would separate them from their loved ones was too much. They fought to keep back their tears as they pushed through the other passengers toward the privacy of their cabin.

The screaming of a child brought Veronica back to the present. A young woman struggled along the sidewalk carrying a heavy suitcase in one hand and dragging the bawling child with the other. She dropped her suitcase next to Veronica and turned to the little girl.

"Now stop your blubbering. I know you are tired—so am I. Your father will be here to pick us up soon. He will not be happy to see you crying." The mother pulled a handkerchief out of her pocket, wiped the child's eyes and face, and squeezed her nose dry. She glanced at Veronica. *"Quel voyage! Bonjour, ma soeur."*

"Bonjour, madame," mumbled Veronica.

"Shake hands with the sister," said the woman, pushing the child in front of Veronica.

"Bonjour, ma soeur," repeated the little girl shyly.

Veronica smiled and started to take the child's hand, then quickly pulled away. *"Bonjour, ma petite.* I cannot shake hands with you. I have . . . I have a sore hand."

"What happened?" asked the mother.

Embarrassed, Veronica replied, "Oh, nothing serious, just—nothing serious." At that moment the gray convent van drove up and stopped opposite her. "Please excuse me. I have to go now. Good-bye."

The driver came around the back of the van and greeted Veronica. The old man had driven for the nuns as long as she could remember. "Welcome home, Sister."

"Thank you, Pieter. I think it is better we do not shake hands. I might be infectious, but I do not think so," said Veronica. The old man heaved her suitcase into the back. They pulled away and in moments were speeding up the autoroute toward Antwerp. Veronica stared out of the window. A low, gray overcast covered the flat countryside and leafless woods through which the highway had been carved. The empty fields were mottled with patches of dirty snow, and clusters of red-tiled farmhouses and barns huddled together against the wind from the coast.

"How are things in Zaire?" asked Pieter, looking at Veronica in the rearview mirror.

"Same as ever." She didn't feel like talking and, anyway, the old man had never been out of the country and understood even less about Africa than Luc did about Belgium. Pieter concentrated on his driving. At the edge of the city, he left the highway and, traveling on back roads, drove into 's Gravenwezel, turning left onto the lane that led to the convent and its school. As the imposing red-brick façade and shuttered windows of the convent's main building came into view, Veronica shivered. Pieter tooted the horn to announce their arrival. He retrieved Veronica's suitcase from the back of the van, then opened the door for her. She stepped out carefully onto frozen slush, then looked up at the windows. Faces peered at her from behind blinds. She followed Pieter up to the huge mahogany door with its polished brass handle. She heard a click as the small metal grill through which visitors could be inspected slid shut. As Pieter reached for the bell the door opened, and Augustina stood at the threshold.

"Come in, and take a seat in the visitors' parlor," she commanded. Veronica walked through the door into the dark little room just to the left of the entrance hall. She heard the great door slam shut behind her.

CHAPTER 22

Veronica sat alone in a straight-backed chair in the ante-room reserved for visitors. Her eyes wandered over the furnishings, mostly gifts from benefactors or liquidated estates. On the wall across the room, a crucifix with an angular, copper Christ hung above the fireplace. A doll dressed in a blue robe trimmed with gold balanced a crown on her blond curls and stood dustless under a plastic dome on one end of the mantelpiece. At the other end, cherubs held a brass world above an elaborate clock whose hands were fixed at noon or midnight. The small brick hearth was partly hidden by an antique prie-dieu, its intricate ivory inlays gleaming in the gray light that filtered through the window shade. It was a room for strangers, where the clash of odds and ends made little difference. Before she had sailed to Africa, Veronica occasionally rescued friends from this somber place and led them to the more comfortable parlor near the staircase, reserved for the families of nuns. The silence was oppressive, like that of the potato cellar her mother banished her to when she lost her temper as a child. The opening door startled her; Augustina walked in.

"I have made arrangements for you to have a room to yourself," she said, closing the door behind her. "Now I must call the professor at the institute. He wants to ask you some questions." She sat next to the telephone and dialed.

The professor was the last person Veronica wanted to talk to. The man who'd been so rude to her in Yambuku was about to interrogate her.

"This is Sister Augustina, Professor. Sister Veronica has just arrived. I will put her on." She pointed the receiver at Vero, who walked over to take it.

"Hello."

"So, what have you done, Sister?" asked the professor bluntly.

"What do you mean, 'What have you done?' "

"Sister Augustina has told me that a new case of the fever was admitted to Yambuku Hospital and that you left the mission, apparently without permission." The professor's tone of voice was that of a prosecutor laying a trap for a hostile witness.

Veronica flushed with anger. "That is right, sir, but I was not exposed."

"How do you know that, Sister? You are not even a nurse, if my memory serves me well."

"I know because I lived through the whole epidemic and learned about transmission of the disease and the precautions that need to be taken."

"I must ask you, nevertheless, to tell me exactly what happened, who was with you, and what you know about the patient. I will decide, not you, whether you are to be isolated, and I can do that only after I have all the facts. And now, Sister, please let us start from the beginning."

Veronica sat down, closed her eyes, and told him every detail she could remember, from the moment Serafina had suspected the patient had the fever, to her own trip and arrival in Brussels. The professor listened without interruption.

"Thank you, Sister. Now I have a few more questions." She could hear him shuffling paper. "Let's see . . . you say you never touched the patient, that you only talked to him through the window. But how can you be sure that the other sister did not touch him?"

"Because Serafina is a well-trained nurse, and as soon as she realized that the man might have the fever she told Sukato he was the only person allowed near the patient. Sukato has antibodies."

"Yes, I remember him," said the professor. "But how do you know that the sister did not touch the patient before she made the diagnosis? Surely, if she is as good a nurse as you say, she would have examined him before arriving at the conclusion that he had a deadly disease."

"I only know what she told me, which was that she did not touch the patient."

"Maybe she lied. Maybe she was scared to tell you the truth."

"Sisters do not lie, Professor." She glanced at Augustina, who looked away.

"Did you have any physical contact with Sister—Sister Serafina?"

"Of course not!"

"Did you not shake hands with her when you left?"

Veronica paused to think back. "No. I embraced her and thanked her for coming when I needed her."

"Did you kiss her?"

"No! Certainly not! I don't remember. . . . I doubt it."

"But you do not know," said the professor, a note of triumph in his voice.

"I know that Sister Serafina had no contact with the patient and could not have been contaminated. As I told you, I was present throughout the epidemic. I know that only those who touched a patient with the fever became infected and died."

"I am aware of that, Sister. I am simply trying to confirm

that you, yourself, did not touch any person who might have been exposed to the patient."

"I repeat, I had no such contact."

"Did you shake hands with Sukato when you left? Did any one of you touch any member of the patient's family?"

The questions went on and on. What physical contacts had she had with the French nuns in Gbadolite, with Collard, and with the passengers on the plane? Veronica was already exhausted when she landed in Brussels; now her head began to swim. This man on the other end of the phone had the persistence of a mosquito. She knew that sooner or later, because of her fatigue and growing confusion, he would find a way through her defenses. She looked toward Augustina for support, but the older woman's eyes were fixed on her hands in her lap.

"Sister, I asked you a question," said the voice in her ear.

"I am sorry, Doctor, my attention wandered for a moment."

"That is just the problem, isn't it? Your attention may also have wandered over the last few days and led you to do things which would have placed others in danger." His attack was relentless, and the questions came like bullets. Veronica's answers became shorter and shorter: "Yes, sir. No, sir," said in a flat voice. Finally the professor conceded that she was probably not contagious. However, to be safe, she was to have no physical contact with anyone; she must use only her own dishes and towels; she must sleep in a room by herself for two weeks. Every day she would record her temperature. If she developed a fever, or any symptoms at all, she was to call him, day or night. Veronica handed the telephone to Augustina and buried her face in her hands. Augustina acknowledged the professor's orders and hung up. She stood quietly next to Veronica for a moment, then said, "Come, I will take you upstairs. You can wash and join us for lunch."

Veronica picked up her suitcase, and as they left the room, she asked, "Where are Antonie and Father Dubonnet?"

"The father is recovering from surgery on his throat, and Antonie is in a nursing home. She has wrapped herself in a shell and needs special care."

Veronica followed Augustina up the dark stairs to a small spare room. Dropping her bag on the bed, she washed her face and hands in the sink. She saw her reflection in the mirror—how haggard and old—and pressed her face into a cold washcloth. *Two weeks of isolation in this dark convent!*

Augustina was waiting for her when she came out, and they walked downstairs and along the tiled corridor to the refectory. As they stepped into the room, the black-veiled nuns turned to stare; conversation stopped. Veronica was acutely aware of her white missionary uniform. Her friend Ursula raised her hand in greeting, but dropped it quickly. Matilda's own sister, a confidante of long standing, smiled briefly and turned away. Veronica followed Augustina to the end of an empty table. The conversation in the large room resumed, first in spurts, then normally, as though nothing out of the ordinary had happened. A young sister served them potato soup from a large tureen. Augustina and Veronica ate in silence.

How different from the last time Veronica had returned to the convent. Then, she had been on home leave after four successful years with her agricultural projects. Membership in the cooperative was growing beyond her expectations; the rice harvest had beaten all previous records. The sisters had gathered around her during her first meal, and she had regaled them with stories of her trips to hidden vil-

lages and of the youngsters who were learning new ways to
plant crops and take care of the soil. She'd been so happy
then, so proud.

After the meal, Veronica returned upstairs to unpack. She
showered, then dressed in black, pulling on a black cardi-
gan to counter the chill. She stood in the middle of the
room and stared through the voile curtains over the narrow
window. The bare branches of the trees next to the empty
parking lot jabbed into a leaden sky. The only sound that
reached her was the muted rumble of trucks and buses on
's Gravenwezel's Principalstraat. She closed her eyes and
pictured, framed by the window in Augustina's office, the
flame tree in full scarlet bloom next to Masangaya's house.
Fatigue made her light-headed and dizzy. She quickly
opened her eyes and steadied herself on the bedside table.
She fought the urge to complete her isolation by going to
bed and curling up in a ball. Turning away from the window, she walked to the door, opened it, and stepped out
into the corridor. An old nun, her head bowed in meditation
over folded hands, passed by without a sign of recognition.
Veronica made her way downstairs through the halls to the
chapel. She walked slowly to the altar rail, clasping her rosary, then knelt and tried to pray. Images pushed into her
mind of the dying man, of Gabrielle and the others standing
on the convent steps, of the long forest tunnel. She repeated
Hail Mary's, Glory Be's, and Our Father's like a robot, and
pleaded with the Holy Mother to ease her burden of guilt
and shame. She heard footsteps behind her, looked over her
shoulder, saw Augustina approaching, and stood to meet
her. But Augustina stepped into a pew and knelt. Veronica
turned back to the sanctuary and continued her recitation to
Mary as she fingered her rosary. After a while she heard
Augustina's retreating footsteps. She was alone again. Lowering her head onto her folded arms, she closed her eyes.

Moments later, the rosary slipped from her fingers and the rattle of it hitting the marble floor roused her. She stood, genuflected, and left the chapel for her room. Once in bed, she fell into a deep sleep. Awaking around midnight, she turned on the light and saw that someone had brought her a bowl of soup and some bread and left it on the table by the window.

Her first thought on waking was the confession she would have to make before the morning service and communion. She dressed quickly and was the first in line when *le père* Anselmus, the wizened old father confessor, shuffled in with his cane. She was relieved to see him, glad that it was not the younger priest whom she had met during her last home leave and who reminded her of Father Gérard at his most severe. She stepped into the cubicle and, after the usual invocation, admitted her transgressions, fears, and desertion of duty. The priest, a perceptive old man, who had listened to the sins of nuns for years, encouraged her to continue. She listed her moments of pride and intolerance, her quick temper and lapses of submission. With a feather touch, he probed the corners of her conscience, and she told him of her talks with Dr. Aaron, then, hesitatingly, described the episode in the hut during the storm. The priest waited silently—long enough to allow her to say more. Then, satisfied that her confession was genuine and complete, he absolved her of all her sins, real and imagined. As penance, for the next seven days, she would read Biblical passages in the presence of all the sisters. He would choose the readings for her; she would receive them before the evening service. Veronica had not kneeled as a penitent before the whole community since her days as a novice. Her face flushed with shame as she stepped out of the confessional. The old man's gentle voice called her back.

"Sister Veronica, never forget that big falls come only to those who risk much for the faith."

"*Oui, mon père.* Father Dubonnet, I mean Father Jef Maas, said something like that to me before he left Yambuku. Have you seen him since his return?"

"Yes. He is recovering from his surgery but still has trouble speaking. When you are released by the Mother Superior, pay him a visit; it would be good for both of you."

Just before vespers, Augustina handed Veronica an envelope from Father Anselmus. She opened it and found the readings he had chosen for her to fulfill her penance. With the sisters filing past her, she stood by the chapel door and marked the passages in her Bible. After all were seated, the bell for vespers tolled, Veronica walked slowly up the aisle, her hands clasping her Bible in an attitude of reverence. She stepped through the opening in the rail and knelt on the marble step in front of the altar. The bell stopped ringing. She opened the Bible, took a deep breath, and read aloud so all could hear: "Saint Paul's letter to the Philippians 2, III: 'I pray you to give me the utter joy of knowing you are living in harmony, with the same feeling of love, with one heart and soul, never acting for private ends or from vanity, but humbly considering each other the better man, and each with an eye to the interests of others as well as to his own.'

"Proverbs 16, XVIII and 18, XII: 'Pride ends in disaster. . . . Haughtiness ends in disaster: to be humble is the way to honor.' "

She scanned the paper. In closing, the priest wrote that she might choose as her final reading her "favorite passage from the Holy Scriptures." She closed her eyes and recited: " 'Consider the lilies of the field, how they grow; they toil not, neither do they spin: and yet I say unto you, that even Solomon in all his glory was not arrayed like one of these.' "

She bowed her head, and the Mother Superior started vespers. Veronica remained immobile for the next hour. The chapel was cold, and her knees ached from the chill of the bare stone.

By the end of her seventh day of penance, in front of all those who gathered in the chapel each evening, she felt superior to no one.

But God forgave more readily than His chosen servants.

Veronica passed the next week in silent torment. Few sisters spoke to her, and those who did covered their disapproval with a veil of chilly formality; most remained silent in her presence. During one noonday meal in the refectory, the director of the primary school read aloud part of a letter she had received from Sister Clarysse of the Binga mission: " 'The Zairian Church aims to take over all missions. Naturally, that is their right, but we hope there will be enough time to make a proper transition. The local politicians, especially the youth wing of the party, have been quite aggressive in wanting us out. Of course, they covet our vehicles and supplies. We pray that God will guide us in His wisdom.' "

In the conversation around the table that followed, one of the sisters turned to Veronica and Augustina. "What do you think our missions should do?"

Augustina replied, "We must stay as long as we can to train Zairians to be responsible for their own affairs. Although our Africans have given us very little trouble I am sure that as the politicians become bolder our lives will become more difficult."

"But, of course," cut in the school director, looking straight at Veronica, "if life in Zaire becomes too risky, we Catholics could just run away." Veronica opened her mouth to reply but was stilled by Augustina's grip on her arm. Furious, she rose, left the table, and ran down the corridor. As she started up the stairs, she spun around and faced Augustina, who had followed her.

"The Africans are more Christian than some of our sisters. A thief caught stealing walks up and down the village road with a dead chicken around his neck for a few days, then he is readmitted to the community. Here, they revel in my guilt."

"You are not in Africa now."

"Really?" exclaimed Veronica. "How silly of me to forget." She stomped up the few remaining steps to the landing.

"Veronica!"

"I'm sorry, Augustina. But I have had as much of being treated like a pariah as I can take."

"Never mind," said Augustina. "I spoke to the professor this afternoon: your quarantine is officially over today. Now get your coat. Your father and mother are anxious to see you. They have been calling every evening. I have told them only that there were problems in Yambuku, and you had returned . . . for discussions."

"Why didn't you tell me?"

"I did not want you crying into the telephone and upsetting them."

That evening Veronica composed a letter to Gabrielle.

's Gravenwezel
December 1976
Gabrielle, my very dear sister,

I write to you because I know you will understand. Although I am your older sister, I pray that you will never put me on a pedestal.

For the past two weeks I have been walking alone through a dark tunnel. How gray and chilly are the winters in Antwerp! How cold are the hearts of our sisters toward one of their own.

With Augustina I went to see our parents this afternoon. They are both well. Father as silent as ever, and Mother in full control. It was difficult because they do not know why I came back and trust that it has something to do with our mission work. I was grateful they did not pry.

It is hard for them to realize that home for me is Africa. I do miss all of it: the clouds, the flowers, the gentle people, especially the children with their bright eyes, and, of course, the sun and even the heat. I miss meeting my agricultural friends in the villages. I even miss the storms at night. But, after the convent, the warmth of the fireplace in our parents' house is welcome. I wish I could spend more time with them. Maybe I will.

I hope to receive a letter from you soon telling me that you are well and that you understood that I did not have the courage to be responsible for everyone and everything in Yambuku in the face of another epidemic. I am not imperturbable like Augustina. I am almost afraid to ask whether you have any news of more patients with the fever.

I will write again soon. Pray that I may find peace again in my heart. With all my love, your sister and Sister in Christ,

Veronica

The next day she set out for the House of the Pères de Scheut, a twenty-minute walk from the convent. The morning was windless, and snow fell softly on the path before her as she turned down the winding lane bordered by chestnuts that led to the monastery. The fresh white mantle on the trees reminded her of a glass ball her father had given her one Christmas. A happy little snowman with a black top hat and red jacket stood in a swirling snowstorm she could cause by shaking the globe. It had been a favorite possession and one of the hardest to leave when she entered the convent. Today, blinking through the white flakes on her eyelashes, she felt like that snowman. She hurried toward the old stone mansion crouched among gnarled oaks. Its deep-set windows and stubby, crenelated towers reminded her of history book pictures in which homes were hovels or castles. Would Dubonnet feel out of place and cramped in this ancient, dark monastery? How different the winters were here from all those they had spent together in the tropics. How would he greet her? How much did he know? When she had called earlier to ask permission for the visit, the sister in charge of invalid fathers had avoided her questions about him.

She pulled the bell handle next to the iron-studded Gothic door, and after a short wait, it was opened by a very old and bent priest with a white beard down to his waist like Father Time. He straightened up, as much as he could and ran a thin hand over the few wisps still sprouting from his parchment scalp.

"Sister Veronica of Yambuku?" he asked, his small blue eyes squinting in the glare from the snow.

"*Oui, mon père.*"

"Come in, come in. We have been expecting you. Dubonnet—yes, we call him that, too—is in the solarium, waiting."

Veronica stepped into the front hall. "How is he?"

The old man closed the door. "Let me take your cloak." She handed it to him, and he shook off the snow.

"How is he?" he repeated, hanging her cloak on a rack. "No different than he has always been, except for the hole in his neck. You know about his surgery?"

"Very little."

"They cut a tumor out next to his voice box and put a tube in so he could breathe while things heal. He puts his finger on the hole to speak. Sounds like an old bullfrog. But he is doing well, considering." He stuck out his hand formally. "I am Brother Boniface, the doorkeeper and general factotum for the fathers. I am honored to meet you, Sister."

"Honored . . . ?" Gently, she took his frail hand.

"You are the sister who rides through the forest on a red Vespa. He has told us all about you. But come; he is waiting."

Veronica smiled and followed him out of the entrance hall, down one side of a cloistered, snow-covered garden, and into a large solarium. In a corner by the back wall, Dubonnet, in a spotless white cassock, was stretched out on a wicker chaise longue. He lay under a sprawling broadleafed rubber plant fixed to a trellis in the shape of a canopy. One one side a potted sentry palm stood guard; on the other, a red hibiscus plant and lady ferns graced a card table on which papers and books were scattered.

"*Voila,*" said Boniface, with a sweep of his hand. "This is the nearest thing to a jungle we could manage."

She laughed, "Oh, *mon père* . . ."

"*La soeur* Veronica, herself," announced Dubonnet, in a hoarse whisper. He pulled his hand out from under his beard.

She reached for it. "How are you, Father?"

His lips moved, and a windy cough shook his chest. He pulled his hand away from her and groped around his neck. "As you can see . . ." he croaked, "I am living in regal splendor. Our Boniface keeps me supplied with good cognac and Bukavu cigars." He reached behind his back and pulled out a bundle of dark cheroots bound together with raffia. "We have to hide them from the witch of a nun who has appointed herself my guardian. She says they are bad for me, but the truth is she has no appreciation of fine, native tobacco." Veronica laughed and sat on the chair that Boniface pushed against her legs.

"Tea? Coffee? Or something stronger for a winter day?" he asked.

"I would love a cup of coffee," said Veronica.

"She likes it strong with lots of sugar," said Dubonnet. "And put in a little of our fresh cream."

"And you, Father?" asked the old man, fussing with papers on the card table.

"A glass of your good port might do wonders for my voice and weak blood," replied Dubonnet. Boniface shuffled off.

Dubonnet looked at Veronica; for a moment their eyes met, and she looked away. "And you, Sister Veronica, how are you now?"

"Now?" she asked. He nodded.

"The better for seeing you, Father. Have you been told everything?"

"No, but enough to have prayed daily for the revival of your spirit and that you would be spared bitterness."

"My spirit is struggling."

"It is a law of nature that when pride is crushed, the spirit often founders."

He snatched a handful of tissues from the packet on his lap, pushed his beard aside, and after a deep, whistling inspiration, broke into explosive coughing that cleared the phlegm from the metal tube in his trachea, but left him gasping for air. Veronica jumped up, then hovered over him, feeling useless. Sweat ran down his forehead, and his skin looked like wet putty. At that moment Brother Boniface returned to the room, quickly deposited their drinks on the table, then hurried away, saying, "I will go for Sister Chantal."

"No!" wheezed Dubonnet, groping for the opening in his neck. He plugged it with his finger and tried to breathe, but started another coughing fit.

"Father, try to relax," pleaded Veronica.

"Relax!" His finger was back on the hole in synchrony with his breathing. He puffed away, then looked up at her and smiled, waggling his bushy eyebrows. "I will be better when I learn to play this pipe like a flute," he rasped. "Anyway, you don't know Chantal. She washed my beard with bleach when I was still groggy from the shots they gave me after the operation."

"I thought there was something different about you," exclaimed Veronica.

"I smelled like a diaper laundry."

"Now he smells like *une fumière*, a dung heap," said a gentle voice from the door. Sister Chantal stepped up to the chaise longue, assured herself that the priest had recovered from his spell, and turned to Veronica. "You must be Sister Veronica. We are grateful for your visit. Father Jef has spoken of you often, and in glowing terms. How did you and Sister Augustina ever deal with him?" Chantal's smile and soft voice were disarming.

"We didn't," replied Veronica. "He dealt with us." She was struck by the serenity in the face of this beautiful nun.

"Maybe bringing cleanliness and good manners to the natives of the dark continent is less arduous than trying to civilize some of our Christians," said Chantal, resting her hand on the priest's shoulder. He ran his fingers through his pristine beard and looked up at her like a comfortable, shaggy dog. Boniface guffawed in the background. Chantal handed Dubonnet his glass of port and Veronica her coffee.

"Now I will leave you. I am sure you have much to talk

about." At the door she turned, "Call if you need anything. My office is just down the hall." Veronica acknowledged her offer with a wave and turned back to Dubonnet.

"I expected a witch to ride in on a broom. She is kindness itself."

Dubonnet pursed his lips. "Sweetness can be a velvet pad that softens the shackle."

"You're impossible!"

"I know. It has taken me a long time to arrive at such a finely tuned state." He paused. "And now, Veronica, I want to know. How are you?"

She sat down. "Expiated and raw. The passages the father confessor gave me to read struck at my heart. Do you know him?"

"He lives in the room next to mine."

"Did you . . . ?" Dubonnet looked at her wide-eyed. "Oh, *mon père* . . ."

"Oh, *mon père*, oh, *mon père*," croaked the priest. "You are beginning to sound like one of those cracked records you used to play in the refectory." With his blue eyes fixed on her face, he persisted. "And now, Veronica, how is it with you?"

She cradled her coffee cup in her hand. "Starting right now, at this very moment, I am less empty than I have been for weeks."

"That is good." He reached for his glass with one hand and covered the hole in his neck with the other. "When I was a young priest, an old Polish lady worked here in the garden. She had a way with roses and an intolerance of weeds. Once, on her rounds of the flower beds, she caught me sitting on the stone bench in the bower, feeling sorry for myself." Dubonnet sipped the port and licked his lips. "She paused to look at me and declared, 'A sad Christian is indeed a sad Christian,' then continued on her way." He drained the last drop from his glass and handed it to Veronica. "You should spend time with your family and work outside. Rake away the debris of winter, *ma soeur*, and prepare for the spring."

"I will do that, Father. Now I must leave, or Sister Chantal may think I have exhausted you."

"Never mind her! You have made me a happy old Christian." His eyes were bright in the way she remembered so well. "You will come again?"

Taking his hand, she squeezed it. "Of course." She turned quickly and left.

As time went on, Veronica was given permission to spend nights with her family between vespers and matins. One evening she walked home to find a letter on the table next to the front door. It was postmarked Antwerp, but she recognized the writing. She ran upstairs to her room, closed the door and, with trembling fingers, ripped open the envelope.

Binga Catholic Mission
Republic of Zaire
December 1976
Dear Veronica, my beloved oldest sister,

I imagine that by now you have been able to get the rest you needed so badly. So that you do not worry, I have to tell you that we had word from Luc that things are going along quite well at Yambuku. He mentioned that after the man died, no more patients with symptoms of the fever have been seen.

As you asked me, I said nothing about the situation and the reason for your leaving until after I had been back at Binga for a few days. Because everyone here knows you and respects you, there was only a little difficulty. When I informed the Mother Superior that we thought a patient had come in with the fever, I was ordered to take the usual precautions. I told her that I had not even seen the patient, but she insisted. The disease spreads fear, like rabies or the plague. Now everything is back to normal, and I am fine.

Veronica, knowing you as I do, I cannot think that you will be very happy in Belgium. I hope you will come back soon. I am sure everyone in Yambuku misses you, as you must miss them.

Please give our father and mother big hugs for me, and have them embrace you in return. I must take this over to the house of the fathers now as Father Verlinden is leaving for Lisala and Belgium and agreed to take this letter with him.

My prayers and love are with you. From your own sister and Sister in Christ,

Gabrielle

Veronica put the letter down on the bed and took her pillow and hugged it as she would have liked to hug Gabrielle. She rocked gently, her nose and lips brushing the top of the pillow. *My little sister, thank you for being so warmhearted and so guileless. I have not been such a good example for you to follow, but that does not change your love.* She knelt by the bed for a few minutes, taking the letter between her hands, then got up and hurried downstairs. Her mother glanced over her shoulder and continued stirring soup on the stove.

"I can see you received good news."

"You can read the letter for yourself," said Veronica, putting it on the kitchen table. She went over to her mother and, taking the wooden spoon out of her hand, spun her around and gave her a hug. "This is from Gabrielle."

Her mother returned the hug. "I'm so happy to see you coming out of yourself."

"It's about time," said Veronica. "Where is Father?"

"In the front room. Tell him to come and eat," replied her mother, retrieving the spoon from her daughter. She looked up at the ceiling and said, "Thank you, Blessed Virgin."

The old farmer was reading the evening paper by the fire.

"Supper is ready, Father," said Veronica, walking in. He folded his paper carefully and put it on the table next to his chair. He stood, took the pipe out of his mouth, and put it in a rack on the mantelpiece. She hugged him and rested her head on his shoulder.

"That must have been a very good letter to bring a smile to my oldest daughter's face," he said quietly.

"It was, Father. Gabrielle sent you her love. She is so understanding and so free of judgment." He kissed the top of her head.

Sitting around the fireplace after supper, Veronica told her parents about her last two months in Yambuku.

The next morning Veronica told Augustina that she wanted to work in the convent's cemetery and gardens. The leaves and sticks left by the winter winds needed to be gathered and burned.

During the following weeks, Veronica worked outside every day and visited Dubonnet regularly. Sometimes, wearing a yellow slicker like the fishermen on the Scheldt, she went about her tasks in the rain or blustery squalls that swept over the lowlands. Then, almost overnight, life returned to the grass, and a new vigor and resilience crept into the bushes and fruit trees as sap pushed upward to meet the spring.

Father Dubonnet was slowly losing weight but not his sense of humor. One day, toward the end of the month, she informed him that she was ready to return to Yambuku. He motioned her to push her chair up close. "Are you sure you are ready?"

"I am ready, *mon père*," replied Veronica. He pointed to a letter on the table, then put his finger over the hole in his neck.

"From the Bumba mission ... the riverboats are paralysed ... no fuel." He coughed and sucked in air. "The party thugs appropriated the mission truck ... teachers, who have not been paid for months, are on strike." He reached out to the table.

Veronica handed him his glass. "Surely the worse things are, the more they need us, Father."

He swallowed a mouthful of water and made a face. "Boniface forgot the cognac, or that guardian angel has locked it up." Veronica retrieved the glass.

"Do you want me to call her?" He shook his head, looking at her as he would a silly child. After a moment he continued.

"They do need us ... but in a new way." He took some deep breaths and continued in short bursts. "When you return ... back the Zairians when you can ... in all good conscience. Be a supporter ... not an intruder. And Veronica ... temper discipline with compassion." He stopped to rest. "No doubt someone has taken over your work with the cooperative.... Are you ready to accept that?"

"I think so," she said dubiously.

The priest fixed her with his eyes. "Sister, are you prepared to take orders ... from a Zairian?"

She looked at him, gave a little shrug of her shoulder, and stood up. "I will think about that."

As the days went by, dawn came earlier, and the faint

smells and feel of spring replaced the chilly dampness of winter. One morning in late March, Veronica noticed that little nubs had appeared among the branches on the oak trees over her head. Picking up a twig, she fingered the point of green peeking out from a soft brown shell that was sticky between her fingers. Her visits home had always been in the summer; she had not seen spring for twenty years.

During the days that followed, she thought about Dubonnet's admonitions as she pruned the fruit trees in the convent gardens—an art that Sister Matilda had taught her when she was a novice.

"We had a message from the missionaries in Bumba," said Adeline one morning at breakfast. "One of them drove up to Yambuku two weeks ago and reported that the hospital was running surprisingly well with Sukato in charge, but that many of the children straggled in late for their lessons and were loud and uncontrolled in the classrooms. You knew, of course, that Dr. Collard asked Dr. Miatamba to cover the hospital until a permanent doctor was assigned to Yambuku." Augustina and Veronica nodded.

Adeline continued, "The father said that the gardens are being maintained, but because of the lack of fuel for the trucks, the rice and manioc are piling up in the fields and rotting. His conclusion is that the sisters need to return to take charge again."

"Vero, have you seen any newspapers during the last ten days?" asked Augustina.

"I've seen the headlines about another crisis between Zaire and Belgium," replied Veronica. "We have been through the same thing before. The pressure builds up, a few concessions are made with no loss of face by either side, and things return to their normal chaotic state."

"I think it is more serious this time, at least for us who

work in Zaire. It has to do with budget allocations and the Belgian-Zairian Cooperation Programs. President Mobutu has stopped Sabena flights to Kinshasa, and our minister of cooperation has countered by forbidding Belgian teachers and technicians to return to Zaire after their Easter vacations."

"That is ridiculous," replied Veronica. "The Africans need us. So long as we produce rice and take care of the people, I am sure the Zairian authorities will leave us alone."

"I hope you are right, Veronica. Anyway, I think you should plan to return to Yambuku shortly," said Augustina. "But I will not be able to travel with you for the time being."

"Why not?" asked Veronica. "You are much more needed there than I."

"The doctors have found a growth in my breast."

"A growth? A cancer?"

Augustina nodded.

"How long have you known?"

"I felt something before leaving Yambuku." She avoided Veronica's eyes. "When I returned here a doctor checked me, obtained an X ray, and did a biopsy with a needle. The day before you arrived they telephoned me with the results."

"And you said nothing to me about this?"

Sister Adeline put her hand on Veronica's. "You were hardly in shape to deal with more problems," she said quietly.

"Will they operate?"

"Yes. In ten days," replied Augustina.

"I will wait for you to recover, then we can go together."

"No, Veronica. You must leave in the next few days. I do not know how long I will have to stay after the surgery.

Other treatments may be necessary, depending on what they find."

Veronica pulled Augustina to her feet and put her arms around her. "I have been such a poor friend to you."

Augustina freed herself. "On the contrary. Your courage in the face of your pain will help me through my own."

Veronica walked slowly down the lane to the monastery. Arriving at the studded door, she paused, decided not to tell Dubonnet about Augustina, then pulled the bell. In a moment she heard the latches drawn back, and the door was opened by Boniface.

"Good afternoon, *mon frère*. I have good news for Father Dubonnet," she announced. They shook hands and the old man closed the door.

"Good news is what he needs," he mumbled as Veronica hurried to the solarium.

Dubonnet was slumped down in his chaise longue, his head thrown back on a pillow, with his mouth open. Short hard breaths from his neck tube puffed through his beard. His eyebrows and whiskers could not hide his fragility. She turned at the sound of footsteps, and Sister Chantal stood beside her, a finger to her lips.

"What has happened?" whispered Veronica.

"The tumor has spread below his neck. He can hardly swallow," replied the nun softly.

"Is he in pain?"

"Not when he allows us to give him an injection."

"How long . . . ?"

Chantal raised her shoulders a little, shook her head, and put her arm around Veronica. The wicker chaise creaked. The sisters looked down at Dubonnet. Following a feeble cough, he had pushed himself up and was scrutinizing them with bright eyes. His hand fumbled for the tube, and in a husky voice, he exclaimed "*Ça, alors! C'est du jamais vu:* nuns hugging . . . in a monastery!" He reached toward a glass of water on the table. Chantal stepped forward and helped him. "Thank you. Only vultures would hover . . . over an old man without . . . serving him."

Chantal turned to Veronica. "When the time comes for our dear father, I wonder what he will say to Saint Peter?"

"Probably, 'Don't just stand there. Open the door,' " replied Veronica. The old priest pursed his lips and nodded firmly. Veronica turned to him.

"*Mon père,* I have come to say good-bye, and to ask for your blessing. I leave for Yambuku in the next few days."

The priest closed his eyes and was silent for a moment. "You return with a new objective?"

"Yes, Father. I will try."

"Then kneel." Both sisters knelt beside him. He traced the sign of the cross on Veronica's forehead with his thumb. "In the name of the Father . . . and of the Son, and of the Holy Spirit . . . I commend you to His care. Go with God . . . to serve . . . not to command."

The sisters stood, and when the priest looked at Vero, a smile rose to his face and wrinkled his deep-set eyes. "*Kende malamu, ma soeur.*" Go well, my sister.

CHAPTER 23

Sister Vero did indeed return to Yambuku soon after her last conversation with Father Dubonnet. Her resolve to work under an African was put to the test the day she arrived. Her "baby," the Agricultural Cooperative, had been taken over by an ambitious Zairian.

The next year she was given the task of turning over the Yambuku Mission to Zairian sisters.

At present she is teaching school in Binga, a long day's drive southeast from Yambuku.

EPILOGUE

After the first explosion of Zaire's Ebola virus in 1976, the country continued on its inexorable decline into economic collapse and political chaos. A different strain of Ebola erupted in south Sudan three years later. As before, it came . . . it killed . . . it disappeared.

Ten years after the tragedies in Yambuku, I had settled into a remote rural medical practice in Wyoming. One morning I opened the newspaper and read that the United States Army intended to build an aerosol lab at Dugway Proving Ground near Salt Lake City to test hemorrhagic fever viruses, including Ebola, for "defensive purposes." With Salt Lake only a three-and-a-half-hour drive from my Wyoming home, I felt a tightening in my gut: there would be no defense against a laboratory accident. An outcry from the people of Utah delayed the project—for the time being.

Four years ago, Zaire was again on the front pages. Like a coup de grace, a violent mutiny gripped the country by its throat. The troops, backed by a desperate, hungry population, rampaged through the major cities and destroyed what little remained of industry, commerce, and the rotting infrastructure.

In August of 1994, I returned to Zaire at the invitation of the Prime Minister of the transitional government, Mr. Kengo wa Dondo, an old friend. With Zairian and Belgian colleagues, we reviewed the medical crises that continue to overwhelm the country. Sleeping sickness, river blindness, goiters and cretinism, and malaria had been under effective control during the decades before independence and into the sixties and early seventies. But, with the disintegration of Zaire's economy, exacerbated by gross corruption and mismanagement, by the early 1990s these diseases were again ravaging large segments of the population and AIDS played out its slow-death scenario in every city. I visited the capital city's general hospital, called "Mama Yemo" after the president's mother. Her bronze bust still stands among fetid, skeletal buildings of what had been a proud and efficient referral center of two thousand beds. Old midwives walk four hours to come to work. Doctors thumb rides to be on call. The personnel is there, trained and ready to work, but there is no equipment, no medicines, no IV fluids worth mentioning. The medical staff come, still hoping that they can do something for people.

Prime Minister Kengo's government has started up the long and dangerous road to reforming the national economy. This means eliminating powerful and wealthy forces that have profited from the virtual collapse of government. This means countering political egos and stepping on sensitive toes. Communications, schools, medical services, and normal government functions like tax collecting and customs at the ports of entry must be rebuilt from scratch. For this to happen, roads, telephones, postal services, water supply, and sewer systems must function properly. The disintegration of these combined services signifies an infrastructure that has plummeted to catastrophic levels. In such conditions, it is not surprising that major epidemics are flourishing, and devastating diseases like hepatitis, AIDS, "red diarrhea," and now, once more, Ebola, are threatening the population and, possibly, the world.

In 1976, Zaire was still a client state of the West, and although President Mobutu's long, all-powerful dictatorship had stifled progress and milked profits for himself and his entourage to the detriment of his people, some services were still working, especially the mission hospitals and schools. Today this situation is far worse. Zaire, Rwanda, and Burundi are examples of countries whose strategic value to the West all but disappeared when the Berlin Wall came down. "Africa has fallen off the horizon." "We will help you, Mr. Kengo, when you have straightened out the country." Catch-22 nonsense dressed in meaningless, diplomatic jargon and papered with documents that begin, "We deplore . . ." It takes a corrupter to exploit the leader of a client state.

The present resurgence of Ebola in Zaire, the deaths in Kikwit of patients along with their Zairian doctors, nurses, hospital workers, and Italian nursing sisters, can either generate fear and more panic-provoking films, or it can give rise to an awakening in all of us. We live in a small community of nations. When one nation coughs, others cannot sleep. When the people of one nation are crushed by destitution, disaster from revolutions or plagues are inevitable. Then, countries such as ours, which with small amounts of timely assistance could have prevented the worst from happening, are forced into more massive involvement. Recent history proves the point.

Devastating diseases breed in the cesspools of poverty. Many Zairian doctors and nurses are well-trained, competent professionals, but they have little or nothing with which to work. Maintenance and even the most basic supplies are lacking in government hospitals because of the gross mismanagement characteristic of regimes that preceded Mr. Kengo's government. We must graduate from judgment and neglect to realistic actions, and we must encourage the handful of men and women now struggling against monumental odds in countries all but abandoned by the West.

I am sad that the occasion for the publishing of my book *Ebola* coincides with another outbreak of this African hemorrhagic fever in Zaire. My heart joins the many who mourn. I bow to the courage of those who take care of the sick and dying. Whether this resurgence is caused by our trifling with nature's balance or by some other tragic circumstance, let us hope that Ebola's hiding place will be found this time.

If this book opens hearts, stimulates minds, and broadens our human perspectives, it will have played a small part in surmounting an immense challenge.

W.T.C.
Big Piney, Wyoming

GLOSSARY

abacos: A tailored jacket with short sleeves with an ascot popularized by Zairian President Mobutu (Lingala).

adieu: "good-bye" (French).

akoufi: "dead" (Lingala).

allez, allez: "go on, go on" (French).

allo, oui?: "hello, yes?" (French).

Americains: "Americans" (French).

ancien régime: "former regime" (French).

les autochtones: "the natives" (French).

Banda mikolo boni ozali na mpasi?: "How long have you been sick, mama?" (Lingala).

bangi: "marijuana" (Lingala).

la belle époque: "the good old days" (French).

Bima!: "Get out!" (Lingala).

bokende malamu: "go well" (Lingala).

Bonjour, monsieur le scientiste: "Good day, Mr. Scientist" (French).

Bon voyage, et bonne continuation: "Have a good trip and keep up the good work" (French).

Bon voyage, ma soeur, et bon retour: "Have a good trip, Sister, and come back soon" (French).

botikala malamu: "stay well" (Lingala).

Ça, alors! C'est du jamais vu: "Well, that is something never seen" (French).

Ça ira, peut-être: "It will be all right, maybe" (French).

Ça n'va pas?: "Is it not going well?" (French).

Ça n'va pas du tout: "It is not going well at all" (French).

Ça ne se fait pas!: "It is not done!" (French).

C'est comme ça: "That's the way it is" (French).

chanvre: "marijuana" (French).

chicotte: a rawhide rhinoceros whip (Lingala).

chikwangue: fermented manioc rolled in a thin tube of banana leaf (French).

Compagnie Maritime du Congo: maritime company of the Congo. S.S. *Elizabethville*, flagship (French).

confrère: "colleague" (French).

le Congo Belge: "the Belgian Congo" (French).

débrouillez vous: "work it out any way you can" (French).

de reigueur: "compulsory" (French).

deuxieme bureaux: "mistress" (French).

docteur: "doctor" (French).

la doctoresse: "woman doctor" (French).

elamba: a long cotton print cloth wrapped around the lower body and tied at the waist (Lingala).

Elles ont pris fuite: "They have escaped" (French).

Entrez: "Come in" (French).

"Épidémie": The title of a song to which prostitutes danced during the Ebola epidemic (French).

les évolués: "the civilized" by Western standards (French).

Ezali pamba, Nza akufi: "It is no use. Nza is dead" (Lingala).

féticheur: "sorcerer," "witch doctor" (French).

Flamands: "Flemish" (French).

Formidable! Formidable!: "Terrific! Terrific!" (French).

une fumière: "dung heap" (French).

fungula: "key" (Lingala).

fÿnproevers: "gourmet" (Dutch).

Gauloise: brand of French cigarettes.

gendarme: "policeman" (French).

la grande France: "the great country of France" (French).

la grippe: "flulike infection" (French).

iyo: "yes" (Lingala).

kaput: "all gone, destroyed, used up" (German).

kende malamu: "go well" (Lingala).

kisi ya basenji: "native medicine" (Lingala).

Kitisa motema!: "Calm yourself!" (Lingala).

Kota, kende: "Get in, go" (Lingala).

kwanga (like *chikwangue*): a long roll of fermented manioc wrapped in banana leaves (Lingala).

laissez-passer: "permit, pass" (French).

Lakisa ngai mwana: "Show me the child" (Lingala).

libela, libela: "forever, forever"; also, the name given to Father Gérard by Zairians (Lingala).

liputa: "sarong" (Lingala).

longwa: "go away" (Lingala).

lotoko: "banana liquor" (Lingala).

makayabu: "smoked, salted fish" (Lingala).

makila: "blood" (Lingala).

Malembe, mama. Kobanga te: "Easy, mama. Do not be frightened" (Lingala).

Mangez. Mangez bien: "Eat. Eat well" (French).

masanga: "wine" or "beer" (Lingala).

masanga ya mbila: fresh palm wine, only faintly fermented (Lingala).

matanga: "mourning" (Lingala).

mbondo: the poison certain tribes in Zaire mix with their banana liquor to prove their innocence by defying death (Lingala).

mbote: "hello" or "good day" (Lingala).

mbuta muntu: "respected elder" (Lingala).

Merci, ma soeur: "Thank you, Sister" (French).

Merde!: "Shit!" (French).

mère: "mother" (French).

mikolo minso: "every day" (Lingala).

mikolo sambo: "seven days" (Lingala).

mindele: "the whites" (Lingala).

mobali: "male" (Lingala).

mokumi: "an honorable man" (Lingala).

molimo: "our souls" (Lingala).

mondele: "white man" (Lingala).

mon Dieu: "my God" (French).

mon frère: "my brother" (French).

monganga: an expert in white medicine (Lingala).

motumolo: "older brother or sister" (Lingala).

Movement Populaire de la Révolution: in 1976 the single, all-powerful political party in Zaire, controlled by President Mobutu (French).

mpondu: the coarse green leaf of manioc (Lingala).

MPR: see *Movement Populaire de la·Révolution* (French).

mwambe: an African dish with chicken or fish, spices, peanuts, and palm oil (Lingala).

mwana: "child" (Lingala).

mwana kitoko: "good child" (Lingala).

mwana ngai: "my child" (Lingala).

mwembu: "voodoo man" (Lingala).

Nayebi te: "I do not know" (Lingala).

Nazali na pasi awa: "I have pain here" (Lingala).

ndoki: "evil spirit" (Lingala).

nganga: "medicine man," "native healer" (Lingala).

Nini?: "What?" (Lingala).

nkoko na ngai: "respected father of mine" (Lingala).

nkumu: "big chief," "person of note" (Lingala).

noki-noki: "quickly, quickly" (Lingala).

nonnette: slang for "nun" (French).

Nsoni!: "Shame on you!" (Lingala).

ntonga: "injections" (Lingala).

nyonso: "all over" (Lingala).

Ô mon Dieu: "Oh, my God", (French).

oui: "yes" (French).

oyeh: "Hurrah for . . ." (Lingala).

Papa akufi, akei!: "Papa is dead, he is gone!" (Lingala).

pasi na lokolo: "pain in my leg" (Lingala).

père: "father," "priest" (French).

petit: "small or little one," "child" (French).

pirogue: dugout canoe.

pondu: vegetable dish made from ground manioc leaves (Lingala).

poso moko: "one week" (Lingala).

primitif: "primitive" (French).

pulupulu: "diarrhea" (Lingala).

Quel idiot!: "What an idiot!" (French).

Quel voyage!: "What a trip!" (French).

Sango nini?: "How are things?," "What's up?" (Lingala).

santé: "health" (French).

sese: strong Budja wine (Lingala).

si didactique: "so didactic" (French).

Sik'oyo nini!: "Now what!" (Lingala).

Sikoyo, pema makasi, tata: "Now, breathe hard, Father" (Lingala).

simbas: "lions," name given to rebels in Zaire (Swahili).

soeur: "sister" (French).

tata: "father" (Lingala).

tata na ngai: "father of mine," a respectful greeting to an older person (Lingala).

tata-nkoko: "esteemed old father" (Lingala).

te: "no" (Lingala).

teeeeeee: Said with a finger pointing behind, meaning "a long time ago" (Lingala).

tika: "wait" (Lingala).

tikala malamu: "stay well" (Lingala).

Tolongwa awa: "We must flee from here" (Lingala).

tonga: "needles" (Lingala).

voilà: "there," "behold" (French).

Yo, kobwaka te: "You, hold on" (Lingala).

Zaire: country in Africa where the village of Yambuku is located, formerly the Belgian Congo.

zaire: national currency of Zaire.

zela moke: "hold on" (Lingala).

zoba: "idiot" (Lingala).